Praise for the Grigori Cycle

"Unrelenting is a tapestry of emotion that effortlessly weaves the threads of grief and obsession into a supernatural thriller."
    -Mary Robinette Kowal, Hugo Award winning author

"A fast-paced, supernatural thriller that will keep you turning the pages long after you should have gone to sleep."
    -Dan Wells, New York Times bestselling author

"Unrelenting effortlessly blends supernatural fantasy and thriller into one cohesive, wholly accessible story."
    -Pipeline Media Group

"I could not stop reading! A thunderous debut with real heart. Epic powers, villains you'll love to hate, and a plot that doesn't stop make for an amazing story."
    -Dan Eavenson, The Fantasy Book of the Month Podcast

"...a unique take on magic wrapped within a finely-crafted conspiracy."
    -Geoff Habiger & Coy Kissee, authors of *Wrath of the Fury Blade* and *Unremarkable*

"...a twisted but entertaining world of mystery and unexpected danger."
    -Hugh Fritz, author of the *Mystic Rampage* trilogy

UNDENIABLE

Book 2 of The Grigori Cycle

by JES HONARD
and MARIE PARKS

Published in the United States by
www.NotAPipePublishing.com

Trade Paperback Edition

ISBN-13: 978-1-956892-72-7

Cover Art and Design by Lauren Raye Snow

DEDICATION

For Marlene and for Nancy.

And for you, who endures, even when it feels impossible.

ONE

Bridget never imagined a cup of tea could fill her with so much dread.

She sat on a wooden chair beside her sister's, their knees almost touching. Across from them, Nuriel placed a mug on the walnut kitchen table, then leaned forward in his seat. He brushed back his dark curls and gave Dahlia an encouraging "Go ahead."

Bridget gripped her knees tightly as she forced herself to watch. Dahlia lifted the mug in one hand. The word "Cleveland" was emblazoned across it, below a drawing of the city skyline. But Bridget's eyes gravitated to her sister's wrist. There, an intricate tattoo of ominous, swirling lines darkened her naturally tan skin. Its twin, she knew, was inked on Dahlia's back. This was the tattoo that had changed their lives forever.

She's still Dahlia, Bridget told herself. She wore what

Bridget called her game face—a familiar, determined expression where the tip of her tongue stuck out as she concentrated.

It was a reminder for Bridget to check in with her own expression, and she forcibly smoothed away the grimace—though she could do nothing for the knot in her chest. This was wrong.

Slowly, a stream of green tea lifted above the porcelain rim, thin as a straw. It turned clockwise, stirring itself. Dahlia's gaze grew more focused, and the tea straw gained speed.

Goosebumps prickled along Bridget's arms, and she dug her fingers into her jeans. It had barely been a week since Dahlia's rescue. She'd found her sister, not gone, but not the same either. She was, strictly speaking, no longer human.

The liquid straw twisted into a tiny waterspout under Dahlia's command, the mouth widening into a cone. She lifted her palm, and it widened further, and further, and...

...it wavered and fell into itself, sending a spray of lukewarm tea in every direction.

With a groan of dismay, Dahlia plunked the mug down on top of that morning's newspaper. She sat back in irritation, wiping flecks of water off her sketchbook.

"It's okay. It takes practice," Nuriel assured Dahlia. He'd taken out a pack of cigarettes while watching her, and now he stuck one between his lips. Dahlia wrinkled her nose.

"I've *been* practicing, ever since I was rescued." She looked down at her spattered t-shirt with a frustrated sigh. It was a thrift store find, promoting a high school track championship from five years ago.

He took the mug from her and set it down on the table. "I know. It does become easier, with time. And the faster you learn, the more helpful your abilities might be." With a brief flick of his fingers, the water rose, curling in on itself as it formed a long, shimmering snake.

Dahlia leaned in, watching the swirl of liquid intently. The hunger in her eyes made Bridget uncomfortable. Ever since discovering she was one of them—an immortal, magic-wielding Grigori—Dahlia had eagerly sought to learn more.

Bridget had seen Nuriel use his water ability to create a barrier of ice, trap a man within a tempest, and scald his foes with boiling projectiles. So long as the liquid wasn't contained in a pressurized system or a sealed container, he could put Poseidon to shame. If Dahlia could someday wield that kind of unnatural power, what would be left of the little sister Bridget loved?

She spoke up for the first time in several minutes. "You said she'd be helpful. But why should she try to be? We barely survived the last fight." *And only because I killed a man.*

Nuriel let the water slide easily back into the mug, without a single drop spilling over. "We're safe, for now. But Tannin is still out there. We need to prepare for the worst."

Bridget broke Nuriel's gaze. She didn't want to think about how dangerous her sister's kidnapper was. It was his obsession with uncovering ancient Grigori symbols that led to this whole mess. They had made dangerous enemies in the previous weeks—Grigori with horrifying powers at their disposal. Abilities to invoke choking, sulfurous smoke. To infect with disease, to create a destructive tornado.

After a week of moving from motel to motel, they'd settled at their current location. Viri, another Grigori, had welcomed them under his roof with open arms, despite the dangers pursuing them.

Dahlia reached for the mug again. "It's fine, Bridget. I want to learn. I need to protect myself."

Nuriel nodded in agreement. "Especially as a mimic. Your ability to borrow powers is too rare and volatile to leave to chance."

The chair squeaked as Bridget sat upright. "She shouldn't have to protect herself. She should be worrying about a summer job or spending time with friends."

It wasn't rational; neither of them could return to their normal lives. How could they, with the ash of battle still scratching her throat? Or with nightly dreams that reminded her of everything lost in the search for her sister. How could she ever return to normal when James, her friend and confidante, lay cold in a morgue?

Still, Bridget hoped to carve out a piece of the life she'd lost. For herself, for Dahlia, and for James.

Before Dahlia could respond, a familiar voice interrupted. "Nuriel, we need to speak with you." Gaul stepped into the room, his red hair the only thing bright about him.

Bridget tapped her fingers against the fabric of her jeans in immediate response to his presence. Even though she had been reassured by the others that they were safe around Gaul, it remained hard to trust him. He held malice towards her sister—a lack of trust based on nothing Bridget could see. When she'd reminded him she had known her sister all her life, and she was no threat, his response had chilled her. *No. You've only just met her.*

He looked between the three of them. "Still training?" His tone was sour.

"She's progressing well." Nuriel removed the unlit cigarette from his lips.

"What are you meeting about this time?" Dahlia started to rise from her chair.

"You're not invited. Nuriel, come on."

Nuriel favored the sisters with an apologetic smile and obediently stood. "We'll continue later, Dahlia."

Without another word, he followed Gaul out of the kitchen. They retreated down the creaky wooden hall.

Dahlia sunk back into her seat, lips twisting into a scowl. "Why do they still not trust us?"

Bridget shook her head. "He was like that the whole time I was trying to find you. Anyway, it's best if we *don't* get involved."

"We're already involved, Bridget. Maybe they're gearing up to fight back." Her eyes sparkled at the idea. It sent a pang shooting through Bridget.

"That's one more reason for us to steer clear, Dahlia. We'd be a liability."

"Really? Who killed Kai, again? Sure as hell wasn't any of *them*."

Bridget's stomach twisted. The memory of Kai, spasming from the gunshot wound to his neck, surfaced with nauseating clarity. "It doesn't matter. We need to focus while we have a few minutes on our own."

"On James," Dahlia said, tone cautious.

Bridget drew in a slow breath at his name, and she pushed down a familiar pang of guilt—and hope. If she dwelled on it, she knew grief would overtake her. Instead, she returned her attention to the nascent plan to bring him back to life. "With them in a meeting, no one is watching us. Now's a good time to get your sketches back."

She had lost track of the drawings—stolen from Tannin's underground museum by Gaul when he'd grabbed the papers instead of breaking Dahlia free of her cage. A bitter ball of disgust still formed in her throat when she thought about that decision. But now they were both here, and the sketches pointed to James' only hope for survival. The potential magic locked away within the drawings could revive him, just as Dahlia had been revived. Then they could get the hell away from the horror show their life had become.

"Is it even worth it, Bridget? I spent *months* trying to replicate my sketches, but only one ever worked. Grigori Artists like Nuriel or Kai train for decades."

"We have to try. We owe him that much."

Dahlia still looked reluctant. "If the others find out, they might destroy the drawings." She could too easily imagine Gaul casting the drawings into the fire or burying them deep in the earth. He hadn't destroyed them yet because he hoped Nuriel could learn from them. But if he knew Bridget's plans for them, that could quickly change.

Frustration locked Bridget's jaw. James' final moments, gasping as blood spilled from his chest, haunted her even more than Kai's death. At least Kai had deserved it. "We won't let them find out. Why are you fighting me on this? Do you have a better plan?"

Dahlia gave her sister a wry grin. "No. It's just easy to poke holes in yours."

Bridget pressed her hands flat on the table and stood. They'd both been in that cold basement, when Kai's scissors pierced James' heart. Did she not care?

"Come on." Her tone was flat.

She led the way into the hall. It was lined with ferns and succulents. A few vines drooped down from baskets hanging near the ceiling. An enormous monstera filtered light from one of the wall sconces, and the gentle smell of jasmine drifted in from somewhere deeper in the house. Viri didn't seem to distinguish between indoor plants and outdoor plants. They all belonged everywhere.

Bridget pinpointed the source of the voices: a closed bedroom door farther down the hall. They passed the wide wooden stairs that led to the second floor and the open doorway of Viri's library.

Crossing the high-ceilinged foyer, they followed the murmur of conversation toward the ground floor bedrooms. She couldn't make out what Gaul was saying behind the closed door, but his voice was a low, urgent rumble.

The sisters hurried past the occupied room to the next one—Nuriel's guest room. Bridget gripped the knob and slowly pushed it open.

The hinges squealed, and she froze, listening. The voices paused. Bridget held still, heart pounding in her ears.

It would be terrible to get caught before they even began. Gaul's face, twisted in anger, flashed through her mind. But the conversation started again, this time with Nuriel's calmer tone. Bridget let out a relieved breath.

"Go," Dahlia whispered urgently. They slipped inside and Bridget eased the door closed behind them. The hinges protested again, but not as loudly this time.

The room was made for guests, with a single twin bed and a sturdy wooden dresser. The faint scent of cigarettes hung in the air, intruding on the heady honeysuckle covering one wall.

Dahlia went straight for a stack of papers on the nightstand, starting to dig through them.

Bridget went to the desk. There, sitting under a set of drawing charcoals, were a few more loose pages. She flipped over the top sheet. It was a portrait of a woman. The barest hint of a smile touched the subject's lips as she stared up from the page. Bridget had watched Nuriel sketch her only a day after the fight with Tannin.

Every page under it was another drawing, many of the same woman. Others were landscapes, clearly inspired by the urban sprawl of Cleveland, but most were portraits. She paused on a drawing he'd done of Dahlia and Bridget. In the sketch, both sisters sat on the bed of the first hotel they'd escaped to. Bridget's likeness leaned overbearingly close to her sister, brows furrowed in concentration.

Dahlia, by contrast, was propped against the pillows, one hand outstretched. Above her palm, a clump of dirt hovered. On the surface, it was a perfect portrayal of her, right down to the wave of her hair. But Bridget's throat felt tight as she touched the drawing with her fingertips. She wasn't sure what felt discordant. Maybe the tilt of Dahlia's jaw, or her tight expression, but even though it *looked* like Dahlia, it didn't feel like her.

"Nothing here." Dahlia's voice tugged Bridget's attention back to the room.

"Or here." Bridget put the drawing away. She wasn't surprised. Nuriel was meticulous, and she doubted he would leave something so important out in the open.

"Maybe they're looking at them in their meeting." Dahlia ducked down to peer under the beds.

"We're not giving up that easily." Bridget walked to the dresser, pulling open its top drawer. It held a neatly folded stack of clothing, rescued from the destroyed house they'd been forced to abandon.

Finding nothing in the remaining drawers, Bridget turned to the closet. There were still voices coming from the other room. If anything, they seemed louder. Were they arguing?

She went to the closet. Several shirts hung from the rod, but the small space was mostly empty. Except for a black metal box in the corner.

"Dahlia? I found a safe."

Dahlia scrambled up from the floor and hurried over. "Open it!"

The door held fast when Bridget tugged. She inspected the front of the safe. It was a simple digital keypad lock.

Dahlia hovered over Bridget's shoulder, inspecting the lock. "Uh, try 1-2-3-4?"

Bridget rolled her eyes but gave it a shot. *ERROR* scrolled across the readout.

"Do you know his phone number?" Dahlia asked.

Bridget shook her head. "No, only the Detective's."

"Do they even have social security numbers?" She wrinkled her nose. "Oh, what about his birthday?"

Bridget shook her head, then paused. "His birthday..." She typed in 1-7-9-4.

The lock whirred. The readout flashed to *OPEN* in blocky letters. "Yes!" She swung the door open.

"How'd you know that?"

"I don't know his birthday. But it's the year he became a Grigori." She reached inside and pulled out a thin stack of folded papers, which she offered to Dahlia.

"This is it." Dahlia thumbed through the pages, and Bridget leaned over to watch. Some had a single, large symbol drawn in intricate detail. Others featured dozens of smaller sketches, with slightly different arcs and twists to the pencil lines. They reminded Bridget of when Dahlia was in middle school, taking her first art classes. She'd draw the same figure over and over, in slightly different positions, until she got the shape just right.

"Nuriel's been modifying them. See this?" Dahlia's finger traced a precise, angular shape drawn on top of the original. "That's not my work." She handed the pages back to Bridget.

She took them and flipped through more slowly. "Why is he changing them?"

Dahlia shrugged. "Think about it. He's an Artist, and he suddenly has a whole stack of new, incomplete drawings that could unlock ancient Grigori powers."

There was only one type of symbol Bridget was interested in. She examined the page Nuriel had edited, but the design looked the same as any other—an intricate weaving of lines that was beautiful, but meaningless to her. "Can you make a copy of his work?"

"I can try. But we're talking about copies of copies, at this point. They're going to get even less accurate." Dahlia retrieved her sketchbook, flipped it open to a blank page, and went over to the bed. "Bring them here."

"Do your best." Bridget set the drawings down beside her. Dahlia pulled a mechanical pencil from her back pocket.

Bridget watched anxiously as Dahlia worked. These images were exactly what they needed. If even one of them could create a new Grigori, they could use it to revive James.

The same way Dahlia had been revived. Kai's last words still burned in Bridget's memory. *Your sister is dead. I killed her myself.*

She shoved them back as she watched Dahlia draw. *It will be alright*, she told herself. They were facing a monumental task in saving James, but at least they were facing it together.

If there was anything she could trust, it was that Dahlia was still her confidante. Her best friend. Her sister.

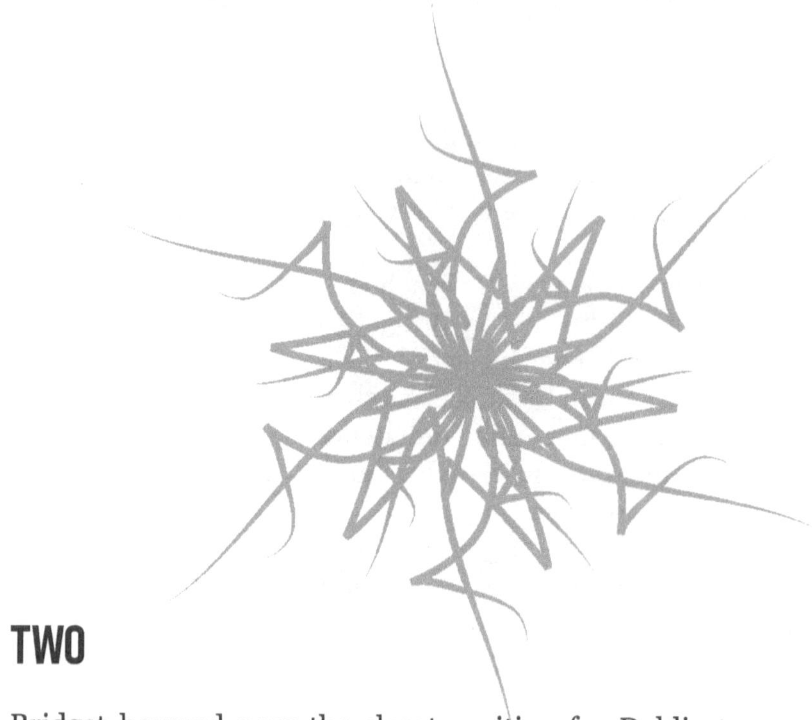

TWO

Bridget hovered near the closet, waiting for Dahlia to finish sketching. It was impossible not to think about the meeting taking place, just on the other side of the bedroom wall. "Come on, hurry up."

Dahlia shot Bridget a scathing look. "I'm going as fast as I can."

Blowing out an anxious sigh, Bridget paced past the neatly made twin bed to the window and peered out. Nuriel's room looked into the backyard, with a view of the impressive gardens Viri had created.

Bridget was about to urge her sister on again when a squeal of hinges startled her. The bedroom door inched open, followed by a sardonic voice. "What are you doing?"

Dahlia snapped her notebook closed, stuffing the original drawings between the pages. Tension rode up Bridget's shoulders as the last person she wanted to see entered the room.

With disheveled blond hair and a permanent smirk, Danel made Bridget want to kick his teeth in. This man had manipulated Dahlia. He was responsible for the kidnapping that led to her death.

"Get out." Dahlia's voice burned like hot coals.

Danel ignored her, closing the door behind him. Bridget moved in front of her sister, fingers curling at her sides. He didn't flinch at their glares, though he did keep his distance. Not that it mattered. If he wanted, Danel could be at their throats before she could blink. His inhuman speed had saved their lives in the battle against Tannin, but it also meant he was always a threat.

Now, he looked utterly at ease as he leaned against the door. "If you're going to ransack someone's room, at least make sure no one will walk in on you."

Dahlia got to her feet, standing shoulder to shoulder with Bridget. "I told you to leave. You're not wanted here."

Danel's gaze lingered on Dahlia, then drifted to the notebook gripped in her hands. "Ah. You're still convinced those drawings can save James."

"What do you want?" Bridget didn't need to justify herself to him. His motives were a mystery to her, but they always seemed rooted in selfishness. Even his relationship with Dahlia had been fake—a ploy so he could ultimately bring her to Tannin's cages.

Danel tilted his head, his mussed hair falling to the side. He didn't seem bothered by the harsh reception. "While you were pilfering through Nuriel's belongings, I was eavesdropping on their meeting. I thought you might want to know what they're talking about."

"We don't," Bridget said. They were going to make

their own plan, and once James was safe, the three of them could figure out their next steps.

Dahlia shot her sister an annoyed look before responding to Danel. "Tell us what you came to say and go away."

To Bridget's surprise, Danel complied without asking for anything in exchange. "Word finally got out about Kai and the guards who were killed."

Bridget froze, cold trickling into her gut. "The police know it was me?"

"No, Eisheth's got your back where law enforcement is considered. I'm talking about the Grigori."

"And nobody's happy about it," Dahlia guessed.

"Nope. There aren't a lot of us. Killing someone is kind of a big deal, and it comes with pretty hefty consequences. People are going to expect Tannin to avenge those deaths."

Avenge. The word settled in her chest like heartburn. "How?"

"They'll want Tannin to make sure those responsible never hurt anyone else." He eyed Bridget. "You, in particular, being human and all."

Dahlia moved halfway in front of Bridget. "You're telling me my sister is a target?"

"I'm telling you more people are paying attention now."

"Don't you people have due process? I shot Kai in self-defense. Plus, *they'd* already murdered Dahlia and James."

"Two measly humans, in their eyes. Do yourself a favor, and don't try to rationalize it. Our justice system is as contradictory and convoluted as any human one."

And now the others were discussing her future

without her. Her earlier relief at being excluded evaporated. "What plans are they making?"

"Gaul wants us all to leave, this time out of state. Whatever you need to do in Cleveland, do it fast."

A lead weight sank into Bridget's stomach. "We can't leave town yet." If they left, James would be out of reach. The sketches, completed or not, would be unable to revive him.

"We need to work faster," Dahlia murmured, looking down at her half-finished copy of the sketches.

Danel pulled out a phone from his back pocket and held it out. "Maybe this can help."

Bridget eyed the device suspiciously. "Where did you get that? I thought we weren't supposed to have any technology on us."

Danel scoffed. "Gaul is a dinosaur. He doesn't understand these things can work *for* us as easily as against us."

"I seem to remember you don't get along with technology too well yourself," Dahlia said stiffly.

"At least I don't reject it outright. Go on, take it."

Bridget eyed him. "This is a trick."

"Consider it an attempt to make amends." Danel set the phone on the twin bed between them.

"Amends?" Dahlia's voice pitched higher. "Are you serious? You think a *phone* is going to make up for how you got me killed?"

"Shh," Bridget hushed her. "They'll hear us."

Danel raised his hands in a placating gesture. "Use it to take pictures of the sketches so you won't tip Nuriel off."

Dahlia scowled, then darted forward and grabbed the phone. She moved so quickly Bridget's breath caught.

With Danel standing close, Dahlia could feed off his power, using it for herself. She wasn't as fast as him, but it was still disconcerting. Even Danel looked uneasy.

As Dahlia flipped open her sketchbook and pulled out the loose papers, Bridget scrutinized Danel. It had only been a few days since he'd been her enemy. He'd been the perfect person to lure Dahlia into Tannin's clutches. Lean and muscular, with confidence that bled into arrogance, he was exactly Dahlia's type. He made Bridget's stomach curdle.

But she had no reason to think he was lying now. The deaths of Kai and Tannin's two guards—Ketill and Dolos—hadn't been subtle or well hidden. "Do the Grigori have, like... a court?" Bridget asked as Dahlia took photos.

Danel pried his gaze away from Dahlia. "Nothing so bureaucratic."

"What, then?"

He licked his lips. "We all have mentors. People who were supposed to train us and teach us. Part of their job is to make sure the laws are followed."

"You break laws all the time," Bridget pointed out.

"I break human laws, not Grigori ones—at least, not the capital offenses. Anyway, I'm not exactly mentee material. I stay away from Gaul as much as I can."

"And *that* doesn't break a law, to avoid your mentor?"

Danel waved the question away. "It's not typical. But Gaul lets it slide. Anyway, everyone who died worked under one of Tannin's contracts."

"Doesn't that make him look bad?"

"Sure does. And Tannin's own mentor is going to want to make sure he saves face. Publicly."

"Tannin has a mentor?" The idea of someone even

older and more powerful than him was unsettling, to say the least.

Before Danel could respond, Dahlia interrupted, "Okay, I have photos of all of them." She offered up the sheafs of paper with her original work. Wordlessly, Bridget took them and strode back over to the safe. Silence followed her. Dahlia didn't seem eager to talk to Danel, and the room felt heavy with unspoken words.

"So, um, I've been meaning to ask, how are you—" Danel, of course, was the first to try and initiate conversation. Dahlia cut him off immediately.

"Don't. We're not friends. I don't want anything to do with you." Her voice was laced with ice.

Bridget locked the safe and looked over her shoulder as Danel raised his hands, palms out. Somehow, even confronted with Dahlia's anger, he managed to look at ease.

"Alright, alright. I'm leaving. You'd best do the same, if you don't want to get caught." He turned and opened the door, slipping into the hall.

Dahlia exhaled, her shoulders relaxing. "I hate him."

"I know." Bridget had nothing more to say. Danel deserved every bit of anger Dahlia directed at him. And, at the same time, Dahlia might not be here if not for him. He, like everything else in her life lately, was another complication.

"He's right, though. We should go." The plant-adorned walls felt like they were closing in, like Tannin's so-called justice.

Bridget closed the closet door, gently latching it. She took the lead, striding to the door and peeking out into the hallway. Empty. The murmur of voices next door had gotten louder, but Bridget didn't stop to listen. She glanced back at Dahlia, who made a shooing gesture. Wiping sweaty palms on her jeans, Bridget picked up the pace.

Her mind snagged on their conversation with Danel, replaying it. If he was right, Gaul, Nuriel, Ret, and Eisheth were discussing her fate behind closed doors. The four Grigori who had helped her most in the hunt for Dahlia were now trying to protect her from the consequences of her actions.

She didn't regret killing Kai. He was a cruel, violent man who tormented her sister and murdered James. If anything, the greater Grigori population should *thank* her for getting rid of someone so volatile. But that didn't mean his death didn't haunt her.

Bridget stepped into the sunny kitchen, but even the bright room felt small. The mug of tea from Dahlia's practice session glared at her from the table, a reminder of how much had changed in their lives.

Dahlia approached the mug, staring at it. The surface of the water started to ripple.

Bridget's breath felt thin. She glanced toward the window, and the blue sky beyond. It beckoned to her. "I need more space. Come on."

Dahlia sighed in frustration and stalked in front of her sister into the sunroom.

Warmth settled over Bridget like a blanket fresh from the dryer. Dahlia led her past white wicker furniture topped with faded floral cushions. Viri's plant theme continued, and she walked around thick stalks and vibrant green leaves. The screen door to the backyard opened easily.

Taking in a gulp of fresh air, some of the tension in her body worked itself loose. The backyard bled into rolling hills and, distantly, a wall of trees. Bridget guessed the house had once been surrounded by a farm, but former fields had been reworked into an intricate series of gardens.

Dahlia stayed ahead of her as she walked toward a small copse of dogwood trees, tucked away from view of the house. The shade inside the stand of trees was cool and welcoming, and overhead the branches created a ceiling of pink and white flowers. Bridget stopped by one of two wrought-iron benches, while Dahlia plopped down on the hard-packed dirt. Sitting cross-legged, Dahlia set her sketchbook on her lap, with her new phone on top.

"We should hurry. Especially if Danel's right about us leaving." Bridget wrapped her fingers around the cool bench. She paused. "How do you know when you get it right?"

Dahlia's gaze was flat. "I guess you try it on someone and see what happens."

Oh. Bridget's mind flung itself back to an icy freezer in Tannin's lair, filled with body bags. Beside the freezer stood a sterile room with a tall, metal table and tattoo equipment. Goosebumps rose along her arms, and she tried to rub them out. "We don't have anyone to try them on."

Dahlia shrugged and flipped her notebook open to a blank page. "We're going to need to get to James anyway. We can try them on him until one works."

Bridget stared at her sister. "You want to, what, cover him in tattoos? He's not a blank sheet of paper, Dahlia."

"At the moment, he kind of is."

The off-handed comment burrowed into her. She watched her sister start to draw long, swooping marks on the blank page. *Is this what Gaul meant when he said she would be different?*

Dahlia must have seen the horror on Bridget's face, because her annoyance eased a little. "I'm messing with you. We'll know when we have one that works. It glows for a second when everything clicks."

Bridget stared at her, confusion and irritation mounting. She let out an awkward laugh. "Okay. Why didn't you just say that?"

Dahlia shrugged. "If you're going to be weird about me practicing, I'm going to be weird about your plans. How are we getting to James, anyway?"

With some effort, Bridget shoved aside the dark thoughts about her sister. "I'm still working on that part." Viri had assured them news of James' death hadn't yet spread beyond Grigori circles. It was a small comfort. Eventually, someone would need to tell James' family and return his body to them.

If Bridget had her way, there wouldn't be a body to return.

To that end, Dahlia wasn't wrong. Tattoos were a small price for a second chance at life.

The crunch of gravel interrupted them. Bridget shot Dahlia an urgent look, and her sister snapped the notebook shut and tucked the phone away.

A moment later, Ret came into view. He was on crutches, left leg ensconced in a cast. The injury was a physical reminder of their fight with Tannin. Ret couldn't use his healing ability on himself, even through Dahlia's mimicry. So, while everyone else's broken bones and burns were gone, Ret was still in pain.

"I'm sorry for interrupting," he said when he noticed them. His dark skin had a light sheen of sweat, as if he'd been working out. "I didn't realize anyone else was back here."

Dahlia threw on her sweetest voice—the one reserved for when their mom brought home an unexpected guest. "It's alright. Did you need something?"

Ret looked between them, forehead creasing. "No, I was taking my leave from Gaul's meeting. It's getting progressively louder, and I'm not sure my presence is useful."

"Why wouldn't they want you there? Aren't you senior to all of them?" As far as Bridget knew, Ret was millennia old, and Gaul held a great deal of respect for him.

Ret glanced at the bench opposite Bridget. "Do you mind if I sit? These crutches aren't particularly comfortable."

"Sure," Bridget said, and Ret sighed with relief as he settled down. "Well?"

Dahlia sighed in exasperation. "You'll have to forgive my sister. She doesn't understand tact."

Ret chuckled softly, reaching into his pocket and pulling out a handkerchief. He mopped his forehead with it. "You've both been through a difficult situation. I don't blame you for wanting answers. This is going to sound a bit crass, but I'm not sure how else to put it. Have you ever babysat?"

Bridget frowned. "What?"

"Well, when you watch a group of children, sometimes you have to simply let them argue. They don't want interference. They want to speak their piece. And when they're ready, they will look for guidance from their elders."

Dahlia snorted a disbelieving laugh. "Are you really calling them children? Nuriel's like three hundred years old."

"And Gaul is over a thousand. That doesn't mean he wants me hovering over him or his mentees." His focus moved to Dahlia. "How have you been doing?"

Dahlia shrugged, closing off. She clutched her sketchbook tightly. "Fine."

"It's never an easy transition into our world."

Bridget glanced over at Dahlia, then down to her notebook. "I've been thinking about what happened. You're right, we both still have a lot of questions."

Ret looked between them. "I'll answer what I can."

"Thanks." She considered where to begin. "How exactly did the tattoo turn Dahlia into a Grigori?"

"Ah." His fingers drummed on his crutch thoughtfully. "The tattoos create a small fissure between our worlds. That fissure allows one of us to slip through, into the body carrying the tattoo. It wasn't always this way, of course. The tattoos were simply insurance. As it turned out, they saved our lives."

"What do you mean?" Bridget leaned forward.

"We had a war with humans long ago. Before then, there was an open Gateway between our worlds."

"Like the portal?" Dahlia asked.

Ret held up a hand, wobbling it from side to side. "Bigger. Portals are tiny tunnels. The Gateway was a door, and it was guarded by a gatekeeper who monitored the flow of magic between worlds. Back then, we could come here freely and find a suitable human candidate. But in the war, humans attacked the Gateway, leaving the tattoos as our only anchor to this world. They're better than nothing, but they do create some instability."

"How?" Dahlia asked.

"If they're damaged, the anchor is destroyed. And every time one is created, it pierces the fabric between worlds. Enough holes, and they could turn into rips."

A glimmer of an idea prodded at the edge of Bridget's mind. "Where was the Gateway?"

Ret's gaze snapped into focus. "Why?"

"I find it interesting."

His expression turned guarded. "It was locked and destroyed, along with its key. Our method for opening it was lost during the war, along with so many lives."

Bridget bit her lip, suppressing the urge to ask more. As much as she wanted to press him, she recognized the tense set of his shoulders. It was the same way she'd looked whenever someone had told her to forget about Dahlia. Or James.

If she wanted more information, it would have to wait. "Thanks for telling us about what happened. We'll get out of your hair."

The hardness in his eyes receded. He cast them a small smile as she stood. Dahlia got to her feet, brushing gravel from her jeans.

Ret touched Bridget's shoulder as she passed, bringing her to a stop. "Please be cautious. We will protect you as much as we can, but our world is dangerous. Most humans don't survive it long."

THREE

Once, Dahlia would have loved finding herself in a big, old house in the middle of nowhere. It was the perfect location for late-night parties.

But with her life turned upside down, a curtain had fallen over her usual optimism. She could feel Ret's gaze following her as she walked through the garden toward the house and beside her, Bridget radiated tension. Instead of planning a night out with friends, she was scheming to reanimate a corpse. Not exactly the type of party she usually went for.

Rebirth really did a number on one's sense of self.

Death and captivity had sharpened her soft edges to points. She carried a constant, jarring sense of *wrong*ness. Of *too much*ness. Of *not enough*ness.

The sensation welled up every time she looked in the mirror and saw the same old face covering a newly forged heart. It lurked in the shadows of her mind when Bridget called her name and hugged her close. It taunted her when she thought about the naïve college student she'd been—who waltzed foolishly into a dark, abandoned building, believing the promises of her then-boyfriend.

Before Danel, she'd thought of herself as easygoing and quick to forgive. Now, the idea of forgiving him made her physically ill.

Was that her trauma circling the drain on events she wished she could unwrite? Or was it Grigori magic, changing her in ways she didn't fully grasp? Making her angrier, more vindictive, more callous.

Sometimes her new self was clear as day. When she practiced with Nuriel, the wrongness faded away. She could *feel* herself grow whole as she channeled his ability through her mimicry powers, weak as they were.

But those moments of clarity were few and far between, and frequently chased by confusion and guilt.

Bridget's voice pierced Dahlia's dark thoughts. "Do you think we could find it?"

Dahlia blinked. Somehow, they'd arrived on the stoop outside the sunroom, her body continuing to move while her mind stuck to her past like an insect trapped in tree sap. Bridget, as always, was on a mission. "Find what?"

"The Gateway. What else?"

The question sent a spike of annoyance through her. God love her sister, but working alongside her tested every inch of Dahlia's patience. "One second you want to steal sketches, now you want to find a lost, mythical door. You're grasping at straws."

"One of those straws might work," Bridget said firmly. She held open the screen door.

Dahlia's shoulders seized up with growing frustration. Despite Bridget's promises to help Dahlia understand her new identity, her sister shut down every time it came up. And yet, when it came to reviving James, Bridget's interest in Grigori magic had no limits.

She hid her unsettled emotions beneath a scoff and strode past Bridget, deeper into the kitchen. Lowering her voice, she said, "This Gateway is from an ancient war or whatever. Let's focus on what we already know works. I want to take a closer look at the changes Nuriel made to the sketches."

They emerged into the empty hallway. The meeting was still in full swing further down the hall. They were too far away to make out any words, but Dahlia could feel the gentle pulse of their powers. It was a new sense she'd picked up upon her resurrection, and the clearest reminder she'd changed. Once fully trained, she'd be able to tell each Grigori's ability apart, make them her own. At least that's what Nuriel had told her. Right now, the powers jumbled together in an indistinguishable cacophony.

Dahlia followed Bridget up the stairs, stepping lightly to avoid making them creak. She didn't return to her normal gait until both she and Bridget were in the room they shared, the door locked behind them. Their sneaking felt like being a teenager again, returning home after curfew—something she'd done more than her fair share of times. Those memories felt fuzzy now. Not quite like they belonged to someone else, but more like they'd lost their shine.

She sat down among the rumpled sheets marking her side of the queen bed they shared. She hadn't bothered tidying after another night of tossing and turning. Bridget, of course, had pulled her half of the sheets up perfectly.

Bridget perched beside her now. Dahlia flicked through the photos she'd taken of the sketches, trying to ignore how close her sister sat. It was no different from the million other times they'd huddled together over a shared project, but today her skin prickled.

Dahlia paused on one particular drawing, overlaid with pencil lines.

"Is that the one Nuriel tried to change?" Bridget leaned in closer, and Dahlia tried to subtly shift away. Would it kill her to stop hovering for ten seconds?

"Yes." She zoomed in on the sketch, turning the phone to inspect it from another angle.

"Why that one?"

She forced back an exasperated sigh. "I don't know, maybe because the other ones are barely legible? Mind giving me some space?"

Bridget sat back. "Okay, okay. Don't disturb the cranky artist at her work."

She rolled her shoulders, forcing them to relax. She knew she shouldn't be so harsh with Bridget—she loved her sister and owed her her life.

With some effort, Dahlia turned her focus back to the photographs. Even incomplete, the symbols were beautiful. Each was circular and symmetrical, with swirls and finely detailed turns around which the pattern orbited. Unfortunately, the original stone tablets were lost. Most of the drawings were filled with gaps and guesses.

And, despite their beauty, the drawings left a tangled

mess of emotion in the pit of her stomach. She'd drawn these while trapped in Tannin's cage for nearly nine months. Under his orders, Kai had used knowledge as a carrot, doling out bits of understanding about her transformation in return for her work.

Bridget isn't like either of them, she reminded herself firmly as she pulled out her sketchbook. Besides, Dahlia had agreed to help revive James, and she had no intention of breaking her promises. She owed both of them more than she could ever repay.

The drawing was beautiful, so long as she put distance between herself and her memories. Once, she'd loved art. For months, she'd agonized over which passion to follow in college—art or science. In archaeology she'd found a way to blend the two, decorating her field notes with detailed recreations of their finds.

Maybe she could recapture some of that enjoyment. She took her pencil from her bag and began laying out the barest outline of the sketch. Instead of focusing on her time in captivity, she thought back further, to when she and her classmates had uncovered the stone tablets on a spring break archaeology dig in Tunisia. At the time, she'd been thrilled. It was more than she'd ever expected to find, and the stonework entranced her. She loved the symbols so much she'd gotten one tattooed on her wrist.

Another stupid decision in the long line of dominoes that had led her to her murder and imprisonment.

She glanced at Bridget. Her sister was toying with the frayed edge of the bed quilt, watching a braided money tree with more attention than it deserved. It was obvious she was trying as hard as she could not to peek at Dahlia's work.

"You know," Dahlia ventured, softening her tone a little. "It's kind of nice to work on these in a way that actually helps someone. Maybe Nuriel could teach me how to be a real Artist."

The words had an immediate effect on Bridget. Her shoulders pulled up, the corners of her eyes tightened, and her voice flattened out. "Why would you want to? Once we have James back, we can get ourselves out of this mess."

Dahlia's cheeks went hot. "Right." She didn't push the topic; she knew the edge in Bridget's tone too well.

Bridget, for her part, didn't hesitate to push. "I know you're excited by all of this, but we have to be careful. You don't want to get involved in their politics again."

"Yeah." Disappointment washed over her. She turned back to the drawings.

The unfairness of it settled over Dahlia. She'd never asked for this. How could she have guessed dating Danel would lead to her own murder and subsequent resurrection? And even her revival had gone wrong in ways Dahlia didn't fully understand. Gaul's warnings about an "unstable match" haunted her increasingly prevalent nightmares.

Dahlia was coming to realize Bridget's promises came rife with caveats. She could explore her new identity, but only if it helped James. Right now, recreating the symbols was the best way for Dahlia to explore her new world without triggering Bridget's never-ending quest for normalcy.

As if they could ever go back to the way it was.

Dahlia turned the phone, then zoomed in further, examining Nuriel's work. He'd trained under Kai, though centuries ago. She wondered if he'd been as cruel to Nuriel as to her—if that was why Nuriel was such a patient instructor himself. He clearly knew what he was doing. The alterations he'd made were precise, even if they weren't the direction she would have gone.

In fact, they almost made it seem as if the lines were—

"Oh!" Dahlia's exclamation drew Bridget's attention again.

"What is it? Did Nuriel figure it out?"

"He didn't finish, but I see what he's doing. Grigori writing has to be symmetrical, or a repeating pattern radiating out from a central point, right? But see this swoop here?" She pointed at a line looping through the intricate pattern like a ribbon. "This line interrupts the entire pattern and ruins the symmetry. But that's by design. I think I know what to do."

Heart pattering, she flipped her notebook to a new page. There, she started a fresh drawing, attention swinging between the phone and the paper. The design took shape haltingly, with so many eraser marks the page rubbed thin in places. A rush of exhilaration coursed through her.

She'd found the key to Nuriel's additions. With no prodding, no formal training. Just her own intuition for the shape and feel of the lines. For a moment, she recaptured the childhood thrill of willing her imagination into the real world with nothing but pencils.

She made another mark and turned it around to show Bridget. "This line starts again here. Because this isn't two-dimensional. The line goes *behind* the pattern. There's more to this than we can see."

Bridget looked confused. "So, they're three-dimensional? Did Kai ever teach you how to draw them that way?"

"No, but Kai only showed me foundational principles. I guess he didn't think it was relevant." A triumphant smile pulled at her cheeks.

"Or maybe he didn't know. Maybe Nuriel picked up on it."

"Maybe, but he didn't finish. Look." She laughed, dragging the image to the corner where he'd written in the margin, *Que diable?* "It must have stumped him."

Bridget's lips curved up. "Wow. You did it." She wrapped an arm around Dahlia's shoulders and squeezed. Warmth flooded through her.

"Can you finish it?" Bridget asked.

Some of her excitement ebbed. She tilted her drawing, inspecting it from various angles. "I can try. I'm going to need help, though. This is way beyond what I've learned."

Bridget pulled her arm back. "We don't have the time. Keep trying."

The command stung like a hot poker. A flash of iron bars, of Kai's hard eyes. She gripped her pencil in a stranglehold. "I'm doing my best, Bridget."

"I know, but hurry, okay?"

Dahlia shifted away from her sister. "Stop pushing me so damn hard. You're acting like Kai."

A bright red flush colored Bridget's cheeks, and her eyes widened in horror. "No, Dahlia. I'm sorry. I didn't mean to pressure you."

Dahlia glared at her. "Too late. What are *you* contributing?"

"I'm—I'm going to make sure we can get to James."

"Good. You do that." Dahlia flipped to a fresh page of

her notebook. She could feel Bridget's eyes on her, but Dahlia refused to take the bait and look up. Just because Bridget had been a bossy second mom in their childhood, that didn't give her the right to push her now. Not with the echoes of Kai's demands still ringing through her nightmares.

Bridget finally heaved a sigh and stood. She let herself out of the room and closed the door behind her.

Dahlia listened to Bridget's footsteps recede, then returned to her notebook. She tried to recapture the glimmer of excitement, but Bridget's rigidness consumed a dark corner of her mind.

Practicing her newfound abilities with Nuriel, working on the sketch—all of it felt natural and *right* in a way Dahlia couldn't put to words.

The Grigori world pulled at her like a magnet, making her past feel brittle and faded. Somehow, she had to find a way to hold onto her humanity, and her sister. But not at the expense of suffocating this new part of herself. If anything, she needed to understand it more, so she could convince Bridget it wasn't dangerous or evil. She was still herself—just more.

She picked up her pencil and got back to work.

FOUR

Irritation fizzed through Bridget as she walked along the upstairs corridor. Dahlia was helping her, but for the wrong reasons. Where Bridget ached for the peace and predictability of her North Carolina apartment, Dahlia didn't seem to miss any of it—not home, not school, not even her friends. Any time Bridget mentioned them, her sister would look bewildered, like she was trying to remember why she *should* care.

Stopping at the top of the stairwell, Bridget let her frustration bubble up. If she was being honest with herself, it wasn't really her apartment she missed. Or even North Carolina, though she'd never lived anywhere else. Home hadn't felt like home ever since Dahlia left for college.

What Bridget wanted—what she *craved*—was the little sister she remembered.

The rift that had started when Dahlia moved to Cleveland had only grown wider since their reunion. Even with Dahlia physically near, she could feel her distance.

The clanging of pots sounded from the kitchen below, and she let the sound pull her from her thoughts. Two voices, Nuriel's and Gaul's, carried up the stairs as they discussed lunch. The meeting must have finally adjourned.

Two immortals discussing egg salad *would* have been funny, if they hadn't just finished a far more consequential conversation. Who knew how quickly Gaul would move them to a new, supposedly safer, location? Tannin could be prowling Cleveland right now, to both avenge Kai and retrieve the sketches. Viri's house wasn't exactly hidden, or secret. They were staying on borrowed time.

She pushed those thoughts aside. Before she could leave town, she needed to focus on James. And with the threat of Tannin looming near, she needed help from someone she could trust—someone who might agree with her. That certainly ruled out Gaul.

She made her way down the stairs, hand running along the wooden banister. In fact, she didn't need Gaul, or Nuriel. Right now, she needed Eisheth, the Grigori detective originally in charge of Dahlia's case. She and Bridget had once been at odds, but they'd formed a tentative allyship. Even if she didn't understand, she would listen.

Bridget found the detective in the library, sitting on a low sofa and rubbing her temples. Danel lounged in a chair across from her. Bridget paused in the hallway, not wanting to interrupt.

"If we're going to leave, we should do it right," Eisheth was saying.

"But you want to stay." Danel's mouth twitched into a smirk.

"Don't grin at me like that. Of course I want to stay. I'm not letting Tannin drive me from this city." She glanced over, noticing Bridget. "Yes?" Her dark hair was pulled back in a tight bun and her expression was etched into a frown.

"Ah..." Bridget glanced at Danel. She had no intention of speaking to Eisheth while he was around. "Can we talk?"

"Okay." Eisheth eyed Bridget suspiciously.

"Alone?"

Danel laughed and got to his feet. "Alright, hint taken." He sent a mock salute Eisheth's way as he left, earning an eye roll.

"What do you want?" Eisheth gestured to the chair Danel had vacated.

Bridget walked into the room. "You were saying we're leaving again?"

She sounded sour. "Probably. That's what Gaul wants. It's not as if we're well-hidden here."

Bridget settled herself on the edge of the deep leather chair. The room embodied coziness, with its dark paneled walls, potted plants, and handsome bookshelves. The stately fireplace was currently dark, but it was swept clean, and there was fresh wood in place, ready for a chilly morning. "How fast does he want us to move?"

"He *wants* us to go as soon as we can pack. I've convinced him to let us remain for a few more days." She sat across from Bridget, drawing her feet onto the spacious chair with her.

"Why do you want to stay?" Bridget said, fixing her with a level look.

Eisheth folded her arms. "We all have lives we've been dragged from. Friends we've abandoned, jobs we've lost. We'd like to tie up loose ends, as much as we can."

That gave Bridget pause. She'd come to think of the Grigori she knew as a cohort who lived, worked, and socialized only among themselves. But of course, Eisheth had her job at the police station. Nuriel was a museum docent, and Viri spent more time at his hospital job than at his house. It stood to reason that their work lives extended to social lives, as well. She wondered how they maintained relationships with humans while knowing they would outlive them?

Eisheth seemed to sense Bridget's questions. "We're used to leaving people behind, but I personally prefer to do it with some sense of closure. I've been put on administrative leave at work. I want to see the process through, if I have any hope of restarting my law enforcement career. Besides, running is a short-term solution."

"You think Tannin will find us anywhere we go."

The detective shrugged. "If he wants to badly enough, he'll make it happen. I'd prefer to face the problem directly than go on the run for who knows how long."

Bridget wrapped her arms around herself. As much as she wanted to put Tannin out of her mind, it was impossible to avoid him. Even though he might track her down anywhere, there was no question staying in Cleveland was a greater risk than leaving. "He's coming for me, right?"

"What makes you think that?"

"Danel told me."

Tannin's name evoked the memory of his powers—his toxic, black smoke. She'd seen him take out an entire parking lot with a single earthquake. Watched Kai defer to him, bowing to his authority. Tannin wasn't just strong. He was calculating and charismatic. It would take all of them to stand against him, and even then, it might not be enough.

Eisheth sat back in the chair. "I told Gaul we should invite Danel to the meetings. He's going to listen in anyway."

"Did you tell him to invite Dahlia and me too?" It was easier to be annoyed by Gaul's gatekeeping than it was to give breathing room to her fear.

"Of course. You're as involved as any of us. If going home was difficult before, it's even harder now."

Bridget dropped her gaze, running a finger absently over the back of her palm. "Why, though? It's not like I can tell anyone anything."

Eisheth followed Bridget's attention. "Tannin doesn't know about the silencing contract Gaul gave you. Even if he did, he's receiving pressure from too many people."

"What people?"

Eisheth paused. "One moment." She stood and disappeared into the hallway. Bridget waited, curiosity curling around her anxiety.

The detective returned with a few pieces of paper in hand. She offered them to Bridget, who pulled them close. They were printouts of conversations, written in blocks of text with little formatting. "What is this?"

"It's a forum we created to communicate with one another. Viri printed off a few pages."

"You couldn't have started a group chat?"

"I'm loathe to be the one to suggest *change* to this particular group. The forum barely gets any use, but lately activity has spiked. They're very eager for Tannin to even the scales, as they put it."

Bridget skimmed the posts. The thread was titled "WHERE IS JUSTICE?" and was followed by dozens of angry comments.

Tannin needs to fix this. He employed Dolos and the others. He promised them everything and look what happened.

I spoke with Ketill's partner. She said he only took the job because Tannin pressured him into it for his strength. And we all know how Kai is.

How Kai was. He's dead too. Three of us gone in one night. When was the last time that happened?

And all under Tannin's jurisdiction.

Does he read these threads?

I'm sure he does, but it doesn't matter. I'll pay him a visit. Make sure he knows how critical this is. No one should get away with the cold-blooded murder of our people. He needs to see that they are avenged. Immediately.

The room seemed to tilt around Bridget, and the nightmares she'd been nursing came back full force, accompanied by a twisted sense of nausea. She shoved the papers back at the detective.

Eisheth sighed as she took them. "We'll keep you safe. As safe as we can."

"What does that mean? If we avoid Tannin long enough, will he give up on avenging them?"

She shrugged, expression pinching. "I don't know."

"Even if he does, he still wants the sketches we took."

"I know. We may never be free from his attention. Not during your lifetime, at least."

Bridget's grip on the chair tightened. It was a grim picture the detective painted. In some ways, Bridget agreed with Gaul. Under any other circumstances, she would want to get as far away from Tannin as possible.

And she would, once James was at her side. She drew in a deep breath, then exhaled slowly. She'd come to Eisheth for a reason, and it wasn't to talk about Tannin.

"I want to ask a favor."

Eisheth sat back with a snort. "This ought to be good."

"I want to see James. If we're about to leave, I won't be able to say goodbye to him. And everything ended so abruptly—" She cut off as her voice cracked with genuine emotion.

"And you want to revive him."

Bridget started. "I—"

The detective gave Bridget a knowing look. "Do you think I believe for a second you want to see him *just* to gain closure?"

Warmth crept up the back of Bridget's neck. Like it or not, Eisheth knew her well. "I need to try."

"You don't *need* to try. It's tragic, Bridget, but death is the natural order of things. James died far too young, but he was always going to die."

"Nothing about James' death was natural or okay."

The detective softened. "I'm sorry, that was insensitive of me. But Bridget, we can't go down this path."

"Why not?" The response sounded petulant, even to Bridget's ears, but she stood firm.

Eisheth sighed, leaning back against the chair. "Because then we have to ask ourselves where it ends. Who gets to live, and who dies? Whose choice is it, or should it be no one's choice?"

"Isn't someone already making those decisions?" Bridget pointed out. "Look at Dahlia."

A grimace stretched across Eisheth's face. "My point exactly. Do you really want to replicate what Kai did to her? Immortality with no choice in the matter? Taking closure away from his friends and family?"

Guilt pressed on the edges of Bridget's plans. Would someone search for James with the ferocity she had searched for Dahlia? The memory of those awful months of not knowing was still fresh, and she wouldn't wish the experience on anyone. She thought of her mother, who had now lost two daughters, with no hint of what had happened. Letting her know they were okay would only draw her closer to a dangerous world.

"I'd still like to see him before they alert his parents." This step in her plan, at least, wouldn't cause anyone undue pain. She could see James, map out the funeral home, and take the information back to Dahlia. Then they could figure out their next move.

Eisheth pressed her lips together into a thin line.

"Please?" Bridget pressed. "At least give *me* a chance to get closure."

The detective sighed and stood from her chair.

A flutter of anxiety washed through Bridget. "Where are you going?"

"To get Viri. He knows the funeral home director."

They found Viri in the front garden, tending an intricate array of pollinators. He was a tall, serious-looking man who held gazes during conversations with earnest clarity that bordered on unsettling. Bridget hadn't had much occasion to speak with him since they'd moved into his home, but she always felt intensely *listened to* when she did.

As she and Eisheth approached, Viri lifted a palm, coaxing fresh sprigs of lavender from the dark soil. They unfurled, stretching toward the sun with little bursts of purple flowers.

Viri looked up at them. "Lavender has always been one of my favorites. It makes me think of home."

"Where was home?" Bridget watched a bumblebee fly inelegantly towards the fresh flowers.

"Portugal." He lowered his hand and turned his full attention on them. "How can I help you?"

"Bridget needs a ride to the funeral home," Eisheth said.

Viri lifted his eyebrows. "How was your top-secret meeting?"

The detective blew out a sigh, then briefly recounted the morning meeting. Then she explained Bridget's desire to say goodbye to James. She didn't mention her suspicions about resurrection, for which Bridget was grateful.

Scratching his short beard, Viri considered. "I hope Gaul wasn't planning to leave without saying goodbye."

"That's between the two of you. Can you give us a ride?"

Viri nodded. "I owe Charlie a visit anyway. I'm afraid they're not entirely thrilled with the arrangement we've agreed to. Give me a moment to clean up."

He strode past them, disappearing into the house. Bridget went over to the newly grown lavender, bending to smell it. The bumblebee ambled past, drunk on pollen. "Before he died, James was making a list of everyone and their abilities."

"Oh?" Eisheth didn't sound impressed.

"He would've loved learning more. I don't think he ever imagined gardening as a superpower."

Eisheth responded with a disgruntled snort, and Bridget lifted her gaze to the second-floor windows. If she gave Dahlia some space, maybe she'd finish the sketches quickly. In the meantime, she had a funeral home to scope out.

FIVE

In the silence of the bedroom, Dahlia hunched over her notebook. It had been at least an hour since Bridget left for the funeral home, but she'd barely moved from the bed. All of her focus was on the drawing in front of her. Sketch, erase, sketch, erase. Memories of endless drawing under Kai's command lurked at the corner of her mind.

This was different. She *wanted* to help her sister, and she wanted to help James.

Alone in the bedroom, she still felt watched. Not by Bridget, or even the memory of Kai, but by herself. The new her, and the old her, both eyeing her hands as they skipped across the page.

Would James resent his new life, if they were successful? Sure, there was a shiny veneer of new abilities and a long life. But he'd also have to contend with a muddled, shadowy sense of self, and the unsettling reality of death and rebirth.

For almost ten months, the sense of *wrong*ness had chased Dahlia into her sleep. Disturbing dreams plagued her almost every night, filled with dark shadows and strangers' cries for help. She often awoke sweating, body coiled with tension.

And the dreams were followed by uncanny valley wakefulness. Every day brought a new discordant moment where something completely familiar felt utterly alien. Coffee dripping into a mug looked like a pool of murky oil. Music she'd loved sounded tinny and false. The word "sister" felt like a foreign language. Instances like these were happening more frequently—or maybe they were more noticeable when she was with Bridget. More than once, Dahlia had said something that *felt* natural, and her sister had responded with a look of surprise. As if she were a stranger.

The eraser tore through the page, ripping across her symbol.

"Damn it!" White-hot anger flashed across Dahlia's vision. She threw her pencil at the wall where it bounced off and rolled under the dresser. She knew Bridget would be upset if she didn't make progress. But her sister only valued her for what she could *do*, not who she *was*.

The torn drawing stared up at her, waiting. Dahlia slammed the notebook shut. In her youth, drawing had been her escape. She'd used it to retreat from the pressure of exams and fights with her family. Now, her private sanctuary was poisoned with new expectations and dark memories.

Some unexplored, alien part of her mind grasped her

irritation, fanning the flames. Fury seethed beneath her skin, sending heat crawling up her neck.

She needed to get the hell out of this room.

Hiding the phone and notebook under the mattress, she stalked into the hall. It felt good to move, and even better to swat at a fern hanging outside the door. It swung precariously, leaves whispering in protest.

Why did everyone insist on using her? Like one of her mom's old CDs, the feeling of injustice skipped and replayed.

The other Grigori didn't get treated this way. What made them so great, anyway? Gaul made people sick—some great power. Eisheth created fire faster than a Boy Scout, good for her. Nuriel could make it rain in a city renowned for gloomy weather, amazing. Danel could win in a sprint, good for him. And Viri? She scowled up at the fern again.

Her? She was either a tool or a problem. To Bridget, she was a means to an end. To the others, she was an unknown element, a human body connected to a symbol that didn't quite fit, granted rare mimicry abilities that put them on edge.

Bold of the others to think they were so damn special—because they knew who they were. The way they looked at her felt patronizing at best.

She growled and kicked over a ceramic pot. It cracked and spilled a succulent onto the hardwood.

A door across from her opened. "What's going on?" Spots of anger popped in her vision as Danel peered out. His brow furrowed. "Dahlia? Is everything alright?"

False concern. The mere sight of him made her want to scream.

Power flickered at the edge of her perception, radiating from Danel. His speed and the manipulation of earth tangled together. She tugged at the sensation, and spilled dirt rose around her, a constellation of soil hovered above her outstretched hand. With a sharp jerk of her wrist, she hurled it at Danel.

He yelped in surprise, darting behind the door in a blur. The damp dirt splattered against the wood with a hollow thump.

"What is *wrong* with you?" Danel demanded from inside the room. "This is what I get for trying to help?"

Dahlia made a low sound in her throat she barely recognized. Pressure built behind her eyes, warm tears clouding her vision. He should *know* what was wrong. He was the one who caused all of this. He stole her life, ruined everything.

In her rage, she sought out another thread of power and darted after him. The world slowed around her, and she kicked his door forward. Time popped back to its standard pace as the door swung in swiftly, met with an "Ow!" on the other side. Danel hopped into view, holding his foot. "Dahlia! Cut it out!"

He couldn't even take a stubbed toe? She snarled, raising her hand and feeling another clump of dirt float into the air behind her. She squeezed her fist, and it coalesced into a loose ball.

A sudden tug. The dirt jerked out of the air and fell to the ground, peppering the carpet runner. Dahlia started, looking behind herself.

"That's quite enough," Gaul said. He stood in the center of the hallway, hand outstretched to his side, fingers splayed. With her attention diverted from Danel, she could now sense his earth-based power. It was stronger by orders of magnitude, pulsing like a second heartbeat around him.

With a low growl, Dahlia tried to raise the dirt from the floor, but it held firm. Gaul's strength outweighed hers by millennia of life, and the harder she tried the more her own strength slipped away. Weariness washed over her.

Gaul pressed his lips into a thin, irritated line. "You're going to hurt yourself. Stop."

With a shaky sigh, she released her hold on his ability and slumped against the wall.

Danel came out of his room, eyeing Gaul warily. "I didn't do it this time. I swear."

"Take a walk, Danel. Dahlia, come with me." Gaul descended the stairs without waiting to see if either would obey.

She could feel Danel trying to catch her eye, but she pointedly turned her gaze away. Straightening, she followed Gaul downstairs, leaving Danel behind. Her pulse began to even out, adrenaline draining away.

Embarrassment mingled with frustration. Gaul had watched her make an idiot of herself, while stopping her with barely a thought. Danel probably could have done the same, if he hadn't been taken by surprise.

She stepped into the kitchen, steeling herself for a reprimand. Gaul was opening the bar cabinet as she entered. "Whiskey?"

She paused. "Um, sure."

He gestured for her to sit at the kitchen table as he brought out a bottle and two glasses. Afternoon sun filtered through the vines encircling the window and encroached on the door to the back porch. It lit his red hair ablaze.

She pulled out the same chair she had used that morning, watching as he dug whiskey stones out of the freezer, then poured the amber liquid over them.

Gaul sat across from her at the table with the whisky and glasses, sliding one of them in her direction. She took a sip. It was smoky, and it burned. Which was, as it turned out, exactly what she wanted right now.

He set his glass down, and said, "I'm sorry you have to stay in the same building as Danel. I imagine it's hard to share space with him."

Dahlia eyed him uneasily. "You're not going to chastise me?"

He lifted a shoulder and sat back in his chair. "You couldn't have caused any real damage."

The statement stung. "Danel looked nervous."

"You're acting in a way he doesn't expect." Then he sighed, shaking his head. "This isn't my first time being around young Grigori, you know. Danel and Eisheth had similar outbursts early on. Even Nuriel had his moments."

"So what, we're kids having temper tantrums to you? Ret said the same thing about *you*."

Gaul didn't look bothered by the comparison. "In a manner of speaking. You're testing your limits. That's a trying experience."

She scowled at her drink, then took another sip. "I guess my limits are pretty pathetic."

"For now. But your strength will grow. *Is* already growing. Training can help."

"Then why haven't *you* been willing to train me?"

Gaul took a sip of whiskey. His gaze lifted to the ceiling, where the fan turned in a languid circle. When he spoke, his tone was thoughtful. "There's a lot you still don't know."

"That's a bullshit answer and you know it." Dahlia set her glass down hard enough to make liquid slosh up the edges. "I won't learn if you don't teach me."

Gaul lifted his eyebrows, looking back at her. "You're far more direct with me than your sister is."

"That's because I'm not afraid of you." She'd confronted far worse than a prickly redhead with a penchant for whiskey.

A flicker of amusement crossed his face. "She's afraid of me, is she? I suppose I've earned that."

Dahlia brushed past the comment. The burn of the whiskey was soothing her fury, allowing her to focus. The shadow in her mind shifted, eager for answers. "Why have you been avoiding me?"

Gaul's smile faded, stoicism returning. "Unstable matches like you are dangerous. So are mimics in general."

Frustration fluttered through her. "Are you going to tell me what that means, or keep speaking in riddles?"

He lifted his drink, swirling the liquid. "Which part?"

"What does it mean to be an unstable match? Why would Kai use a symbol that doesn't work right?"

Gaul shook his head. "It works fine, clearly. The problem is the personality of the Grigori and personality of the human are at odds."

She tightened her grip on her tumbler. "Which means?"

He gestured to her. "That little temper tantrum

upstairs. Would it have happened in your previous life?"

She paused. Her outburst earlier had felt natural, but before her kidnapping, she'd prided herself on staying level-headed during conflict. She never flew into an uncontrollable rage. But at the same time, who knew how her traumatic months trapped in Tannin's cage had changed her? Who was to say the hatred she was incubating had anything to do with being a Grigori. She was due some rage toward Danel. Right?

He tipped the bottle over her glass, giving her another splash of the drink. "You look like you're going to need more."

She nodded her thanks, glaring down at the table. "What about the other part? The mimicry? I fail to see what's so dangerous about having no abilities of my own."

Gaul sipped his drink. "Plenty. There are two consequences to your mimicry. The first you've already caused without knowing: if you use my earth ability when I'm nearby, it depletes my own reservoir."

She exhaled slowly. "I didn't realize it lessened what you were able to do."

"Yes. Although it's negligible at this point, so it hasn't been an issue."

He loved to remind her of that. "What's the second aspect?"

"Permanent siphoning. Some of the strongest mimics in our history have collected a vast array of abilities. They don't need to be in proximity, if they are strong enough, or rather, all of Earth is within their proximity."

Her eyes widened. "As in, I could have permanent access to *every* power? By draining those around me?"

He held up a finger. "A: that would be rude. But B: yes, give it a few millennia."

She stared at him. "So, I could theoretically take away Tannin's powers?"

Gaul shook his head sharply. "That's a stupid idea. He's already two thousand years your senior and will be even stronger by then. My hope is this feud will be long forgotten by the time you have that kind of strength. But even if not, it comes with serious consequences. Holding too many of them at one time can destroy your mind. Not to mention your relationships with other Grigori."

The revelations were important, but they were still distractions. "You don't want to train me because you're worried I'll steal everyone's powers in several thousand years? I don't buy it."

A frown etched itself onto Gaul's face. "No. That's not why."

"Well?" She leaned forward, as if getting closer would allow her to yank the information from him.

Gaul sucked in a breath, seeming to steady himself. "Ret created me after the war, but mimics still had quite a reputation, and I was advised to give them a wide berth—those who had survived."

"*All* mimics? That's not fair." Dahlia clicked her nails against her glass. "You shouldn't hate a person for something they can't control."

"That's what I thought too. Only a handful remained, and I had the occasion to meet one. He was..." Gaul trailed off, expression contorting. "He didn't seem like the villain I'd been told to fear."

His words were measured and precise in a way Dahlia wasn't used to hearing from Gaul. She thought she saw pain behind those ice-colored eyes.

"He was someone you cared for, wasn't he?"

The moment shattered in an instant. Gaul's scowl settled back into place. "He tricked me. Took advantage of my youth and my abilities."

So, his refusal to work with her stemmed from a jilted lover centuries prior? That hardly seemed fair.

"Was it really that bad?"

Gaul met her gaze. "Have you ever heard of the Black Death?"

Coldness seeped through her. "Oh. Shit."

"Hartu had lost close comrades during the war. In the millennium after, he experienced more heartbreak and abuse from humans, not to mention his own kind. In his misery, he found only anger and a desire for vengeance."

Gaul sighed, turning his glass on the table. It rasped with each rotation. "The sickness spiraled beyond what even he imagined was possible. It caused centuries of devastation. I got sick myself, tending to those who were infected. I nearly died, but Ret found me, healed me, and traveled with me for a time, so I could continue atoning."

She watched his faraway expression with interest. This was not the Gaul she expected. It seemed there *was* a heart, deep down there. "Whatever happened to Hartu?"

"He died of the bubonic plague a century after he began it," Gaul replied hollowly.

An ache spread through her. She knew how it felt to be betrayed by someone you trusted. "I'm sorry."

Gaul rolled his shoulders back, as if shrugging off the grief. "In a way, his actions led me to Viri. For that, at least, I'm grateful."

"To Viri? How?"

"You'll have to ask him." Gaul tipped back his whiskey and drained the glass.

"You know, I'm not Hartu. You don't have to treat me like you would treat him."

"No?" He set his empty glass down with a thump. "You wear his naming symbol on your back."

Ice prickled her heart as the pieces clicked into place.

Hartu died centuries ago, but his magic persevered, living on in her. Was it his influence that caused the bursts of anger she didn't recognize? Was his latent personality the cause of her rage?

The *rightness* of the shadow within her seemed more sinister now. It pressed on her, larger than her twenty years of experience, urging her to accept it *as* her.

But the way Gaul told it, that shadow was the echo of a vindictive, vengeful person who'd caused centuries of suffering. No wonder he was hesitant to train her.

Was this her inheritance? Her legacy?

A realization struck her. "Is that why, when you and Ret snuck into Tannin's place, you made time to get my *drawings*, but not free me?"

He had the decency to flush, but his eyes remained steady on hers. "Yes. I had seen a photo of the tattoo on your wrist. If you were with Tannin, we knew he'd likely used the same symbol to revive you. Hartu was back. We believed it was for everyone's safety."

"But I'm *not* Hartu." Saying it out loud made her feel better. She *wasn't* a centuries-dead man who'd drowned in his own desire for revenge. "I have a different human mind, a different human background. And what about *my* safety?"

Gaul made a low rumbling sound. "I *do* regret it now."

"If Bridget hadn't come back for me, I'd still be there."

"Yes."

His brashness took her aback. It reminded her of Tannin—someone so old and removed from human suffering he'd forgotten how to care.

He softened as he watched her. "Dahlia, I'm sorry. I let my personal feelings get in the way of practicality. It's far safer to keep you with us than allow you to stay with Tannin."

The way he spoke about her, as if she were a powerful but delicate weapon, set her teeth on edge. "Tannin is an enemy to all of us, and I deserve to know how to fight back. At the very least, I need to know how to control my abilities, so I don't hurt any of you when I'm stronger."

She would never allow herself to become Hartu.

Gaul considered her, then stood from the table. He went to the sink, soaping up, then rinsing out his glass. Setting the clean tumbler aside, he returned to her, leaning over to rest his hands on the table.

"Fine. Let's go out to the garden."

SIX

Bridget peered through Viri's car window as it rolled up to the funeral home, trying to take in as many details of the funeral home as she could. She didn't know which would be important when they came back for James.

The building itself was a single story, its once-white siding gone gray from years of rain and snow. A dark green sign read Stevenson Funeral Home in gold lettering, with a small bed of flowers underneath. The building's yard was one massive parking lot. Viri pulled into an empty space next to the only other cars: a battered Volvo and an aged hearse.

"Let me do the talking. Charlie and I are friends, but the situation is unusual." Viri opened his door.

A glass-paned front door marked the entrance. Bridget glanced up at the awning, searching for cameras. Finding nothing, she relaxed a little. Their rural surroundings were working to her benefit. The only visible security measures were the intricate metal grates covering the windows.

Viri opened the door and a warbling electronic chime sounded from deeper inside. The heavy smell of lilies greeted them as they passed into an entryway wallpapered with tiny pink flowers. The dizzying pattern was interrupted by two open doorways and several framed cross stitch patterns with sayings like, "In loving remembrance" and "Hope is the thing with feathers."

Bridget stepped lightly. It felt wrong to make unnecessary noise, even though the low-ceilinged chapel to her right sat empty. She started to make a mental map of the facility. It was unlikely she and Dahlia would enter through the front door, but she noted a larger side entrance beyond the chapel, as well as a set of stairs descending into the basement.

Viri called out, "Hello?"

A petite person with a violently pink undercut and purple horn-rimmed glasses rounded the corner. "Dr. Barbosa, good to see you." Their voice was light, but they looked wary. The light from the wall-mounted electric candelabra glinted off their nose ring. Everything about them clashed with their surroundings.

He smiled warmly. "Good to see you. These are my friends, Bridget and Detective Elizabeth Ivanova." He turned to them. "Meet Charlie. They're the best mortician in the county."

"The only in the county," Charlie quipped. "What can I do for you?"

"Sorry for dropping by unannounced, but we were wondering if we could see James. It's nearly time to return him to his family, and they wanted to say goodbye."

Charlie hesitated. "Are you certain?"

"They're about to travel, so this is their last chance."

They glanced uneasily at Bridget and Eisheth.

Viri added, "It's alright. They know about the arrangement."

Charlie didn't look encouraged. They lowered their voice. "I can't keep him here for much longer. It doesn't sit right."

Viri took Charlie's hand, squeezing it. "I know. I appreciate all you've done for us. It's been an immense help."

Charlie's gaze softened, but a moment after Viri let go, they shook their head. "All the same, James needs to be returned to his family."

"You have my full support in returning him, once we leave town. Isn't that right, Detective?"

Eisheth shot Bridget an apologetic look. "All of the necessary reports are ready to file. We appreciate your patience. This was a tricky situation, and the police department didn't want to release anything prematurely."

Bridget didn't meet the detective's eyes. She considered Eisheth and Viri allies, but in James' future they were united against her.

Charlie's expression remained polite, though they sounded reluctant. "Of course. Happy to help."

"Can we see him now?" Bridget asked. She didn't relish the idea of looking at his body, devoid of life, but they'd been standing in the entryway long enough for Bridget to create a mental map of the area. She needed to examine more of the funeral home.

Resignation flashed across Charlie's gaze. "Right this way. Watch your step."

They started down the stairs. The wooden stairs were even, and they made hollow *thumps* with each footfall. As the group descended, the sharp smell of ammonia and formaldehyde burned her nose. It was a far cry from the musty smell of her own childhood basement.

Bridget partly expected to emerge into a vast, macabre space, filled with shadowy corners. But the stairs only led to a well-lit hallway extending in both directions, with white walls and more cross-stitch decor. These ones took on a less austere tone. The framed piece nearest her pronounced "F*CK CANCER" in purple and black stitching.

To Bridget's left, the hallway was lined with doors. To her right, another stairwell led up, with an exit sign glowing above it. Daylight filtered through windowpanes on a door at the top.

Two entrances, then. Bridget tucked away that bit of information for later.

Charlie led them down the hall to the left. They opened one of the doors, leading them into another tiled room, this one with a stainless-steel table in the center. Bridget froze in the doorway. The table reminded her of the one in Tannin's basement, where James had been killed. That room, too, was a repository of the dead.

As Charlie flicked on the light switch, Bridget steadied herself and followed the others. This wasn't Tannin's lair, and no one was going to die today.

The room had six rectangular metal doors set into the back wall. Bridget recognized them from shows as mortuary freezers. A laminate counter wound around the sides of the room, topped with machines Bridget didn't recognize.

Once they were all inside, Charlie approached one of the metal doors and turned the latch. The door swung, and they slid out a long, metal tray. Bridget's heart sank with dread at the white sheet, laid gently over the entirety of James' body. From across the room, all she could make out was the curve of his feet.

Charlie turned to them. "I'm very sorry for your loss, and I'm glad to give you time with your loved one. However, I need you to understand that this situation is highly unusual." Their voice was soft, like they were speaking to a nervous horse. "Since James' family hasn't yet had a chance to recover his body or let me know what they wish to be done, I haven't prepared him. You may find it a bit disturbing." They gestured to the counter. "There's a tissue box in the corner, and there's water in the break room across the hall. Take all the time you need."

Charlie slipped into the hall and silently closed the door.

A hush fell over the three of them, and Bridget stared at the shrouded body. Her stomach clenched, and she felt rooted to the spot. She'd come here to learn the layout of the funeral home under the guise of saying goodbye to James. Now that she was here, now that she had the information she needed and was confronted with his death, she felt the urge to run.

But Viri and Eisheth were both watching, waiting for her to move toward the freezer. She braced herself. She had to see this through.

Giving the two of them a grim nod, she walked to the tray. She swallowed, throat thick. The sheet gave only an impression of what waited for Bridget underneath, and her palms were sweaty as she reached up to take the corner between two fingers. Slowly, she pulled it back.

James' hair was as curly as ever, but his skin was an unnatural gray color, bloodless and gaunt. His eyes were closed, thankfully. The area beneath them held dark shadows. A large swatch of gauze had been placed over his chest, blocking the fatal wound from view. He looked peaceful, but no one could ever mistake him for sleeping.

Her vision blurred, and warm tears slipped from the corners of her eyes. There was no world in which she wouldn't fight to revive him. She and Dahlia were both making progress, and he'd be okay. He'd died because of them, so it was only right that they brought him back.

She closed her eyes, picturing him as he'd been in life—grinning, bounding with energy, nerdy to the max. It was through his urging that Bridget had followed the right trail to Dahlia. His excitement kept her hopeful when it felt like all was lost. Their brief time together had changed her life. Standing over his still body, Bridget made a silent promise to do right by him. Whatever it took.

"Do you know why I became a doctor?" Viri's voice was close enough that Bridget started and opened her eyes. She hadn't heard him move forward.

"No." Her voice was thick, and she cleared her throat.

"One of my abilities is tied to emotion. Under my touch, I can manipulate how someone feels. I thought, arrogantly, that I could use it to take away the suffering of others. To help them find courage to face their diagnosis."

Bridget glanced up at Viri, but he wasn't looking at her. His eyes were on James.

"It didn't work?"

"Oh, it did. But as soon as I left, the grief crashed down harder than before." Viri sighed and turned his attention to her. "In my attempts to help, I made it so much worse. I learned that my job wasn't to eliminate suffering. It was to be there to support them through it. Humans, Grigori—we're all shaped by the hardships we've endured. We can't cheat our way out of grief; we have to coexist with it."

Bridget looked back at James, setting her jaw. "He didn't deserve what happened to him."

"No. But all you can do is move forward, and honor him as best you can."

"I will." Her way of honoring him might just be different from what Viri was imagining.

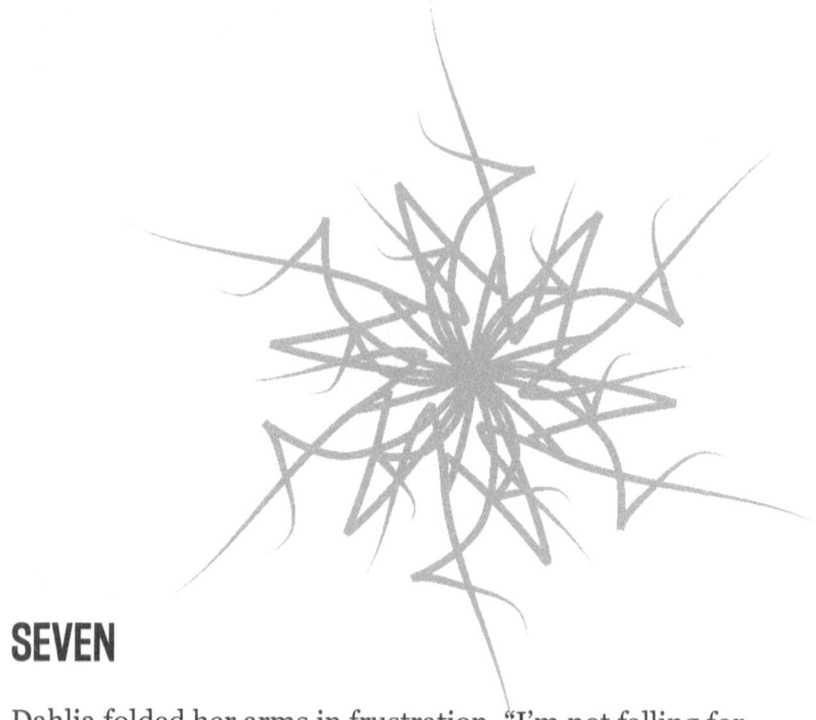

SEVEN

Dahlia folded her arms in frustration. "I'm not falling for that again."

"Strength isn't only a matter of age." Gaul and Dahlia stood among the hedges of Viri's labyrinthine gardens. The house was fifty feet away, and between here and there was an abundance of rose bushes, fountains and bird baths, and ivy-covered trellises.

An empty flowerpot rested on the ground between them. He'd asked her to move it with her abilities as he used his own to hold the fired clay in place. "Strength is also derived from creativity."

"What do you mean?"   The drink had helped her rally, but she didn't have anything close to Gaul's stamina with Grigori powers.

"I've seen Eisheth cause an explosion with nothing more than a spark." Gaul looked down at the flowerpot. "Don't push. *Think.*"

Dahlia sighed and shook out her arms. "Think. Right."

Gaul's powers were there for the taking, twin pulses she could sense. They were jumbled, intertwined, hard to distinguish. But when she focused, she could catch glimmers of how they differed. One felt rich and moist. The other stank of decay and darkness.

Suppressing a shudder at the sensation, she grasped a tendril and held it between her hands. It wasn't substantive, really. There was nothing to see or touch. But it was accessible. Cupping her hands together made it feel like she could scoop the power up and mold it to her desires.

She sought out the flowerpot between them. The same rhythm of Grigori magic surrounded it—Gaul holding it in place with his strength.

She gave a tentative nudge, but the pot held firm. Pushing harder, she flared her borrowed ability. Sweat broke out on her forehead, and she clenched her fists as she siphoned as much of Gaul's power into herself as she could muster. Giving one last shove, she focused all her energy into the pot.

It didn't move. Gaul yawned.

The earthen ability slipped from Dahlia's grasp, and she staggered backward. She panted, glaring at the offending flowerpot. Gaul had centuries of experience. She'd never be able to overpower him.

There had to be another way. This is what he wanted her to learn. "You just want me to move it?"

He nodded. "Make it budge."

It was like staring at the drawing in her sketchbook upstairs, trying to figure out which line to draw next. This was a puzzle to solve, not a trap to escape.

After a moment of consideration, she released her attention on the flowerpot, seeking the dirt beneath it instead. With a tug of Gaul's earth, she pulled the soil toward her.

It piled up, and the flowerpot tilted downward into the new divot.

"Excellent," Gaul said with a rare, full smile.

Nearby clapping startled Dahlia. She released her hold on Gaul's ability and looked across the lawn. Ret approached them, grinning. "How long did it take Danel to learn that?"

Gaul's scowl returned. "Too long. But he never bothered showing up to practice."

"Well, it's nice to see you helping. You're a good teacher." The compliment earned Ret a surly glare from Gaul, which the other man simply laughed off. "Dahlia, well done. I'd like to have some lessons with you too, if you're amenable."

"Now?"

"If you'd like."

Gaul gestured for Dahlia to go ahead. She reached out for Ret's abilities. Ethereal air and sparkling healing surrounded him. The pulsing was even stronger than Gaul's—so present, she found them hard to ignore. Now that she'd been taught what to look for, it was hard to believe she'd never noticed the auras before her training had begun a week ago.

She squared off in front of Ret. "What do you want me to do?"

"Knock the flowerpot over with my power," he said.

She glanced at it. "With Gaul holding it?"

"This time, try for brute strength."

Dahlia frowned, not sure what he was getting at. If she hadn't been able to push the pot over before, how would this be any different? But she obediently pulled a tendril of the magic toward her. It was cool and inviting. She shaped the currents, then *pushed*.

The pot shuddered, then fell neatly on its side. The terra cotta shattered into large shards.

"I did it!" Dahlia exclaimed in shock. "Did you see that? I knocked it over!"

Gaul bent and began gathering the broken pot pieces. "And now you see how the different abilities react to one another. If we're both trying to move the same clay pot, my strength far outweighs yours. But earth and wind interact differently. I can't defy the laws of physics."

Ret chuckled. "I think most humans would argue we defy the laws of physics every day."

Dahlia's pulse raced with excitement as possibilities unfolded in her mind. With so many possibilities at her fingertips it didn't matter if she was young and new. She could find creative ways to bend the magic to her will. Her strength could come from her flexibility and innovation.

Gaul's voice brought the world around Dahlia back into focus. "At this rate, she'll have a new name before we know it."

Ret shook his head. "Don't pay him any mind, Dahlia. You don't have to choose a new name until you're ready. No one will rush you."

The shift in topic leached away her excitement. Nuriel had told her about the Grigori practice of renaming oneself, but she'd tucked the information aside for a much later time. It was a ceremonial shift they'd observed for as long as any of them could remember. It had become a symbolic way to indicate the readiness to fully leave their old, human existence behind and embrace life as a Grigori. To reinvent themselves. To become their true selves.

She thought of her sister, determined to reclaim the life they'd both lost. "What if I never take on a new name?"

Ret shifted his weight. "That's your decision. And one we can never take away from you."

"It's also not likely," Gaul said. He seemed back to his usual bad mood.

Ret heaved a sigh, leaning on his left crutch so he could smooth back his dark, wavy ponytail. "There may come a time when you no longer feel your past life suits you. When—*if*—that happens, we'll support you. And if it doesn't, we'll support you in that, too."

"Have there ever been Grigori who didn't change their name?" Dahlia asked.

Ret shook his head. "Not to my knowledge. Nuriel was the last to, and one of the youngest of our kind. The older we get, the more we feel the need to seek out a more fitting identity."

Dahlia didn't like to think of time in terms of centuries and millennia. It seemed too big, too unwieldy to grasp.

Ret's attention flickered back to Gaul. "I originally came out here to tell you I've made some progress in locating Eris."

The name was a memory in Dahlia. "The person Danel worked for before Tannin?"

"Yes." The corners of Ret's eyes tightened. "We were colleagues once. Eris, myself, and Tannin."

Surprise hitched Dahlia's breath. "You worked *with* Tannin?"

"A long, long time ago. Eris and I got to know him quite well."

Gaul straightened and brushed dirt from his khakis. "We can continue this conversation later." He shot a pointed look at Dahlia.

She balked at the dismissal, turning to Ret. "Is she trustworthy?"

"That's what I hope to find out. Don't worry, Dahlia. You have enough on your plate right now. Focus on your training and I'll handle the politics of the situation."

It was still a dismissal, though Ret no doubt meant it to land more softly. Resolving to speak to Ret in private later, she rolled her shoulders back, turning to face Gaul. "Fine. Again."

"Are you certain you don't need a break?" He nodded to Ret as he gave them both a wave and headed toward the front of the house.

Dahlia watched his retreating figure, then turned back to her once-reluctant instructor. "You don't get breaks in a fight."

"Well put. Let's get back to it."

They returned to their positions. Dahlia held her hands up, ready to push, but Gaul stopped her.

"Let's try something different." He gestured to the ground in front of them. It split and cracked, revealing softer soil underneath. "Bring the dirt into three separate piles of the same size."

"Is this another puzzle?"

Gaul raised his eyebrows. "A different kind of practice. Finesse is as powerful a skill as strength."

Moving dirt around couldn't be nearly as difficult as knocking the pot over. Focusing on his abilities, she drew at his earthen power. Instead of pushing, this time she tried to wrap the ability around the exposed soil.

Instead of piling up, it pulled together into a tight ball, rolling toward her. Surprised, she loosened her grip, and it collapsed into a crumbling pile.

Pressing her lips together, she shifted her focus, trying to tidy the dirt. The soil churned, as if a mole were nosing it around, then it settled into a loose spray.

Gaul's smirk was on full display. "Not so easy, is it?"

She glared at the uncooperative ground. "Why won't it work?"

Gaul shrugged, twisting his hand in a way that drew the scattered dirt into a neat pile. With two more gestures, he created two identical piles. "We've only scratched the surface of what you can do with a *single* power. Most Grigori have two powers to master, but you have all eight, on top of their derivations."

"How many of those are there?"

"Countless. For example, Tannin and I both can manipulate earth, but for me, that means soil and stones. For him, it manifests as volcanic output. You'll need daily training sessions, with a rotation of what is available to you here."

She wrapped her arms around herself at the mention of Tannin. "I've already been doing that with Nuriel."

"Nuriel won't push you hard enough."

He was probably right. Nuriel's teaching style was gentle and exploratory. Prickly as Gaul was, she appreciated the way he challenged her. She squared her shoulders. "I don't mind working hard."

"Good." The ice in his eyes softened ever so slightly. "I am sorry this is the world you've been shoved into. Most of us have decades to grow accustomed to our new lives."

Dahlia pushed her weariness aside. "It's a good thing I'm a fast learner then. Let's go again."

They practiced for another hour before Dahlia was so tired she could barely stand, let alone think of creative ways to move dirt. When Gaul declared they were done, she plopped right down on the ground, breathing hard.

"It will get easier." Gaul swept his hand in an outward motion. The divots and mounds of soil smoothed out, removing any sign of their training session.

"I hope so." She rubbed the sweat from her forehead.

The earlier conversation with Ret resurfaced, and she looked up at Gaul. "Can I ask you a question?"

"Fine."

"How did you choose your name?"

He cast his eyes to her. "The idea stuck, did it?"

She shrugged. "I'm curious."

"It's different for everyone. Danel's name came as the result of a drinking game, if I recall correctly."

Dahlia rolled her eyes. "Somehow I don't think you'd be so cavalier about the whole thing."

"'Gaul' is the name of my people. At least, it's what the Romans called us, before they drove us nearly to extinction. I wanted a name that would remind them we weren't all gone."

Romans? Not for the first time, it struck Dahlia how ancient some of the Grigori were. When Gaul's lover had unleashed a plague on the world, he'd already been centuries old.

A thousand questions bubbled up, but Gaul was saved from further prying by a blur of motion. Danel hurtled to a stop, almost colliding with them. His cheeks were bright red, and he doubled over, hands on knees as he panted.

"Danel? What's wrong?" Gaul's tone was on instant alert, and both he and Dahlia stood.

"Back at the house." Danel gasped. He turned his head to the side and spat, then cleared his throat. "Tannin's here."

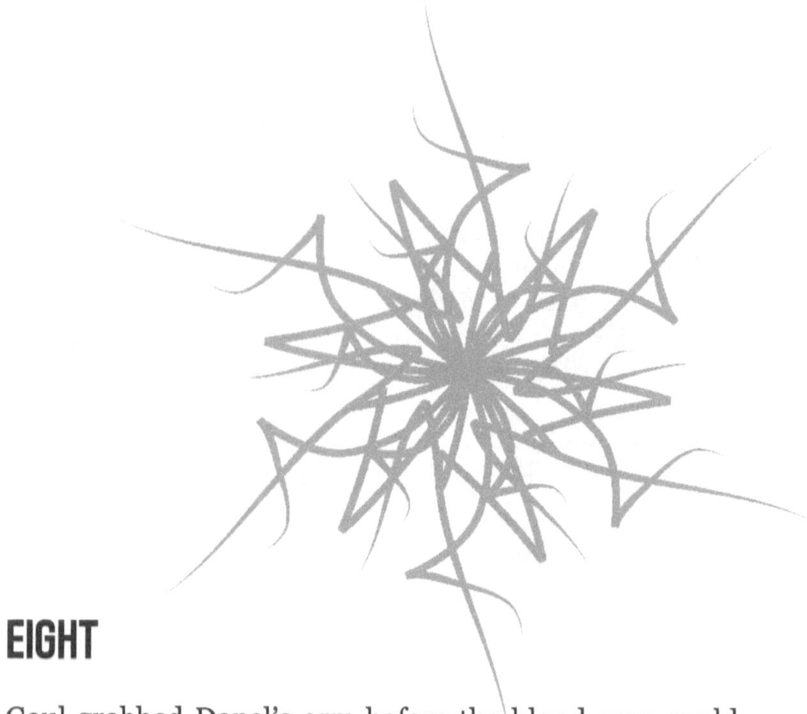

EIGHT

Gaul grabbed Danel's arm before the blond man could disappear. "Did he see you?"

Danel's grimace provided answer enough.

Dahlia's mouth went dry as she got to her feet. If there was anything she knew deep in her bones, it was that she absolutely could not be recaptured by Tannin.

Gaul craned his neck to look toward the front of the house, but it was out of their field of view. "I'll handle this. You and Dahlia wait here. Stay out of sight."

He set off around the house.

Dahlia watched the stiff set of his shoulders as he walked away, keenly aware of how her heartbeat pulsed in her ears. The edges of her vision were closing in. Tannin was here. He'd found them—or maybe he'd known where they were all along.

Thank God Bridget wasn't at the house. She, at least, would be safe. But that wouldn't stop Tannin from trying to collect the sketches or dragging her back to Athens.

"Hey." Danel's gentle voice cut through her fear like barbed wire. She stiffened further. "We won't let him take you."

She swallowed back the acrid taste of bile. Letting Danel see her freak out wouldn't help anything. Besides, she wasn't in captivity anymore.

"I know." She inhaled deeply to rally her strength. Letting her arms drop to her sides, she shook them out.

Danel eyed her. "Okay. I'm going to get closer." He blurred away before Dahlia could respond, leaving behind the rustle of leaves.

She stood alone in the garden, feeling cold despite the sweat matting her hair. Looking back at the house, she wavered. She could stay here, as Gaul had directed, and let the others handle Tannin's appearance. But then she'd be in the dark—again. At the very least, she could listen in to their conversation, safely out of sight.

Steeling herself, she made her way to the sunroom. Closing the door quietly behind her, she entered the kitchen, then stood still and listened. Voices carried from the foyer.

"—what you want." Gaul's voice was flattened by the closed door between them.

"Two things." Dahlia's throat clenched at hearing Tannin's baritone. It was like a velvet-wrapped knife. "I want my drawings back. And I want the justice I'm owed: the sisters, and yourself."

"They aren't your drawings. And we aren't in the practice of handing over sacrificial lambs."

Dahlia gripped the handle to the kitchen door so tightly her knuckles ached.

"Then let's begin with something you *can* trade in. The sketches, Gaul, Ret. Don't make me take them by force."

The speed with which he dropped his request for so-called justice made her insides twist. In her experience, Tannin operated with surgical precision. If he was willing to shift his demands so easily, it was intentional. And it meant he was confident he could snatch them another way, outside of this negotiation.

The sketches were clearly his priority, and he couldn't be allowed to get them. No one but Bridget and Danel knew about her copies upstairs. But the originals, locked in Nuriel's safe, were at risk.

"They're gone. We destroyed them." Ret's lie sounded smooth.

Tannin responded with a disappointed scoff. "You wouldn't destroy a piece of our history."

Gaul snorted. "Ret's sentimental, but you're vastly overestimating *my* ability to give a damn."

She focused on the press of powers coming from the open foyer. They mingled together, difficult to discern. The only one she found herself confidently pinpointing was Gaul's now-familiar ability to move the earth.

Gaul was speaking. "You stole that girl's *life*."

"And gave her immortality. I fail to see the problem."

Tannin's words crawled up Dahlia's skin, leaving her lightheaded. Just being near him made her want to scream. She thought she could at least listen in on the conversation, but hearing him speak left her body shaking.

"There you are." A voice behind Dahlia sent a shock through her. She whirled around to see an unfamiliar woman entering the kitchen, through the backyard. She had blonde-and-gray curls pulled back from her face and wore jeans and a plain sweatshirt. "We've been looking for you." She spoke with the tone of a playful mother.

Dahlia had been so focused on Tannin she hadn't

noticed the flicker of strength behind her. Now, the woman stood squarely in Dahlia's escape path. A jolt of panic sent her heart racing.

"Let's go join the conversation, shall we?" She made a shooing gesture with her hands.

Dahlia's breath came in short gasps. She shook her head and took a step back, but the closed door blocked her path. She couldn't face Tannin. Not now. Her fury toward him was utterly buried under panic.

In a desperate rush, Dahlia tried to push past the stranger. But her hand shot out and snatched Dahlia's wrist. The physical touch sent a shock of electricity up her arm. More surprising than painful, she gasped and yanked her hand back, stumbling to a stop.

"That was a warning, sweetie. Let's not make this difficult." The other woman gestured toward the door, little arcs of lightning flicking up and down her arms.

Dahlia took a step back. In a panicked gesture, she tried to siphon off the woman's lightning. But the powers were unfamiliar, and Dahlia was exhausted from her training session. Blue light flickered and sparked in her palm, then fizzled out.

She clamped down on her fear. Losing her grip would only make her situation worse. She was valuable to Tannin; this new threat wouldn't kill her. So, she darted forward again, ducking past the woman.

White flashed in front of her eyes. An electric shock zapped down her spine, accompanied by a sharp stab of pain. Her legs gave out underneath her, and she collapsed, landing on her shoulder.

The woman hauled her to her feet with a tutting sound. She gripped Dahlia's arm and pushed her into the hall. "Found her for you, sir."

The conversation came to a standstill. Gaul and Ret

turned in unison to look at them. They flanked the front door to the house, blocking Tannin from entering. Beyond them, she caught a glimpse of tan skin and a well-cut suit. Shifting into full view, Tannin's lips smoothed into a thin smile. "Dahlia, there you are."

All her attempts to fight back panic failed. She couldn't take a full breath. She was back inside a cold, steel cage. Trapped. Regarded as a tool, not a person. Pacing endlessly, drawing line after line for the reward of a meager meal.

Tannin was still speaking. It took all of her willpower to listen to the words. "I see you've met my newest recruit, Cyrie. She's quite the prolific Artist."

He'd already found a replacement for Kai. It had only been a few weeks—were that many people willing to serve him? To placate themselves in front of his desire for Grigori dominance? Perhaps the lure of his massive collection was enough for them.

She forced herself to stand steadily as she faced down her captor. "Tannin." Her voice was raw, like sandpaper scraping across stone.

"I'm glad you decided to join us. We were just discussing you."

A tight ball of fury lodged itself in her throat. Dahlia swallowed it back and leaned into Ret's earlier lie. "We don't have your sketches."

Tannin responded with a disappointed sigh. "I don't believe you. Now that you're here, let me be plain. I never should have allowed Kai to imprison you. For that, I am deeply sorry."

Suspicion tightened Dahlia's shoulders.

"What do you want?" She hated how weak her voice sounded. Where was the fury she'd worked up with Bridget?

"Direct as always. I appreciate that about you."

She flinched. The compliment was coated in poison.

Tannin spoke with a business-like clip. "I would like to hire you, Dahlia."

The offer was so unexpected that surprise burst through Dahlia's fear. "What?"

She caught a glimpse of Gaul's murderous expression. Remembered his story about Hartu, the Grigori she'd inherited. Was *that* what Tannin was interested in?

"Not a chance." Dahlia hoped she sounded firm and confident, that he couldn't see the way her hands were shaking.

Tannin sighed, then nodded to Cyrie, who went to his side.

The relief Dahlia felt at the distance between herself and Cyrie was short-lived. With the two of them standing shoulder to shoulder, it felt even more like a stand-off. Dahlia approached Gaul and Ret, stopping between them.

Tannin adjusted the cuffs of his suit jacket, the picture of a casual businessman. "Even if working for me will clear your sister's name? I'd be willing to overlook her murder of Kai if you come with me."

Ret cut in. "Be reasonable, Tannin. Those deaths were *all* in self-defense."

Revulsion built up in the back of Dahlia's throat. Tannin truly thought he could overcome months of captivity with a few paper-thin offers. "I have no reason to trust you."

"Don't you wonder why these two keep you around? They're scared of you, child—Gaul, particularly. Of what you represent, of who you once were. If you come with me, I can help you *claim* your destiny, instead of hiding—*oof!*"

Tannin grunted and stumbled back onto the porch. A heavy terra cotta pot fell to the ground, splintering. Dirt rained down on the wood.

Gaul unclenched his fist, glowering. "Leave. Now."

The pungent smell of sulfur hit Dahlia. As Tannin straightened, black smoke bubbled out from around his feet. "That was exceptionally foolish, even for you."

Gaul hissed and made a grab for Tannin. He and Cyrie darted out of Gaul's range, and she spread her hands wide. Electricity crackled between her fingers.

Ret hurried on his crutches to put himself between them. "There's no need for violence. Tannin, please leave. Now."

The look Tannin gave Ret was filled with distaste. "Your friend shouldn't have started something he doesn't intend to finish." The stench of sulfur grew stronger.

Dahlia scrambled for the powers of those around her. Unlike her training sessions where she'd focused on one person at a time, a multitude of abilities pressed in on her. She picked out Gaul's through the cacophony, but beyond him was a seething torrent of sensations. The sheer amount of power left her lightheaded.

Burning pain sliced through her leg.

A sharp *tug* yanked her feet out from under her. She hit the floor hard, one of Tannin's dark tendrils of smoke tight around her ankle. Her nerves screamed, pinpricking with fire as she kicked frantically, trying to break free.

A grunt came from the porch, and the vice grip on her ankle loosened and vanished. Dahlia looked up to see Tannin thrown back against the railing, tackled by Danel.

She skittered back, her ankle screaming, as she tried to make sense of the fight.

A coil of smoke snaked around Danel's torso, throwing

him into one of the porch's support columns. He cracked into it with a cry and slumped to the ground, dazed.

A sharp wind kicked up from around Ret, twisting the smoke into dissipating eddies. The wind howled out the door, pushing Tannin further back onto the porch. "Leave, Tannin."

Tannin let out a low growl. "Cyrie, to me!"

A plume of smoke billowed against the gust. It thickened and hid Tannin from view. The woman stepped up beside him, into the swirl. Dahlia could barely make out her shadow. The air became heavy, like the calm before a lightning storm. The sharp tang of ozone burned Dahlia's nostrils. Then, the cloud crackled with blue lightning, exploding outward with a blinding flash.

It hit Ret and Gaul in their chests, knocking them backward. Ret hit the stairwell banister with a crash, his crutches clattering to the ground. The wind sputtered out. Gaul landed on one knee, panting and gripping his heart.

Heat rolled over Dahlia, thick with the cloying scent of rotten eggs. Gaul had been knocked back, down on one knee in the corner, furious glare on Tannin. Danel was nowhere to be seen.

"I'm capable of admitting when I was wrong." Tannin's voice was like oil as he approached. "I treated you poorly, Dahlia. Return with me, help me recreate the symbols, and I promise I will drop all charges against your sister."

A manic sensation of disbelief rose in Dahlia's throat, bursting free as a laugh. Not two minutes ago he'd been *bartering* for her and now he was bargaining with her?

Tannin's voice was firm as he continued. "You can be a part of the world we rebuild. Not this misguided attempt to diminish ourselves."

Filled with revulsion, she seized his smoke ability. Thrusting her hand forward, a thin rope, black as tar, extended from her fingers, coiling itself around Tannin's outstretched arm.

Tannin's eyes bulged wide. He snatched his hand back with a hiss. The tendril disappeared almost immediately.

"How *dare* you use my powers against me." Tannin rubbed his forearm, eyes glittering like polished jet. A wave of darkness piled up around him, blotting out the light from the open doorway.

Dahlia hurried back on her hands and knees until she pressed against the wall. Tannin stepped closer and the wall of smoke followed obediently.

Dahlia couldn't see Gaul or Ret anymore, but she heard a crackle of electricity, followed by a whine of pain. She reached for his powers, for any powers, but they were a tangle in her mind, impossible to grasp with Tannin looming overhead.

He's too strong. She couldn't fight back—not with any hope of winning. All of them together weren't enough to overpower him.

"Stop!"

Tannin's gaze flickered. Dahlia twisted, looking toward the voice.

Nuriel stood in the hallway wearing a determined expression. He held his sketchbook. "I'll give you what you want."

NINE

Guilt followed Bridget up the stairs to the main level of the funeral parlor. She hated leaving James alone in a dark basement. At the same time, she took solace in the fact that his situation was temporary. She would be back here soon, and she'd walk out with him.

Charlie was waiting for them at the top of the stairs. "Viri, a moment? I'd like to discuss our next steps."

"Why don't the two of you go wait in the car. I'll be right there." Viri handed the key to Eisheth.

They were almost certainly going to discuss Charlie's plans for James, and Bridget desperately wanted to stay for the conversation. But she suspected she'd already pushed her luck enough.

She followed Eisheth out, taking a deep breath as soon as she emerged into the sun. It hadn't smelled *bad* in the funeral home, exactly, but the fresh country air was a welcome change. The breeze blew strands of blonde hair across her face, so she gathered it back into a ponytail, securing it with an elastic around her wrist.

Eisheth wrapped her arms around herself, thin shoulder blades defined under her cardigan. She looked uncharacteristically distraught.

"Are you okay?" Bridget asked.

She scowled. "He shouldn't be here at all. But as long as he is, someone should stay with him."

The declaration surprised Bridget. Eisheth had barely known James and was clearly exasperated by the idea of reviving him. "You mean like a guard?"

Eisheth exhaled and shook her head. "No. It's a tradition from—never mind. It's from my life before... all of this." She waved vaguely at the parking lot around them.

They got into the car, Bridget sliding into the backseat once more. The inside was pleasantly warm. Eisheth left her door open, letting in the spring breeze.

"Do you ever miss it?" Bridget asked.

"Miss what?"

"Your home. Your human life."

"No."

There was enough ice in the word that Bridget knew she was treading on dangerous ground. Bridget and the detective had come a long way from their initial antagonism towards one another, but she would never be warm and cuddly.

The detective turned her stony gaze on Bridget. "You need to let him go, Ms. Keene."

She started. For a moment, she'd let herself forget that the detective had intuited her plans. But Eisheth certainly hadn't forgotten, even if she'd remained quiet during their visit. "I can't."

Eisheth pursed her lips, her disapproval plain. But she didn't push, and Bridget let the conversation lapse, turning her attention to her memory of the funeral parlor's layout. It didn't matter what the detective thought; Bridget's plans were already underway. Her fingers itched for a pencil, so she could draw it out before she forgot anything important.

The front door swung open, held by Charlie. Viri stepped past them with a wave, making his way back to the car. Opening the door, he slid into the driver's seat, turned the key and pulled them onto the road.

Bridget asked, "What were you and Charlie talking about?"

Viri glanced at her through the rearview mirror. "They were letting me know they can keep James for another week or so, but no longer. It's important we return him to his family soon."

Eisheth turned towards him, seatbelt rasping. "I asked one of my colleagues to explain a sanitized version of the situation to his parents when I give the go ahead. But I'm waiting to receive the okay from you first."

"Did they revoke your position, then?"

Eisheth's jaw twitched. "I'm on leave during their investigation. Which tends to happen when you let your cruiser get burned to a crisp."

Bridget looked between them in concern. A week. Even if Gaul *didn't* relocate them, the clock was ticking.

She drummed her fingers on her knee and watched the fields blur by. They'd been gone for almost two hours. Was that enough time for Dahlia to finish the sketches?

She tried not to get her hopes up. After all, Dahlia had spent months working on them under Kai's tutelage, to no avail. But they hadn't had Nuriel's additions then, or Dahlia's realization about their complexity.

"Do you smell that?" Eisheth asked as they turned onto the street leading to Viri's house.

"What?" Bridget opened the window further. She inhaled deeply. It smelled like the countryside. Fresh grass, manure, and spring flowers, all overlaid with the acrid tang of—

"Smoke."

"I have a bad feeling." Viri stomped on the gas pedal, and the car picked up speed down the country road. As they drove, Bridget tried to keep herself from jumping to worst-case scenarios.

Maybe someone was simply burning their trash. That happened all the time in the rural communities around Winston-Salem where she'd grown up.

Viri peeled onto his long, gravel driveway at gut-wrenching speed. The burning smell grew more intense.

Bridget's heart was in her throat as they raced up the windy drive.

As they cleared the trees, the house came into view. Bridget's stomach dropped. The front porch was black, the railing ripped free. The glass had blown out of the windows, and a blue shutter hung limp from its hinge. "Dahlia!" Bridget flung open the car door as it skidded to a stop in front of the house.

"Bridget, wait!" Eisheth's cry went unheeded as Bridget pushed the car door open and tumbled out and rushed toward the ruined porch. Behind her, Eisheth cursed.

As Bridget ran, heart in her throat, she felt transported. The last time she'd smelled this much smoke was during the battle for Dahlia's life. The way it clung to her nostrils and clawed down her throat nauseated her.

"Dahlia!" Bridget cried again. She had to find her sister. Had to—

Fingers closed on her arm, and she jumped, spinning around.

"Whoa! It's me." Danel gripped her firmly. He'd appeared out of nowhere, his blond hair darkened with soot. A dark red burn stretched down one cheek. "Everyone's okay."

"What's going on?" Eisheth came up behind Bridget.

"Tannin paid us a house visit."

Bridget didn't stay to hear the detective's response. Pulling free from his grip, she thundered up the porch and into the house. A haze of gray greeted her in the foyer, and she skidded to a stop. The entryway was empty, but the rotten-egg smell of sulfur lingered, sending a chill up Bridget's arms.

"Hello?" she called out, then coughed, covering her mouth with her arm. Faint voices sounded deeper in the house, carrying sharp edges. "Dahlia?"

"—put us all in danger." Gaul's low, rumbling voice shook with fury. Bridget hurried forward, arms outstretched as she navigated through the thinning smoke.

"What other choice did I have?" Nuriel sounded exasperated. Pained.

Viri entered the house behind her, and they followed the voices through the hall and into the kitchen. It was empty, but through the window she spotted Gaul, Nuriel, and Dahlia on the back patio. They stood facing one another, shoulders tense.

Relief flooded through Bridget. She hurried towards them.

"What's this all about?" Viri asked. For the first time since she had met him, he sounded angry. He strode past Bridget and into the sunroom. She followed him to stand next to Dahlia, taking her hand.

"Dahlia, are you alright?" Up close, she could see her sister's hair was a mess of tangles. Soot covered her cheeks, and the corners of her eyes were tight.

"I'm okay," she said, grasping Bridget's fingers. "Thanks to Nuriel."

"At what cost, though?" Gaul's hands clenched at his side. His attention was fully on Nuriel, who stood back, shoulders hunched.

"It doesn't matter," Nuriel insisted. "It *shouldn't* matter. Grigori and human lives are worth preserving, even over keeping our symbols out of Tannin's hands."

"He took the symbols?" Bridget's eyes widened.

Gaul glowered. "No, Nuriel *handed* them to him."

Viri looked askance at Nuriel. "I struggle to believe you would do so without good reason."

"He was going after Dahlia. There weren't enough of us here to overpower him *and* Cyrie. It was the best I could think of."

Gaul started to snap a retort, but Viri stepped forward, holding out his hands. "Enough. Stop bickering. At least everyone is safe."

Dahlia's voice was quiet, but it drew the attention of the room. "Nuriel did the only thing we could do. And I'm grateful. But now Tannin has the drawings."

"And an Artist," Nuriel pointed out.

"What?" Bridget asked in surprise.

"Her name is Cyrie," Nuriel explained. "I've met her a few times, and honestly, I'm not surprised she agreed to work with him. She's a historian, so the promise of new symbols would have been incredibly tempting."

Gaul cut in, "And now she has everything she needs to expedite her work." He shot a pointed look at Nuriel, who shifted his weight and turned his head away.

Bridget was starting to understand Gaul better. His prickliness was a manifestation of his anxiety—which made her own bubble up. With the drawings in hand, Tannin would see the changes Nuriel had made, and Cyrie would have a head start. If she finished first, they'd be back where they started, with no help for James and a dwindling timeline.

Gaul continued. "The sketches are gone. There's nothing we can do about that. But the threat of retribution is still very real. It's clear he's been watching the house. Otherwise, why wait until we're split up to approach?"

A guilty look spread across Viri's face. "I'm sorry. I thought you would be safe here. Very few people know where I live, and—"

Gaul waved the apology away. "It's done. So long as he knows where to find us, we're in danger. Dahlia, get your ankle healed. Bridget, pack your bags. Nuriel, get Eisheth and Danel."

Bridget pressed her lips together to hold back a protest.

Viri reached out to touch Gaul's arm. "Surely we can find a compromise."

Gaul smacked Viri's hand away, not even looking at him. "No. Not without reinforcements, at least."

Viri grimaced, eyes darting down as he withdrew.

Gaul continued, "Tannin *will* return. We need to be gone when that happens."

Viri offered a small, sad smile. "Could I persuade *you* to stay, at least?"

They met one another's gaze and Bridget shifted uncomfortably. It felt as though she was intruding on a private moment.

Gaul shook his head. "I need to protect them."

"It's not as if Nuriel hasn't found his own way over the past three centuries," Viri sighed. "And he can guide Dahlia."

Gaul scowled. "I'm not certain I trust him right now."

Nuriel started, looking taken aback. "Gaul."

Ignoring him, the redheaded man continued, "It's time to put as much distance between ourselves and Cleveland as possible."

The conversation was beginning to circle. If it followed the same path as their closed-door meetings, they would debate logistics for the next hour. Bridget placed her hand on Dahlia's arm, nudging her backwards. "Come on."

Dahlia took a reluctant step back, eyes on the two men. Then she broke away from the conversation. The two of them moved back into the kitchen, where the smoky tang of burnt wood lingered. With luck, Gaul would assume the two of them were simply following his orders.

She turned back, realizing Dahlia was lagging behind. "Are you okay?"

Dahlia grasped the kitchen counter as she followed.

"Burned my ankle."

Protective anger seeped through Bridget, and she moved forward to help her sister through the kitchen and into the hall.

They found Ret in his guestroom, the same one where the meeting had occurred. He was sitting on the bed, broken leg stretched out in front of him and crutches leaning against the dresser.

Dahlia knocked on the doorframe to announce them.

He looked up from the light suitcase he was loading on the comforter. "Come on in."

Bridget waited in the doorway as Dahlia limped over and pulled up her pant leg. The skin beneath was red and raw, blisters running along the curve of her ankle.

That's it. I'm never leaving her side again. If Gaul was right, Tannin had waited for them to separate. For a chance to attack while her back was turned. It made her sick.

Ret bent, grunting at the awkward position. Even though his touch on her skin was gentle, Dahlia hissed in pain. He glanced up at her. "Just breathe."

A gentle glow settled over her skin. Even from Bridget's vantage point, she could see the blisters shrink and the redness fade. There was *some* beauty in Grigori magic—when it wasn't being used for destruction. "We're lucky you're here."

He turned his eyes up to her. "I've always felt fortunate to have this power. Any other scrapes, Dahlia?"

She shook her head. "No, thanks. Sounds like we're going. Gaul's all worked up."

Ret was sporting a few new bruises—ones he couldn't heal. "It's unsettling that Tannin knows exactly where we are. I won't be joining you all, though."

"You're staying here?"

"No."

"You're going to talk to Eris," Dahlia said.

Bridget frowned. "Who?"

"Danel's old boss."

Ret nodded. "I know Gaul wants to wait, but Tannin has escalated the situation. It's time for an intervention from those whom he may consider equals."

Dahlia tested her weight on her ankle. "He didn't seem to think too highly of you today."

"No. But if Eris and I can present a united front, I'm certain he will listen."

Bridget wasn't so sure, but it also wasn't her decision to make. She didn't intend to partake in any negotiations with Tannin, anyway. "Come on, Dahlia. We need to pack."

Dahlia lingered. "Be careful, Ret."

"You too."

Dahlia turned away and Bridget led her up the creaking stairs, but when they reached the top landing, her sister stopped. She gripped the balcony tightly, her shoulders hunched. Dark waves of hair shielded her face.

"What's going on? Are you still hurt?" Bridget asked.

Dahlia shook her head. "No."

They went into their bedroom. The bright space, with its hanging plants and open curtains, failed to cut through her anxiety. As long as they found a way to stay near James, they could continue their plan. But now everything was going out the window.

"Grab your bag." She pulled the door closed behind her and went to the old-fashioned chestnut dresser. Her few remaining possessions—primarily thrift store clothing—took just a moment to gather and toss onto the bed. It was only after she'd emptied the drawer that she realized Dahlia was standing in front of the window, gazing out at the smoking porch.

Bridget set down her hairbrush. "Dahlia, how are you really?"

"I'm fine." Dahlia forced herself to look at Bridget. She smiled, but her dark eyes were haunted. "The attack caught me off guard, is all. I'll be alright."

Bridget hovered, not sure how to help, but desperately wanting to heal the invisible wounds her sister carried.

Dahlia must have noticed Bridget's anxiety, because she arched an eyebrow. "Don't go into mom-mode on me. Come on, tell me your plan. I'm guessing you don't want to stick with Gaul like a good girl?"

"Nope." Bridget pushed back the desire to fix everything. She needed to pay attention to what she could control. "It'll be pretty easy for us to get to James' body. But we have to hurry. The owner is planning to call his parents soon."

"You want to try waking him up there?"

"Yeah, I think that'll be easiest." Bridget couldn't imagine trying to move his body again. "There's not much in the way of security. No cameras or anything. If we sneak in after hours, we'll have as much time as we need. With luck, James will be able to walk out with us."

Dahlia's expression resolved into determination. "Okay. Where are we going in the meantime?"

"Somewhere you can finish the drawings—before Tannin has a chance to first."

Dahlia went to the closet. She shoved clothes into her

bag, placing the notepad and drawings carefully on top. "We're lucky we have pictures of the sketches, but Bridget, I can't finish them faster than a real Artist."

Bridget eyed her. "Did you make any progress while I was gone?"

"Enough to know I need help. It's too advanced."

For every bit of progress they made, another obstacle appeared. They were so close Bridget could feel it. But she couldn't ask her sister to replicate centuries of experience on a whim.

The bedroom door creaked open, and Bridget jumped. Danel stood in the frame with eyebrows raised. "What did I tell you two about locking doors?"

Any softness in Dahlia's countenance evaporated. She glared at him, a t-shirt balled up in her hand. "Get out of here."

"You really need to stop treating me like your enemy."

Bridget scowled. "Then stop acting like one."

"Oh?" He shot Dahlia a scoffing look. He put a hand over it. "So, I *didn't* help fight off Tannin?"

Dahlia rolled her shoulders back, as if talking to Danel was a physical burden. "I appreciate your help. That doesn't mean I want you bothering us."

Danel's cheeks went the color of rust. "I'm no more eager to wind up under Tannin's thumb again than you are. If you're planning to leave, we may as well go together."

Bridget wondered how much of their conversation Danel had listened in on before opening the door. "Why not go on your own? No one is keeping you here."

"Because, despite your endless suspicion of me, I *do* want to help."

Dahlia snorted. "You're not going anywhere with us."

He reached into his pocket and pulled out a set of car keys, dangling from their ring. "But I have something *you* need. Unless you were planning to walk?"

Bridget and Dahlia exchanged a look. Dahlia lurched forward to try and snag the keys, but this time Danel was anticipating her. Before Bridget could blink, he blurred and reappeared in the back corner of their room, leaning against the wall. "That's rude, you know."

"It's rude to kidnap your girlfriend and turn her over to a bunch of zealots," Dahlia retorted.

He flushed and, for once, didn't seem to have a clever comeback. "Look, do you want a place to go, or are you going to let Gaul drag you around?"

Bridget winced. "It *would* be helpful to have somewhere to hide."

"Bridget!"

"I can take you somewhere safe—somewhere close by—where you can regroup without worrying about anyone breathing down your necks. But whatever you're doing, decide quickly. I'm leaving in five." He strode over to the door, slipping out before Dahlia could snap back at him.

She glared at the open doorway. "We aren't actually going with him, are we?"

Bridget shifted her weight as she considered their choices. Danel was one of the last people she trusted, but she didn't have time to explore every option.

"We'll be careful," Bridget said. "For better or worse, Danel is good at disappearing. This time, we can disappear with him."

Dahlia yanked the zipper of her backpack closed. "Not

without help. I told you, I can't finish this on my own. Let's ask Nuriel to come with us."

Bridget shook her head. "Would he disobey Gaul?"

"He didn't exactly follow protocol giving the sketches to Tannin," Dahlia pointed out.

Bridget considered. "He *did* already make a lot of progress. But you realize it means bringing him in on our plan with James."

Dahlia shrugged. "We'll get him to understand." She stepped into the bathroom to grab her toothbrush and toss it into her bag. "Ready?"

Maybe it would work. Nuriel was the easiest solution to finishing a drawing quickly, and he was in a precarious position. Bridget hefted the backpack onto her shoulder.

"Ready enough. Let's go get us an Artist."

TEN

Dahlia let Bridget lead the way downstairs. They passed the door to Eisheth's room, which was closed tight. The faint sound of irritated muttering trickled through, followed by the sharp zip of a suitcase.

Dahlia's surroundings felt far away. Adrenaline had carried her through the initial aftermath of the confrontation with Tannin, but now it was crashing down.

Part of her wanted to crawl into bed and burst into tears. Pulsing anxiety left her head buzzing. Seeing Tannin again, feeling his powers press on her, had brought memories roaring to the surface. His attempt to entice her back into his fold made her skin crawl. He hadn't even been subtle in his manipulations. As if she'd ever take him up on *any* offer.

The shadowy part of her she now knew belonged to

Hartu stirred. It wanted vengeance Dahlia was all too inclined to allow. Tannin certainly deserved it.

But no. She forced herself back to the present, adjusting the straps of her backpack as they descended the stairs. Tannin was far more powerful than she was. In a face-off, she'd be crushed.

For right now, Bridget's plan was the best course of action. Lay low. Work on sketches. Build her strength and train up.

She still didn't see why Danel had to come.

Based on the muffled voices drifting through the house, at least some of the group was still on the back patio, arguing about their next move. Step one would be to get Nuriel's attention, pulling him away from the others.

Bridget pulled her to a stop in the kitchen. "Okay, here's the plan. If we can catch his eye through the window—"

Dahlia rolled her eyes. As direct as Bridget could be, she also spent way too much time overcomplicating everything. She moved past her sister and opened the screen door. "Nuriel? Can I see you for a sec?"

Nuriel seemed relieved to break away from the conversation. "I'll be right back."

Dahlia shot Bridget a raised eyebrow. "Simple."

Bridget laughed. "Alright, don't rub it in." She beckoned Nuriel deeper into the house.

His expression was somber, but when he entered the foyer and focused on the sisters, it neutralized. "What is it?"

"Bridget and I are going off on our own."

He looked between them in surprise. "That isn't a

good idea."

Predictably, Bridget's voice gained an obstinate edge. "We can't leave Cleveland yet. I owe James my life. Dahlia owes him her freedom. We're going to revive him, and we need your help."

Nuriel rubbed his temples. "Bridget, you know our rules about creating new Grigori. Besides, the drawings are gone. I can't recreate them from memory."

"You won't have to." Dahlia reached into her backpack and pulled out her sketchbook. "I have my own copies."

Dahlia felt a small thrill of satisfaction as Nuriel put a hand over his mouth in surprise. He stared as she flipped through the rough drawings. "Where did you get those?"

"I'll tell you later. But we really need to go." She closed the book and shoved it back into her bag.

Bridget stepped closer, eyes bright. "This is our chance, Nuriel. We can help James *and* prevent Tannin from using at least one of the symbols. But you need to come with us."

"No, he does not." Gaul's voice fell over them like a mallet. He walked into the hallway, followed by Viri. "It's already been decided. We're leaving together."

Dahlia froze. Then her sister turned to face Gaul, jaw set. "*You* decided. We disagree."

"Your opinion isn't needed."

A flush of irritation washed over Dahlia. She came forward beside Bridget. "Oh? Am I *your* prisoner now? I thought we'd finally started to understand one another."

"If we had, then you would know when to listen."

"Excuse me?" Heat rose up her cheeks. That strange, comforting rage loomed closer. She clenched her hands to prevent herself from grabbing his powers.

Bridget edged in front of her. "Let's just calm down, alright? We're better off if we split up. Tannin can't chase after all of us." Bridget gestured to herself, Dahlia, and Nuriel. "We can hide while you stay here."

A pair of red eyebrows lifted. "And what do you expect us to do?"

Nuriel responded. "You can help Viri repair his home while you wait for Ret to return with news of Eris."

Gaul rubbed his forehead. "You know what? Fine."

Bridget started. "Really? You're not going to stop us?"

"I'm tired of endless arguments, and Nuriel has a point about Ret. Once we add Eris' voice to ours, maybe Tannin will listen to reason. They always got along."

Nuriel looked satisfied, but Gaul quelled the expression with a glare. "I don't like this. But—shocking me most of all—you're all adults. In the spirit of keeping you safe, go. Don't tell me where you're headed, and I'll be here if you need me. Assuming Viri will allow that."

Viri put a hand on his shoulder. This time, Gaul didn't push him away.

Dahlia exhaled slowly, the rage funneling out with her breath. He'd been reasonable. Thank goodness. As Hartu receded, the human part of Dahlia even felt a small tickle of affection for Gaul and Viri.

Nuriel looked surprised by Gaul's change of heart, but he collected himself quickly. "We'll stay hidden." He glanced over at Dahlia. "Give me a moment to get my things."

As he turned toward his bedroom, Bridget eyed Gaul. "No tricks? No contracts?"

He fixed her with a level stare. "Just don't do anything foolish."

"We won't."

"I don't believe you." He managed a weary chuckle.

Of course, if Gaul knew Dahlia had already copied the sketches, he'd stop them in an instant.

Viri dropped his hand from Gaul's shoulder. "Before you go, let me give you a way to get in touch, if you need us."

"I thought the rule was no phones," said Bridget.

"It is." Gaul's voice was firm. "And the rule remains in place while we're separated. It's too easy to trace these newfangled devices."

Dahlia had to press her lips together not to snort. She certainly wasn't going to tell him about the phone Danel had slipped her. Besides, it was in airplane mode.

"This is something different." Viri walked past them, disappearing deeper into the house. When he returned, he was carrying two small, sandstone discs in his palm. He handed one to Bridget, and Dahlia leaned in to inspect it. A Grigori symbol had been carefully etched into the otherwise smooth surface.

"A drink coaster?"

"I wouldn't recommend setting your beer on it. It's a beacon. The writing on yours matches the writing on mine. If you press on it, both will light up."

"Will it tell you where we are?" Dahlia traced the symbol with her eyes. It was different from the complex design she'd been working on for James' revival. Simpler, with fewer overlapping lines.

He shook his head. "No, but it will try to find the fastest path to its match. The closer they are to being reunited, the quicker they will flash."

"Thanks. Hopefully we won't need to call for help."

Bridget handed the beacon to Dahlia. She unslung her backpack and slid it into the front pocket.

Straightening, the group regarded one another. For a moment, no one seemed to know what to say.

Viri broke the silence. "Be safe. We'll activate your beacon when Ret returns, and we have a new plan."

Dahlia hesitated. "If Tannin comes back..."

"We'll take comfort knowing you're safely out of his path."

A lump formed in Dahlia's throat. She barely knew Viri, and yet he'd offered them his home. Even after it had been attacked, he still offered to protect her. She nodded, blinking back tears as she turned to follow Bridget to the front porch. With her anger leeching away, all that was left was a low, steady hum of anxiety. It pressed on her as she wrapped her fingers around the blackened porch railing.

Bridget looked over. "This is the right move."

Dahlia glanced at her. "Are you trying to convince me? Or yourself?"

She huffed a small laugh. "Both of us."

They fell silent, looking out at the driveway. Soaring trees boasted fresh, spring leaves. A robin chirped and flitted closer, oblivious to the complicated world below.

It *was* the right move, and for more reasons than Bridget knew. Yes, it would give Dahlia room to work on the sketches, but it would also give her a chance to think. Tannin's attack had come so quickly, and she'd reacted on instinct.

How much of Hartu lived in her? How much of her rage was his? Or had his rage *become* hers? It was all jumbled together, and Tannin's looming presence only made it worse. She couldn't tell if the lingering smell of sulfur was in her imagination or reality. As comforting of a presence as Viri was, his house now carried an association of danger her body couldn't shake.

The front door opened again, and Nuriel stepped out, carrying his suitcase. A worn leather messenger bag was slung over one shoulder. "I have a few ideas about where we can go, but none of them are local."

Bridget shook her head. "Danel has something close."

"Danel?" Nuriel's eyebrows shot up.

"I made the same face," said Dahlia.

"You didn't mention he was involved."

Bridget shrugged. "I know, but he can keep us close to Cleveland."

"Why not Eisheth?"

Dahlia glanced over. "Yeah, why *not* Eisheth? She's not an asshole."

Bridget shook her head. "It's better if the detective stays here. The fewer people involved, the better."

"Let me guess: she knows what you're planning for James and doesn't approve."

Before Bridget could respond, Danel pushed through the door with a bulging grocery sack. "Road snacks."

"We'll take my car." Nuriel unzipped his messenger bag and fished through it.

"Sure thing. Looking for these?" Danel pulled a keyring from his pocket. "I'll drive."

Nuriel stared at Danel in exasperation. "Is nothing safe around you?"

"Come on, it's Nuriel's car," Dahlia said.

Danel grinned. "And I'm the one who knows where we're going."

"It's fine, Dahlia." Nuriel heaved a defeated sigh.

They crossed to the car and Bridget slid into the front seat, which was perfectly fine by Dahlia. The further she could keep from Danel, the better.

Dahlia slid in beside Nuriel, setting the backpack on the floor in front of her. She glanced at him. "You sure about this?"

He nodded, fixing her with a small smile. "A change of scenery will be nice. And the company's *mostly* good."

She nodded and looked back up at the house with its burnt porch. It felt strange to be splitting everyone up, but at the same time, she knew she was taking the next right step.

Danel started the car, its engine humming to life. "Let's get the hell out of here."

He pressed down on the accelerator, kicking up gravel as they sped away. Dahlia turned her attention forward. She had no idea where Danel was taking them, but leaving the house behind felt like breaking free.

ELEVEN

Bridget fidgeted as they drove past green fields, putting distance between themselves and Viri's house. It was a relief to make forward progress, but the urgency of their task weighed heavily on her.

She was desperate to talk with Dahlia and Nuriel alone. She wanted to share what she'd witnessed at the funeral home, to urge Dahlia to pull out her sketchbook and pencil. Most of all, she wanted to take action. Sitting in the car, watching the miles rush by, doing nothing—it left her anxious.

It was Danel who finally broke the silence, as he turned onto a highway entrance ramp. "So, when do we resurrect your boyfriend?"

Bridget bristled, but she didn't bother to correct him. It wasn't worth the effort of engaging with assumptions about her sexuality.

"Look, if I'm dragging you somewhere safe, I deserve to know what you're doing."

Dahlia scoffed from behind the passenger seat. "You're as loyal as a rabid animal, Danel. We don't owe you anything."

Danel laughed. "I'm perfectly loyal."

"To yourself, maybe."

"I've been helping you, haven't I?"

Bridget fought back the urge to lash out, instead balling her hands into fists and turning to the view outside. "We're still figuring out the details. But don't worry, we won't ask you for any more help."

"Good." Danel pressed the accelerator, speeding up to punctuate his satisfaction. "I'd rather not continue overexerting myself." He paused, then added with a smirk, "Unless I'm getting paid, of course."

Bridget was fairly sure he meant the last part as a joke, but it still made her stomach curdle. Dahlia made a sound of blatant disgust.

"Ever the opportunist," Nuriel murmured. Bridget glanced at him, surprised. He usually kept his opinions to himself. But he was gazing at the back of Danel's seat with his eyebrows puckered together in concern.

Bridget licked her lips. "Sorry we're dragging you into all of this, Nuriel."

He tore his attention away from Danel. If anything, he looked more worried as he considered her. "I appreciate that, but it was my choice to accompany you. I only hope we're not making a terrible mistake."

"We're not." Bridget turned back to the front, holding the affirmation close. Saving someone you care about was never a mistake. Doing everything you could to help a person who'd been treated unjustly was always worth the effort.

Eventually, the highway arched over a hill, and Cleveland's skyscrapers appeared in the distance. Lake Erie extended towards the horizon on their right, sparkling in the late-afternoon sun. As they got closer to the city, familiarity left Bridget cold. They weren't far from the lakeside park where she had last faced Tannin— working alongside the others to save Dahlia. Where she'd killed Kai.

As rush hour traffic grew more congested, Danel barely slowed down. He weaved in and out between cars, and Bridget gripped her seatbelt tightly.

A mile shy of reaching downtown, they exited the highway onto a lakefront road, passing beaches, parks, and museums. Bridget let out a sigh of relief, prying her fingers free as Danel turned into a parking lot at the water's edge.

"A marina?" Bridget asked, taking in the rows of docks. "Why?"

Nuriel let out a long-suffering sigh. "His boat."

Dahlia groaned. "I should have guessed."

"Problem?" Danel asked lightly as he turned off the car. "If Tannin comes looking for us, we'll be harder to track down on the water." Danel slid out of the car. "Besides, I'm sick of land."

"I don't know," Bridget said reluctantly as she grabbed her backpack and opened the door. "We won't go far, right?"

"Have any other bright ideas?" Danel asked. "Maybe you've got a secret house somewhere you forgot to mention?"

At her silence, he turned and headed for the docks.

Bridget eyed the lake warily, but Danel was right, she *didn't* have any better ideas. Slinging her backpack on, she followed him, with Dahlia and Nuriel trailing behind. The slip gently bounced under their weight, floating atop the marina's placid water. A small sailing yacht waited for them, its mast stretching high overhead, sail neatly furled. Its hull was painted dark blue, with white script scrawled along the side.

"*Mercy*?" Bridget read, raising her eyebrows.

"Yeah, he named it after the last thing he deserves," Dahlia muttered. She stared at the boat in distaste, and Bridget realized this must be a familiar sight to her. How many times had Danel taken her sailing, back before their relationship turned out to be a sham?

Danel hopped over the rail and onto the deck without responding to either of them.

Bridget followed him on board, using the rail to steady herself as she climbed in. "This boat is really yours?"

"Bought and paid." He unlocked the cabin door and disappeared inside. Bridget turned to help Dahlia onto the deck. Nuriel climbed in last.

"This is a terrible idea," Dahlia said once they were both on board. "True Crime 101: Do *not* get on a boat with the ex-boyfriend who got you murdered."

"I'm not happy about it either." Bridget eyed the open door to the cabin. "But as much as I don't trust him, I honestly don't think he wants to hurt us."

Dahlia responded with a snort, brushing past her. "Maybe not now. But what about when he decides we're too much of an inconvenience? For all we know, he's planning to sell us off to the highest bidder."

"That's not going to happen," Nuriel said quietly.

"It could."

He rubbed the back of his neck, frowning at the open cabin door Danel had disappeared through. "Let me speak with him."

He ducked into the cabin, the door latching behind him.

Dahlia walked along the deck, clearly not interested in going below. Bridget followed. With only the two of them on deck, the *Mercy* felt spacious. It was well-appointed with a gleaming white deck turned golden in the sun's lowering light. Ropes extended upward, attached to the mast in an incomprehensible pattern. But Bridget's attention was drawn to her sister more than the boat.

"Are you okay?" she finally asked, after they'd made nearly a full circuit of the deck.

Dahlia shrugged, pausing to touch a thick rope. "I don't like being here. It reminds me of how stupid I was to trust him."

"You weren't stupid," Bridget said gently. She decided not to mention how frequently she'd told Dahlia to be careful with the cute older man who was promising her the world.

"I was. And look what happened." She wrapped her fingers around the rope, gripping it tightly. "I thought I could handle seeing Tannin again. But... no, it was like being right back in his stupid cage."

Bridget's heart ached at the tightness in Dahlia's eyes, the tension in her posture. She reached out to squeeze her shoulder. "I'm listening."

Dahlia met her sister's gaze. "Let's walk and talk."

She shrugged out from under Bridget's touch, then led

them in a slow circle around the deck. Dahlia quietly recounted the events at the house, from Tannin's initial attack to Nuriel's decision to hand over the sketches. From the haunted look in her sister's eyes, Bridget suspected she was holding back a little, but she didn't push. Clearly, talking about Tannin was a challenge.

They'd made several circuits by the time Dahlia fell silent. She stopped at the rail and leaned against Bridget. Together, they looked across the water, watching a flock of seagulls squawk and circle.

"Nuriel doesn't like the idea of resurrecting James," Dahlia said.

"I bet he likes the idea of Tannin resurrecting a freezer filled with bodies less," Bridget pointed out.

Dahlia grasped the railing, staring up at the jagged Cleveland skyline. "I do feel better having him here."

"Me too." Bridget let silence stretch between them.

A cool breeze kicked up and sent a shiver prickling down her arms. "Come on, let's go inside."

Bridget led them to the cabin door and walked down a short flight of stairs. The interior was as upscale as the deck. Wooden surfaces gleamed beneath high windows that let in plenty of early evening light.

Two compact leather couches faced one another. Nuriel sat on one, wearing an exasperated expression as he watched Danel put away the food. Behind the cabinet he was unloading snacks into was a small, tidy kitchenette. Toward the bow of the boat, Bridget could see a sleeping area.

Dahlia looked around the cabin. "Bridget and I get the bed."

A trickle of warmth bubbled through Bridget. The

proclamation was reminiscent of the many times Dahlia had called shotgun when racing to the car as preteens.

Danel looked up, a scowl on his face. "It's *my* boat."

Dahlia simply glared at him until he gave an exasperated sigh. "Fine. But don't touch anything that isn't yours."

"Precious, coming from you."

Danel stiffened. "I'm not joking. You can use the cabin and go up on deck. The cockpit controls are off limits. The storage area under the bow is off limits."

"Anything else? Should we pay you for passage, too?" Dahlia asked, saccharine.

"Okay, stop," Bridget urged. "If we're going to be stuck in this tiny space together, we need to not murder one another."

Dahlia shot Bridget a baleful look.

She winced. "Bad choice of words."

Nuriel looked between them. "Can we at least avoid arguing? It won't get us anywhere."

"Sure, but I want to know why Danel's *actually* helping us. I don't believe for a second it's only because of guilt," Dahlia said.

"Does it matter?" Danel finished shoving snacks into the cabinet and looked up at them. "I'm still helping."

"It matters to me."

He sighed irritably. "I'm not exactly on Tannin's good side right now. And he's only *one* business deal gone sour."

"You mean Eris." Dahlia looked him over. "I don't understand why Ret is trying to reason with her if she's upset with you."

Danel shrugged. "Because she's old and powerful and

they were colleagues once. Let's just say I'd rather stay off her radar."

Dahlia folded her arms, staring him down. "You're racking up quite the list. Anyone else you want to avoid?"

"The three people on the *Mercy* with me, for starters."

Nuriel sighed and rubbed his forehead. "Danel, be reasonable. You offered your ship—"

"Boat. Yacht, technically."

Nuriel lifted his eyebrows. "You offered your *boat* up to us. If you're going to make life difficult, we can find our own way."

Danel looked between them. For a moment, Bridget thought he might actually kick them off the *Mercy*, simply to prove a point. But then his gaze landed on Dahlia and lingered.

"I'll get us underway." He turned and climbed out of the cabin.

Bridget took a seat at the dining table. Whether or not they trusted Danel, this was their best solution right now. It was time to refocus. "Come on, let's figure out our next steps."

Nuriel stood and paced to the window, where he watched Danel untie the boat from the slip. "So, are you going to tell me how you got a copy of the sketches?"

Dahlia slid into the booth opposite Bridget. She unzipped her bag and brought out some supplies—the unlit stone beacon, her sketchbook, and the phone. She activated the screen and pulled up the photos.

"Where did you get that?" Nuriel strode towards them.

"Danel gave it to us so we could take pictures of the sketches."

"You broke into my safe." Nuriel frowned as he took a

seat beside Bridget.

She gave an apologetic grimace. "I'm sorry, it was my idea. But at least we have something to work from. We just want to do right by James."

"I can sympathize, but it doesn't make James' resurrection a better idea."

Bridget gestured at Dahlia's sketchbook. "Aren't you at least curious about how to finish these? Wouldn't you rather *we* do, before Tannin?"

He considered, dark eyes holding hers steadily. If she'd read him correctly, the opportunity to avoid further confrontation with Tannin would be enough to make him overlook the small betrayal—especially since it meant his work wasn't lost. There was still more for him to discover.

Finally, he nodded. "I *would* feel better if I had a deeper understanding of what these did. And if this one *is* meant to create a new Grigori, I suppose I'd rather we use it than Tannin."

Bridget's stomach fluttered in relief. "Thank you."

Nuriel squared his shoulders as if preparing himself for battle. "Alright. Let's see what we can make of it together, Dahlia."

"Well, I already did some work."

He leaned forward in interest, watching her pull out her notebook and open it flat. Using her pencil, she tapped the first drawing on the page. "There are two lines that go behind the design."

"Ah, you figured that out." Nuriel almost looked proud. "Tell me why you started with this one."

"Well, it's the most complete, for one. Plus, it's the one most likely to create another Grigori. Right?"

The corners of his eyes tightened. "How did you

determine that?"

"Nothing fancy," Dahlia admitted. "I don't know what any of them can do, but I figured Tannin would start with whatever was most powerful, and so would you. What's more powerful than creating more Grigori?"

Nuriel tipped his head in acknowledgment. "Nothing I know of. Although this particular one is more complicated than other binding symbols I've seen. There are a few tricks we can try to complete it, but we may be forced to figure this out through trial and error."

"That could take forever." Dahlia looked at Bridget. "How long do we have before the funeral home can't keep James anymore?"

"Viri bought us another week."

"A week? Kai and I worked for months."

Bridget tapped her fingers on the table. "Can I help you two?"

Nuriel turned his attention to the phone, zooming in on the pictures. "We will need space to work. And supplies. A ruler and calculator would be helpful."

That was something Bridget could handle. "Well, I bet the phone has a calculator on it. And I'm sure I could find a tape measurer somewhere around here." She pulled a blank sheet of paper closer to her. "Okay, so let me—"

"Make a list?" Dahlia guessed. Bridget glanced up to catch her smile. "You're nothing if not predictable."

"Lists are helpful. They give us marching orders." Bridget snagged Dahlia's pencil and wrote at the top, *Next Steps*. Then she paused and added in front of it, *Operation Save James*. He would appreciate giving their plan a nerdy name.

"Alright, what else do we need?"

"A symbol that actually works," Dahlia said, deadpan.

Bridget rolled her eyes, but wrote, *Ruler/tape measurer* followed by *Completed symbol.* "We'll also need a way to apply the tattoo."

Nuriel sucked in a breath, then stopped himself.

"What?" Bridget asked.

"I have what we need."

Bridget looked up at him skeptically. "You have tattoo supplies? I thought you worked at a museum."

"I do. Did. I also work at a tattoo studio downtown."

Dahlia laughed incredulously. "Really?"

Bridget was equally surprised. She thought tattoo artists were usually covered in ink, wearing art as a badge of honor. She'd never noticed any tattoos on Nuriel, except the Grigori symbol between his shoulder blades.

Nuriel shrugged. "It keeps my skills honed. Besides, I enjoy work that gives me creative freedom."

Pursing her lips, Bridget wrote, *Tattoo supplies* on the list, then added a check mark beside it. "Why do you have everything with you?"

"It's not so unusual for a tattoo artist to have their own supplies. As for having mine on hand... I have Kai to thank for that. He taught me to always be prepared for anything, as an Artist, so I keep a portable kit with me."

Dahia furrowed her brow. "If we figure this out, do you know how to activate it?"

Nuriel pulled a fresh cigarette out, tapping it on the table. "When Kai taught me, there were no available naming symbols; we thought they'd been lost to time. But I know the theory, so... yes, probably." He looked like he had more to say, but he stopped himself, sticking the cigarette between his lips.

Dahlia sat forward. "We'll need access to James' body."

Bridget wrote *James*. Then she added, *Plan to break into the funeral home.*

Nuriel leaned over to read the list. "We will need someone to keep watch while we're at the funeral home, to make sure we aren't interrupted. It will take hours to tattoo him."

"Got it," Bridget said, writing *Guard duty.*

The boat lurched as the engine rumbled to life. Bridget glanced up through the high windows. It was nearly dark out now, the horizon a purple smudge.

Bridget turned her attention back to the others. "Anything else?"

Dahlia sighed. "Tannin to not find us? Danel to find a conscience? More realistically, graphing paper?"

Bridget wrote down the new request, then looked up as the boat shifted in the water. She craned her neck to look through the windows. They were gliding out of the slip and past the docks. Bridget watched the masts of other sailboats pass, then the breakwater, and then nothing. The *Mercy* was in open waters.

She turned her attention back to the paper. "Okay, I think this is good enough for now. Unless you wanted to add some—"

"—ice cream? Yes." A wide grin split across Dahlia's face. "And maybe some Cheerwine."

Bridget couldn't help but laugh. "We'll have to get supplies, if we're going to be here for a few days. I'm sure we can find ice cream. Cheerwine will be harder up here."

"Or beer. I'd take that over ice cream, at this point." She brightened and headed to the kitchenette. "I bet

Danel already has some."

Bridget looked down at her list while Dahlia raided the fridge. Half the items seemed impossible, and it was all set against the hope they'd finish before James was returned to his family. Or before Tannin made his own progress. On top of that, they were on a boat with a man they barely trusted, heading deeper towards the inky blackness of Lake Erie.

"Are you alright?" Nuriel looked her over with concern.

She let go of a long breath. If she'd learned anything from James, it was to accept the help she was offered. They'd figure it out together. "Yeah. I'm good. Let's get started."

TWELVE

The rocking of the boat left Bridget's stomach churning as she tried to sleep that night. When she finally drifted off, the motion followed her into her nightmares. Nausea pressed around distorted memories of James' sightless stare, Kai's blood soaking the dirt. The shock of a gun's recoil in her hand. Dahlia, eyes sparking with vengeance as she shot Tannin's guard over and over again.

Bang. Bang. Bang.

She bolted upright, instantly alert. Her t-shirt stuck to her, sweaty and twisted. Water sloshed against the side of the boat.

What had woken her? She searched the dim cabin, but it was too dark to see well.

A moan, inches from her, sent her heart into her throat. It took her a panicked moment to realize it came from Dahlia, curled up beside her. Her sister cried out, tossing violently in the bed.

"Hey!" Bridget hissed, reaching over to shake her. Dahlia flailed, smacking Bridget's arm in the process. "Wake up."

Dahlia drew in a sharp breath. The sheets rustled as she sat. "Bridget?" She sounded confused.

"I'm here. You're okay, it's me." Bridget kept her voice calm and low, despite her thudding heart. "Do you want me to turn on the light?"

Dahlia made a quiet sound of affirmation, and Bridget groped for the switch on the wall. It lit up the bed and cast a dim glow throughout the cabin. Sweat beaded on Dahlia's forehead, plastering dark, wavy hair to her face.

"Let me get you something to drink." Bridget slid out of the bed and gave the cabin a cursory look. The couch—where Nuriel was supposed to be sleeping—was empty. He must have gone on deck with Danel. She made her way to the refrigerator. Inside were several bottles of chilled water. She selected one and walked back, offering it to Dahlia.

"Thanks." Her voice cracked. She took the bottle and untwisted the cap. Half of it was gone in a single, long swig. "I'm sorry. Did I wake you?"

"No, I was already up." Bridget sat on the corner of the bed, taking the bottle back from Dahlia and sipping it. She could only imagine the kinds of dreams that plagued her sister after months of captivity. "Do you want to talk about it?"

Dahlia brushed her hair back, eyes distant. "No. I

don't really remember what I was dreaming about."

"You were yelling."

Dahlia shook her head slowly. "I'm not sure why. Don't worry, okay?"

"But—"

"It's a dream, Bridget. It can't hurt me." She tempered the sharp tone with a forced, shaky smile. "I'm going to get some air."

Bridget angled her wristwatch toward the moonlight; it was a cheap digital one from a thrift store. "It's four in the morning. You should get some more sleep."

Dahlia shrugged and scooted over to the bedside. She reached into her backpack, pulling out her bra. She shimmied it on under her t-shirt. "I'm fine. Don't follow me, okay?"

A protest bubbled up within her, but she bit it back. Arguing would only make the situation worse—the unfamiliar, angry glint to Dahlia's eyes made that clear enough. "Alright. Be careful."

With a roll of her eyes, Dahlia stood and crossed to the stairs. As soon as she closed the door behind her, Bridget sank back down onto the mattress and pulled the covers over her. She felt like bursting into tears. What was happening to her little sister?

She tried to distract herself by focusing on the sway of the boat, but that only left her nauseated. Danel's footsteps creaked overhead, mingling with the snap of sails. She muffled the sounds by burying herself fully under the covers.

After twenty minutes of tossing and turning, Bridget

gave up. She shoved the blankets off and padded to the kitchen table. Her list was still sitting there, on top of Dahlia's sketchbook.

She read it over, running the tip of her finger over each line.

Operation Save James: Next Steps
Ruler/tape measurer
Completed symbol
Tattoo Supplies ✓
James
Plan to break into the funeral home
Guard duty
Graphing paper

Beneath the list, she'd jotted down the name of the funeral home and a blocky map of the layout—her attempts to solidify their plan to get closer to James.

"Just a little breaking and entering," Bridget muttered to herself. The pencil she'd been using had rolled onto the ground with the boat's sway. She bent and picked it up, then began adding details to her sketch. She didn't have her sister's artistic talents, but she could make a simple map. She added the covered porch and the parking lot, and indicated the two exterior doors she knew about: the front door she'd entered through and the basement door.

As the outside gloom brightened, the windows of the boat drew her attention. If she tilted her head far enough, she could see Nuriel and Dahlia talking near the bow.

Bridget was grateful for his presence. He'd helped her search for Dahlia, taken up mentoring her sister, and shown genuine sympathy for them both. She trusted

Nuriel's kindness, and Dahlia clearly trusted his Artist training.

Bridget almost felt guilty dragging him into their scheme. But despite his reservations about the whole affair, he seemed willing to try.

She looked back down at the map, returning to the problem at hand. *Plan to break into the funeral home.* This was a problem she could chip away at, while the others focused on the drawings.

She hadn't seen any security cameras, but that didn't mean one wasn't hidden out of sight, or that the doors weren't alarmed. And the barred windows were out as a possible entry point. Which meant they *had* to go in through one of the doors—both of which would likely be locked.

The last time she'd been in a situation that required getting past a lock was in Tannin's collection room, breaking Dahlia out of her cell. Her sister had guided the process and later told her that everything she knew about lockpicking had come from Danel. Because of course it had.

As much as she hated to admit it, they needed his expertise as much as Nuriel's.

A flash of light caught her eyes. The beacon. It was flashing ponderously—a slow, silent tempo alighting the lines of its symbol.

Her breath caught. She picked up the stone and pulled it closer. Despite the glow, it was cool in her hands. It pulsed steadily, the light growing brighter then dimmer. Someone at Viri's was tracking them. Or trying to alert them.

Maybe Ret was already back with Eris. Or, more worryingly, perhaps Tannin had returned to the house. Maybe someone was hurt, or Gaul had decided to leave Cleveland after all.

But any distraction could cost them precious time.

She hesitated, then slipped the tablet into one of the inside pockets of Dahlia's backpack, out of sight. They could deal with it later.

Right now, she had to focus on the problem at hand. Namely, Danel. Going back over to the bed, she pulled a sweatshirt and long pants over her pajamas.

The air on deck was chilly, with a stiff breeze blowing over the lake. The boat dipped up and down on the waves, and Bridget grabbed the rail, her stomach turning over unpleasantly. She'd emerged directly in front of the wheel, which was surrounded by fiberglass seats.

Danel lay across one of the benches, arms behind his head, staring upward. He looked over at the sound of the cabin door opening. "The stars are nice."

Bridget turned her gaze upward. This far out on the water, the glow of light pollution had faded away. Even with dawn impending on the horizon, the sky was dominated by the wide swath of the Milky Way. "It's like we're in the middle of the ocean."

Danel shook his head. "It doesn't feel like the ocean at all. For one, the smell is all wrong. And the waves aren't caused by a tide, just wind. Can't you feel it in the way the boat moves?"

"I'd rather not think about the boat moving. What's

wrong with the smell?"

"No salt. The Great Lakes are big, but they're fresh water. Plus, they're miniscule in comparison to any ocean. If I sailed us north, we'd be able to see the Canadian coast before long."

Bridget took in the quiet of the waves and the darkness of the sky. The glow of a cigarette appeared, then vanished, near the bow.

"I would think Nuriel would be the one with a boat," Bridget commented.

Danel scoffed. "Nuriel wouldn't know rigging from a rudder. Just because he can manipulate water doesn't mean he *appreciates* it. It's a waste, if you ask me."

"Right. Because super speed and manipulating the earth is meaningless."

"Do you have any idea what running that fast does to my shoes? Besides, he'll gain strength with time. We all will." Danel sighed and stood, going to the wheel, and checking the readouts behind it.

Bridget watched the bow. Every time she thought she'd figured the Grigori out, they surprised her. She'd never even considered whether they *liked* the powers they'd inherited.

Dahlia and Nuriel formed two dark silhouettes against the gray sky, their backs to Bridget. With Dahlia's hair whipping in the wind, she looked like a phantom.

The instinct to go to her sister, to keep her close and safe, flared up. But *Operation Save James* was fresh in her mind.

Demands wouldn't go far with Danel; she'd need to

approach the conversation with care. "Were you a sailor? Or... a fisherman? Back before you became a Grigori."

He glanced at her, the corner of his mouth twitching. "Something like that." He didn't offer any more information, and Bridget didn't press.

Instead, she settled into the seat by him. "It's a lovely boat."

Danel responded with a low laugh. "What do you want, Bridget?"

She winced. Dahlia was right; tact had never been her strong suit. She was far better at being direct. "I want you to keep helping us."

He snorted. "I'm not a part of your elaborate plans. I'll drop you off on shore once you're ready. Otherwise, my help ends there."

"I'm glad to see your guilt only carries you so far."

Danel gave the wheel a languid turn. "You *want* me on your side now?"

"I'd rather keep you close than let you run back to the enemy."

He made a low, disparaging sound. "I see why you get along with Eisheth and Nuriel."

Bridget frowned. The way he said it, it was clearly meant as an insult. "Eisheth and Nuriel saved my life more than once."

"Yes, of course they did." He rolled his eyes.

Bridget bristled. She hated the sarcastic way he spoke. "You say that like it's a bad thing."

"Nuriel has an insufferable moral compass. Eisheth..." He trailed off, then shook his head. "You're seeing this in black and white terms. Good versus evil. Enemies and allies. The real world isn't so neat."

She tensed as the boat turned into the early morning wind, sails filling. She gripped the edge of the seat. "What Tannin is doing is evil. Kai was evil, too."

"Kai was a sanctimonious asshole and Tannin's ego leads him to make questionable choices. But neither are evil."

Bridget laughed incredulously. "Tannin tried to kill you. He very nearly succeeded!"

"I betrayed him."

"You've betrayed a lot of people," Bridget pointed out. "What about Eris? What happened with her?"

His fingers clenched the wheel. "I'll deal with Eris. Go back to playing God."

The sneer in his voice startled her. "James deserves another chance."

Danel glanced at her. "Who are you doing it for? Him? Or you?"

Heat flooded her cheeks, a sharp contrast to the chilly breeze. She stood abruptly. *Time to try the direct approach.* "I don't have to justify myself to you. You're going to help us."

He glanced over at her, eyebrows lifting. "I am?"

"We need someone who knows how to pick locks without being seen. And if something goes wrong, we need someone who can get us out of there quickly."

Danel scowled. "I told you, I'm not part of your little scheme."

"You *caused* this. If not for you, Dahlia never would

have been kidnapped by Tannin. She never would have been *killed* by Kai. I would never have needed James' help, and James would have never died trying to save her."

Anger bubbled through her as she recounted the chain reaction Danel's selfishness had set off. She fought to keep her voice steady.

"I've already helped." Danel gestured to the boat around them.

"It's not enough. This isn't some business transaction. This is someone's *life*. Isn't there anyone you care about enough that you'd do anything to help them?"

Something unreadable passed over Danel's face, so quickly Bridget wondered if she had imagined it. Tense silence passed.

Danel turned the wheel. "Maybe you should go back to worrying about your sister."

A hiss of irritation rose from Bridget. "What the hell is that supposed to mean?"

Danel looked past her and toward the bow. "Something I overheard from Gaul. Apparently, the symbol she's wearing belonged to a pretty nasty fellow before her."

She folded her arms. "You're trying to distract me."

His gaze snapped back to hers. "Doesn't mean it's a lie. She's been having nightmares, hasn't she?"

Bridget faltered. "Nuriel says it's part of the process."

"It is. But do you know what those nightmares *are*?"

She wanted to tell him it didn't matter. That he should focus on the issue at hand. But her stomach knotted in a way that had nothing to do with the moving boat.

Danel continued, not waiting for her to respond, "They're her Grigori self, bubbling up. The core of who she is now, trying to reconcile itself with a human body and human memories."

"Bullshit." The wind stole Bridget's words, making them sound thin.

Danel shrugged. "Believe what you want. But you're lying to yourself."

The warning hung between them, and Bridget almost took it to heart. Hadn't Gaul also told her as much? Hadn't she *just* witnessed Dahlia sweating and crying in her sleep? But she'd also been there for the aftermath, and the scared look in her sister's eyes.

"Stop pretending you know her better than I do, Danel."

She turned away from him, stalking as best she could with the boat rocking beneath her. It was only when she'd reached the bottom of the stairs that she realized Danel had completely distracted her from asking for help.

"Damn," she whispered. She went over to the table, where her list waited. She'd have to find another way to persuade him.

THIRTEEN

Dahlia glanced behind her at the sound of the cabin door closing. Bridget had gone back downstairs. Good. The last thing she wanted was to talk with her overbearing sister right now. She turned to look back out over the lake.

"You alright?" Nuriel looked over. They'd barely spoken since she'd come up on deck, interrupting his cigarette break.

She nodded, but it felt like a lie. She *wasn't* alright. Her nightmares were getting worse. The feeling of disjointedness had only amplified since they'd left Viri's house. She didn't know if it was Gaul's revelations about her past life or Tannin's unwelcome return, but it felt as if she were two pieces of Velcro, slowly being torn apart.

Nuriel brought his cigarette to his lips and inhaled deeply. When he spoke, his words formed a smokey haze.

"You're doing a great job with all of this."

A surprised laugh burst free from her. "Am I?"

"Decoding our written language, adjusting to life as a Grigori, learning how to use your abilities—none of it is an easy process. Do you want to talk about it?"

"Not really."

They lapsed into silence again. For some reason, though, that only sparked her irritation. Both Bridget and Nuriel wanted to help, but where Bridget had been too overbearing, Nuriel was the opposite. He never pushed.

"Gaul says you go too easy on me during training," she blurted with more anger than intended.

He looked over. "Does he?"

She doubled down. "He took me through a session yesterday and it about wiped me out. How come you never do that?"

"You want me to exhaust you?"

Dahlia gripped the rail tightly and let out a huff. "I want you to teach me. Without holding back. Why is everyone always trying to protect me? I'm not a doll."

She knew it wasn't fair—she wasn't actually mad at Nuriel. She was mad at the situation. At being trapped in a body and mind that felt foreign, at feeling used by her sister, at the fractured sense of self she couldn't get her hands around.

"What do you want me to teach you to do?" Nuriel was infuriatingly placid.

"To fight. To defend myself."

He took another drag of his cigarette. "I know it feels like a new battle is around every corner, but I assure you it isn't usually this way. Most of your Grigori life will be downright boring. Mine has."

She drew her brows together. "I don't care. Tannin is a threat *now*."

"Do you intend to fight him? Dahlia, you've seen how strong he is."

She looked away. She hadn't intended to imply a plan for retribution. Logically, she *knew* it was a terrible idea. Vengeance was a fantasy—a counterbalance to the nightmares—but it couldn't actually happen. At best, she could hope for Ret to leverage some sort of truce between them, with Eris' help.

She scowled and came away from the rail. "You know smoking is disgusting, right?"

Before Nuriel could respond, she turned and stalked away. She'd hoped his presence would be calming. But right now, she didn't *want* to be calm. She was seething with leftover energy from her nightmare.

She paused near the mast, resting a hand against the cool metal. She'd been here before, what felt like a lifetime ago. On an early date, she and Danel had sat on the deck while he taught her different knots. They'd laughed as she fumbled with the movements and made lewd jokes about tying one another up. She remembered feeling *alive* with the energy of their banter. He'd been so charming, had hid his motives so well.

The memory felt like it belonged to someone else. Someone naïve and in love. Someone who hadn't yet been betrayed.

She strode to the bench seat where he lay. "Get up."

"Huh?" He propped himself up on his elbows.

"I said get up. I want to practice, and I need to use your powers."

Warily, Danel pulled himself to sit on the bench. "You

want to practice now? It's the middle of the night. Doesn't anyone around here sleep?"

"Shut up."

He held up his hands in a plaintive gesture. "Okay. Got it. I'll sit here and not talk to you while you use my abilities for... whatever it is you're going to use them—"

Dahlia snatched the thrumming aura surrounding him. Earth was useless on a boat in the middle of the lake, so she sought his speed. She grasped it, then tugged it toward her.

The world stuttered. Beneath her, the rocking of the boat fell still. Danel's mouth wasn't quite frozen, but moving in slow motion. She went to the wheel and turned it a few degrees.

She released her focus, and the world sped up again. The boat fell back into a regular motion and began to list.

"—for," Danel finished his sentence. Then he blinked, realizing Dahlia was in a different spot. "Hey! What did you do to my boat?" He leapt up, pushing her off the wheel. Near the bow, Nuriel stumbled. It looked as if he'd dropped his cigarette.

"What else can you do?" Dahlia asked Danel.

"What do you mean?" He didn't take his eyes off the readouts.

"Gaul showed me a bunch of different ways to use his earth ability. And I'm sure he can cause a dozen different diseases. What else can speed do?"

Danel grunted. "Makes getting take-out a breeze."

She planted fists on her hips. "Are you going to help me or not?"

He sighed and ran a hand through his hair, turning to face her fully. "You and your sister are certainly related."

"What's that supposed to mean?"

"Nothing. How can I help?"

"Gaul said I needed to train with all of the abilities. You're the only person here with access to speed."

Danel responded with a scoff. "You really want to spend time with me?"

She fixed him with a deadpan stare. He knew how she felt about him. But he was here, so she may as well take advantage of it. She shook out her arms and planted her feet. "How do we start?"

Danel's lips twitched into the jaunty smile she used to love. He patted the bench beside him as he sat again. "By learning some finesse."

FOURTEEN

The next morning broke with heavy clouds. Groggy, Bridget skipped breakfast, instead mentally reciting *Operation Save James* to distract herself from the boat's movement. The slightest swell in the waves left her stomach turning over unpleasantly, especially after a night of broken sleep.

Dahlia had stayed up even later than Bridget, but that hadn't stopped her from getting up early. She and Nuriel had already set up their workstation at the dinette, huddling over coffee as they laid out their papers.

"You look like you're going to throw up." Dahlia looked her up and down as she forced herself out of bed.

"I'm fine." The sensation reminded Bridget of the one time she'd accidentally activated Gaul's contract. Her decision to even hint to Dahlia's old roommate about Grigori magic had triggered the stipulations and left her vomiting.

Nuriel set his coffee down, watching Bridget with concern. "Perhaps you should spend some time on deck. The fresh air may be better for you."

Bridget shook her head. "I want to help."

"We don't need your help right now," Dahlia said.

The words stung, echoing the previous night's conversation. She looked over the table, with its sketchbook and pencils laid out. "Can't I do something?"

Dahlia gave Bridget a level look. "You can not throw up all over our work. Go on deck. We'll be fine. It's just going to be us drawing."

Bridget held back another protest as her stomach gurgled. Dragging herself to her feet, she grabbed a bottle of water.

"Good luck," she murmured, then hauled herself upstairs.

Danel looked up from the cockpit as she emerged into the cold morning air. "You look terrible."

"Thanks." The biting breeze felt like a smack to the face, but it did start to clear her head.

"You'll get your sea legs eventually."

"Somehow I doubt it." She staggered over to one of the fiberglass seats near where Danel stood.

"We'll be back on land soon. If the clouds weren't so damn low, you'd be able to see the shore."

Bridget groaned. "Why aren't we there yet? I thought you said Canada was only a few hours away."

"It is, but I was waiting for stores to be open. I'd rather spend as little time at the marina as possible."

"Why? Do you think we're being followed?" She'd assumed they would be safe outside of Cleveland—hoped

Tannin would be distracted enough by his retrieved sketches to pause his search for justice.

Danel shrugged but didn't answer. Instead, he tipped his head up, eyes lingering on the boat's unfurled sails. They were full, catching the morning wind.

"You don't like land very much, do you?"

He exhaled and returned his attention to the cockpit, gently nudging the wheel. "Land is fine, but it's limited. The water gives me freedom."

Bridget didn't understand the appeal, but she could see how true it was for him. He seemed more at ease on the boat than he had at Viri's house.

"There." Danel pointed towards a dark smudge on the horizon, separating itself from the wash of clouds. The smudge solidified into a lighthouse, squatting on the edge of the lake. Behind it, buildings and boats started to blur into existence.

"Where are we?"

"A small enough town to get supplies quickly and without a car. You have your shopping list?"

Bridget nodded. *Operation Save James* was folded in her pocket, where she'd stashed it after her late-night ruminations.

"Good. There are a couple of stores about ten minutes' walk from the marina. I'll point you in the right direction when we dock."

"You're not coming?"

He shook his head. "I have my own plans."

Bridget snorted, but her stomach turned, and she hunched over.

"Maybe you should add anti-nausea meds," Danel quipped.

With a groan, Bridget stood and hurried over to the rail. She clung to the metal bar with both hands, counting slowly as she inhaled. The nausea ebbed and she relaxed her grip. The port town came into more clarity. Morning light filtered through the clouds, illuminating distant buildings, budding trees, and the masts of boats docked in a marina.

Bridget didn't move until they pulled up to a slip and Danel cut the engine. He passed her, going to the rigging. As he walked by, he said, "Take the others to shore with you. It'll be best if you stick together."

"Don't we need to go through customs or something?" Bridget had never been to Canada, but she'd seen pictures of the snaking lines of cars at border crossings.

Danel shot her a lopsided grin. "Let me worry about that."

Knowing better than to ask questions, Bridget turned away, crossing to the cabin door. Now that they were docked, the boat felt steadier under foot.

As soon as she opened it, the sound of excited conversation floated upward.

"Excellent!" Nuriel sounded eager. Proud.

"I can't believe I did it!"

Bridget's heart leapt. She hurtled down the stairs, taking them as quickly as she could without pitching forward. If they'd already finished, she wouldn't have to spend more time on the boat. They could head straight back to Cleveland, and—

She halted at the bottom of the stairs. Dahlia and Nuriel were in the same spots she'd left them, but the sketches were stacked in a neat pile at the end of the table. Their pencils and the cell phone were on top, untouched.

"Bridget!" Dahlia looked over, eyes bright. "Come look."

She gestured to a bowl of water in front of her. No, not water. As Bridget came closer, she realized the bowl was filled with a solid hemisphere of ice.

"What's going on?" The excitement Bridget had felt in the stairwell crashed down around her, leaving her hollow.

"I managed to freeze it." Dahlia tipped the bowl in Bridget's direction, as if she couldn't see it.

Nuriel beamed. "It's a tricky skill to learn. She's doing very well."

Bridget felt as if she'd been slapped in the face. "Okay. But why are you doing this? You're supposed to be working on the sketches."

Surprise, then pain crumpled Dahlia's expression. Her voice went sour. "Because we're still waiting on some of the supplies we need. We decided to take a break. Is that a crime?"

"No. It's just—we don't have a lot of time. James could be returned to his parents any day now." And if that happened, it would be over. She'd never get him back.

Dahlia's eyes narrowed. "Anything that isn't *your* mission is a waste of time to you."

The barb only made Bridget stiffen. "Well, it's important."

"So is my training. Besides, we don't have everything on your list yet."

"Well, we're docked at a town. We can get the supplies here."

Her sister's glower deepened. "Why don't *you* do the

shopping? I want to keep practicing."

Nuriel touched Dahlia's hand. "It's alright. You should rest for a bit. And stretching would do us some good."

Dahlia made a sound of exasperation and pushed the bowl away. "Sometimes I can't believe you," she muttered to Bridget as she slid out of the bench seat.

"I'm trying to keep us focused."

Dahlia swept past her without response, going straight for the stairs.

Bridget watched, then turned back to Nuriel. "I'm sorry if I seem harsh. I just don't think we should get distracted."

Nuriel stood, taking the bowl over to the kitchen sink. "Your sister cares about you deeply. She takes your words to heart."

"I care about her, too."

He looked up, pain flickering across his face. "Yes, I know."

"Do you think I'm wrong?"

"I think you're scared." The bluntness of his response caught her off guard. Nuriel was usually gentle with his words. But, as usual, he was also right.

"Of course I'm scared. I don't want us to fail James. I don't want Tannin to hurt anyone else."

Nuriel shook his head. "I don't think that's what you're most scared of. You're scared of who your sister is becoming, so you're holding her as tightly as you can."

Bridget fell silent, cheeks growing hot. She didn't have a good response.

"Please trust her," Nuriel implored. "Everything she's doing is normal. But she needs space to explore her new identity."

A lump formed in Bridget's throat. As soft as his words were, they cut deeply. She gave him a curt nod. "I'll meet you on deck."

The three of them followed Danel's instructions to a sleepy strip of shops. After a brief stop-off for coffee, they found their way to the general store.

It served up a hodgepodge of groceries, hardware supplies, clothing, and fishing gear. Bridget found a ruler and some graph paper in the art section, then went in search of anti-nausea meds while Dahlia and Nuriel wandered the rows, talking quietly.

The frustration she'd felt on the boat nipped at her. She was glad Nuriel was with them but couldn't help feeling he was part of why Dahlia was pulling away. But she also knew confronting her sister about it would only make matters worse.

Best to give them some space.

"I'm going to take this stuff back to the boat." Bridget poked her head down the aisle they were in. Dahlia and Nuriel weren't even looking at the shelves. They were immersed in conversation.

Dahlia glanced up. "Sounds good. We'll be right behind you."

It took all of Bridget's willpower not to intrude further. She paid with Canadian bills Danel had given her, then hurried back out into the cool morning air, heading for the marina.

She was halfway to the docks, walking past a not-yet-open bookstore, when she caught a flash of blond hair.

Danel was exiting a coffee shop, a tote bag slung over one shoulder. He didn't appear to notice Bridget as he walked in the direction of the marina.

Why did he have *two* paper coffee cups?

Making a snap decision, Bridget began to follow him. The streets weren't busy, so she hung back a block.

He peeled off the sidewalk onto a small side street and out of sight.

She picked up her pace, skirting around a young couple strolling toward the general store. The street Danel had ducked down was tucked between an ice cream shop and a ceramics store. She paused at the corner, peeking around it.

He wasn't there. It wasn't a street at all, but a short alleyway that dead-ended into a faded wooden fence. Recycling bins lined one side, opposite a set of exterior wooden stairs leading to the second floor.

She scowled, annoyed with herself for thinking she could follow Danel. With his access to super-human speed, who knew where he was. Maybe he hadn't turned at all but blurred away.

A sharp knock came from above her. She looked up. The stairs led to a small wooden porch, and through the slats she could make out the movement of a person. They knocked again, and this time the door opened with the protest of a sticking door frame.

"What are you doing here?" The voice was unfamiliar. Bridget held perfectly still.

"I brought you coffee. Sugar, no creamer, right?" Danel.

A pause, then a noisy sigh. "Come in. I was starting breakfast."

"I won't stay long." His footsteps moved off the porch.

She waited until the door closed, then carefully set her shopping bag on the ground. Walking around to the base of the wooden stairs, she took them slowly, bracing her toes on the edges of each stair to avoid making them creak.

The small porch boasted a single flowerpot bursting with spring tulips. The only other decoration was a pink doormat with black cats silhouetted along the edges. She edged closer to the door, listening.

"Just take it." Danel's voice was muffled, but he almost sounded as if he were pleading.

"Why now?"

"Because I want you to have it. Don't ask too many questions, alright?"

Beyond the door, a single window overlooked the porch. Bridget crouched down to approach, peeking through the glass. A gauzy curtain blocked out most of the interior, but she could make out the silhouette of two figures. One was unmistakably Danel. The other appeared to be a tall woman with flowing hair and a long skirt. Bridget pulled back before either of them could notice her.

Who was she? Bridget's mind flickered immediately to Eris—but no. The way Danel was speaking to the woman wasn't deferential *or* defiant. He sounded concerned. Almost paternal.

The woman spoke again in a deep alto. "I will never understand you, Uncle Dan."

Bridget could hear a smirk in Danel's response. "Good. I like to keep people guessing."

A sigh. "Whose side are you on? You're going to have

to choose eventually."

How many times had she asked herself the same question about him?

And whose side was this woman on?

He sidestepped the question entirely. "Just be safe, okay, Morgan?"

"Follow your own advice."

"No promises. Life needs a little excitement."

Holding her breath, Bridget moved away from the door. Danel was many things, but an uncle? Had he docked them at this marina for the express purpose of meeting up with this woman?

Bridget hurried back down the stairs, as quietly as possible. She grabbed her shopping bag and hurried around the corner onto the main street. As she made her way through the stirring town, she parsed through the exchange. It felt more implausible by the second. Danel had family. Not just family, but family he met with and gave gifts to. Was she also a Grigori? Or was she human?

And—besides the coffee—what on earth had he given her?

It was not lost on Bridget that she'd found the leverage she needed to make Danel compliant. She sat down on the deck, took an anti-nausea pill, and waited.

He arrived shortly after, a single paper coffee cup still in his hand. He looked troubled, eyes on the deck as he boarded.

"How was your visit?" Bridget asked.

He raised the single paper coffee cup still in his hand. "Caffeinated."

"That's not what I mean. Your niece lives here?"

He looked at her sharply, then groaned and sunk into

the bench seat. "You followed me."

"I did. So, you *do* have someone you care about."

Danel set his jaw. "Are you trying to blackmail me?"

"Maybe. Does Gaul know you're connected to this Morgan person?"

"It's none of his business."

"Of course not. I don't blame you for wanting to stay close to family."

Bridget couldn't help but feel immense satisfaction as Danel's shoulders stiffened. He set his coffee aside with a scowl. It felt good to have him under her thumb for once.

She pressed her advantage. "What did you give her?"

Danel bristled. "*That's* none of *your* business. Let's skip to the end of this conversation, alright?"

"Depends. What's the outcome?" Bridget held his gaze.

His jaw set. "You stop asking me questions. And in return, I'll help you get into the funeral home."

"Deal." At last, something was going right.

FIFTEEN

On their fourth morning on the yacht, Dahlia curled up in the dinette, staring out the windows as she cradled her coffee. The sleepless nights pressed on the back of her eyelids, but there was no time for brain fog. Bridget's continued insistence that they hurry grated on her.

She sipped her drink, hoping the caffeine would cut through the haze. Clouds had returned, and with them a strong wind that rocked the boat and sent Bridget sprinting into the bathroom. Danel was on deck, as usual. That left Nuriel, preparing them a scant breakfast.

"You haven't been eating much." He slid a bowl of dry cereal her way.

Dahlia caught it before it could pitch to the floor. The rough water had her stumbling this morning. With her other hand, she brought her coffee closer. She inhaled the steam, glancing through the window to see ominous clouds gathering.

"Or sleeping," Nuriel pressed. "I've seen you up at night, working on the drawings. The more you push yourself, the slower you'll go."

Dahlia picked up her spoon. "Could you bring me the milk?"

He sighed and turned away to search the refrigerator.

She looked down at the open notebook page on the table. She could see clearly what the symbol needed to do. What it *wanted* to do. It desired to curl in on itself, loop through its own pattern, and stretch outward. It was like a living creature—a spindly sea star.

It could almost speak to her. When she closed her eyes, she saw it dancing, breathing.

But every time she attempted a new drawing, it felt so lifeless. How could she capture it in a static form?

"Tell me when." Nuriel voice brought her back to the cabin. He was pouring milk into her bowl.

"That's good, thanks."

He returned to the kitchen to make his own breakfast, then settled into the seat beside her. "Every time I look at this, my eyes cross." He nudged the notebook away from his bowl.

"I feel like I'm so close to getting it."

Nuriel gave her an understanding look. "I feel much the same. But this design is odd. I'm starting to wonder if it's even for a resurrection."

"Really?"

He shrugged. "Whatever it is, it contains a lot of power. I just hope we finish before Tannin."

Dahlia's chest tightened. During the daylight, she tried to put him out of mind, but her nightmares had been frequented by his billowing smoke. Most mornings she woke up clutching her neck.

She turned toward Nuriel, spoon pinched between her fingers. "If Tannin *does* beat us, we'll try another one." She tapped the phone, where pictures of a dozen sketches waited.

Nuriel didn't look optimistic. "Yes, but he'll have this one, and he'll apply it to one of his victims. The possibility makes me incredibly nervous."

Dahlia chewed on that for a minute. "How do you reckon he's going to control the Grigori he creates? What if the people he resurrects don't want to listen? I didn't."

"I don't know. It's likely he's working up some sort of contract to coerce them."

Dahlia stared down at their work. Then she heaved a sigh and took a few bites of cereal. Nuriel was probably right—it was almost certain Tannin had prepared for these complications.

The sound of the bathroom door opening caught her attention. Bridget emerged, looking green.

Sympathy stirred in Dahlia. "Morning, sunshine. Hanging in there?"

She groaned. "How in the hell are you eating?"

Nuriel gave a sympathetic tut as he took out his pack of cigarettes. "Medicine not working?"

Instead of responding, Bridget shuffled back to the bed, falling onto it with a *fwump*. Dahlia watched her for a moment. Since arriving on the yacht, the sisters hadn't had many opportunities to speak alone. In some ways, it was for the best. Dahlia kept turning over Tannin's words in her mind, his offer to withdraw his claim to Bridget in exchange for Dahlia's help. As much as Bridget would hate it, the offer did present an opportunity for Dahlia to get closer to Tannin, if necessary.

Nuriel drew her attention as he spoke, staring out the upper window at the tilting horizon. "It's hard to make progress with the boat rocking like this."

She gave him a flat stare. "Nuriel. You can literally control water."

He looked surprised, then laughed. "True." Extending a hand outward, palm down, he closed his eyes. Then he paused, cracking one open with a gleam of amusement. "Would you like to help me?"

Her heart skipped at the offer. Following his lead, she turned both palms downward. Then she reached out with her mind, searching for Nuriel's primary ability. She took a small sliver of it into her own hands, extending it downward and outward, beyond the cabin and into the lake's tumult. *Calm.* Tapping into Grigori power was more invigorating than coffee—it filled her with life.

The sway of the boat lessened, then stopped altogether. Breathless, Dahlia didn't dare stop channeling energy outward. When she glanced over at Nuriel, he was smiling. "You're getting good at this. Unfortunately, it won't last long."

"No?" Then Dahlia remembered her training. "It's because of the wind, right?"

"Yes. You can ease off. I'll hold us steady for as long as I can."

Dahlia released her focus. She turned her attention to the drawing, cupping it in her mind's eye. She imagined it turning, swirling, dancing. Then she took pencil to paper and began drawing. Lines flowed from her almost unconsciously. She was so close she could taste it.

"What the hell are you doing?"

Danel's harsh tone broke her flow. The yacht lurched as Nuriel lost his concentration.

"We're working."

"I'm trying to sail here." Danel's attention dropped to the box of cigarettes near Nuriel's empty cereal bowl. "If you light one of those in the cabin I *will* throw you overboard."

Dahlia's scathing response was interrupted as the boat rocked to the side and Bridget bolted up from bed. With one hand clasped over her mouth, she raced past them and back into the bathroom, slamming the door behind her.

"Maybe we should put a pause on the sailing," Dahlia suggested. "At least until the waters calm down."

Danel eyed the bathroom door distastefully. "I can't anchor here. It's too deep. We need to keep moving."

"Can you get us somewhere you *can* anchor?" she asked.

"Give me twenty minutes." He trudged up the stairs. The whistle of wind accompanied him as he opened the door. It shut with a bang, leaving Dahlia and Nuriel alone once more.

Dahlia stared forlornly at their graphing paper. "I was making good progress."

"I know. I was watching you draw; you're getting very close." He rose—using the table for balance—and gathered their empty bowls. "More coffee?"

"Absolutely." She passed him her mug.

He took the dishes to the kitchen and set about washing and wiping them down. "Do you want to tell me more about the nightmares you've been having?"

Dahlia looked up from the notebook. "Sorry I've been waking you up."

"It's not a problem." Nuriel set the bowls into the cabinets inlaid with rubber liners to keep the dishes stationary. "I just want to make sure you're alright."

"I'm fine. I know it's part of the process."

Nuriel brought her a fresh mug. "Unfortunately, you're likely having a more difficult time of it than I did."

The coffee mug warmed her fingers, but Dahlia felt cold, nonetheless. "Because I'm a mismatch with... with the person my tattoo belongs to." She didn't say Hartu's name out loud. Acknowledging him felt like a step too far.

"Yes. On top of the trauma of how it happened."

Dahlia took a sip of coffee, but it tasted acrid and bitter. She set the mug down. "No one really has told me what that means. I know you usually match a symbol to a particular person, but what actually happens when you don't?"

"From what I understand, it's a lot harder to settle into your new identity. Parts of yourself feel fractured because, well, you are." He sat down again, picking up the pencil and tracing a few lines. "These are contracts that bind us together, right? But all contracts require agreement between parties. Ours are no different."

Dahlia thought back over the last few weeks. To when she said something and her sister did a double take. To when she felt like she was inexplicably in two places at once. To the insidious nightmares with their inverted lightning.

More than once, she'd woken with lingering, angry heat burning in her gut. It simmered beneath the fear, reminding her of how much had changed. How much she'd lost. Was that Hartu, slipping in? Could she reconcile herself with someone who'd lived in the pursuit of vengeance?

"You're lucky." Nuriel gently pulled her back to their conversation. "In some ways, you already have a head start on many."

"How?"

Nuriel nodded toward the bathroom. "You have someone who cares about you. Someone who can help reconcile your human self with your Grigori self."

Dahlia followed his gaze. Her sister hadn't emerged yet. "I don't feel very much like the person she knows anymore." It was the first time she'd admitted it out loud. Somehow it lifted a weight from her.

"Also to be expected. But you *are* still her. You're just also someone else."

"That's not how Gaul talks about it. According to him, the human I was is nothing more than a bunch of old memories."

Nuriel shook his head. "Gaul has his own unique perspective of our world, but that's all it is. A perspective. Remember, he's over a thousand years old; he hardly remembers those first few years of his life as a human. You could meet a hundred Grigori, and we'll all have a different view of ourselves and our human origins."

Dahlia gave a humorless laugh. "That is way too vague to help."

His smile was gentle. "My point is, there's no wrong way for you to feel. You're changing, you're grieving, you're staying the same. All at once. That's difficult for anyone to navigate."

Dahlia lowered her voice. "I've been thinking of a

name."

"Oh?" Nuriel's eyebrows lifted.

"I mean, I..." She hesitated. How to put her tangled thoughts into words? "Gaul told me who had my symbol before me."

Understanding crossed Nuriel's face. "I can see how that would be unsettling."

Dahlia shrugged, looking down. "I don't have any memories of that life. It doesn't feel like mine, that person doesn't feel like me. But..."

Nuriel tapped his fingers thoughtfully on the table. "The name you use is an incredibly personal decision, Dahlia."

"I know. And I don't have anything in particular in mind. Even if I did, I wouldn't do it now. It would destroy Bridget."

He stilled his tapping, looking to her. "When you're ready, Bridget will need to accept that."

If only it were so simple. Getting Bridget to accept anything beyond what she'd set her mind to was like trying to cut a boulder with yarn. "I don't know if that'll happen."

"Then that's *her* battle to fight, not yours," Nuriel said firmly. "You're the only person who gets to say who you are. Not Bridget. Not any past iterations of yourself."

The words sounded good. Hopefully she'd find it in her to believe them one of these days.

Exhaling slowly, she looked out of the windows; the gray clouds were still there. The roll of the boat had stilled over the course of their conversation. "Do you think we anchored?"

Nuriel shook his head. "No, we would have heard it.

The wind died down."

"Let's hurry and make some more progress, before it picks back up again." She grabbed the notebook, setting their conversation aside. As usual, Nuriel had given her a lot to think about.

"Can I make some adjustments?" He held out a hand and she slid the notebook to him.

They fell into a familiar rhythm. Nuriel worked for a few minutes, then passed the paper to her. Dahlia sketched up a fresh version of the drawing, adding or subtracting what didn't feel right. Then she returned the sketch to him.

Back and forth they went, until it was impossible to tell where one Artist's work ended and the other's began. Swooshes and flourishes wove in and out like a Celtic knot.

Then, suddenly, they didn't have any lines left to draw.

Time stood still. They stared at the design, then Nuriel waved her in closer. "Press here."

She put her index finger on the center of the symbol.

A shimmer of gold rippled outward from her touch. It trailed along the curves, extending to the spiraling arms and illuminating the entire drawing with a glistening light. Dahlia gasped. The edges of the design held the shimmer for a striking moment before fading to black. Lightness filled her.

"We did it," she whispered.

SIXTEEN

Dahlia froze, staring in disbelief. Then she was laughing, hugging Nuriel. "It works!"

He smelled of cigarettes and shampoo, and when he pulled back, his eyes were dancing. "Excellent work."

Dahlia looked back at the sketch. They'd done it. *She'd* done it. Against all odds, with minimal training, she'd finished a sketch. In days, she'd accomplished what she couldn't do in months of captivity. *Fear is a terrible motivator.* All of Kai's threats couldn't do what Nuriel's gentle, steadfast support managed.

The door to the bathroom opened then, and Bridget staggered out. Her skin was pale, but based on her hopeful expression she'd clearly heard them celebrating. "Did you say you finished?"

Dahlia urged her forward. "Come and see."

Bridget took a few steps forward, then paused to catch her breath.

"Here." Nuriel got up and snagged a water bottle from the refrigerator, offering it to her. "Drink this."

"Thanks." Bridget took the bottle and approached the table. Dahlia watched as her eyes grazed over their workspace. To Bridget it probably looked like a haphazard spread of notebook pages—not the systematic process she and Nuriel had devised together.

"How do you know it's done?" Bridget uncapped the water bottle and took a generous swig.

"Look." Dahlia selected the final sketch and turned the paper toward Bridget. Once again, at her touch a gentle shimmer spread outward, glimmering like the sun off water. When she pulled her finger away, the glow faded.

Bridget looked up at them both, and her breathless excitement sent a pang of joy through Dahlia. Her older sister might not understand the intricacies of the work, but she could appreciate the results. Maybe it was a sign she could someday accept the other changes in Dahlia's life.

She felt herself grinning widely. "We can work on the other symbols, if you want, but I think we should give this a shot with James."

Dahlia looked back down at the pattern, eyes tracing its lines. It was beautiful, somehow *feeling* complete without feeling familiar. A brand-new name, ready to join with a human vessel.

Assuming they could get it to James fast enough, of course. It had been nearly a week. During that time,

James could have been returned to his family. Or Tannin could have made his own progress, rendering it useless to them.

"Do you know what it will let James do?" Bridget asked.

Nuriel shook his head. "We don't. This symbol, like Dahlia's, comes from a set lost long before I was created."

"But it will work?"

"I'm fairly certain. It has the proper structure to bind with a human."

Something in his tone gave Dahlia pause. "You still think this is a bad idea, don't you?"

He turned to her. "There are inherent risks in sealing a newly recovered contact. We don't know how it will behave. We don't even know if James is the proper recipient for a Grigori, much less *this* one."

Bridget didn't look bothered. "Dahlia wasn't the perfect match, and she's fine. She hasn't changed at all."

The comment hit Dahlia in the heart. Her joy fizzled away, leaving a tight feeling in its wake. She looked away, pulling one of the unfinished sketches closer. Uneasy silence enveloped the trio.

Dahlia could feel Bridget and Nuriel watching her. After a few uncomfortable seconds, Nuriel cleared his throat. "I'll tell Danel we're ready to head back to Cleveland."

He pressed his fingers lightly on Dahlia's arm as he stood. It was a gentle reminder of his support, and she was grateful for it. The pain didn't lessen, though. How was she supposed to explain to Bridget she was deluding herself? That she *wasn't* the same person, that she never would be? Even without the tattoo on her back, her experience of imprisonment had left her altered.

Bridget waited until the door to the cabin closed behind Nuriel. "Dahlia?"

She looked up from her pile of drawings, eyes burning. Bridget slid onto the seat, taking the spot where Nuriel had been. "Hey, I'm sorry. Did I say something wrong?"

Of course she had. Bridget had always been an expert at blurting out the worst thing with the best of intentions. Growing up, Dahlia had weathered it by charting her own path. Where Bridget had remained fastidiously focused on her responsibilities, Dahlia sought out her own joy in life. But this wasn't a situation Dahlia could ignore or shrug off with a night out on the town.

Dahlia sat beside her sister, putting the sheet of paper down. "Sometimes, I have trouble believing this is my life now." It was something she hoped Bridget could relate to. Everything had changed, for both of them.

Bridget looped an arm over Dahlia's shoulder. "I know. You've been through so much."

Dahlia tried not to flinch back from the physical contact. It felt heavy and wrong, completely unlike Nuriel's reassurance. She could feel her heartbeat in her ears.

She distracted herself from the sensation by picking up another piece of scrap paper, folding it in half. "And then sometimes, the part that feels unbelievable is my human memories."

"What do you mean?"

She took a deep breath to steady her pulse. "Everything I am now feels *real*. I mean, of *course* I'm a mimic. Of *course,* I'm having trouble caring about the degree program I'll never finish, or my friends, or seeing Mom again. It just doesn't feel important." To give her hands something familiar to do, she folded the paper over itself again.

Bridget scoffed. "You don't mean that. Your archaeology program means everything to you. You can finish school when everything settles down, and Mom... I was thinking we should go see her as soon as we can."

Frustration roiled up. It was so on-brand for Bridget to not listen. She blurted viciously, "Sometimes I forget about you, too." Dahlia's throat felt hot and her eyes stung. She folded the paper in half once more, trying to channel her irritation into the creases.

Surprise flickered across her sister's face, followed by pain. Bridget retracted her arm and cleared her throat. "What do you mean?" Her blue eyes watched Dahlia uncertainly.

Dahlia had meant to be hurtful with the words. But now, seeing the wounded look in her sister's eyes, her heart sank. Sometimes family was suffocating, but it didn't mean you wouldn't do anything for them.

"You know, never mind. I'm glad you're here with me, Bridget." The words were true, a messy web of contradictions and complexities.

Her sister's voice was small. "Yeah. Always."

The words twisted in Dahlia's gut. She looked down at the paper under her fingers, folding it several more times until it became a thick knot, impossible to crease again. Grief overpowered her anger, and she whispered, "But you *won't* always be here, will you?"

It was the part they never said out loud. The centuries of life she'd inherited were incompatible with Bridget's existence. Every frustration, every conversation, every moment together... someday they would be in Dahlia's distant past.

Tears threatened to build up again, and Bridget put her hand over Dahlia's. She gently pulled the folded paper from her grip and slipped her hand into Dahlia's. "A human lifetime is still a long time. It's all either of us were going to get, before this." This time, Dahlia didn't flinch back at the touch. She turned her palm upward and tightened her grip.

"Listen, Dahlia," Bridget said. "Time is going to pass, no matter what. We can't help that. But we *can* focus on what's in front of us. What's here and now."

Sometimes, her sister *did* know what to say. "Yeah, you're right."

"I'm proud of you, Dahlia. I mean, look what you and Nuriel did."

She wiped her tears as she looked down at the completed drawing. "Thanks. I hope it's enough. Just... make sure this is what you want, okay? If it works, James will be different." *Like me.*

Bridget squeezed Dahlia's hand. "We're all doing the best we can to give him a second chance. That's the most we can ever do."

SEVENTEEN

No one wanted to risk sneaking into the funeral home in broad daylight, which meant whiling away the day in an anxious haze as Danel sailed up and down the coastline.

From inside the cabin, Dahlia could hear Bridget pacing above her. She had to assume she was only on deck for the fresh air, not for the company.

Sitting at the dinette, Dahlia and Nuriel sat side by side, replicating the symbol on transfer paper they would eventually copy onto James' skin. It was one thing to sketch lines in a notebook. Tattooing them permanently onto a corpse was another matter entirely, and there was no room for error.

They reconvened as a group over a hurried dinner of peanut butter sandwiches. Bridget brought out her hand-drawn map of the funeral home. "Danel is going to help us pick the locks."

"He is?" Dahlia looked over at Danel in surprise. The last she'd spoken to him, he'd been adamant about staying out of the heist.

He rolled his eyes. "Don't look so surprised. It's not like any of you could do it."

She thought she saw him exchange a quick glance with Bridget, but the moment passed in an instant. They returned to their planning.

A few hours later, Danel brought the yacht into a new marina—closer to their destination, according to him. He and Nuriel hopped off the boat first, looping thick ropes around the metal cleat. It was nearing midnight, and the boats around them were empty and dark.

The wind had fallen still, a misty coldness settling in its wake. Dahlia wrapped herself in a hug, wishing she'd brought more than a threadbare hoodie. The weight of her backpack, with the finished sketch nestled inside, felt comforting—a promise of progress.

"You ready?" Bridget asked Dahlia. Her sister was practically buzzing with eagerness.

Nuriel turned his head and exhaled a cloud of smoke. He had his messenger bag with him, and he kept one hand resting on the flap, nervously toying with its edge.

Danel walked up beside them and surveyed the sparse parking lot. "Let's find our ride."

Bridget, predictably, looked uneasy. "I still don't like this part of the plan."

Danel shook his head. "Nuriel's car has probably been towed by now, so we need to find a new one."

Bridget opened her mouth, but Dahlia cut in. "It's not like we won't return it. Assuming we can get past whoever's in there." She nodded toward a gatehouse near the marina's entrance. It was a small, whitewashed structure sitting between the parking lot entrance and exit. A single light shone from within.

Danel looked at the guard house thoughtfully. "Hm. Well, maybe we *don't* have to steal a car. Technically."

Nuriel went stiff. "Out of the question."

A wolfish grin crawled across Danel's face. "Come on, it'll be easier this way. And cleaner, far less suspicious."

Nuriel shook his head. "I don't even know if it will work."

"If it doesn't, we'll go with Plan B."

Dahlia glanced curiously at Nuriel. She'd spent enough time with him recently to learn many of his mannerisms, but this was something new.

"You okay?" Dahlia nudged him gently.

"He's squeamish," said Danel with a mocking laugh.

Nuriel glared at him. "It's not right."

Danel tapped his wrist. "Tick tock. The longer we stand here arguing, the more time Tannin has to get the jump on us."

With a sigh, Nuriel tipped his head back, eyes on the clouds. He looked as if he were praying, though Dahlia had no idea what sort of gods Grigori might believe in. Then he sighed and dropped his cigarette, putting it out with one shoe. "I can try, but no promises. I'm going to need some money."

"Pay me back." Danel slipped five dollars from his pocket and passed it to Nuriel.

Taking the bill, Nuriel rolled his eyes. "I'll buy you a coffee." He bent down and picked up the cigarette to find a place to dispose of it.

Dahlia watched him go, curiosity gnawing at the edges of her mind.

She turned to Danel. "What's going on?"

"While the rest of us have to rely on charm to get what we want, Nuriel can be quite persuasive when he wants to be."

The words clicked, and Dahlia's eyes widened. "Is this his other ability? How does it work?"

Danel shrugged. "Haphazardly, in my experience."

"I want to see." Dahlia took off after Nuriel.

"If you go with him, you'll make him lose focus," Danel called.

But Dahlia didn't stop. She knew nothing about Nuriel's second power. He refused to talk about it, let alone train her in it.

A hand snagged her wrist, slowing her down. She looked back to see Bridget had followed.

"Hang on. We don't want to interrupt him."

Reluctantly, Dahlia slowed her pace. They followed Nuriel at a distance, close enough to eavesdrop but far enough to go unnoticed.

Nuriel knocked gently on the guard house's window. Dahlia and Bridget ducked behind a pickup truck. Staying within the pool of shadow it created, Dahlia peeked over the top of the bed.

The window slid open with a grating sound, and the guard came into view. He was bald with a long beard, and he gave a wave with a notebook and pen clutched in his hand.

"How can I help you?" The guard's voice carried the rawness of someone who hadn't slept much lately.

"Sorry to bother you," Nuriel said. "My car got a flat while I was out on the lake."

"Sorry to hear that. I can call you a tow." The guard set his notebook down and reached over, presumably for a phone.

"Actually, I was wondering if I could borrow yours."

The guard paused. "My... car?"

Nuriel leaned in to read the name badge stitched

across his shirt. "Mr. Gorman, right? It would help me out quite a bit."

The guard shook his head. "Call me Benjamin. And sorry, I don't think so. I'll call you a tow, or I can lend you a jack."

"Ah. Alright, no worries. Thanks anyway." He extended his right hand for a shake. In his left, he procured the crisp five-dollar bill. "For your hard work here. I know night shifts are no fun."

Looking flabbergasted, Benjamin accepted the handshake and reached for the tip. Dahlia inched closer to watch as Nuriel kept his hand in a firm grip. She focused on Nuriel's powers; sure enough, his mysterious second ability flared to life. Wisps of gold spread between their clasped hands.

Benjamin's expression underwent a subtle transformation. The wary skepticism in his eyes faded, transforming into trust. She couldn't see Nuriel's face, but his shoulders were rigid. When he dropped the handshake, Benjamin slipped the money into his pocket. His hand reemerged with a set of keys. "Bring it back full."

"Of course." Nuriel took the keys and turned away quickly. There was a light sheen of sweat on his forehead. His eyes met Dahlia's for a split second, then darted away. He pressed the key fob, and a battered Volvo flashed its lights. He went directly toward it.

A twisting sensation wormed its way through Dahlia. Benjamin continued to look hopeful as he watched Nuriel walk off.

"Mind control?" Dahlia asked Bridget quietly.

Her sister shook her head, although she also looked uncomfortable. "He told me once he can suppress emotions. I've never seen it work, though."

Huh. So, his talents were an inverted version of Viri's. Instead of drawing up a specific emotion, he stifled them. Which, when she thought about it, was essentially the same. If Nuriel stifled all of the emotions Benjamin felt *except* his sense of altruism, how was that any different from Viri expanding on that emotion?

In both cases, the Grigori power manipulated someone's own feelings, bending them to a specific desire.

The revelation left a bitter taste in her mouth. Nuriel, more than any other Grigori, had been by her side to help her understand her new world. She trusted him.

Had he tricked her, like Danel had? Tweaked her emotions to make him more affable?

She hurried after Nuriel, joining him at the car. "What happened back there?"

"What did it look like?" His voice was gruff as he opened the driver's side door and sat inside.

She knew Bridget would want the passenger's seat after her days-long bout with motion sickness, but she slid into it anyway. "It looked like you can control people."

Nuriel's lips tightened. He didn't say anything as Bridget and Danel piled into the backseat, which had a fine layer of dog fur inside. The car started with a sputter, and Nuriel drove them out of the parking lot. He kept his gaze firmly fixed ahead as he passed through the exit, avoiding making eye contact with Benjamin.

Once they turned onto the street, Danel spoke. "I knew you had it in you, Nuriel."

"Be quiet." Nuriel's voice had an edge Dahlia had never heard before. She took in the tightness around his eyes and didn't know what to say.

He'd always seemed quietly embarrassed of his ability

to manipulate water, for reasons she didn't fully understand. This was something different. This was shame.

Dahlia wanted to press him, but his mood settled over the car like a storm cloud. So instead, she kept quiet, watching the road. Once, she glanced back at Bridget. Her sister was tapping her fingers against her knee in a steady rhythm, no doubt counting the seconds until they reached James. Danel's eyes were on the passing scenery as it became increasingly rural.

Dahlia returned her attention out front, trying to force the knot in her stomach to unwind. Nuriel had given her no reason to distrust him. He clearly didn't like to use this second, lesser power. And if Bridget had gotten a whiff of coercive control from Nuriel, she would have put a stop to it.

But after everything she'd experienced, Dahlia couldn't help but doubt herself. Once, she'd had total confidence in her instincts about who was good and bad for her to be around. Now, her faith wavered.

If she couldn't trust herself, what kind of eternal life would she have?

Twenty minutes passed before the car rumbled to a stop on the side of the road. The headlights illuminated a dark rural stretch of road and, about a hundred feet ahead, a driveway.

He cut the engine. "We're here."

EIGHTEEN

Bridget stepped out of the car onto the narrow shoulder. A grassy drainage ditch extended along the length of the road. With the headlights off, it looked impossibly deep.

Heavy clouds trapped the moon, diffusing its glow. Dahlia was a shadow beside her. The corn fields were a swaying smudge that *shushed* in the breeze. Stripes of gray marked the road's gravel edge.

"See you at the back door." Danel started to run, then stumbled, catching himself on the hood of the Volvo. He straightened and stared at his feet.

"Danel?" Bridget whispered.

He glanced back at her, then shook his head and took off at a jog.

Dahlia sighed, leaning into Bridget. "I wish we didn't have to bring him."

"Me too, but he'll make this a lot easier in the end."

"How'd you finally convince him to help?"

Bridget shook her head. "It doesn't matter." She'd promised to keep Danel's confidence about his niece. She'd break his trust for her sister in a heartbeat, but there wasn't any need. Besides, she needed Danel's cooperation right now.

The plan was to give him a head start, letting him locate and cover any exterior cameras Bridget might have missed, then soothe the lock into submission. If it didn't work, they'd have to figure out how to break in through the barred windows.

Bridget started down the road. As the only person from their group who had been inside the funeral home, her job was to guide their movements. She stopped on the edge of the parking lot, listening. The old hearse still sat in silent vigil, but the lot was otherwise empty.

As Bridget moved down the property line, she ran through the litany of everything that could go wrong. She wasn't so worried about gaining access to the building as she was about the symbol proving inert.

But she could overcome even that. If this one didn't work, they'd try the next. And the next. It didn't matter how long it took. Tannin couldn't steal them all. And while he was busy raising his Grigori army, she could rouse James.

And then what? The question poked at Bridget. What would she do when James was revived as an immortal, like Dahlia? The disturbing conversation she'd had with her sister was a splinter she couldn't quite work free.

A moment later, Danel poked his head around the corner and waved. Bridget shoved down her thoughts and led the three of them along the edge of the lawn, brushing past boxwoods.

The back of the building was a mirror of the front, sans the portico, plus a bit more grime on the siding. Danel led them to a concrete stoop in front of a simple, whitewashed door. It was marked with an "Employees Only" sign.

Danel shook his head in dismay as they approached. "Not a single camera. And the lock was simple. It's almost as if they *want* to be robbed."

"Some people have faith in the goodness of others," Nuriel said.

Danel rolled his eyes. "Stay here until we know it's clear."

The door swung open with a quiet creak. Danel slipped into the darkness beyond, and Bridget followed before he could tell her to stay, too. Nuriel and Dahlia came in last.

Tired wooden steps groaned a soft protest under her weight as she descended. Bridget tried to chase away the lingering apprehension of breaking and entering. By now, she should be used to it. And yet, a lifetime of being told right from wrong made it difficult to stay calm as they crept downward.

Danel reached a hand back to halt her.

"What?" she hissed.

"There's a light on." He gestured toward the end of the hallway, and she peered over his shoulder. The hall was dim, but a white light shone from beneath the door to one of the rooms. The room where James waited.

Danel held up a hand, then snuck forward, peering into corners—presumably hoping for the conciliatory challenge of interior cameras—and edging toward the room.

Bridget waited at the foot of the stairs, trying to breathe calm into her veins as she waited.

Less than a minute later, Danel returned. He leaned in and whispered, "Someone's definitely in there."

"Probably Charlie." Bridget waved them back up the stairs to regroup on the landing. "Nuriel, can you do the same thing you did in the car lot?"

A scandalized look passed across Nuriel's face. "No."

"I understand you don't like it, but this is a special situation."

He shook his head. "Just because I am capable of something does not mean I should wield its power. Besides, it's difficult for me to use it again so soon."

"But can't you at least *try*?" Bridget pressed.

It was Dahlia who shook her head. "Let it go, Bridget. He's telling the truth—he tapped out that ability last time."

Bridget's mouth went dry. "You can tell something like that? How?"

Before Dahlia could respond, Danel cleared his throat. "While this conversation is fascinating, can we focus on the goal?"

He was right. Their primary plan had relied on Charlie *not* being present. After all, who worked in a morgue in the middle of the night?

She tapped her fingers against her thigh. "It's time for a distraction: I'm going to ring the doorbell."

All three of them stared at her in disbelief.

"After I spent all that energy breaking in?" Danel dropped his arms, eyebrows drawing together.

Bridget rolled her eyes. "It took you five minutes. You just complained about how easy it was. Here's the new plan. I go around the front. When Charlie comes to the door, I'll keep them talking. While they're distracted, you can sneak down these stairs and into the room with James."

"Administering the tattoo will take hours," Nuriel said. "We were planning on working for most of the night. You can't keep them occupied for that long."

"I have a plan for that, too."

"Like knocking them out?" Danel asked.

Dahlia shot him a scathing look.

"What? It's an option!"

Nuriel looked unsettled. "I'd prefer not to harm anyone, if possible."

Bridget rolled her eyes. "I'm not going to hurt Charlie. I'm going to tell them Viri needs their help."

"You have no way of knowing if that will work," Dahlia said. "I mean, they could literally call him."

Bridget shifted her weight. Tension crackled through her veins. They were so close. She wanted to *move*. "Well, there's another option. I keep Charlie distracted for a few minutes while you sneak James into the car. We take him back to the boat and apply the tattoo there."

"You want us to steal a corpse?" Nuriel asked sharply.

Danel eyed Bridget with something bordering on respect. "I like it."

"It's what we have to do." Bridget's words felt raw, like someone had rubbed sandpaper along the lining of her throat. She remembered the weight of James' limp body all too well, as she dragged it back to Cleveland from Tannin's collection. The sensation of helping Nuriel lift him into his car haunted her at night.

Dahlia reluctantly nodded her agreement, but Nuriel was watching Bridget with concern.

"Are you certain? If our symbol doesn't work, he will decompose swiftly without refrigeration. Getting him back to his family will become more difficult."

She swallowed. "It's the simplest option, especially with Charlie here."

Dahlia's hand found hers, then squeezed. "If anything happens, run for it."

"You mean if Charlie calls the cops on me for breaking and entering?" Bridget tried to laugh, but it fell flat. She cleared her throat. "James' body is in the top center freezer. Please be careful with him."

"Do you want assistance at the front?" Nuriel asked.

Bridget shook her head. "No. It'll take at least two people to carry him and someone else to keep a lookout. I'll be okay." She dropped her sister's hand. "I'll meet y'all at the car."

Dahlia's smile was tense. "You know Bridget is stressed when her North Carolina comes out."

She rolled her eyes. "Good luck, everybody."

The sound of crickets followed her as she walked

around the building. The ground was wet from a recent rain, and her shoes squished in the muck. Not very discreet, but then again, Bridget had never done well with sneaking.

She felt conspicuous as she walked beneath the portico and walked to the front door, cleaning her shoes on the mat. Through the glass, the upstairs was dark. Bridget had a feeling Charlie didn't spend much time on the main floor unless they were with a client.

Bridget ran through her options. She needed to keep Charlie preoccupied while the others snuck in. She also didn't want to come off as a threat, which was all too likely with a midnight knock at the door.

She could come up with a lie, but she worried she was too blunt to fool anyone. She filled her belly with a long, slow breath. "You'll figure it out," she whispered to herself. She always did. Steeling herself, she rang the doorbell. A pleasant chime rang inside.

All Charlie needed was a reason to pay attention. All Bridget had to do was give them something to pay attention *to*.

While Bridget waited, she focused on the memories she'd avoided most. Not only the horrible, final moments of James' life, but the times when he'd made her laugh. The trust he'd placed in her, and the earnestness with which he'd joined her hunt for Dahlia. For the short time they'd known one another, he'd been such a true friend.

The lights stayed dark. She rang the bell again.

Nothing. Maybe Charlie couldn't hear the doorbell over their music. She held the button down. A steady cacophony of chimes spilled out.

It shouldn't be this hard. She shouldn't have to sneak around to save her friend. James never should have died in the first place.

He'd only been good to her. He'd listened when no one else would—helped when everyone else fell away. His eyes shone with excitement when he learned about the secret world of the Grigori. Only to have those revelations end his short, bright life.

By the time Charlie's pink hair appeared on the other side of the door, pressure had built up behind Bridget's eyes, and tears rolled freely down her cheeks. The funeral director's surprise barely registered to Bridget as they unlocked and opened the door.

They flipped on the porch light and looked Bridget up and down. "Is something wrong? Are you hurt?"

Bridget realized she must look wild. Between the lack of sleep, the mud on her shoes, and her mussed hair, she may as well have crawled out of the nearest moonlit cornfield. She opened her mouth to answer Charlie, but a sob broke free instead.

"You're Dr. Barbosa's friend, aren't you? Come in. What happened?"

Charlie ushered Bridget into the entryway. Before she could respond, Charlie was turning away. "Here, let me get you some water." They moved into the deeper recesses of the building.

"No!" Bridget's cry stopped Charlie in their tracks. "Please, I don't want to be alone right now." She searched her mental map of the facility, from her trip earlier that week. "Can I sit in the chapel?"

Looking relieved to have some direction, Charlie gestured. "Of course. Come this way."

They led Bridget into the side room she'd seen on her first visit—on the opposite side of the building from where James was. It was unchanged, with chairs facing an empty altar, ready to take up the vestiges of whichever religious gathering was present. A table pushed against the wall had various religious texts shelved neatly.

"Are you sure you don't want water?" Charlie asked.

Bridget sank into one of the chairs. Her tears were ebbing, and she wiped her eyes. "Stay with me?"

Charlie pursed their lips, then sat as well, leaving an empty chair between the two of them. "It's Bridget, right? What are you doing here?" Their voice was gentle, but carried an edge. "You realize it's the middle of the night."

"I know." Bridget toyed with the hem of her shirt. She wasn't much of an actress, so she decided to tell Charlie the truth. "I'm sorry, I couldn't stay away. I know Dr. Barbosa was going to have you contact James' family soon."

"Tomorrow," Charlie said, and the edge in tone grew stronger. "I can't keep him here any longer, and they have a right to know."

Bridget's heart thumped. What would have happened if it'd taken Dahlia and Nuriel a day longer to finish the tattoo?

"I just... I miss him. I feel like it's all my fault." That much was painfully true.

Charlie's eyes softened. "Losing a loved one is never

easy, especially to violence."

Fresh pressure welled up behind her eyes. The moments before James' death were a swirling panic in her memory. Flashes of it threatened to overtake her. The smack of a body hitting the wall. The horrible sensation of stabbing her attackers. Kai's vindictive smirk before he sent Bridget's weapon flying from her hand into James' chest. The memory of his blood sat at the back of her throat, a sharp tang.

"Bridget? I'm going to call Dr. Barbosa, okay?" A hand on her shoulder brought her back to the present. Charlie was watching with growing concern. Bridget swallowed back bile and started to speak.

Her words were interrupted by a scraping sound, deeper within the funeral home. Charlie froze, then turned in their seat.

"He didn't deserve to be murdered," Bridget blurted, voice pitched too loud. Hopefully loud enough to cover any other sounds.

Charlie looked at Bridget, brows furrowing. "It's a terrible situation."

There was no way she could tell them what actually happened. Who knew what Gaul's contract would do to her? "It really is," Bridget said. She had to keep talking. Keep Charlie's attention. "He was only trying to help me. And instead, I got him killed. It's my fault he's gone. I don't—"

"Shh." Charlie held up a hand. In a smooth motion, they stood. "Stay here, Bridget."

She shook her head. "Wait. No, don't leave me."

"I'm not going far." Charlie turned toward the hall, and Bridget hurried to her feet.

"Please, I can't be alone." Grief stung at the corner of her eyes. Hot tears spilled over. "Not right now."

Charlie shushed Bridget again, moving into the hall and toward the basement stairs. Bridget followed and, in a fit of desperation, swiped a floral-printed vase from its table.

It smashed to the ground, shattering into pieces. Charlie jumped at the sound, whirling back to face Bridget.

"I'm sorry! I ran into it!" she cried.

Charlie eyed Bridget. "Wait in the chapel." The sympathy was gone from their voice, replaced by firm suspicion. "When I return, we'll talk about why you decided to knock on my door in the middle of the night."

They turned away and strode purposefully toward the stairs. Biting back the desire to call out a warning to Dahlia and the others, Bridget skirted around the shattered glass and followed a few feet away. "Do you think someone's there?"

"That's what I'm trying to find out," Charlie whispered. They were having a hard time keeping their irritation at bay. "Did you come alone?"

"Yes," Bridget lied, hoping her voice carried as far as the basement. "I'll come with you in case you need backup."

"Shh!" Charlie glared at Bridget. "Don't follow me." They descended.

Bridget hovered at the top of the stairs, wiping the

tears from her cheeks and waiting. As soon as Charlie was out of sight of the bottom landing, she followed as quickly and quietly as she could. Her pulse beat wildly in her ears as she slipped downward.

The basement hallway was silent. Ahead of her, Charlie flicked the light on, and Bridget blinked against the bright overheads.

"Hello?" Charlie called.

No answer. Bridget hung back as Charlie made their way forward. The door to the morgue was cracked open, light spilling into the hall. Had Charlie left it that way, when they'd gone to answer the ringing bell? Surely it hadn't been long enough for the others to remove James' body yet.

"Maybe we should call the police," Bridget suggested, panic nipping at her edges. The back door was closed.

Charlie whirled around. "I told you not to come downstairs! Stay back."

"If there's someone here, you might need help." Bridget ignored Charlie's warning and moved further down the hall.

It was clear Charlie wasn't happy about Bridget's continued presence, but they turned their attention back to the morgue's door.

Bridget tensed, trying to keep her breath steady. If her friends were in the room, she'd need to intervene quickly.

Charlie nudged the door with their foot. It swung inward, light spilling into the hallway.

A body came into view. Bridget's heart twinged, but then she took a closer look. It wasn't James. The body belonged to an elderly man without a stitch of clothing on him, arranged respectfully on a metal bed. Bridget looked away quickly, but not so fast she didn't notice the tube attached to his neck. Charlie must have been in the process of embalming.

The room beyond was otherwise empty. No Dahlia. No Danel or Nuriel.

And no James.

Her heart leapt again, this time in relief. The freezer door that had held his body was ajar, revealing a dark, empty hole. They'd done it.

Charlie spun on Bridget, jaw slack with horror. "What did you do?"

Bridget took a step backward. "Nothing."

"Where is he?" Charlie reached for her, looking shell-shocked.

Bridget pulled away. She needed to leave, and fast. With an apologetic grimace, she turned and ran toward the stairwell that led outside—the same one she and Danel had initially descended. Behind her, Charlie shouted for her to stop.

She'd hit the first step of the stairwell when the exterior door swung open.

A new, cold voice made her heart stutter.

"Stop right there, Ms. Keene."

NINETEEN

Bridget stumbled to a halt. The familiar silhouette of Eisheth stood in the back door, outlined by hazy moonlight.

What was *she* doing here? Bridget backed up, running straight into Charlie. They grabbed Bridget by the arm and spun her around. The shock was gone, replaced by an angry red that rode up their cheeks. "Where is the body?"

With a yelp, Bridget twisted free of Charlie's grip. She shoved them back and bolted for the main stairwell. Her heart skittered as she took the stairs two at a time.

"Bridget!" Eisheth's voice followed. Charlie's boots thundered behind her.

Bridget didn't stop as she reached the first floor. She had to get to the car, and the front door was her only option.

In the hall, Charlie tackled her, and Bridget fell to the floor with an *oof*.

Charlie's voice was hot against Bridget's neck. "Do you have any idea how illegal this is?" They shoved her flat and pinned her limbs.

Bridget gasped, cheek smashed into the hallway runner. A shard of porcelain from the broken vase was an inch from her eyes.

She twisted under Charlie's weight, trying to throw them off. "Get off me!"

"Not a chance," Charlie growled. Their grip tightened on Bridget's wrist, and she hissed in pain.

"You can release her, Mx. Stevenson." Eisheth's smooth, business-like tone left a pit of dread in Bridget's stomach. Her shoes came into view as she strode over, glass grinding into the carpet. She knew how Eisheth felt about Bridget's desire to help James.

"This woman is *stealing* a *body*." Charlie's rage was so palpable their words vibrated. "She broke into *my* funeral home."

"I understand you're upset, but Bridget isn't going to run away. Are you, Ms. Keene?"

Bridget opened her mouth to respond, then closed it tightly. Fighting her way out wouldn't work. Not against someone who could summon fireballs at will. She hoped she'd caused enough of a distraction to keep both Charlie *and* Eisheth away from the others.

"No, I won't run." She didn't need luck to guess Danel wouldn't wait too long for her. Not if it meant saving his own hide.

"But—" Charlie spluttered.

"Mx. Stevenson, release her before I bring you in on assault charges." Eisheth had put her sharp detective voice on.

The pressure on Bridget's back eased. She let out a long, ragged breath and pushed herself upright. Her cheek felt raw and her wrists ached, but she was otherwise unharmed. Eisheth stood in front of her, hands on her hips, fixing both of them with her signature glare.

Charlie scrambled to their feet. "If anyone should be arrested, it's her. Not only is she trespassing, but she's conspired to remove one of the bodies from my morgue."

Eisheth's glower found its mark on Charlie. "So, she broke in?"

"I rang the doorbell," Bridget said.

The flush returned to Charlie's cheeks. "In the middle of the night! And then she began feeding me some sob story about her murdered friend."

Eisheth's dark eyebrows inched upward. "I'll admit, a mortician isn't the person *I'd* go crying to, but Bridget has always been a bit strange."

Bridget scowled as she braced herself against the wall and climbed to her feet. What was she playing at? She couldn't figure out if Eisheth was angry at her or helping her. Possibly both.

"You're not taking this seriously!" Charlie's cheeks were mottled with indignation.

"Oh, I'm taking this quite seriously, Mx. Stevenson. Did you ever see Bridget with the body?"

Charlie's eyes narrowed. "No."

"Do you have any idea where she might be hiding a body?" Eisheth looked around the room as if a corpse might be propped against the cabinetry.

"*No*. She obviously had help."

"Was anyone else on the premises? Do you have cameras?"

"I don't have cameras, but—"

Eisheth held up a hand. "You accuse Bridget of breaking and entering, when she rang the doorbell and you, presumably, let her inside. Then you accuse her of stealing a body, even though she's been with you the entire time. You have no footage to prove she had help, and nothing but empty accusations. Is that correct?"

"I have a missing body! Come down to the morgue and see for yourself. A bit odd he disappeared minutes after she rang the doorbell."

"Ah." Eisheth gave them a thin smile. "You mean the body of James Schuster, no doubt. A man who, if I recall correctly, you took in as a favor for Dr. Barbosa. A man who, at his request, was never entered into your register, and who, officially, has never been on the premises."

The words hung between them, a covert threat. So, Eisheth was still on her side, even if she disapproved.

Charlie paled as they realized what was happening. "Do you have any idea how much trouble I could get in for helping Dr. Barbosa?"

"Yes. The very same trouble you're trying to throw on Ms. Keene here." Eisheth folded her arms.

Charlie coughed in disbelief. "You're covering for them. You—"

"I'd choose your next words very carefully, Mx. Stevensen. I think we can both agree this would best be resolved by ignoring it altogether. I wouldn't want to interfere with your professional relationship with Dr. Barbosa."

The breath Charlie took was filled with indignance, but then they deflated. "I'm responsible for the people who pass through here."

Their words sent a pang through Bridget. They were an echo of her own sentiments about James.

"He's important to me," she blurted. It was raw and true. She didn't have a grudge against Charlie, and they were only trying to protect themselves and their business.

Charlie wrang their hands with anxious anger, backed into a corner. "Does Dr. Barbosa know about this?"

"No," Bridget said honestly. "He approached you as a favor to me, but this has nothing to do with him."

Eisheth cut in before she could offer up any more information. "Here's what's going to happen next. I'm going to leave with Ms. Keene. You are going to clean up and go home. It's late, and you've had a long night."

Charlie's jaw snapped together in frustration, but they didn't protest.

"Call Dr. Barbosa if you want. I'm sure he'll be happy to listen." Eisheth focused her attention on Bridget. "As for you, come with me."

Before Bridget could respond, Eisheth turned on her heel and stalked toward the front door at an urgent, clipped pace. Bridget spared one last apologetic look to Charlie, then hurried to catch up.

Eisheth cursed as Bridget met her on the front stoop. She scanned the parking lot. The hearse had been joined by Viri's car, parked at an angle, as if the driver had been in a hurry. The only sound was the rhythmic rise and fall of crickets.

Eisheth ran a hand over her forehead, staring out at the empty road. "Idiot. Of course he didn't wait for us."

Some of the tension fled from Bridget. As she'd hoped, Danel had driven away without her. James was probably safe in the car, heading back to the marina. Dahlia was likely furious, but for once, Bridget was on Danel's side. James was more important than sticking together.

Eisheth rounded on Bridget. She looked sallow in the porch light. "Where were they going, Ms. Keene?"

She jutted out her chin. "Are you planning on stopping them?"

Eisheth blew out a frustrated sigh and turned away. She marched over to the car and held open the passenger side door. "Get in."

Bridget hung back. "Eisheth—wait. Let me explain."

Her eyebrows pinched. "Do you have any idea what you left me to deal with?"

"I—hang on. You're not mad about James?"

She huffed in response. "Of *course* I'm mad about James."

"I'm sorry—"

Eisheth held up a hand, cutting her off. "Save it. I've heard all of your arguments."

Flinching, Bridget approached the passenger side of the car. "You were spying on the funeral home, weren't you?" She glanced back at the building. The lights inside were still on, but Charlie hadn't followed them. "How long have you been here?"

The detective's gaze was tight. "We don't have time for this, Bridget. Unless you'd prefer to hike alone?"

She would not. The marina was miles away, and Bridget had no idea how to get there. With a sigh, she settled into the car.

"Finally," Eisheth muttered, slamming the passenger door closed and walking around to the driver's side. Bridget gripped her knees, waiting in silence until the engine started. She watched, nerves flickering.

"How long have you been waiting here?"

Eisheth sighed and looked over. "On and off since you left."

"It's the middle of the night. Have you not been sleeping?"

Eisheth glanced at the dashboard. Viri's small, stone beacon rested there, its design dark. She remembered tucking away its counterpart on the boat during their first night aboard. Had that glow been Eisheth, trying to find them? "You've been tracking us."

"When you decided to leave without me, I wanted to make sure you were somewhere safe."

"But you didn't follow?" Theoretically, the beacon could have led the detective straight to them, no matter where Danel sailed.

"I decided to be helpful on shore."

"So, you've been hanging out at the funeral home for a week?"

Eisheth pulled the car into reverse. "I told you he shouldn't be left alone."

A surprising warmth alighted in Bridget. Somehow it made her feel better to know James hadn't been by himself this past week.

"I—thank you."

The detective flicked her hand dismissively, but there was hurt in her eyes. "Didn't you pause to think *maybe* with you gone, Viri would move more quickly to return James to his family?"

Bridget's next breath came up shallow. Oh. "You've... you've been making sure he stays here."

An annoyed twitch passed over Eisheth's face. "I assumed you would return for James eventually. I wanted to make sure you had someone to retrieve. Even though—and I'll keep saying this, Miss Keene—I still believe you should *not* revive him."

Bridget gripped the strap of her seatbelt. "I'm not going to stop the process."

Eisheth didn't answer. Her fingers were white on the steering wheel. "I'll ask one last time. Which marina?"

Bridget hesitated. If she refused, the detective could simply use the beacon. But she'd taken the time to ask, which meant she wanted to work together.

"I can give you the name."

Entering the marina into her phone's GPS, Eisheth turned onto the main road, headlights flashing.

Dark rows of corn and soybean fields flickered past, ghostly in the moonlight. Bridget guessed Danel had at least a ten-minute head start, maybe more. Once they were out on the water, it would be impossible to track them down without a boat of their own.

As they drove, she noticed the tense set of Eisheth's jaw. Her gaze kept darting away, as if waiting for someone to jump out of the cornfield. She seemed jumpy, which struck Bridget as out of character.

She's scared. The realization sent a pulse of fear through her. She'd watched the detective face down Kai and stand up to Tannin, all with grim determination. Nothing scared her.

"What's wrong?"

Eisheth's eyes narrowed, and she flicked on the car's high beams.

"Eisheth?" Bridget's voice slid higher. "What aren't you telling me?"

"Ret's visit to Eris didn't go as planned." Tension laced through her mostly measured tone.

The words sent a tendril of dread creeping across Bridget's skin. "What do you mean?"

Eisheth's fingers tightened on the steering wheel. "He wanted to see if Eris would join us in standing against Tannin. Instead, she has decided to work *with* Tannin."

Bridget frowned, watching Eisheth as the world passed in a dark blur beyond her. "What do you mean?"

The floor of the car rumbled as Eisheth picked up speed. "Ret's dead, Bridget. Tannin and Eris murdered him."

TWENTY

Dahlia kept the car window cracked open as Nuriel pulled onto the highway. The fresh air helped center her.

She had only helped carry James a few minutes, but his stiff, unnatural weight lingered in her hands. Seeing him lifeless was shocking. She wasn't sure if she fully agreed with sister's insistence to revive him, but if he *was* going to be brought back from the dead, she wanted him to wake up surrounded by friends. Especially because he had been killed trying to help them. He was the only one who helped Bridget follow Dahlia's trail to the Grigori, who went with her through the portal to Tannin's lair, who broke Dahlia out of her cell.

A hot coal stirred in her stomach.

Before tonight, the last time she'd seen James was during his final battle with Kai. She'd been nearly unconscious when Kai drove scissors into his heart, but she still remembered hearing Bridget's cry and seeing a flash of shocking red spread over the polished floor.

Shocking and familiar.

She'd seen so much blood lately. It had become a backdrop to her life. Later, upon her escape from Tannin, she'd shot one of his lackeys over and over. Even after he was dead, she'd kept firing, transfixed by the damage of each bullet—by the changing landscape of his expression.

Bridget had averted her eyes as she skirted past, but Dahlia saw it as another form of art. A creation of vengeance and righteous anger.

"Dahlia? You alright?" Nuriel's voice tugged her to the present.

"What?" She cleared her throat, graphic images fading.

"I was asking you if you're going to be ready to start once we get back to *Mercy*, or if you need to rest first."

Dahlia let the car come back into focus. They'd turned onto a main highway, leaving the dark country roads behind. The dashboard clock blinked at them, showing the late hour.

"You could celebrate for five seconds," Danel chimed in from the backseat.

Irritation flared through her again. "Celebrate what? We're only halfway through our plan, and we abandoned Bridget."

Nuriel sighed. "I feel terrible about that."

"She'll be fine. It's not like Eisheth is going to hurt her." Danel's voice dripped with exasperation.

Dahlia ignored him. It was too easy for her to slip into anger, especially when she spoke to him. Instead, she looked at Nuriel. "I'm ready to start as soon as we get back." The image of the bloody guard re-emerged in her mind, but this time it felt hollow. She wrapped her arms around herself and turned toward the open window. Sometimes, she didn't recognize herself. Now, she supposed she knew why—she was half Dahlia, half Hartu. She needed to shove the dead Grigori down. She wasn't like him. She wouldn't *let* herself be like him. She was a good person.

This was her opportunity to reinvent herself. Maybe Nuriel was right, and she should give some thought to coming up with her new name.

The mood in the car remained uneasy as Nuriel turned down the road that led into the marina. He cleared his throat as the guard house came into view. "We may have a problem."

Dahlia looked out the window. A police cruiser had parked next to the little building, its lights off. A figure stood by the guardhouse window, talking with Benjamin inside.

"He called the cops?" Danel sounded affronted.

"We *did* steal his car. My persuasion has probably worn off." Nuriel frowned, glancing in the rearview mirror. "What if we leave the vehicle and make our way on foot?"

Dahlia chewed her lip. "They'll still see us. Especially carrying a body."

"Good point. Danel, can you run with James? If you're

fast enough they won't notice."

"No." Danel's response was gruff. He cleared his throat. "Too heavy."

Slow resolve trickled through Dahlia. They'd come this far. "I don't think we can get out of this situation without some conflict, Nuriel."

He looked affronted, slowing as they approached the marina. "Conflict? I'm not fighting them. They didn't do anything wrong."

"Conflict doesn't have to mean throwing punches. Pull up closer."

Nuriel glanced at her. "What do you intend for us to say to them?"

"The truth. Sort of. Come on, they've already seen you."

The officer turned toward the car, shielding his eyes from the headlights. He was plump, with a receding hairline and a spray of freckles across ruddy cheeks.

From the guardhouse, another head popped out. "That's my car!" Benjamin exclaimed, half hanging out of the window.

With a sigh, Nuriel eased off the brakes and rolled forward until he pulled even with the guard house. "Officer."

The policeman bent down to peer into the driver's side. "Sir, show me your license and registration. And I need you to turn the engine off and step out." He peered into the backset, at Dahlia and Danel. "All of you."

On shaky legs, Dahlia unbuckled and let herself out onto the concrete drive. She circled around the front of the car, forcing an innocent smile. "Is there a problem, Officer?"

He swung a no-nonsense glare at her. "Sit on the curb, miss. You too." He jerked a thumb at Danel in the back seat.

Danel got out of the car and joined Dahlia as they sat. Nuriel remained standing, speaking to the officer as he dug around in his wallet.

Benjamin scowled as he approached from the guardhouse, long beard swinging. As he drew nearer, she realized he was younger than she first imagined. "What do you think you're playing at? You can't go taking people's cars."

Dahlia shook her head, watching Nuriel pass the keys over to the officer. "We didn't take it. My friend asked, and you said yes."

"Why would I say yes?" Benjamin pointed a knobby finger in Nuriel's direction. "I was just minding my business, working on my novel, and that guy came up out of nowhere. He manipulated me. I'm telling you, there's something strange about him."

Danel's voice was flat. "Sounds like you're the strange one, giving your car to strangers."

Benjamin glared at Danel. "I've *had* it with you people."

"Alright, enough." The officer cut in. He came around the car, Nuriel following. "Sir, this man says you loaned him your vehicle. Is that true?"

"Absolutely not," Benjamin said.

Dahlia leaned forward, poised to stand.

"And you don't know him? Do you want to press charges?"

"Maybe!" Benjamin folded his arms and gave Nuriel a glower.

"This is ridiculous," Danel snorted.

The officer turned to give Danel a warning look. "Don't move. Sir, do a quick search of your car to make sure everything is there."

Benjamin peered into the front seat, leaning in and opening the center console. Dahlia's breath caught as he grabbed her backpack, but he set it on the ground and resumed his search.

"Looks like everything is here," Benjamin said.

"Do you have anything in the trunk?"

Dahlia's throat squeezed tight. He absolutely could *not* open the trunk.

She shifted her weight, muscles tense as Benjamin walked around to the back of the car. The officer followed, keeping a close eye on them.

As soon as Benjamin leaned down to pull the trunk's lever, she lurched forward and grasped his bare ankle. In the same motion, she reached up and grabbed the officer's wrist. He jerked in surprise, but she held on. Then she seized Nuriel's ability, funneling it into them as hard as she could.

A cacophony of emotions pressed on her from all sides. Indignation and rage and boredom and exhaustion pummeled her, threatening to drag her under. The parking lot faded away, and she was left only with a bubbling mess of feelings.

It's their *feelings*, she realized. The indignation came from Benjamin, realizing he'd been conned into loaning his car. The boredom belonged to the police officer, who saw this as another routine stop during his long night shift.

She clamped down on the officer's desire to be done with this, back in his cruiser and taking a break before his next stop. At the same time, she picked out Benjamin's weariness from working night shifts.

Boredom and exhaustion. She hugged those two emotions closer. They felt wispy and thin, like they might dissolve from her grip at any moment. Hurriedly, she tamped every other emotion down with an instinctual mental *push*.

With it, she gave a firm command. *Leave us alone.*

Golden light brought her back to the curbside. It eked from her fingers into the skin of both men. The officer faltered, fingers slackening. A bored look spread across his face. Benjamin yawned.

Dahlia could feel the tenuousness of the power she held. Quickly, she pushed forth another command. *Go take a nap.*

She didn't expect it to work. At most, she hoped they would step back a few feet and give Danel space to make a run for it. Heavy or not, he could get further with James than she or Nuriel.

But to her shock, Benjamin rubbed at his forehead and pulled back from the still-closed trunk. "It's empty." His voice was thick. "Let's drop it, alright?"

Relief broke over the officer's face. "Sure. So, you're

definitely not interested in pressing charges?" Dahlia didn't miss the hope in his tone. She was still making contact with him, could still feel the rush of his emotions. The last thing he wanted was a mountain of paperwork.

"Nah. No harm, no foul," Benjamin said. He was already pulling away from Dahlia. As soon as she broke contact with him, his emotions faded away from her awareness. But Benjamin still seemed to feel the impact. He strode back to the guard house, let himself in, and flopped into the chair, slouching out of sight.

The officer gave Dahlia and Danel a distracted nod. "Just a warning this time." Then he wandered over to his patrol car without looking back. He got in, started the engine, and drove away.

Danel let out a low whistle. "Damn."

Heat crawled up Dahlia's cheeks. That had worked far better than expected. "Come on, let's move. I don't know how long it will last."

As she hurried around to the trunk, she risked a glance at Nuriel. He hadn't moved. As their eyes met, a coil of shame blossomed in Dahlia's stomach. She'd expected anger, but he looked horrified.

She pushed aside the twisting unease. "Danel, pop the trunk."

"Yes ma'am." Danel eyed her with a level of respect she hadn't seen before. He went to the driver's door and leaned in to pull the lever. The trunk latch clicked. For a wild, impractical moment, Dahlia worried the body would be gone. But no, James was still there, curled awkwardly around a spare battery, his cheek pressed against a small scattering of old, faded receipts. He was naked, a thick bandage covering where he'd been stabbed.

Danel came up beside her, reaching in for James' arms. Dahlia took his legs and, together, they pulled James from the trunk.

"Let me help." Nuriel's carefully measured voice sent a cold tendril down Dahlia's spine. He slid his hands beneath James' shoulders, taking over for Danel. "Why don't you go get the boat ready?"

Danel looked at Nuriel's grim expression, then to Dahlia. "Yep. On it."

Nuriel nudged the trunk closed and tossed the keys into the open car door. They slowly began carrying James through the parking lot and toward the docks. The corpse was heavy enough that, mercifully, they couldn't talk while transporting him. That didn't lessen the disappointment radiating off Nuriel. Dahlia tried to ignore it, focusing instead on the sweat beading on her forehead as they walked him to the slip.

She had only used his power for the greater good. Couldn't he see that? She hadn't hurt them. Benjamin got his car back, and the officer could get on with his night. They could move James to safety. Everyone won.

But if that was true, why did she feel so guilty?

TWENTY-ONE

Eisheth's proclamation knocked the wind from Bridget's lungs. She gripped the edges of her seat as the detective drove well above the limit.

"Ret's dead? How? He didn't hurt anyone." The straight, flat road stretched out before them, two lanes crowded by cornfields and bordered by white stripes.

Eisheth didn't look over. "He's been helping all of us, and he's the most senior Grigori of our group. Apparently, that was a justifiable reason to execute him."

"I don't understand." Ret had been their source of healing, and their window into the distant Grigori past. She hadn't always agreed with him, but she couldn't imagine their little group without him.

"A life for a life," Eisheth said. "Grigori justice is simple. It doesn't technically have to be the killer who is killed."

"But isn't part of the issue that there are so *few* Grigori? Why kill more of them?"

Eisheth shook her head. "I've been asking myself the same question. My best guess? Ret was seen as a threat to Tannin's bigger plans."

Bridget felt weak. All this time she'd been worried for herself and Dahlia—she hadn't imagined retribution could come for Ret. Unease hung over the car.

"Ret's symbol can't be reused? We can't bring him back?"

"Not for two centuries, according to Gaul."

Bridget rubbed her palms on her jeans as if she could rub away the horrible feeling that had settled over her. She licked her lips and murmured, "I hate to ask, but is it done? Will Tannin stop getting pressure to avenge the people who died?"

The detective glanced over. "That's Gaul's hope, but it's unlikely. Powerful as Ret is—was—he was one person. We caused three deaths."

By saying *we*, Eisheth was including herself. But it wasn't her finger that had pulled the trigger, even if it was her gun.

For the rest of the ride, Eisheth gave monosyllabic responses to Bridget's questions. Gaining little traction, she stewed in her fears. With Ret gone, they lost a layer of protection. And now Eris posed another, new threat.

More reason than ever for Bridget to go into hiding with Dahlia and James, far from Grigori politics. Guilt washed over her at the thought of abandoning the others, but she couldn't risk Dahlia's life. Or James'.

Surely Dahlia was almost to the *Mercy* by now. She itched to be there with them. To be there for James when he woke up, and to congratulate Dahlia on her success.

There was nothing she could do to help Ret. James, however, she could still save.

"This is your last opportunity to back out, you know." Eisheth's hands were tight on the steering wheel, knuckles standing out like a mountain range.

"Why would I do that?"

She shifted her weight, seatbelt rasping gently. "Have you ever thought it might be worth letting James go?"

Her heart thumped painfully. "Everyone acts like that's so easy."

"No, not easy. But perhaps necessary." Eisheth kept her eyes on the dark horizon. "When you live as long as we do, you get well-acquainted with goodbyes. They're a part of being human."

"But you're not human," Bridget pointed out.

"Part of me is." Eisheth lifted a hand to her chest. "There's a human heart beating in my ribcage. I've been a human, loved humans, created a human—one who is now long gone. Death is one of the realities of this world that keeps me grounded in my human half."

Bridget looked up at her. "You had a child?"

Eisheth ignored the question. "Death equalizes us, allows our stories to end. Almost every Grigori I know has longed for it at some point."

"Easy for you to say. You don't really die. You go back to your world." Bridget looked down at her lap.

"True. But none of us remember what it's like there. And if we ever get the chance to return, we won't be the same person. It's still a very real loss."

Her eyes stung, and she raised her hand to wipe away a tear. "I'm not ready to let him go."

"I know. But at the end of the day, this isn't about you. It's about James, and what's best for him. Remember that."

Bridget nodded, but she felt more unsettled than ever. She trusted Eisheth's opinion more than Gaul's, but she was still immortal—centuries old. For all her talk of being "grounded," how could she really understand?

"What's this?" Eisheth's voice interrupted her thoughts. The car slowed, and Bridget turned her attention back to the window. They'd made it back to the marina, but the entrance was blocked by the Volvo they'd borrowed from Benjamin.

"Let's pull over." Bridget pulled her jacket tightly around her, waiting until the car came to a stop before unbuckling and letting herself out.

She hurried to the Volvo. Its trunk was open, as was the driver-side window. Frowning, she spun in a slow circle, searching for any sign of Benjamin. She spotted him through the window of the guard house, snoring gently under the fluorescent light. His notebook was open on the front counter, bookmarked by a pen, and a framed photo of a wolf-like dog looked over him like a guardian.

"Come on." Bridget urged Eisheth forward, toward the boats.

Against the backdrop of stars, Dahlia stood in front of the *Mercy*, waving to them. Nuriel was beside her, kneeling by a shadowy lump that had to be James.

Bridget kept her eyes carefully averted from the body. "Don't mention Ret to them yet."

Eisheth shot her a sharp look. "No?"

"One problem at a time."

"We may not *have* a lot of time, Bridget. We need to regroup."

Bridget shook her head. "I can't change what

happened to Ret. But I can help them stay focused on James. If we tell them now, they won't be able to think about anything else."

The detective sighed, squinting at the yacht. "Then let's be quick about this."

Bridget hurried across the dock and to the *Mercy's* slip, giving James' body a wide berth and tucking Dahlia into a firm hug.

Against Bridget's hair, Dahlia said, "Glad you made it okay." She extended her arms, still holding onto Bridget.

The anxiety coursing through Bridget quieted as she watched her sister.

"What happened?" Dahlia looked past Bridget to where Eisheth approached.

"She helped me get past Charlie."

"She looks upset."

"I'll catch you up later."

Nuriel's voice, surprisingly curt, interrupted them. "Help me get James onto the boat."

Finally, Bridget looked down at James' body. He lay unmoving on the weathered wood, one arm draped over his chest, the other to his side. He looked unnaturally pale and thin.

She sucked in a breath and squatted down beside him. It was time to see this through. "We'll lift him."

They hefted him up and over the rail, teetering with the effort of pushing the limp limbs. Nuriel climbed on deck and helped from above. As he pulled him over, he staggered back under James' weight.

"Are you alright?" Dahlia called.

"Fine." Nuriel gently laid James down, then brushed himself off. He reached down to help Bridget and Dahlia on board.

"Ugh." Danel walked over from the wheel, looking down at James. "There's no way you're taking him downstairs."

Dahlia climbed onto the boat. "We need to be able to see what we're doing."

"Bring the utility light so you can work on deck. It's in the cabinet under the couch."

Nuriel wordlessly walked around James and to the cabin door. Tension radiated off of him like a tuning fork as he opened it and disappeared inside. What Bridget had originally thought was urgency felt deeper.

"What's wrong with him?"

It was Danel who answered, leaning back against the cabin wall. "He's jealous Dahlia saved our hides."

"Danel Bridgeport, you colossal pain in my ass." Eisheth's voice interrupted Bridget's next question. The detective stepped onto the boat, eyes snapping to him like a magnet.

In response, Danel's face underwent a cascade of emotions. Surprise, chased quickly by annoyance and guilt. "Eisheth. Hi."

She arched an eyebrow at him. "You left me behind."

Danel cleared his throat. "Nothing personal. We were in a rush."

"Mm. You and I are going to have a little chat. In private."

He glanced at Bridget and Dahlia, then back to Eisheth, brows puckered. Their usual banter was stilted, Eisheth's cheeks pale.

He coughed. "I need to get *Mercy* underway first."

"I'll wait."

As much as Bridget enjoyed seeing Danel's discomfort, Bridget had a more important task. She turned to focus on James. He lay sprawled on the deck, curls covering his face. "Help me lay him on his stomach."

Together, she and Dahlia turned James over. Bridget paused to brush back his hair. The soft strands were the only part of him that didn't feel ravaged by death.

She thought of Eisheth's vigil over him. Would anyone be there to do the same for Ret's body? To send him on his way with dignity?

A swell of grief swirled through Bridget, making her heart heavy. She hadn't even thought to ask how he'd been killed. For all she knew, there might not *be* a body anymore.

She ached to tell Dahlia, but bit back the words. James first. The detective wasn't trying to stop them at this point, so she needed to see this through.

From the wheel, Danel muttered, "If this doesn't work, I'm dumping him overboard."

Dahlia rolled her eyes, getting to her feet. "I'm going down to get James some clothes. And wash my hands."

"You're seriously worried about germs right now?" Danel asked with a laugh.

Dahlia rolled her eyes. "You're disgusting."

The annoyed banter felt far away to Bridget. She remained by James' side, adjusting his position lightly. The skin of his back was mottled; she hoped it wouldn't hurt their ability to apply the tattoo.

"You'll be okay," she whispered to him. "Hang in there a little longer."

TWENTY-TWO

Dahlia went to the cabin door, taking the steps slowly so she didn't rush in on Nuriel. Since the incident with the cars, he'd refused to acknowledge her.

Bridget's arrival with Eisheth had provided a temporary distraction. It was a relief to see them both, especially once it had become clear Eisheth wasn't here to drag James back to the funeral home.

Descending into the cabin brought the tension between her and Nuriel crashing back.

He was on his knees, rummaging through a compartment built into the base of the couch. He didn't acknowledge her entrance, though he had to have heard the door.

Dahlia went to the kitchen and turned the tap. As she washed her hands, she felt his eyes on her.

"Danel doesn't seem to think he needs to clean up," she said lightly as she worked the lather between her fingers.

The words were met with an exasperated huff. "Danel is disgusting."

"That's what I said." Terse silence fell over them once more. "You're angry with me."

"You had no right to do what you did."

Frustration simmered within Dahlia. She finished washing her hands, then dried them on a nearby cloth. "I got us safely to the boat, didn't I? If I hadn't intervened, we would have gotten arrested, and James would have been taken away."

Nuriel closed the cabinet and stood, a cordless utility light and a pair of shorts in his hand. He strode to her, setting both items on the counter. Cigarette smoke clung to his jacket. "I've been doing this for three hundred years, Dahlia. Do you really think a single police officer and an angry teenager would stop us?"

Fair point. They'd stood up to Tannin and Kai, faced down forces far stronger than they were.

"They might not be a threat, but they were an obstacle."

Nuriel leaned forward, resting his elbows on the table. "You're thinking like Kai."

Dahlia's skin went cold at the comparison. "What do you mean?"

"During my Artist training, he often told me we were entitled to our powers. He thought they made us better than humans—than the families and friends we'd left behind."

Dahlia felt sick. The last thing she wanted was to be compared to that monster. "That's not how I feel at all."

"I know. But you still took something of mine without asking. And you took something from those two men, too."

The tangle in her gut tightened. "Their free will." She hesitated, thinking back to how easily she'd manipulated Benjamin and the police officer. "Why did it work so well? It's your lesser power, and I've had no training with it. I didn't expect it to do much of anything."

Nuriel slipped into her spot behind the sink. "You've practiced with other Grigori. With me, with Gaul and Ret. We can protect ourselves more readily. Humans, *especially* humans who know nothing about us, have very few defenses. Mental abilities, in particular, can be profoundly effective when used on them."

The revelation was jarring. Dahlia had thought of herself as weak, especially compared to people as old as Ret or Tannin. But compared to Benjamin, her strength was immense.

He looked up at her as he soaped up his hands. "None of us are gods, Dahlia. But without rules, we're no better than Kai was."

Memories prickled at Dahlia's consciousness. Kai's frequent ravings that humans were weak and unworthy gained more clarity. Tannin's constant pursuit to assert Grigori dominance, the blind obedience of his followers— it all stemmed from a power imbalance baked into their very existence. Even the weakest of them could dominate their human friends and neighbors.

In their own twisted minds, it was the natural order.

No wonder Tannin thought she'd switch sides so easily.

"Dahlia?"

Nuriel's voice pulled her back to the present. She blinked hard to refocus. Tannin could wait. Right now, she was here, with Nuriel. She watched him dry his hands, guilt swelling up within her.

"I understand. And I'm sorry. Can you forgive me?"

A softness returned to Nuriel's eyes. He twitched his index finger and a small spray of water splattered across Dahlia's shirt. "You're still learning. So, I think I can manage."

The tension between them began to seep away. She didn't feel *good*, exactly. The guilt still simmered, and something dark lurked even deeper under the surface— something she couldn't quite put a name to.

She tried not to linger on thoughts of Kai as Nuriel filled a bowl with soap and water. "Did Eisheth seem more upset than usual to you?" he asked.

Dahlia was surprised by the shift in conversation. "Maybe. I don't know her as well as you."

"What about Bridget?"

Bridget had clearly been relieved to return to the boat, and to find everything going to plan. But now that Dahlia paused, she did sense something off. "It's probably the stress. We haven't exactly had a calm night."

Together, they returned to the deck, carrying the utility light, clothes, and bowl of water. She felt more relaxed in the cool night air. Danel had brought them away from the marina, the soft lights of the suburbs twinkling off the aft side of the yacht. On the bench behind him, Eisheth sat and watched him with a narrow gaze.

Bridget approached Dahlia from the bow. "Can I help?" She looked anxious, her cheeks sallow.

"Let's dress him." Dahlia knelt by James. They silently worked his stiff legs into the shorts under the garish glow of the utility light.

Nuriel unclasped his messenger bag and pulled out an archaic looking tattoo gun with copper coils. It was followed by a small power pack and foot pedal, ink, needles, and a small bottle of disinfectant spray. Sitting beside the sisters, he set each item down on a clean towel.

With James dressed, Dahlia rummaged through her backpack. She brought out her notebook, along with the already-prepared transfer paper.

"Okay. Now what?" Dahlia wished she had paid more attention to the process of getting her wrist tattoo.

Nuriel eyed James' back. "We need to clean the area for transfer. Soap and water first."

Dahlia pulled the bowl closer. The boat tilted and swayed, shifting with the gentle waves. Water sloshed lightly over the bowl's rim. "Danel, can you keep the boat steady?"

"Yes, please," Bridget agreed, pressing a hand to her abdomen. She looked green.

"It's a boat," Danel said pointedly. "We're on water. What do you expect?"

"Just do what you can. We can't afford to mess this up."

Danel responded with an overexaggerated sigh. "Whatever you say."

Why did he insist on acting like an ass? It was honestly

remarkable he'd hidden his real self from her for all those months they'd dated. Where she'd once seen cavalier handsomeness, now she saw someone who made her skin crawl.

At least Eisheth was here now. Danel's behavior tended to improve when she was around. Even as Dahlia watched, he shot the detective a wary look. She arched an imperious eyebrow at him in response.

Nuriel looked up at Bridget. "Why don't you get some rest in the cabin? This is going to take a while. We'll wake you up when we're ready."

She hesitated, brows drawing together. Dahlia could see her trying to formulate an argument. But as much as she understood her sister's desire to see this process through, it would be nice to have a little space. "We promise we won't let you miss it."

Bridget squeezed her eyes closed, then got to her feet, wobbling a little. "Hurry, okay?" Then she left, disappearing into the cabin.

Dahlia met Nuriel's eyes. The calm warmth was back, although there was an undercurrent of urgency. He donned latex gloves, then handed her a pair. While she put them on, Nuriel got to work dipping a cloth into the water and wiping it along the skin of James' back.

It felt disconcertingly intimate, but Dahlia forced herself to watch. Less than a year ago, Kai had stood over her like this, washing her skin with gentle strokes.

"How can I help?"

"There's not much hair on his back, but we should shave it off, to be safe."

"I'll do it." She reached for a thin, disposable razor.

As she ran the blades over the skin along James' spine, she searched for a way to distract herself. "Do you like being an Artist?"

He didn't respond right away, and she looked up at him, wondering if maybe he hadn't heard. But he looked thoughtful, considering her question seriously. "I don't always feel particularly useful. My abilities aren't very strong, and I don't have the same affinity for them as some other Grigori. Art has always been where my talents lie."

"Like tattooing?" The razor scraped quietly down James' skin.

"Tattoos are a practical skill most Artists don't take the time to learn these days. And over time, I realized it was useful to humans, too. My work helps them become closer to their own identities."

Dahlia dropped her gaze to her wrist—to the tattoo that had started it all. When she'd first received it in a shop a few streets from campus, she'd thought of it as a permanent reminder of one of the most exciting experiences of her life. While it hadn't given her any special powers, it *had* garnered Danel's attention.

"It wasn't your fault."

She started and looked up. Nuriel was watching her, eyes soft.

"I know that." She looked away, returning her attention to James. "It feels like it all happened so long ago. Like I'm a different person."

"You are."

He meant it kindly, but the words hung between them, heavy with implications. She remembered the conversations she'd had about choosing a name. They'd said Nuriel was the last of them to shed his human identity. She wanted to ask what had shifted his thinking, what had allowed him to let go. But she also worried the answer would hit too close to home.

Nuriel must have seen her distress, because he turned the conversation back to the work in front of them. "You know, I was the one who insisted Kai properly clean the skin before applying tattoos over a century ago. It was decades into my training when antiseptic began to be used in medical settings. I thought, if it's useful for surgeries, why not tattoos?"

There Kai was again. Nuriel was trying to help, but he'd only steered the conversation into another land mine. Kai, looming in her past, pressing into her present from multiple angles. It was too easy for her to imagine his fingers probing the skin of her back. Bile rose in her throat, and she turned away. Gulps of the cold night air helped steady her stomach, but the shakiness in her hands remained. She'd been unconscious when Kai had tattooed her—no, not unconscious, *dead*—but now she felt ghost fingertips along her back. She hunched away from the phantom touch.

Nuriel's fingers closed over hers, latex separating them. "I'm sorry. Here, let me." He gently took the razor from her hand.

Gratitude washed through her as she backed away. She hadn't expected this to be so hard. Difficult logistically, yes. But she'd been so focused on getting from one step to the next that she hadn't paused to consider how it would feel to take on Kai's role.

She breathed deeply into the wind. How long would it be before she could forget about Kai and his cruel indifference? About how it felt when he sucked the air from her lungs, leaving her gasping and writhing on the ground? She doubted even a millennium could wash it away.

Then again, that span of time was impossible for her to conceive. She might be a Grigori, but all her conscious experience was as a human, with a lifetime scaled to mere decades. It was impossible to know who she would be by then. She'd already changed so much.

She looked at the cockpit. Danel still had one hand on the wheel, but his attention had shifted to Eisheth. The two of them spoke in low whispers, both of their postures defensive.

Dahlia exhaled slowly. She could do this. Applying the tattoo didn't make her like Kai at all. James was exactly the sort of person who would want to become a Grigori. His death hadn't been premeditated or manipulated, like hers. He'd get a second chance, and she wouldn't be so alone on a journey of self-reinvention. As much as Bridget cared, she could never understand.

Resolved, she returned her attention back to Nuriel and James. He'd finished with the razor and was patting James' skin dry. Looking up at her, he asked, "Are you okay?"

"Yeah. Disinfectant next?" Dahlia handed him the bottle and watched as he sprayed it over the freshly shaved skin.

"Now we need to transfer the image. You have the paper?"

Dahlia picked it up. "Yes. I can do this part." Mind over matter—it was just another drawing project. "Walk me through it."

Nuriel lifted the second spray bottle and gave James' back a few liberal spritzes. Then he rubbed the clear liquid evenly over his skin. "When I tell you to, place it face down between and above his shoulder blades."

This would be the tricky part. They had traced the symbol onto special paper that Nuriel promised would replicate its intricacies on James' skin. Without a perfect transfer, they would never succeed.

"Okay, do it."

Dahlia moved in and pressed the paper to James' back. The edges darkened as they sucked up the solution, and she carefully pressed down, working the image smooth.

After she'd run her fingers over every inch of the paper, she looked over at him. "Good?" The ghost of their drawing peeked through the wet paper.

He spritzed more solution on the top of the paper, wetting it further. "We'll find out after it's had a few minutes to sit."

Her hands were starting to sweat inside her gloves, but there was no point in taking them off. They still had the whole tattoo to get through.

TWENTY-THREE

Despite her exhaustion, Bridget dozed fitfully. Every time she woke, her mind raced. She agonized over the slow tattooing process happening on deck. She fretted over what James would think when he learned he'd been revived. And she questioned her decision to withhold information about Ret's death from the others.

She'd tell them what she'd learned as soon as James woke up. And then maybe she could start to process it herself.

When she forced her thoughts away from Ret and James, they landed incongruously on Danel. She pondered her discovery of his niece's existence—how strange it was for someone like him to maintain a family tie. In some ways, it comforted her. Danel wasn't likeable, but maybe he was understandable. Still—why had he chosen *then* to visit Morgan? She resolved to ask him later, once James was back to normal.

Hours of tossing later, the creak of a door pulled Bridget from her hazy half-sleep. She sat up, listening to the footsteps descend.

"I think we're almost done." Dahlia kept her voice quiet, but she had to know Bridget was awake.

She reached up and flicked on the light, foggy and disoriented. "I'll be up in a second."

Dahlia ducked away again, leaving Bridget to crawl out of the bed and to the bathroom. She splashed cold water on her cheeks and threw her snarled blonde hair up into a messy ponytail. The boat's rocking persisted, and twice she had to pause, pressing the flats of her hands on the sink and counting to ten before the nausea passed. No amount of medicine put a dent in her queasiness. She had no idea what Danel could possibly see in being on the water.

The deck's cool, open air provided a welcome contrast to the cabin's warmth. Dawn was creeping close, blotting out the stars with its purple, misty light. Bridget stood still at the top of the stairs, gulping in long breaths.

Danel slept at the cockpit beside Eisheth. The detective watched him with an expression caught somewhere between disdain and affection.

She skirted past them to where James' body lay on the deck, partially blocked by the hunched-over forms of Nuriel and Dahlia. Beside them was Nuriel's messenger bag, the top open. Nestled inside were tattoo supplies— ink bottles, latex gloves, needles. A wad of paper towels had turned black with ink.

Bridget's heart ached to see James like this. She approached him, standing behind Nuriel, who glanced up and moved aside so she could have a better view.

The bandages around James' torso had been cut open along the spine. Even in the pre-dawn gloom, the fresh ink along his upper back stood out sharply. It was, as far as Bridget could tell, identical to the paper sketch.

Bridget's legs felt wooden as she sank down between Nuriel and Dahlia. Although she'd been waiting for this—*hoping* for this—trepidation wormed through her. There was still so much that could go wrong. The symbol could fail. Tannin could have already activated it on someone else. James could resent her for bringing him back or be so changed they hardly recognized each other.

But they'd come this far. Their little group had rallied around this purpose. She knew, no matter what came, she'd see this to the very end.

She looked up at Nuriel and her sister. "Have you activated it?"

He shook his head. "No. We knew you wanted to be here."

Resolve filled her. "Let's do it then."

Nuriel watched her. "This is your last chance to change your mind. Once I activate it, there's no going back."

Bridget swallowed the lump in her throat. She glanced behind her to Eisheth, who was watching in silence.

This was what James deserved. He wouldn't be different. Not *too* different, anyway. He'd be himself, restored, made whole.

"I'm not backing down from this."

Nuriel gave a grim smile. "Dahlia, want to do the honors?"

A flicker of unease crossed Dahlia's face. "You go ahead."

Nuriel removed his gloves, then placed two fingers on the center of the symbol.

Bridget held her breath, and Dahlia leaned against her, their attention fixed on James.

Gradually, a faint light extended out from beneath his hand. Golden strands snaked around the lines of the tattoo. They worked their way from the center of the design to the edges. Aglow, even on the skin of a dead man, it was really quite beautiful. A soft buzz came from the light, growing louder as it brightened.

Within moments, the entire symbol was pulsing vividly enough that Bridget had to look away. The hum became almost unbearably loud, setting Bridget's teeth on edge. It reminded her of passing through the Grigori portal—of the white light, the deafening hum, the brief glimpse into their realm and the distinct feeling she was not a part of it.

The boat suddenly rocked underfoot, sending Bridget falling back. She caught herself with two palms flat on the deck.

Danel awoke with a snort, grasping the wheel and wrestling it back into position.

"What was that?" She pressed herself back up onto her knees.

"I don't know." Nuriel withdrew his hand. The boat was already evening out, and the buzz had faded.

Bridget looked past him at the water, searching for the cause of the disturbance.

A wave radiated out from their boat in an ever-expanding circle along the lake's surface. When the wave intercepted a sailboat two hundred yards away, it wobbled violently, its mast dipping toward the water line.

Bridget looked back at James. The light was sinking into the tattoo, leaving only dark lines behind.

She held her breath, waiting. Seconds passed in silence. James remained still, his skin gray. She touched one of his curls, then pressed a hand to his cheek. It was cold and stiff. A heavy weight settled over her.

"Isn't he supposed to wake up now? Or at least start breathing?" Her voice cracked as she looked up at them. Maybe it *was* the wrong kind of symbol. She pressed a hand against his wrist, but there was no pulse.

Nuriel lifted the paper sketch, examining it. "I don't know. It's the first time I've done anything like this."

Bridget blinked hard, and hot tears spilled down her cheeks. "Has he been dead too long for it to work?"

"No. I have heard of Grigori who were deceased for months."

"Try it again." Her voice cracked.

Nuriel shook his head. "No, Bridget. If it didn't work, then—"

"Try it again!" Her fingers curled into fists at her side. This couldn't be it. Not after everything they'd gone through. Not after she'd promised to save him.

Nuriel held his hands up. "I can't. That's not how it works."

"Bridget." Dahlia touched her arm, but Bridget shook her off.

"You have to try. Please. Just... try. One more time. I promised."

"Bridget! He *did* try!"

"Not hard enough," she snapped.

This *couldn't* be James' end, lying cold and still on a stupid boat in the middle of the stupid lake. A conversation they'd had weeks ago replayed in her mind, about how distraught his family had been at the delay in burying his grandfather. Now, she'd recreated the same trauma for them—and for no reason.

Stronger than the guilt was a growing pit in her heart. Losing James once had been awful. But a second time? "It wasn't supposed to happen this way."

Warmth leaned against her side, and she lowered her hands to see her sister's head resting on her shoulder. "I'm sorry."

She buried her face in Dahlia's dark hair. Its dense texture reminded her of their father's. His was the first funeral she'd ever been to.

Death really was an unavoidable part of life.

Eisheth broke the silence. "We should go back to the marina."

Bridget pulled away from Dahlia's embrace. Her tidy plans for giving James a chance at a good life flickered out. She needed to create a new vision—but she couldn't do it here, on deck, with the others watching her pityingly and James' corpse lying nearby.

"I'm going inside again." She brushed past Eisheth, heading for the cabin door. She was turning the handle when a throaty gasp sounded behind her.

It wasn't any of the others. Which meant—

She whirled around. James was still lying in the same position as before. But the grayish marbling of his skin was receding, replaced with a healthy flush. Slowly, his back rose, lungs filling with air.

TWENTY-FOUR

James' chest rose and fell with a deep, steady cadence. As Bridget watched, the mottling of his skin began to even out, the color returning. Her mouth went dry as she rushed forward, almost tripping over her own feet in her hurry. Nuriel moved aside to give her space.

"James?" The name caught in her throat as she knelt beside him. It was like looking at a completely different person. Grigori magic had woken the blood in his veins, warming his extremities and filling in the gaunt hollows of his turned face. Gently, Bridget touched his shoulder. The skin was warm and soft under her fingers. Alive.

His eyes were closed, but Bridget saw movement beneath the lids. He'd emerged from death and entered a dream. A laugh bubbled up from inside of her as she pulled her hand back.

"You did it."

"We did it." Dahlia's voice, from behind her, was filled with awe.

Danel stepped away from the wheel and approached, bending down to inspect James curiously. "Now what?"

"Now we let him rest." Nuriel straightened and began to clean his tattoo supplies.

"For how long?" Bridget asked. The urge to grab James, to shake him awake and wrap him in a hug, was almost overpowering.

"As long as he needs." Nuriel glanced over at her. "It's tiring, to be pulled from another world and forced into a human form. The Grigori who connected with him will need time to settle."

The words sent a quiver of unease through her elation. They flung her right back to the conversations she'd had with Gaul, after learning Dahlia's fate.

"But James is still in there," she reassured herself.

Nuriel glanced up from his tools, lips pressed together in a thin line. "In a way."

It would have to be enough. James would still be James, just as Dahlia was still Dahlia.

Bridget looked for her sister, to find reassurance. But Dahlia wasn't there. She'd slipped away without Bridget's noticing.

Eisheth pointed her towards the bow. "Over there."

Bridget hesitated, not ready yet to leave James' side. What if he woke up while she was gone?

"It's alright." Nuriel's voice was gentle. "We'll let you know when he stirs."

Bridget swallowed back a lump of gratitude. "Thank you." Turning, she followed the rail toward the front of the boat, letting her fingers graze along the metal. The sun had finally poked free of the horizon, streaking the sky with gold reminiscent of Grigori magic.

Dahlia sat on the edge of the deck, legs dangling off the side. She'd wrapped her arms around the lower section of rail and was leaning over to look into the water.

"Looking for Nessie?" Bridget asked.

Dahlia glanced over, and the attempt at humor fell flat between them. Her eyes were red with unshed tears.

"Hey." Bridget sat beside her. "Are you alright?" She knew the question was wrong as soon as she asked it.

Instead of answering, Dahlia looked down at the water again. It was smooth—a contrast to the jolt they'd experienced a few minutes ago. It was as if that one massive wave had taken the fight out of the lake. It slumbered beneath them, dark and cold and still. Bridget's stomach, for once, didn't turn over.

"Talk to me." Bridget kept her voice gentle.

Dahlia's fingers tightened. "That's what happened to me." Her voice was ragged, a roil of emotions beneath the words.

"Yeah, but—"

"No," Dahlia interrupted. "Don't blow past reality because you can't handle it. That was *me*. A corpse. A dead body Kai and Tannin killed and revived, simply to prove they could."

The sharp edge of Dahlia's words sliced into Bridget, settling beneath her heart. She was right. Ever since learning the truth about her sister, Bridget had pushed past reality, a wall between her and the words Kai had spoken on that battlefield: *Your sister is dead.*

It was an easy truth to ignore, with Dahlia sitting beside her.

"You're here now. That's what matters."

Dahlia shook her head, staring out at the horizon. "I'm *not* here. Not really. I never really accepted it before, but seeing James... Whatever he is now, it's new. Whatever *I* am now is new. I can feel it. Right here." She pressed a fist to her chest.

Bridget's mouth tasted like cardboard. She pressed her lips together, silencing a sharp denial.

Dahlia swung her feet slowly, heels tapping against the hull. "I know what I would've said, before all this. How I would've felt or reacted. How I would have reassured you I was okay. But all of that feels off now. Like a mask. And I'm sick of wearing it."

Bridget wanted desperately to promise her it *would* be okay. Dahlia still remembered their childhood, all the years of Bridget playing with her, caring for her. It was natural for her to change in small ways over time; everyone did. And Dahlia had been through a terrible trauma.

A rush of guilt ran through Bridget as she thought back on the last few days. She'd insisted Dahlia work to help revive James, pushing her to immerse herself in the Grigori world. No wonder she felt triggered.

Bridget forced herself to smile. It felt more like a grimace. "I'm so sorry, Dahlia. I shouldn't have pushed you so hard."

Dahlia looked up at Bridget, reproach in her eyes.

Bridget continued, "I should have leaned on Nuriel more."

Her laugh was derisive. "You don't get it, do you?"

Bridget took Dahlia's hand. "But don't you see? Now that it's done, you don't have to focus on the sketches anymore. Or use your abilities. They're making you feel like someone you're not. You've been through something awful and deserve to be focusing on healing."

Dahlia's gaze hardened, and she pulled her hand away. "You have no idea what you're talking about."

"I understand that—"

"Stop. You *don't* understand." Dahlia's tone was flat, matter-of-fact.

Bridget scrambled for the right words to say. She was reminded, powerfully, of Dahlia's teenage years. The two of them had often battled, especially when Bridget tried to steer her sister away from decisions she knew she'd regret. Dahlia had always sought out adventure, and Bridget had to reel her in.

Except now there wasn't that petulant, accusatory glare she was used to seeing. Just unfamiliar, age-old anger. Dread settled over Bridget. She was losing her.

Bridget wrapped her fingers around the rail in front of her, gripping it tightly. There was no need for dramatics, she told herself. They were all tired, and Dahlia had been working nonstop, only pausing for nightmare-filled sleep. Maybe after some quality rest, she'd feel like herself.

"Why don't you get some sleep? Things will start to feel normal again."

"Normal." Dahlia spat the word like a curse. She turned up her hand, gesturing towards herself. A small spray of water flew upward, covering both of them in a fine mist. Bridget flinched and wiped her cheeks.

"Dahlia..."

"Normal is gone, Bridget. Normal has *been* gone. No amount of pretending will bring it back. I don't want it back."

A chill ran up Bridget's arms. "What do you mean?"

"Did you ever think to ask me what I want to do, once we revived James? Or have you been playing out this fantasy in your head where everything goes back to exactly how it was before?" Dahlia turned to face Bridget squarely, dark eyes narrowing. "Maybe I don't want to live a normal life. Maybe I don't want to go into hiding. Maybe I don't want to go back to college, where I feel guilty I haven't texted you all week. Where I get mad Mom hasn't texted *me* in a month."

The words landed like physical blows. Bridget felt small. "What *do* you want?"

Dahlia held Bridget's gaze. "Justice. I want Tannin to answer for what he did to me—for what he did to all of those people in that horrible freezer. I want him to regret the abilities he gave me. I want to stop him from ever hurting anyone else again."

And there it was, laid bare between them. The desire for revenge shone bright in Dahlia's eyes. As much as Bridget wanted to run from this strange new world,

Dahlia wanted to use it to hurt those who had hurt her.

And Bridget knew Dahlia well enough to know no amount of arguing would change her mind. She sucked in a shaky breath. "Of course he should pay."

Dahlia arched a dubious eyebrow. "Really? You're not just saying that?"

Something deep in Bridget's soul ached. Tannin *deserved* to pay. Not only for the crimes he'd already committed, but for the ones he continued to plan—like Ret's undeserved death.

But at the same time, Dahlia shouldn't have to bear the burden of revenge. She'd already suffered more than enough. "Remember what Mom used to say about Dad?"

There was no question of who she meant. They were half-sisters, with different fathers, but only one of them was Dad.

Dahlia flinched. "No."

"Liar."

She turned her glare on the water. "I don't see what that has to do with anything."

"No?" Bridget watched the wind as it blew the dark waves of Dahlia's hair back. "Mom always said that when he first received his diagnosis, she was so angry. Dad had been telling the doctors something was wrong for months, but no one had listened."

Dahlia snorted. "Of course they didn't. They couldn't possibly believe a Black man's pain was real."

"And he had every reason to be bitter. You were still a baby. I was barely in preschool. And he so wanted to be a part of our lives."

"What's your point?" Dahlia asked gruffly.

"My point is, even though his anger was justified, he didn't let it consume his last year of life. He spent that time *living*. Taking me to school, rocking you to sleep, being with Mom." Bridget's chest tightened. She didn't remember much of him, having only been five when he died. But she did remember firm hugs and a deep, melodious voice. He would sing to her at night, to scare away the monsters.

Dahlia leaned against the rail. "Tannin will keep hurting people."

He already has, Bridget thought. But now wasn't the time to give Dahlia more reasons to go after such a powerful person. "You can't change the past. But do you want to know what the best revenge would be?" At the shake of Dahlia's head, Bridget went on. "Pursuing a life you love. A life you deserve."

Tears filled Dahlia's eyes. She sniffed and turned her attention back to the horizon.

Bridget squeezed her sister's shoulder gently. "I love you, and I want to keep you safe."

Dahlia was silent a long moment before she murmured, "I love you too."

The silence between them felt like physical distance. Bridget searched for the words that would fix everything, but came up empty and hollow. She wasn't fooled into thinking she'd changed Dahlia's mind. But maybe, hopefully, she'd offered her sister a different perspective.

TWENTY-FIVE

Dahlia woke with a disoriented start. The prickly feeling of being watched lingered as she tried to piece the nightmare back together. This time, she'd been visited by the agonized eyes of plague victims, black pustules on their bodies. They had been reaching for her, shouting accusations she couldn't quite remember.

She sat up, wrapping the comforter around her. The dream must have been conjured from her argument with Bridget. She'd drawn from that, and her conversation with Gaul about Hartu, to craft some horrible false memory. The guilt it left behind felt all too real.

Willing herself into the present moment, she slipped off the bed and yawned. Through the windows, daylight illuminated the massive lake. She checked the screen on her phone. She'd slept well into the afternoon.

And she wasn't the only one. Exhausted, all of them

except Eisheth had taken the opportunity to nap. Bridget was fast asleep beside her, and she could hear Danel's gentle snoring from the couch. She padded to the boat's tiny bathroom, past the dinette, which had been folded down into a bed. Nuriel lay curled in a ball on the short mattress, a quilt half covering him.

She closed the door and undressed to take what Danel called a military shower—only letting the water run when rinsing off. He'd warned them their fresh water supply would not last long, considering the boat had no filtration system.

The shower didn't do much to wash away her troubled thoughts. Her argument with Bridget spun around her mind like water in a drain. Some part of her had always known that, once James' symbol was administered, Bridget would try to convince Dahlia to abandon her new life entirely. It still felt like a betrayal.

How could she make her sister understand the possibilities in front of her? As a mimic, she could *help* people. If Gaul was right, she could someday collect multiple abilities for herself, so she could make sure no one ever found themselves trapped, as she had.

If anyone deserved destruction, it was Tannin. Surely Bridget could grow to understand.

Warm thoughts of a world without him hummed through her as she finished showering. She changed into her only remaining set of clean clothes and climbed onto the deck. The air outside was warm, and it held the humidity of the lake close.

A soft orange glow drew her to the cockpit. Eisheth sat on the bench, flames dancing along her fingertips, illuminating the space. The detective looked up at her approach and closed her hand, putting out the fire.

"Sleep well?"

"Not really." Dahlia walked over to James. A blanket had been put over him, and a pillow was under his head. "He's not awake yet?"

"No. Nuriel says it might take a while."

She looked out past the rail. They were close to shore, bobbing gently in calm waters. Danel had anchored them along a narrow beach backed by steep, grass-strewn hills. High above them sat well-to-do houses, wooden steps snaking between the beach and their back decks. The charred remains of a bonfire marred a section of the sandy shore.

Dahlia looked away. "I met Danel at a beach like that. I never really figured out why he was there."

Eisheth looked up from her screen. "Isn't it obvious? He was looking for you." She shifted her weight forward and dropped her legs to the deck. "He likely knew about the artifacts your class dug up and wanted to get close to someone who was there."

Frustration panged inside Dahlia. Of course. The feeling that her entire life had become a sham rushed back. Her skin prickled with the painful knowledge her own intuition couldn't be trusted. "I hate him."

Eisheth shrugged. "I don't blame you, but I wouldn't waste your energy on it. Danel is who he is."

"How can you possibly care about him?" It was no secret Eisheth and Danel had a bond. Love wasn't exactly the right word, but Dahlia didn't doubt either would fight to protect the other.

A smile tugged at the corners of Eisheth's mouth. "Because he is who he is."

Dahlia scowled. "At least I'm not the only one with terrible taste."

"I won't argue there," Eisheth said with a quiet laugh. "But he does have loyalties, believe it or not."

"Only to himself."

"And a precious few others. As imperfect as he is, Danel is part of my family. One of the great privileges of this life is that we get to choose who we let in. Family isn't always the person bound to you by blood or marriage. It's the people who are there for you when everything falls apart."

She scowled. "Everything fell apart *because* of Danel."

Eisheth watched Dahlia curiously. "You're thinking about revenge, aren't you?"

Dahlia started, surprised to find her musings so transparent. "How did you know?"

"It's something I'm familiar with. Do yourself a favor. Channel that anger toward our real enemies, not Danel."

"Danel got me killed." She hadn't actually been thinking about taking revenge on him, but she wasn't ready to shower him with forgiveness either. Tolerating his presence was more than he deserved.

Eisheth turned her full attention to Dahlia. "Yes. He did. It was an asinine decision on his part. But these days, he's also one of your best advocates."

"I'm sorry?" Dahlia's laugh was short and sharp. "When has he ever advocated for me?"

"Constantly. He's been pushing for Gaul to train you since the beginning, and he has been trying to protect you from Tannin since that fight in the park. He gave you a phone and brought you to his boat. He helped you get James out of the funeral home."

"He's trying to make up for literal murder."

"Maybe. But in the end, he chose us. Not Tannin."

Heat climbed up Dahlia's neck, and she bit back a retort. Danel may have decided to turn back on his contract with Tannin, but he wasn't a good person. He'd proven as much when he tossed her aside long ago.

Searching for a distraction, she turned her attention back to James. "Why did you help us revive him?"

Eisheth pursed her lips but allowed the conversation to shift. "As I recall, all I did was bring Bridget to you."

"You didn't try to stop us either."

With a shrug, Eisheth turned her head into the breeze, letting it flick back strands of dark hair. "I know how to choose my battles, Miss Keene."

Dahlia frowned. "Something's wrong, isn't it?"

The detective's eyes snapped to Dahlia in surprise. "Did Bridget speak with you?"

Confirmation swam in Dahlia's gut, mixed with betrayal. What was Bridget keeping from her now? "No. But it was obvious something was bothering her. She's really good at keeping the burden of knowledge on herself. What aren't you all telling me?"

Eisheth considered Dahlia. "Sit down. This may take a while."

Dahlia sank onto the bench across from Eisheth. The fiberglass was warm from the sun, and she laid her hands flat on it. Across from her, she could feel another type of warmth. Eisheth's ability to manipulate fire and to enhance her own physical strength, pulsing around her, ready for the taking. Beyond, emanating from James, she sensed a gentle press of new powers, slippery and ungraspable.

Leaning forward, Eisheth took on the stoic expression of an officer delivering unpleasant news. She spent the next few minutes catching Dahlia up, telling her about how Ret never returned from his visit to Eris, and about the phone call Viri had received from Tannin a day after Dahlia left the house.

As Eisheth spoke, the rage inside Dahlia flared to life. Despicable wasn't a strong enough word for him.

Eisheth looked toward the cabin door. "I didn't tell your sister this part, but the official record states that Ret's death wiped your obligations clean. But Bridget and Gaul are still at risk."

"Why me?" As soon as Dahlia said the words, she knew the answer. She, more than any of the others, was useful to Tannin. He had already tried to strike a deal with her. This was his way of shifting focus away from legal requirements and back toward collecting her.

Dahlia hugged herself as Ret's kind face flashed across her mind. *Will he ever stop?* Tannin's commitment to destroying lives seemed inescapable. His offer stood out in her mind like a neon sign. She'd dismissed it as ridiculous—insulting—but now...

With Ret dead, there was no denying how serious Tannin was. Could she use his offer to find her own leverage?

Bridget's push to go deeper into hiding now made a frustrating amount of sense. She'd been attempting to shelter Dahlia—again. But in doing so, she'd also set her up to abandon the very people who supported her.

That wasn't going to happen. She wasn't going to fade into the shadows while Tannin hurt more people. Bridget's overprotective nature be damned.

Dahlia sifted through the information she had, landing on the unknown element. "What's Eris' deal? She's a collector, too, right? Why does every single one of them want to hurt people?"

"Ret didn't. Collector means something different to us than to humans. Like an Artist, in a way. It's a calling, more than a job."

Dahlia snorted. "That doesn't excuse kidnapping."

"No." Eisheth sighed and uncrossed her legs. "It doesn't. And each person builds a collection for their own purposes. Ret wanted to preserve our past. Tannin wants to recreate it."

"And Eris?"

Eisheth shrugged.

"Does Danel know?"

"You'll have to ask him."

Dahlia squeezed her eyes shut. With Ret dead, everything felt more serious. More urgent. Tannin had proven he really did mean to exact payment for his dead colleagues. "We gotta get to shore."

Eisheth's scowl was testy. "That's what I've been saying. But the anchor's down until James wakes up."

"Maybe I can speed him along." Dahlia stood from the bench and went to kneel by James. She rested a hand on his shoulder and gently shook him. "Hey. Earth to James." His breathing stayed steady, his eyes closed. At least he wasn't so stiff anymore; he looked human again. Not so... well, dead.

She pulled the blanket down. Nuriel had said the process would heal his fatal wounds. Sure enough, the bandage had fallen off, revealing an unblemished torso.

Behind her, the cabin door opened and closed.

Glancing back, her annoyance flared as she saw Danel, hair rumpled from sleep. He went straight to the cockpit, murmuring quietly to Eisheth as he checked the various readouts near the wheel.

Dahlia covered James back up and patted at his cheek. "Wake up. You're worrying us, you jerk."

Still nothing. She stood up and turned away, then froze. The hum of powers emanating from him pulsed, a wave of strength washing over her. James made a low keening sound deep in his throat.

She knelt down again, heart fluttering. "What did you say?"

He squeezed his eyes tight and threw his head to the side. His breathing picked up pace. The aura flared again.

She grasped his arms, sitting him up, but he twisted away from her and thumped back onto the deck, making a low crying sound.

"Eisheth?"

Boots clomped on the deck as the detective approached from behind. "Is he—"

She cut off as James let out another moan, a deep animalistic sound. He thrashed and, for a moment, his tattoo was fully visible. It flashed gold, then went black.

Eisheth stared in shock. "Wake the others. Something's wrong."

TWENTY-SIX

The cabin door opened and yellow lights flickered on. Bridget had only been awake a few minutes, in that strange limbo between exhaustion and alertness. Now, she sat up, heart thumping as Dahlia darted toward her.

"Get up already."

"What's going on?" Bridget slid off the edge of the bed, running a hand through her hair.

"You need to come up on the deck with me. Now." Dahlia turned to lead her past the kitchenette.

Nuriel stirred at the noise. With a yawn, he stretched and sat up. His curls had frizzed during his sleep, leaving him disheveled. The tension in the air caught his notice, as he straightened, getting to his feet.

"Is everything alright?"

"Meet us outside," Bridget said, hurrying after Dahlia. There was only one reason her sister would have woken her up so abruptly.

She burst onto the deck and into daylight, heading straight for James. The blankets had fallen off in a twisted lump. Eisheth knelt beside him, moving the fabric out of the way.

"Is he awake?" Bridget brushed past Danel and crouched beside James.

Eisheth shook her head, and Bridget's heart sank. "No. Look."

James shivered, tremors running up his body like he had a fever. His eyes were still squeezed tight. Like Nuriel, his curls had sprung into frizz. He shuddered, then rolled onto his side with a low moan.

Dahlia looked up at her. "The tattoo started to pulse gold, and then this happened."

"Is this normal?" Bridget asked, already knowing the answer. If it were, they wouldn't have rushed to wake her. "What do we do? Think we can wait it out?"

Eisheth spoke up. "Look at this." She passed Bridget her phone. Bridget took it, but not without a flare of impatience.

The phone was open to a horrendously old-fashioned, 1990s-style website, with the words running off the side of the mobile screen.

"Is *this* the forum?" Bridget stared at the pastel blue background. The printed version had looked less archaic.

"Read it."

Bridget turned back to the open thread, flinching as James whimpered. It was titled: EARTHQUAKE? The author was Prometheus, their avatar a cupcake.

The post read: I felt a massive influx of power, and now there have been a string of earthquakes around the world. What is happening?

Dozens of responses followed.

Whatever it is, the earliest reports are from the Great Lakes region in North America. Who's out there right now?

Gaul was. But he's been unreachable ever since his actions against Dolos came to light. It seems he doesn't care about his crimes.

Do you think he would do this?

No. This is far beyond his abilities. Something is wrong.

Obviously. Turn on the news. Whatever this is, it hit me all the way in Mexico City.

3.4 earthquake here in Santiago. It isn't diminishing as it spreads.

The same in Beijing.

This has to do with the deaths. Dolos and Kai and Ketil all at once? Something is dangerously out of balance.

No. They've been dead for weeks now. This is new. And Tannin is taking care of it.

His method of taking care of it is a mistake. I can't believe Notos approved executing Ret, of all people.

You're missing the point. We have another thread discussing the deaths. This conversation is about who or what caused this earthquake.

The conversation continued, a combination of short, alarmed reports and large, unbroken chunks of text. Bridget skimmed through, a knot forming in her stomach.

"It doesn't sound like everyone is happy with Ret's fate." Dahlia sat beside Bridget.

Bridget looked up from the screen in surprise. "I'm sorry you're finding out this way."

"Actually, Eisheth told me." Dahlia's voice was flat. "I wish you had."

The detective shrugged. "Sorry. She needed to know."

Bridget bit her lip, shame filling her. "You already had enough to worry about."

"Someday, you're going to stop trying to protect me from every uncomfortable thing."

Bridget squeezed her hands together, her feelings too complex to parse. Turning her focus to James did nothing to help. Sweat beaded along his forehead, in spite of the shivers that plagued him.

Behind them, the cabin door opened. Bridget looked over to see Nuriel step out. He walked straight over to them, kneeling beside James, who still writhed on the deck.

"Reviving James may have caused an outburst of power," Eisheth said grimly.

"You think *he* caused the wave?" Nuriel pressed the back of his hand to James' forehead.

"It sure wasn't the wind. And it's spreading outward." She took the phone back from Bridget and scrolled down, then showed them a new post.

I'll take care of this. I have an idea who might be responsible.

"Look at the username," Eisheth prompted. It was a single word: Eris.

Bridget wrapped her arms around herself. If they were in trouble facing one ancient, powerful Grigori, they were *screwed* facing two of them.

Danel spoke up from the wheel, his eyes on the controls. "What are you all muttering about?"

Eisheth straightened from James' side, walked over to Danel, and handed him the phone.

He took it with a frown, scrolling through the thread. As he reached the bottom, the color drained from his cheeks. "What do we do?"

"We need to regroup with the others." The detective gestured back to the deck, and James' trembling form. "Gaul has done this before, right? He'll know how to help."

Danel gave a dark laugh. "He's going to love this."

"He can also protect you from Eris."

He scowled and handed the phone back to her. Turning away, he jabbed an icon on the boat's control panel. There was a clank as the boat's anchor began to lift. "I don't need anyone's protection."

"Not even with your contract broken?"

From the way Danel stiffened, Bridget knew she'd guessed correctly. In the brief time she'd known him, he'd never stumbled in his life—and he never walked when he could run. Part of the effortless demeanor he put on relied on the light-footed speed with which he could move through the world.

Bridget tilted her head. "When you signed your contract with her, the collateral you used was your abilities, wasn't it?"

Danel scoffed. "Let me worry about Eris. She's my problem."

"Eris is everyone's problem now," Bridget pointed out. With Ret dead, she had made it clear she'd chosen to side with Tannin. Now they had *two* powerful, ancient Grigori to contend with.

Or to run from—as soon as James was awake and well.

Danel met Bridget's eyes. "If you want to take James back to Gaul, fine. Let's leave it at that."

Bridget dropped the issue and went back to Eisheth's side. "We should call the house. Let Gaul and Viri know we're on our way back, with James."

The detective nodded. "I'll do it." She took the phone and walked toward the bow.

Bridget took the opportunity to kneel beside Nuriel and Dahlia, who were both watching over James. Something in the way they sat side-by-side struck Bridget. They had worked together, night and day, to create this symbol, and now they were facing its effects together. Even though she was only a few inches from them, she felt miles away.

"This isn't what it was like for you?" Bridget asked Nuriel quietly.

Nuriel started, tearing his eyes from James. "I don't remember my own transition, but everything I've been taught tells me this is wrong."

She didn't ask Dahlia if she remembered anything

from those early days in Tannin's possession. Instead, touched James' shoulder. It was warm and covered in a thin sheen of sweat, so much better than the cold, stiff flesh of the previous night. And yet it still felt *off*. His muscles quivered beneath Bridget's touch, as if he had a fever he couldn't break.

"But he'll be okay?"

Nuriel hesitated. "I don't know. I—"

A massive crash cut him off.

Bridget fell forward as the boat rocked violently to the side. Water sprayed up and over the deck. With a yelp, Bridget grabbed James to hold him in place. Dahlia helped keep him as steady as possible.

The hull dipped low—so low Bridget slid perilously close to the rail. She caught a glimpse of Danel, wrestling the wheel to no avail. Eisheth grabbed onto the rigging, holding tight to keep from falling.

Beside them, Nuriel lurched to his feet and threw himself forward, hitting the rail with a grunt. Bracing himself against it, he pressed both hands outward.

Within inches of the water's surface, the boat began to right itself. First slowly, under Nuriel's influence. Then gravity took hold and the entire vessel lurched backward sharply—before righting itself with another jolt.

Bridget fell back, loosening her grip on James and letting him slump to the side. She gulped in a few deep breaths. They'd gotten soaked by the spray, and her stomach was roiling. Planting her hands flat on the wet, cool wood, she focused on the conversation around her.

"What was that?!" Dahlia exclaimed.

"I don't know!" Danel's response was punctuated by the creak of the boat as he turned it.

"Look." Nuriel's voice was quiet and insistent. Bridget risked a glance up from the deck to see him watching James.

A rainbow shimmer danced around the edges of his fresh tattoo, like oil on water. As Bridget watched, the glow slowly faded, sucked into the ink. James sighed in contentment, settling onto the damp blankets.

Bridget's nausea faded, crowded out by a burst of fear. Bridget locked eyes with Dahlia. In her sister, she saw confirmation. Whatever was happening to James, it wasn't going to resolve itself.

Bridget cleared her throat. "Danel, get us back to shore. Now."

For once, he didn't argue.

TWENTY-SEVEN

They piled into Viri's sedan, laying James across their laps in the backseat.

The entire ride, Bridget held onto him tightly so he wouldn't roll to the floor. Even though he wasn't awake and back to himself yet, he was *alive*. She had to believe everything would be okay, despite their precarious position.

Eisheth flicked the radio on, keeping the volume low. The local classic rock station finished their song before the DJ started talking about the freak global earthquakes. The shaking hadn't caused any damage, but the conversation still filled Bridget with dread. She clung more tightly to James' trembling body.

When the house came into view, the coiled spring of Bridget's insides unwound a fraction. After a week on the lake, the sturdy structure was a welcome sight, even with the blackened front entry. Nuriel's Prius was parked beside the Mustang Ret had borrowed. A pang went through her. While Nuriel's car had been recovered from the marina, the Mustang was back from the airport where Ret had left it. According to Danel, Eris operated out of a shifting array of locations, so it was impossible to know where Ret had flown.

Viri stood on the porch, coaxing thick, woody vines out of the soil and upward. They wrapped around the columns of greenery he'd already created, adding additional support to the damaged structure. He stopped at their arrival, dropping his arms to his sides and watching them drive up.

Nuriel and Danel hefted James between them, climbing from the car first. Viri turned to watch. He looked tired, dark circles etched beneath his eyes, but he managed a weak smile on their approach. "You're safe."

"Where's Gaul?" Bridget asked.

"Inside." Viri gestured toward the front door. "He's already shaken by what happened to Ret. He's not going to be happy when he sees James."

Bridget turned away from his disturbed expression. She'd face enough judgment from Gaul—she didn't also need it from Viri.

"I can catch Viri up." Dahlia put a hand on Bridget's shoulder and squeezed.

Bridget hesitated, but Eisheth stepped forward. "Me too."

"Thanks." She moved into the house. Danel and Nuriel followed more slowly, taking care not to drop James.

"You know, it was a lot easier to carry him when he was dead." Danel grunted as James writhed.

Bridget ignored him, drawn to Gaul's low rumble to her right. She strode over to the open doorway, peering into the living room. Untouched by the fight, it was cozy and functional, decorated primarily with greenery, wooden furniture, and soft yellow lighting. The redhead paced back and forth, phone pressed against his ear, listening.

"Yes. I can be there in a few hours." His attention snapped to Bridget, then to Nuriel and Danel behind her. Finally, he looked to James. His green eyes narrowed to slits.

He hung up and set the phone on the side table.

"Put him on the couch."

They crossed the worn Persian rug and set James on the leather sofa. As soon as they released him, he curled in on himself, trembling.

Bridget made sure he wasn't at risk of falling off, then turned toward Gaul, bracing herself for an argument.

But he wasn't looking at her, instead staring at the freshly inked symbol arching across James' back. "How long has it been?"

Bridget stood beside the couch protectively. "Almost a day."

"And why's he doing... this?" He waved his hand at James.

Nuriel responded, voice laced with guilt. "We don't know. He acts like he has a fever. Sweats, nightmares, trembling. And he won't wake up."

Gaul finally looked at Bridget. "This is highly

abnormal. Botched."

Bridget shifted to put herself between Gaul and James. "Dahlia and Nuriel did everything right."

"Clearly not." Gaul walked to an armchair and took a folded blanket from its back. He shook it out and spread it over James, covering his bare torso. Then he turned his glare on Nuriel. "You've made a habit of poor decisions lately."

Danel threw himself into the chair. "I guess he's been spending too much time with me."

"I'm not sorry we did it," Bridget said.

She winced as James punctuated her statement with a high-pitched whimper. He twisted, and Bridget hurried to place a hand on his arm, preventing him from rolling over. She tucked the blanket around him to keep him in place.

Gaul's jaw twitched, then he turned to Nuriel. "We don't have time for another crisis. How did you even manage this? Tannin took the sketches."

Nuriel sighed and rubbed one arm, looking abashed. "We had copies. Dahlia and I chose one to work from, but..." He trailed off and gestured to the sofa.

"Let me look at this." Gaul approached the couch, turning James onto his side to peer at the tattoo.

"The earthquakes started when we activated it," Nuriel volunteered quietly.

"I see." Gaul straightened and paced over to where he'd set his phone.

"Maybe they'll stop?" Bridget asked hopefully.

The look he gave her was withering. His sharp gaze swept the room. "We need to finalize our plan. Danel, get the others. Bridget, sit down. Nuriel..." He threw up his hands as he took his seat again. "I don't know what to do with you."

Nuriel looked chagrined as Danel hefted himself out of his chair with a heavy sigh, leaving the room.

"What plan?" Bridget asked, sitting on the edge of the sofa, near James' legs.

Gaul sighed. "I'm only going to go over it once."

Dahlia appeared in the open doorway, followed by Viri and Eisheth. Danel entered last. He stayed in the doorway, rocking back on his heels. "I'll be heading out."

Gaul fixed him with a steely glare. "Sit down."

Danel huffed in irritation and remained standing in the threshold.

A cry interrupted them. James twisted, nearly kicking Bridget off the sofa. She jumped up and grabbed his leg to steady him. Worry lodged in her throat. "Hey. It's okay, James. It's okay. You're safe."

His only response was more shivering. With a concerned frown, Viri approached the couch, kneeling by James to feel his forehead with the back of his hand. Then he touched his neck to monitor his pulse. He looked over at Gaul. "I need to examine him."

Gaul closed his eyes and pinched his nose, turning to the others while Viri fussed over James. "We have several problems. Most critically, Ret's murder for crimes he did not commit."

He paused for a beat. His expression didn't change, but the way his eyes clouded hinted at grief that had taken the form of anger.

Clearing his throat, he continued. "The way I see it,

Ret's death should atone for all of us. He was older than Kai, Dolos, and Ketil combined. So, I plan to make Tannin see reason. Even his weak definition of justice should be satisfied."

"Is that who you were on the phone with? Tannin?" Dahlia raised her eyebrows in surprise.

"He wants this situation resolved quickly, and he's willing to talk. He's not out for vengeance so much as to fulfill his duties. To him, this is a distraction."

"Yeah, except now he has Eris whispering in his ear," Danel pointed out.

Eisheth spoke, "How does she fit in? Before she turned on him, Ret thought she might align herself with us."

Danel snorted, folding his arms. "Eris doesn't align herself with anyone."

Bridget considered him. "Is that true? Or are you annoyed she stole your powers?"

Gaul's eyes snapped to Danel. "What?"

Irritation flashed over his face. "It's nothing. I'll handle it."

Eisheth made an incredulous noise in the back of her throat. "You broke another contract, didn't you?"

"I said I'll handle it," Danel insisted.

Gaul buried his face in his hands. "By the old gods, Danel."

He had the grace to look embarrassed.

Gaul straightened and ran his fingers through his hair. "Eris *has* had allies over the years, both Ret and Tannin among them. I suspect she suggested using Ret as a proxy in the first place, though I can't imagine why."

"Did she think he was a threat?" Bridget asked.

Viri straightened from James' side, turning to join the conversation. "Collectors have always had their own sense of loyalty and rivalry. With him gone, his entire inventory is up for grabs."

"It's just like Tannin to outsource revenge," Danel muttered.

"Sure. He already outsources murder." Dahlia's expression was dark.

Danel flushed, looking equal parts angry and embarrassed.

Gaul spread his hands, palms up to refocus them. "Regardless, the best I can do at this point is sit down with Tannin and make sure he agrees that our debts are satisfied—with no further bloodshed."

Dahlia made a sound of disgust. "So, you want to make a deal with our enemy?"

"In this situation? Yes."

Bridget shot Viri a furtive look. He appeared frustrated, and she wondered how long the two men had argued about this idea.

A quiet tinkling sound interrupted them. On the mantle, two crystal candlesticks clattered together.

A low rumble welled up from the ground. Overhead, the light fixture began swaying, making their shadows bounce across the walls. The floor shuddered, and Bridget grabbed the armrests, heart thumping.

A hairline crack snaked across the ceiling, popping the plaster apart. One of Viri's vines followed the crack to mend it.

The shuddering earthquake subsided, and Bridget looked around wide-eyed. "Everyone okay?" She searched for Dahlia, whose back was hunched, and hands covered the back of her neck.

Nuriel spoke quietly. "Look at James."

He'd stopped his shivering and rolled onto his back. Still asleep, his chest rose and fell peacefully.

Gaul went to the fireplace and stooped down, retrieving a picture that had fallen to the floor. "That brings us to our next problem. Three earthquakes now." He cast Bridget a weary look. "And no, I don't think they're going to go away on their own."

"They're tied to James' contract, I'm certain of it," Nuriel said. "I just don't know why. What purpose could a naming symbol like this serve?"

Gaul folded his arms. "I don't know. But the simple solution is to deactivate it."

Nuriel sat upright. "That would kill him."

A flash of protective panic coursed through Bridget. After all they'd done to revive him—after all James had gone through—he deserved this chance. She knew Gaul could be cold, but she never thought he'd be willing to hurt one of his own.

Dahlia spoke up. "Nuriel and I worked our asses off for this. We need to help him."

Before Gaul could respond, Danel cut in, "As much as I hate to admit it, maybe Gaul is right."

Dahlia's eyes narrowed. "Excuse me?"

"We tried. It didn't work. And now the entire world is shaking—literally." Danel shrugged.

Eisheth nodded in agreement. "I'm sorry, Bridget. It's not what I want, but it might be what's necessary."

Bridget felt as if her lungs were in a vice. She'd hoped

coming to the house would present a solution—some way to revive James. Instead, all she'd received was clear confirmation he was not the top priority. Not only that, he was in danger from her allies.

After everything she'd done, after all the work they'd put in, all it had amounted to was a half-revived friend trapped in eternal nightmares. And the best suggestion anyone had was killing him all over again. Up until now, every challenge she'd faced, no matter how difficult, had a path forward. She'd found leads to follow, options to exhaust. Even reviving James had come with an instruction manual of sorts.

Now she had nothing, and it felt like the walls were closing in. Like her chest was being squeezed tight. "We can't—" Her voice came out high and reedy. "We can't condemn him to death again. Please."

"Bridget?" Viri's voice startled her, and she realized she was gasping for air. He still knelt in front of James on the couch, but now he offered her a hand.

She wanted to recoil from the offer, to refuse Grigori magic. But tears pressed at the backs of her eyes, and she felt certain she was going to throw up. Trembling, she took his hand. His bare skin was warm, and that warmth sunk into her own flesh, taking root in her blood and flooding her body. After a few moments, her muscles relaxed, and she found herself able to take in a deep breath. The panic subsided.

"Better?" Viri asked gently.

Bridget pulled back her hand. Some of the warmth faded, but enough remained that she felt able to stay focused. "Thank you."

A hand squeezed her shoulder, and she looked up to see Dahlia had come up behind her. Her sister was watching Gaul with a thoughtful frown.

"I said, the *simple* solution would be deactivating it." Gaul's ice chip eyes were on Bridget. "But that's not the solution I'm advocating for."

Bridget's heart gave a hopeful thud. She swallowed her anxiety, clinging to the warmth Viri had offered her. "Really?"

Gaul turned to Nuriel. "I want you to find every piece of information you can on this symbol. See if there's a way to counteract its effects without hurting James. Or perhaps another one you could complete and apply in its place."

Nuriel nodded wordlessly.

"Danel, Dahlia, help him. Anything you remember about Tannin or Eris could be useful. The rest of you, take care of James and make sure this house doesn't fall down around our ears."

"What about you?" Bridget asked.

Gaul looked from Bridget to Viri, who was silently tending to James once again. "I'm going to have a chat with Tannin in the morning."

TWENTY-EIGHT

Dahlia pressed her fingertips into the back of Bridget's chair, focusing on the ridges of fabric beneath her skin. Gaul's decision to meet with Tannin chafed at her. How dare he consider negotiating with the enemy?

Viri ducked out to gather medical supplies, while Bridget held James' limp hand. Gaul left the room, muttering about wrapping up a few things. A silent conversation passed between Eisheth and Danel as she glared at him and his eyes darted away.

And yet, it all felt distant—as if she were watching the scene play out on a movie screen. She'd contributed where she could, but her mind kept slipping to the earthquakes.

The newest rumblings had caused James' powers to flare once more. Ever since his symbol began flashing, his *presence* had become more pronounced. Now, it almost blotted out the others' powers with its strength—a bonfire surrounded by matches.

His transformation played on a constant loop. The early thrill of success snuffed out by a heavy cloud of dread. All around her, the abilities of the others swirled, a silent, but ever-present whirlpool of possibility and power. And, yet...

"He's so strong." Dahlia didn't realize she'd spoken out loud until she saw the others looking at her.

"Who? Tannin?" Eisheth asked.

Dahlia shook her head, focusing on the sensation of humming, nascent abilities. "James. I can feel his powers. They intensified during the earthquake."

Everyone's attention shifted from her to James, and she let out a sigh. Having them all watch her made her skin prickle. The room was hot and overcrowded. She took a step back, away from the chair.

"I need some space." She turned to leave.

"Wait—" Bridget started to rise, but Dahlia shook her head sharply.

"Please. I don't want to talk."

"But I can help."

A burst of frustration crackled through Dahlia. "I said no. I've already spent an entire week crammed on a tiny boat with you. Give me one damned minute alone."

Bridget flinched as if she'd been slapped. A red flush crept across her cheeks, and a wet shine sprung to her eyes. She tightened her jaw. "Sure. Take as much time as you need." Her tone was carefully measured.

Dahlia knew she *should* feel guilty about upsetting Bridget, but she was allowed her space. It wasn't her fault her sister was so damn clingy.

She could feel their eyes following as she turned to go. She passed through the hall, over the creaking floorboards of the foyer, and onto the front porch. The afternoon sun warmed her shoulders as she crossed the driveway. It was a beautiful day, which only left her sourer. Before all of this, she would have spent hours at the beach or hitting up a house party with her roommate, Nicole. She'd open the windows and watch a National Geographic documentary. She'd take the long way to the coffee shop and watch the dogs at the park.

When she'd first left North Carolina for college, her world finally opened up. She could do anything, study anything, become anything. For the first time in her life, she could make decisions without having to consider Bridget's well-meaning worry.

Now, her life had shrunk back down again. Even her attempts to become her new self were met with friction. Bridget hovered over her. The strength of her allies only reminded her of her limits. Her long imprisonment and inherited identity lurked in dark dreams.

It was all so suffocating.

Dahlia kicked a rock, watching it skitter across the grass. She'd hoped finishing the symbol would make her feel stronger. That it would help her conquer the nightmares and move on with her life. But the victory felt tainted, given James' current condition. She couldn't help but wonder if it was her fault—if she and Nuriel had gotten something wrong. Had they deviated from the original and stumbled upon something new and strange? If she'd been more meticulous, would he be awake right now?

She stopped near the line of trees, pausing to lean against the bark of a tall maple. Turning her eyes skyward through the sunlight-dappled branches, she tried to sort through her options. Constant worrying was Bridget's territory. If the roles were reversed, she knew what she'd tell her sister: what happened was in the past. All she could do was move forward and make the best of it.

Dahlia needed to choose her own path. Ever since meeting Danel, she'd been yanked around, used to fulfill the needs of others. She needed to exert some semblance of control over her life.

The sky overhead was clear, but heavy clouds gathered in the distance. They promised a fresh bout of rain, and their darkness reminded her of Tannin and his choking sulfur.

His offer stirred in the back of her mind. It disgusted her, that Tannin believed she could be bought. She was further turned off by Gaul's decision to work with Tannin.

And yet.

She pressed her fingers against the tree's bark, letting its roughness ground her. It was senseless trying to placate Tannin or trying to find common ground with him. He wanted what he wanted.

That clearly worried Gaul—scared him.

To her surprise, her own fear felt more distant. It had blanketed her when he'd attacked the house, gnawing on her trauma. But ever since learning about Ret's death, anger smothered everything else.

Was Tannin dangerous? Undoubtedly. But he was also weak. Only someone scared would shove a young woman into a cage. Or murder a healer. Or back potential allies into corners.

Clarity shot through her. They'd been going about this all wrong.

Tannin wasn't a person to negotiate with. He was a person to destroy.

She turned his words over again. He'd promised to spare the others if she agreed to work with him. No imprisonment, no more executions. She didn't trust his word, but pretending to agree *would* get her close to him.

And she'd seen for herself how easy it was to end a Grigori. A bullet was all it took, or illness, or a knife at the throat. Immortality would only take Tannin so far.

She considered. Could she do it? Murder someone in cold blood?

No, not anyone.

But a monster like Tannin? Yes. She could do that.

Dahlia let out a long breath, but it didn't release the tension building inside her. Going head-to-head with someone as powerful as Tannin was a fool's mission, but she also couldn't sit by and watch him systematically manipulate the world around his desires. Something had to give.

As she stared out over the gardens, Gaul's conversation about Hartu came back to her. His desire for revenge had ended poorly, but he'd harbored a grudge against all of humanity. Hers was against one person.

Tannin wasn't too different from the flowerpot Gaul had instructed Dahlia to topple during their session a week ago. Everyone had a weakness.

She just had to find Tannin's.

TWENTY-NINE

The first person Dahlia needed to speak to was Danel. She cornered him in the kitchen, dragged him into the library, and whispered her plan.

He hated it but reluctantly agreed to join her. She supposed she should feel guilty for involving him, but he was useful to have around when breaking and entering.

That conversation done, Dahlia made a quick stop in the living room for her backpack. Inside, the stone beacon clacked against her sketchbook.

Then, she went into Nuriel's empty room, pressed *1794* on the safe's keypad, and tucked the sketches away. No reason to bring something so valuable straight to Tannin.

From there, she went to wait on the porch. Viri had covered most of it with thick, woody grape vines, and she took a seat on the sun-warmed steps.

She could do this. She had to.

When Gaul opened the front door, she stood. "You're really going?"

Gaul eyed her as he pulled on his thin suede jacket. "I am."

She nodded. "Be careful, okay? None of us want to lose anyone else."

The corners of Gaul's eyes tightened. He straightened his jacket and gave her a terse nod. "You're a far cry from the Hartu I knew, Dahlia. You'll do well."

His words sent warmth rushing through her—chased immediately by guilt. Gaul had finally begun to think better of her, and here she was sneaking around behind his back. She set the guilt aside. He would understand when Tannin was finally gone.

"Good luck, Gaul."

He strode toward the cars, getting into his shiny red Mustang. The engine rolled like thunder as he brought it to life.

Dahlia waited until he backed up, then leaned down to collect her backpack and began heading down the driveway.

"Danel? Let's go."

He emerged from behind the trunk of a nearby maple. "I'm beginning to feel as if all I do is steal people's keys."

"Did you get them?" She hurried toward the remaining cars.

"Of course I got them. We're in Nuriel's." The locks clicked as they approached.

Dahlia threw open the Prius' driver-side door and slid

in. When she saw Danel begin to protest, she simply held out her hand. He sighed and handed her the key fob, then went around to the other side.

"Hurry," she urged. It would be hard enough to follow Gaul without being recognized. Worse if he got too far ahead altogether.

"I'm going," Danel muttered, pulling the door shut behind him.

"Take this." Dahlia shoved her backpack at him and turned the car on. Through the rearview mirror, she could see the porch was still empty. The knot of anxiety loosened, slightly. It would hopefully be some time before anyone realized they were gone.

A flutter of eagerness raced through Dahlia as she backed out of the spot. It was a small victory, but for the first time in months, she was making a decision for herself. Not to appease Kai or help her sister. Not to keep the peace. To make sure people like Tannin would stop selfishly bulldozing everything in his way.

She sped down the driveway, reaching the end in record time. Looking both ways, she caught a hint of taillights to the left. She turned onto the road. "What happens if you run into Eris?"

"I'll handle it."

She wasn't sure how he'd do that with his powers tamped down, but she didn't argue. She focused on keeping the distant gleam of Gaul's car in view.

"You know he'll want a contract," Danel said, breaking the silence.

Dahlia glanced at him. "I know. I'll have to act before he convinces me to seal one."

"How? Do you have a weapon?"

She shook her head. "Gaul will be there."

The implication hung between them. She didn't miss the worry that flashed across Danel's face, but he didn't voice his concerns.

They fell quiet again, except for the occasional sound of the blinker. Gaul's car stood out as a red beacon as it exited the highway. He'd brought them closer to the city, though they were still in the suburbs. They passed strip malls, neighborhood entrances, and schools. More than one traffic light was dark, with cars stacking up to go through one at a time.

"Power outage?" she asked when they pulled to a stop at their third one.

"Earthquakes will do that." Danel's voice was grim. "Let's hope they don't get stronger."

Finally, Gaul pulled into the parking lot of a squat, abandoned gas station. Dahlia drove past it, craning her head to watch as he pulled to a stop.

She circled the block slowly, fingers sweaty on the steering wheel.

The gas station looked like it had been vacant for some time, with an asphalt lot full of potholes. The windows of the convenience store were broken, and faded graffiti adorned the brick. From inside the building, she sensed the pulse of Gaul's abilities. There was no sign of Tannin. Maybe he was running late. "Let's wait for a few minutes."

"It's okay, you know," Danel said.

She turned to face him fully. "What's okay?"

"Trying to find a way to beat him."

Dahlia bristled. "Am I so transparent?"

Danel shrugged. "I know you, Dahlia. Well enough, at least. No version of you wants people to get hurt."

His words rang false to her. She wasn't the same Dahlia he had dated.

"I want him to get hurt." She reached out to see if Gaul was still inside. His powers hummed steadily in her mind, moving deeper into the gas station. She resisted the temptation to grasp the rank thread of power that promised sickness and decay. Her chance would come.

He winced. "Be careful. There's a reason no one else is trying to strangle him in his sleep."

Dahlia narrowed her eyes at him. "I have to try something."

Danel shrugged. "I don't blame you for trying. But don't go in thinking it'll be easy."

She scoffed, not bothering to respond. Of course it wouldn't be easy. Nothing in her life was. Instead of continuing the conversation, she checked in on Gaul.

His aura was gone. "Gaul disappeared."

Danel sat up, frowning. "What?"

"He's out of range. Or he died. Or... he went through a portal."

Danel groaned. "If there's a portal to Tannin's, this just got infinitely harder."

She let herself out of the car into the sunlight and shoved the keys into her pocket. Pulling her backpack on, she strode toward the old gas station. Plywood covered the windows, making it impossible to see the interior. But she didn't need vision to know the building was empty of Grigori.

He followed her and pushed the door open, entering a dimly lit, open space. Very little light filtered in, casting everything in a grimy grayness. Metal shelves had been largely pillaged of their supplies. Only a few packets of dental floss and a dented box of tampons remained. Grimy dust laid thick over everything, and the checkered tile floor had a layer of dried mud caked along it.

"Tannin always chooses the nicest places, doesn't he?" Dahlia said. She passed an empty postcard rack and moved towards the row of silent refrigerators. Danel's footsteps followed.

It reminded her of the abandoned building where Danel had led her to Tannin—to her death. Empty, dusty, broken. She wrapped her arms around herself.

Danel interrupted the silence. "We're thinking the same thing, Dahlia. I'm sorry."

She turned toward him with equal parts surprise and suspicion. "What, exactly, are you sorry for?"

Danel rubbed at his forehead. "Do we have to do this?"

She raised her eyebrows and said nothing. *He'd* cracked open the can of worms this time.

"Alright, alright. I'm sorry for trying to earn forgiveness for something unforgivable." He ran a hand through his hair, only succeeding in tousling it more. "I never meant to hurt you, but I know that doesn't matter. You were innocent, and you *did* get hurt—"

"Killed."

"Yeah. Killed. And that *is* my fault. I should have fought harder to protect you from Tannin. This time, I will."

His apology hung between them, an offering Dahlia

wasn't sure she wanted to take. She was surprised to find her throat tight with emotion. "I lost everything."

"I know." Danel looked down. "I didn't think about it at first, because that's not how it was for me. When I died—when this body died—it was earned. I was executed for crimes I willingly committed. I didn't *want* it, but it wasn't a surprise either. But you didn't deserve any of this."

Executed. So, he'd always been a con man, through and through. And maybe he was trying to con her now, because he wanted to feel absolved.

She knew she couldn't forgive him, not yet. A rift stretched between them, and it would take time to mend. If it ever could.

But right now, they had a job to do.

She looked around at the dusty, empty shelves. "I can feel your abilities, you know."

Surprise flickered across Danel's eyes. "You can?"

"A hum. Like they're trapped behind a wall or something. But they're not gone. Whatever Eris did, she's just bottled them up, somehow."

Danel swallowed, nodding sharply. He looked caught between pain and relief. "I shouldn't have broken my contract with her."

"Why did you? And how? You've been away from Eris for months, what broke it now?"

He shook his head. "It's nothing."

"Dan." She used his nickname from when she thought he was her completely normal, completely human boyfriend. "No more bullshit."

Danel grimaced. "Her name is Morgan."

She blinked, shocked he'd actually tell her anything. "Who is she? Some old lover?"

Danel choked. "No. Absolutely not. She's one of my descendants. A niece, with a lot of 'greats' in front of it."

"You still keep in touch with your family?" Gaul had led her to believe no one maintained contact with their human relations. If there was anyone who defied this norm, she never would have expected it to be Danel.

He shrugged, fingers tensing and releasing against his thigh. It was clear the topic made him uncomfortable, but he didn't shut it down. "I protect her, best I can. I did the same with her father, and her grandmother. All the way back to my sister, Mercy."

Mercy. "Your ship is named for your sister."

"Boat, but yes. My contract with Eris was predicated on me not visiting Morgan."

"That's a weird stipulation. Why? And why visit her now?"

His expression closed off. "I'd rather keep at least one secret, Dahlia. Come on, Gaul's been through the portal for a while. Let's find it."

The revelation sat strangely with Dahlia. She found it hard to reconcile her own experiences with him alongside this story of a great-niece he'd decided to protect.

She looked over at Danel. "You don't have to come, you know. Especially if it means going to Athens."

"I know." He didn't move, so she led the way forward. A small hallway led off the main area, and she followed it to a door marked "Employees Only." It revealed only a janitorial closet, still filled with mop buckets and cleaning supplies. Directly across from it, an open doorway led into an unlit space—likely where stock was kept. Beside it, the bathroom door hung partially open from one set of hinges, tilted at a precarious angle.

Danel leaned into the stock area, then immediately backed away. "Ugh, it's rank in there."

Dahlia turned to the bathroom instead. She nudged the door fully open with her hip, not wanting to touch the door itself if she could help it.

Light from the hall barely touched the edges of the single-stall room, but it was enough to illuminate the outlines of a toilet, urinal, and sink.

To her left, an all-too-familiar arcing Grigori symbol cut across the whitewashed cinder block wall. Even though she'd been looking for it, the design filled her with apprehension. Going back to Athens—to the place where she'd been held prisoner—made her feel like throwing up. But this time, she would control the outcome.

"Are you sure about this?" Danel's voice was quieter than usual, but it still startled her.

She gripped her backpack straps. For months, she hadn't been sure about much of anything. Her identity, her purpose, her future—all of it was wrapped up in a shroud of question marks. But through it all, she felt certain about one thing.

Tannin needed to be stopped.

"More than anything," she whispered.

THIRTY

Viri slid an IV needle into James' arm with deft, practiced movements. He taped it down then said to Bridget, "Don't let him move too much, or he could pull the needle out. The saline is keeping him hydrated."

Bridget nodded as Viri turned to contend with the drip bag. It was attached to a rolling metal stand he'd brought out from a nearby closet.

"Do all doctors keep hospital equipment in their homes?"

"No, but I like to be prepared."

It was the three of them in the living room. Dahlia hadn't returned from the gardens yet, and Nuriel had gone into the kitchen to put together a meal, murmuring about fortifying himself before diving back into symbology. She wasn't sure where Eisheth or Danel had gone, but she was getting used to the two of them disappearing together.

A quiet whimper pulled Bridget's attention back to James. Since the most recent earthquake, he'd been calmer, but his fingers still twitched like he was having a bad dream. Bridget pulled the blanket higher around his neck. She doubted he knew she was there, but it was the best she could do to reassure him.

"You're a good friend, Bridget."

Bitter laughter caught in her throat. "Gaul thinks I'm an idiot."

Viri pulled off his nitrile gloves. "And you care what he thinks all of a sudden?"

"No. But I'm scared. What if I only made it worse?" She squeezed James' hand, but of course he didn't respond.

"That, my friend, is something I ask myself almost constantly." Viri settled down in the oversized armchair next to the couch. "Not only as a doctor, but as a Grigori. Everything I do has consequences. Of course, that's true of anyone, but our long lives mean we can often see how our decisions reverberate through decades."

Bridget glanced over at him. "So how do you keep from hurting people you want to help?"

His gaze was equal parts kind and sad. "Sometimes I fail. We simply have to do the best we can with the information and wisdom we have." His smile turned rueful. "At least I have a lot of experience asking forgiveness."

Bridget knew he was trying to help, but her throat felt

tight. Unlike Viri, she didn't have centuries to correct her mistakes. She *couldn't* fail where James was concerned. She'd come too far and risked too much. Including Viri's kindness. "Thank you for taking care of him. And arranging everything at the funeral home. I know you stuck your neck out for us."

Viri sighed. "I'll repair things with Charlie one of these days."

"I feel bad for taking advantage of them. But even if I wanted to tell them the truth, I couldn't."

"I know."

Nuriel's head popped around the doorframe. "Sandwiches are ready."

"Why don't you eat? I'll stay with James," Viri told Bridget.

As reluctant as she was to leave James' side, Bridget couldn't remember when she'd last had a full meal. She stood, padding down the hall.

Bridget followed Nuriel into the kitchen, nudging aside an actively sprouting monstera. He went back to the counter, sprinkling herbs on a platter of open-faced sandwiches. Her stomach whined, acutely aware of its recent neglect. "That looks good."

"Cucumber and dill on rye with cream cheese. Grab a plate."

"I didn't know you were a chef, too." Bridget took a small plate from the cabinet and filled it with his offerings.

"We deserve more than peanut butter and jelly after the last few days."

"Mm." Bridget's response came out as a muffled sound of appreciation as she bit into the sandwich. It was heaven.

But her enjoyment was tamped down by the persistent silence around her. Nuriel made up his own plate and sat across from her. A leatherbound book was at his elbow.

"What is that?"

"Something Ret left behind. A history of our people he was working to translate."

Bridget wiped her mouth. "Did Dahlia and Danel remember anything useful?"

"I haven't spoken with them yet."

She still nurtured the spark of hope from the conversation with Gaul. If they all worked together, maybe they could fix James. Maybe this book held the secret.

Bridget started in on her second sandwich. Across from her, Nuriel set down his plate and pulled a chair in. He heaved a long sigh.

"Nuriel? Are you okay?"

He blinked, turning his attention to her. "I've never resurrected anyone before. I always imagined my first time using a naming symbol would go differently. I always assumed I'd work with Kai on it."

She shook her head. "You didn't need him. You did it all on your own."

Warmth lit up Nuriel's eyes. "Your sister and I did it together. She's going to make a remarkably insightful Artist. It was nice to work with someone again. It's been a long time."

The way he talked about Dahlia—with a combination of respect and intrigue—sent up a sudden realization. One that made her feel alien, all too aware of her asexuality. "You like her."

He frowned. "Of course I like her. She's been through a lot, and she's still learning how to navigate that, but at her core she's a good person."

"That's not what I mean. You *like* her. As more than someone to work with."

A laugh bubbled up from Nuriel. "What? No, of course not. She's a colleague." But there was a light flush on his cheeks. Some small part of Bridget was impressed with herself for noticing it. Only years of practice and awkward miscommunication had taught her to identify the signs of attraction in others.

But Dahlia always had been a magnet for that sort of attention, giving Bridget plenty of opportunity to watch flirtation in action. Her sister had reveled in it, while Bridget struggled to understand it.

Even so, she'd never expected to hear an immortal talk about Dahlia with such affection. The realization sent fear and sadness washing through her. It was one more temptation for Dahlia to forget her old world existed. Forget she existed.

Eisheth entered from the hall. "Where's your sister?"

A zip of anxiety hit Bridget. She set down her sandwich. "I think she's still outside."

"I'll check. Hopefully she's not trying to murder Danel."

Bridget held her retort back as Eisheth exited through

the back patio. The screen door slammed shut behind her.

She doesn't need my help. And yet, her heart followed Eisheth, as if her sister had a gravitational pull.

"Bridget?" Nuriel watched her with concern.

She chewed her lip then blurted, "Do you think I'm overprotective?"

The way his expression twisted in discomfort made her regret her words. He fished around in his pocket for his pack of cigarettes.

"It's okay, forget I said anything."

Nuriel flipped the top of the pack open and closed. "You are someone who deeply loves people you're close to and wants what is best for them."

She frowned, hearing the unspoken word in his tone. "But?"

He exhaled. "But the people you love are their own individuals. You cannot protect them from every bad experience this world offers up, and you cannot force them to take the path you've laid out for them. They have their own journey to walk."

Her throat tightened, and she looked down at the notebook in her lap. "What if they get hurt?"

"They will," Nuriel said with such surety it sent a pang of fear through her. "And when they do, they need the freedom to decide how they will face the hurt. As someone who cares about them, all you can do is be there when they ask for your support."

Bridget shook her head. "So, I should shut up and let Dahlia get hurt?"

"No one wants you to shut up, Bridget." Nuriel smiled. "I think we're far better off having your insights."

"Then what? How do I help the people I love without harming them?"

Nuriel tapped a cigarette free. "Trust. That's the key."

She wanted to blurt out that she *did* trust Dahlia but held the words back. She was the big sister, the second mom. Even when Dahlia had left for college, Bridget weighed in on every detail of her life. Sadness tightened her chest. No wonder Dahlia's texts had grown less frequent. Who wanted someone breathing down their neck all the time?

Trust. That's what Bridget was learning. Maybe learning poorly, since her choices kept getting everyone in trouble. But going back to her old ways would only create resentment. The difficulty was she didn't know how to do anything else.

"How do I show James trust? He *can't* make decisions for himself right now."

With a sigh, Nuriel lit his cigarette. "I know. And I feel terrible. We never should have used a symbol we didn't understand. I should have put a stop to it."

Bridget laughed quietly. "Are we going to take turns blaming ourselves? I participated, too. I was the ringleader."

"Perhaps we can find a solution together. Getting a newcomer's perspective on Ret's writings couldn't hurt. Here." He bent down and reached into his messenger bag, pulling out a second tome. It hit the kitchen table with a loud thud.

"How many of these did Ret have?" Bridget asked in surprise, eyeing the thick binding. Going through one could take all day.

Nuriel nudged the book toward her. "Enough to keep us busy. These are the ones he's already translated."

Bridget set her plate aside, opening the book. It was a journal. Gray ink stains marred the yellowing pages, but some of the writing looked quite fresh. Ret's handwriting was filled with cursive flourishes that never lost their tidiness. She flipped to a random page.

Grigori renaming conventions are a peculiar but consistent phenomenon. Long before current technology allowed us to compare experiences across the globe, nearly all Grigori have felt the urge to craft a new name for themselves. Sources of inspiration have included religions and mythologies, folklore, and even regions and cultures (such as in the case of the author's friend, Gaul). It stands to reason that, as our human selves fall away, our fundamental interior change craves recognition through—

Bridget turned the page. The last thing she wanted was another reminder of Dahlia's apparently inevitable changes.

She smoothed her hands over the paper. It would be okay. Change was inevitable with the passage of time, for humans and Grigori both. It didn't mean they'd stop loving each other.

A rumble swept through the house.

Bridget gripped the edge of the table. Nuriel half stood, eyeing the knife as it clattered against the cutting board. Overhead, a hanging plant swung precariously, dropping dirt.

It was over before Bridget could duck for cover. Heart in her throat, she looked over at Nuriel. "Are you okay?"

He nodded, then raised his voice. "Viri?"

"I'm alright." Viri joined them in the kitchen, looking rattled. "We should move James onto Ret's bed, though. He nearly threw himself off the couch."

"I'll help you move him." Nuriel pushed his chair in and put out his cigarette in a nearby ashtray.

"I can keep reading." The earthquake had left her hands sweaty and her veins buzzing with nerves. Bridget lifted her water glass to her mouth and drank the full cup. Steadying herself, she pulled the book closer. She flipped back to the beginning of the book. The first chapter was called "Creation."

While my intent is for this record to contain the story of all Grigori, it's impossible to separate it from my own. Therefore, as the author of this history, I will begin with my beginning. True, there are Grigori older than me, but they speak little of the time before the War, or our true reasons for arriving here in the first place. I have asked Notos, my creator, many times over the years, and he remains evasive. So, I will relay what I remember, and what I have learned during my long years in this world.

A pang of sorrow passed through Bridget. Ret wrote much the way he'd spoken—both thoughtful and academic. She pressed her fingertip against the page, dragging it below the line she was reading to hold her place.

My Grigori life began near the end of the war. Those early days, my first, were confusing, but Notos was an earnest mentor. At the time there were three of us, all younglings, all created to serve.

Back then, the partnership that held our Gateway open still stood strong, and our powers seemed limitless. Even now, I miss the sensation of magic flowing freely between the worlds. At my age, it is not difficult to call upon my abilities, but a resistance still exists that did not in those first few months.

Bridget paused. She'd been told Grigori abilities were always weak when they were young, but apparently that hadn't always been the case. The idea left her skin prickling. She was lucky Dahlia didn't have the degree of power Ret was writing about.

She skipped forward a few pages. As interesting as she found Ret's origin story, she was looking for information about the tattoos. She skimmed, searching until the word jumped out at her, then backing up a few paragraphs.

It's difficult to convey the destruction of that final day. The Key abandoned us, and the Gateway failed. And when it fell, so did almost every Grigori. It's a betrayal still reverberating through our communities today, centuries later.

In the end, only a handful of us remained. My healing did nothing to revive the fallen. Furthermore, my powers had been stifled dramatically. I could barely heal scrapes and bruises. When the Gateway was destroyed, so was the extent of my abilities.

We didn't understand why our lives had been spared until Notos explained the tattoos.

Others had been skeptical about their effect, but Notos had insisted on marking his cohort and himself with a new type of symbol, derived from our base names. A contract, reiterating and cementing our right to inhabit the bodies we possessed.

Tannin, Eris, and I were among only a few dozen survivors of a community that had once numbered in the thousands and stretched across continents. And Notos, of course.

A few centuries later, we discovered we could bring back our companions a few at a time, and no faster, for reasons I didn't fully understand back then. We used the few preserved naming symbols, saved in buried caches around the world. Little by little, Artists—Grigori with an affinity for symbology—rebuilt what they could.

Bridget paused, tapping her finger against the page. When she'd first learned how Grigori were made, Gaul had explained Earth like a ship at sea. Each tattoo formed a small hole, allowing Grigori magic to seep in. Too many holes, and the ship risked sinking.

But what if Earth and the Grigori world were less like a ship and the infinite sea, and more like two rooms, side by side? Dahlia had told her each symbol was more than a contract—it was a key. That's why it needed to be perfect. Just as a poorly constructed metal key would fail to open a lock, an imperfect symbol couldn't carve a pathway between worlds.

Would a more powerful design open a bigger door,

then?

She skimmed back over Ret's words. *The moment the Gateway fell...*

"Holy shit." Bridget sat up straighter and shouted, "Nuriel?"

"Coming!" His footsteps thudded down the hallway. He arrived with Viri behind him. "What is it? Are you alright?"

Her breath felt thin. "James' symbol is the Key."

Confusion puckered his brow. "I suppose they all are, in a way."

Viri looked between them. "But that's not what she means, is it?"

"Not *a* key. *The* Key." Bridget pointed at the book. "Ret told Dahlia and me about a Gateway that used to link our two worlds. He said it was destroyed in the war. But what if it wasn't destroyed? What if it was *locked*?"

Nuriel looked down at the open book. "What do you mean?"

"What if James' symbol is more elaborate because it's designed to allow more Grigori to come here?"

Nuriel's eyes raked across the page. He seemed to be weighing her words with Ret's history. When he looked up at her, fear laced through his expression. "That's quite a leap. The Gateway has been gone for millennia."

"You said it yourself: James' symbol is *more* than a normal naming one. And remember what Dahlia said earlier, about his powers feeling so strong?"

Viri eyed his countertop, where the knife had danced off the cutting board during the earthquake. "Could that be why these tremors are happening?"

Nuriel didn't look convinced. He tapped the pages of Ret's book. "I've never read anything about rampant earthquakes when the Gateway was open. But there's certainly *something* unusual about the symbol." He eyed Bridget. "If you're right, it would change everything."

Bridget's hands felt cold, and she clasped them tightly. "Could we help him?"

"Maybe." Nuriel flipped forward a few pages in the book, still frowning. "But if word gets out about this theory, we may have bigger problems."

"What do you mean?"

He lifted his gaze to meet hers. "If James could actually reopen the Gateway, he will become the most valuable, sought-after person on the planet. Tannin will be after him. Notos. So many more."

Bridget shoved her chair back and stood. "I need to tell Dahlia."

She left them at the table, hurrying out of the kitchen into the backyard. Wind ruffled her hair, but no birds sang. It was too still. She shouted, "Dahlia? Eisheth?"

"Up here!" The detective's voice came from the front yard.

Bridget jogged along the garden path to where Eisheth prowled the nearly empty parking area, all coiled tension.

Dread tightened her muscles as she approached. "Where's Nuriel's car? Where are Dahlia and Danel?"

"They're gone."

THIRTY-ONE

Golden light pooled into the lines under Dahlia's hand. It bled through the swoops, accentuating every delicate twist of the design. The wall turned vaporous under her fingers, and she let her hand slide through. It enveloped her in welcoming warmth.

This was it. Her chance to face Tannin on her own terms. Beneath her fear lurked the hot, angry fire she'd nursed for weeks now. She stepped into the portal.

Inside, the light was bright white. She squinted against it, flinching as a bolt of black lightning streaked across her vision. The air was heavy and thick. It brought with it a high-pitched swarming hum.

From the brightness, figures loomed into view, their forms strange and inhuman. She could feel eyes on her. They whispered in a low hum of voices, speaking no language Dahlia knew, yet could understand. *Sibling,* they sang. *Little sibling, will you kill again?*

She shuddered and looked away from the figures, but that didn't stop the magnitude of their abilities from pressing in on her. The last time she'd gone through the portal she'd felt it as a physical, smothering weight. Now she recognized it for what it was—raw Grigori power, in a thousand forms, swirling around her. It felt both intangible and solid, chaotic and perfectly predictable. She itched to grab it, but she held back. Who knew what touching a live wire would do to her?

It didn't take long before golden threads of light began to split the white sky. Interspersed with flashes of black lightning, the light formed a tunnel that blotted out everything else. The murmur of voices faded, leaving only the portal's electric hum.

An unseen force pushed between her shoulder blades. She fell forward and into the web of light.

Her feet hit solid ground, and she threw her arms out for stability. Spots danced in her vision, clearing as she blinked. The smell of disinfectant and metal hit her. She didn't need to see well to know she'd landed in the basement of Tannin's collection. Every fiber of her being remembered this place.

Danel fell through behind her, and she steadied him. As he regained his footing, the golden light faded out. He looked around, uncharacteristically grim. "So good to be back here."

They were in a long, narrow room with two doors and a single metal table. Her breath caught as she saw it was occupied by a body. It was a woman, laying face down, head turned away. A sheet covered her from the torso down, and her bare, unmoving back was exposed.

Grim curiosity drove her forward, toward the high slab of metal. As she neared, she saw clear signs of an Artist at work. The tool cabinet had sheafs of papers on top of it, weighed down by a book. Inks and needles were spread out on a small tray, and looked to have been abandoned mid-session.

All of that was horrifying, but what made Dahlia freeze were the tattoos.

They spread across the woman's back in a series of half-finished attempts—so close together, Dahlia could hardly see where one ended and another began. Even the woman's arms were covered. In fact, nearly the only piece of her skin not tattooed was a pale, open spot where a naming symbol belonged.

"Shit." Danel had come to a stop right behind her. "What is this?"

Dahlia's throat felt raw as she whispered a response. "Cyrie." Tannin's new Artist, hard at work trying to decode the secrets of the sketchbook.

With an indignant huff, Danel leaned over the body. "What the hell was she doing?"

She swallowed. "Practicing."

Hadn't she joked about this only a week ago, with Bridget? She remembered her sister's horror and felt horrible guilt swell up.

The emotion was followed swiftly by rage.

Cyrie wouldn't be doing this if it weren't for Tannin.

This poor woman, along with all the other bodies hidden away, were nothing more than assets to him. Tools. *Things.*

This place was where Tannin collected his hopes, his projects. The door to her left, she knew, led to a freezer where more bodies were stored. More experiments with Grigori symbols. Her fingers itched to find the circuit breaker and turn off the power, letting his insurance thaw and decay.

It would feel good to destroy his work. To render his projects useless.

But no. The people he'd collected deserved better, and Dahlia's revenge was more personal. Tannin himself needed to suffer.

With effort, she set the temptation aside. Instead, she forced herself to approach the table. "Danel, help me."

He didn't protest, looking almost as perturbed as her. Together, they wrapped the woman more securely in the sheet. Then they gently hefted her off the table, carrying her to the freezer. Inside, at least a dozen occupied body bags lay awaiting their turn with Cyrie. They laid the woman down and backed out of the freezer. They closed the door tightly and Dahlia gulped for air. She felt lightheaded, panic and fury fighting for dominance.

"Hey." Danel rested a hand on her shoulder, and she looked up at him.

His fingers squeezed. For once, there was no humor in his eyes. She saw her own anger reflected. "He'll deserve everything he gets."

She felt buoyed by his reaction. Taking another

breath, slower this time, she straightened.

"Come on." She beckoned for Danel to follow her to the second door. Lights flickered on when she swung it open, illuminating rows of carefully curated objects. Polished floors, unadorned white walls, climate controlled. The objects spanned from books and weapons to vases and jewelry. The only commonality was that each item in the collection was marked with a spiraling symbol, imbuing it with a special power or history connected to the Grigori people. Her people.

She'd spent months in this place, treated with no more humanity than any of the carefully displayed artifacts. Dahlia pressed a hand against her thumping heart. Her vision wavered, starting to tunnel.

"Dahlia?"

"I'm okay." Her voice sounded far away. She leaned against the doorframe to steady the panic. She was not here to be captured again. She was not here to cower or be a pawn, no matter how much her chest constricted.

She needed a distraction.

"Tell me about your niece. Morgan, right?"

By the way Danel pulled his hand away, the question must have taken him by surprise. He took one look at her, though, and acquiesced. "She's a musician—a damned good one. I think she plays three instruments. Maybe four? The flute is her best."

"Does she know what you are?"

He paused. "I've made the mistake of letting other relatives into our world. Telling Morgan's grandfather was a particularly terrible choice. He was a nightmare to deal with."

Her breath was steadying. "Why? Did he get into trouble?"

Danel huffed a laugh. "Not the kind you're thinking. He tried to submit our story to the newspapers. Wound up landing a full-time tabloid job. Stamping the stories out kept Gaul busy for years."

Danel's words conjured an image of a blond, mustached man smoking a pipe and churning out fantastical stories that were secretly true.

"So, you haven't told Morgan."

He looked her over. "No."

Dahlia's panic had finally dropped to a simmer, so she let the topic drop. Brushing past Danel, Dahlia entered the room that had been her prison. She didn't bother to hide herself as she walked past shelves and cabinets. Let Tannin see her.

She stayed to the right, not trusting herself to keep it together if she so much as glanced at the cage along the left-side wall. She did, however, pause and look up at the unblinking red light on the camera mounted above it. Was anyone watching? She lifted her chin, meeting the lens with a defiant stare. Then she strode to a metal door along the wall, holding it open for Danel.

They'd entered an enclosed, marble stairwell. At the top, she paused in front of a second, formidable-looking metal door. She grabbed the handle and pulled, but it didn't move.

"It's locked with a keypad," Danel said.

Dahlia gestured to the door. "Be my guest."

He shook his head. "I'm flattered, but I can't pick a lock like that. It's too high-tech."

"Then what, we camp out here until he opens the door?"

"Maybe. We could—" Danel paused as a low rumble shook the building. Dahlia scrambled to grab the handrail, the stairs trembling beneath her feet. They waited in tense silence until the shaking faded away.

"Quite the global catastrophe we caused," Danel said. "We'd better hurry."

Dahlia set her hand on the lock. "Metal comes from the earth, right?" Digital or not, the inner workings still relied on a manual catch. If she could knock it out of place...

He eyed her. "Yeah, but I don't have my powers."

She shook her head. "Let me try." She reached for the humming of his earth ability. It resisted her, slipping away. Frowning, she closed her eyes, widened her stance, and tried again.

Carefully, she coaxed the power away from Danel. It was sluggish, but obedient. She nudged it toward the metal inside the lock. The entire door rattled, and then a *snap* sounded.

Dahlia beamed as she pulled her hand away. Finally, something was going right.

He made a sour face. "So, you can use my abilities, but I can't. Great. Wonderful. I'm thrilled."

"Stay close in case I need them again." Dahlia opened the door; it swung silently on oiled hinges.

They entered a lobby. It had high ceilings, and every

surface gleamed with polished marble. Or carved marble. Or inlaid marble. With the leather couches and art deco grates, it almost looked like—

"A very fancy, very large bank," Danel said. "One he's converted. It's arranged around a square hallway, but the fastest route to his office is over there." He indicated with a tilt of his head.

It was strange, standing in this space she'd never been allowed to enter. While she'd paced in a cage downstairs, Tannin was surrounded by symbols of luxury and power. A cluster of power hummed nearby, centered in the direction Danel had indicated.

Gathering her courage, she gestured for him to lead the way. Her heart hammered in her throat, and she searched for the anger that had driven her back to this horrid place. It would fuel her far more than fear. Even so, she found her earlier bravado faltering.

Danel led her down the hallway, footsteps almost inaudible. Doors lined both sides, most closed tight. The ones that were open revealed sparse offices, many filled with boxes—an extension of his collection, no doubt.

"Here," said Danel in a hush. He stopped next to one of the closed doors, near the end of the hallway. Light spilled out from underneath, along with the quiet murmur of voices.

Inching forward, Dahlia tilted her head toward the door. She recognized Tannin's low timbre at once, and she shuddered in response. It was followed by a sharp, high-pitched laugh.

"Cyrie?" Dahlia guessed, inching closer.

Beside her, Danel had stiffened. He shook his head. *Eris,* he mouthed.

Dahlia frowned and returned to listening. Gaul's familiar voice joined the conversation; she strained to make out his words.

"—get back to our negotiations."

Tannin responded with a scoff. "You have no leverage."

"I don't want to cause more suffering."

Eris spoke. "Such a noble, loyal creature you are, Gaul. It will be a pleasure to put you down." Her voice was sing-songy.

Danel went pale, giving Dahlia a nod. Definitely her.

"No one needs to be put down. Ret's death is enough. Let us set this behind us."

Tannin's voice turned sharp and business-like. "As much as I would prefer to move on to more important projects, I also suffered losses."

Gaul huffed. "Responding to Grigori death with more Grigori death doesn't undermine your so-called cause?"

"It pained me to return Ret to our world. As it will pain me to do the same with you."

"Speak for yourself." Eris giggled.

Gaul's response was laced in fury. "How dare you. Ret was part of your cohort. You were born together, trained together. As close to siblings as Grigori can be. Do you have no respect?"

"Ret was a sanctimonious fool." Eris' own response turned sharper. "He's spent the better part of a millennium hiding."

"His death had nothing to do with justice, did it? You just wanted him out of the way."

"What's the phrase? Two birds, one stone?"

Tannin's voice re-entered the conversation. "Three birds now, it would seem. I do appreciate you offering yourself up so freely, Gaul."

Gaul's ability burst to life, followed by a sharp crack. "I came here to negotiate, but I will defend myself, if necessary."

A flare of unfamiliar power went up in Dahlia's awareness. The hallway's temperature dipped, and ice fractals radiated out from under the door. "Oh, I think it will be."

Dahlia's stomach churned. She turned to Danel, whispering. "Last chance to back out."

He gave her the flicker of a smile. "What, just because I can't run as fast as usual? Come on. I wouldn't miss their reaction for the world."

Surprisingly comforted by his presence, Dahlia straightened and grasped the doorknob. She could do this. She *had* to do this. For Ret and for the many others Tannin had hurt. For herself.

She turned the icy knob and opened the door.

Across the room, directly aligned with the doorway, was Tannin. He stood behind a sturdy desk, hands flat on the rich, polished wood.

"Let Gaul go. I'm here to take you up on your offer."

THIRTY-TWO

Bridget raced back inside Viri's house with Eisheth, heart in her throat.

Nuriel met them inside the foyer. "What's going on?"

"They followed Gaul," Eisheth said.

Bridget didn't stop to answer any other questions. She made a beeline for the living room, where Dahlia's backpack had been. The floor was empty. Panic leapt into her throat. She turned back into the hall and took the stairs two at a time.

Gasping, she burst into their shared bedroom. It was silent and empty, the bed still neatly made.

Dahlia really was gone.

Bridget touched the foot of the bed, taking in a steadying breath. *Okay. Think. Why wouldn't she tell you?*

Her sister had gone with Danel, and it wasn't like she

cared about keeping him safe. Dahlia must want to protect Bridget. Keep her from following.

But it was still foolhardy. What would Dahlia and Danel be able to do against Tannin? It was a losing battle.

Swallowing back the billowing dread, Bridget turned back into the hallway. Her hands felt numb as she returned downstairs. Viri had joined Eisheth and Nuriel in the foyer, and the three of them looked up at her in unison.

"We have to—"

"Go after them," Eisheth finished. "We know."

Bridget bit her lip, a grateful sound escaping her throat.

Viri looked unsettled as he ran a hand through his dark hair. "We could disrupt Gaul's plans if we barge in."

She shook her head. "Forget Gaul's plans. As soon as Tannin realizes Dahlia is there, he won't care about negotiating with him."

Nuriel spread his palms. "Remember, Dahlia wouldn't have gone without some sort of plan of her own."

Bridget bristled, fingers curling into fists. Her conversation with Nuriel was still fresh. Her question— *Am I too overprotective?* She hadn't expected to be tested so quickly. But was it overprotective to stop someone from walking into clear danger?

Yes, she needed to trust Dahlia. But not with this.

"Whatever her plan is, she hasn't had time to fully think it through. She'll need backup against someone like Tannin."

A crease between Nuriel's brows deepened. "You're assuming she is rushing into a fight."

Bridget thought back to Dahlia's recent words. While

on the boat she'd vacillated between scared and angry. At the time, Bridget had brushed it aside as trauma alone. But thinking back, the darkness in Dahlia's eyes chilled Bridget. "She's running toward an execution."

Eisheth turned to Viri. "So, how do we follow? There has to be a new portal. I can't imagine everyone is traveling by airplane."

"Yes." Viri sounded reluctant, as if he wasn't quite sure how involved he wanted to get.

"Then we find it." Bridget looked around, as if the portal might appear on the wall in front of them. Then an idea struck her. "The beacon."

The detective's eyes brightened. "Does Dahlia have one?"

"It was in her backpack, and I think she took it with her. Viri, where's its match?"

"In the library. One moment." Viri swept from the room, a sense of unease following him.

Bridget watched his departure. "He doesn't like this."

"I don't like it either, Bridget," Nuriel said. "First Gaul, then Dahlia and Danel. Now us. This feels like a trap that keeps pulling more of us in."

"You're welcome to stay behind."

Nuriel didn't respond, instead looking away. The silence that stretched between the trio didn't bother Bridget. Let them stew; she needed to plan. If Dahlia had traveled by portal, she'd probably emerged in Tannin's basement. What would Dahlia do if she truly wanted to hurt Tannin—not just defeat him, but destroy him?

"Here." Viri returned, the coaster-sized piece of stone held in one hand. He offered it to Bridget, who turned it over in her palm. The symbol was dark and the stone was cool.

"How do I turn it on?"

"Hold your fingers against it."

She did. After a few seconds, golden light pulsed outward, letting off a slow glow. She imagined its twin, miles away, also pulsing.

"Then what?" Eisheth asked, looking down at it.

Viri said, "It should seek out the shortest distance between itself and its match. If there's a portal, it will lead you there."

A wordless cry echoed from the hallway, quiet and plaintive. James sounded as if he were locked in a nightmare, trying and failing to surface. Bridget ached to help. Going after Dahlia meant leaving James behind— and just after they'd begun unlocking the secrets of his symbol.

But staying with James meant abandoning her sister to her own nightmares.

Viri followed her gaze. "I'll stay here and keep James comfortable."

Part of Bridget had expected more of a fight. Gaul would have ordered her to stay behind, where she couldn't interfere or weaken their position. Instead, Viri offered help.

"Thank you," Bridget said. "Will you keep looking through Ret's books? See if there's anything in there about how to fix this?"

Viri nodded, though he looked troubled. "I'll do my best."

Nuriel sighed then squared his shoulders. "I'll go with you. But Bridget... don't be surprised if Dahlia isn't happy to see us."

It didn't matter if Dahlia was happy about it or not. Having her sister annoyed with her was better than seeing her killed.

"Be careful, my friends." Viri slipped into Ret's former room, where James was resting.

The three of them hurried outside, piling into Viri's sedan with Nuriel at the wheel. The beacon sat on Bridget's lap. She toyed with it, worried she wouldn't be able to tell when the beacon's pulsing changed. She watched it shimmer brightly, then go dim again, counting the seconds between each flare of light. They pulled out of the driveway and headed toward the city, following the most likely path Gaul had taken.

THIRTY-THREE

Four sets of eyes turned to Dahlia. Her gaze locked with Tannin's first. He stood directly across from her, behind a heavy mahogany desk. Cyrie stood to the side, looking uneasy. Dahlia hadn't counted on her being there, too.

Two chairs sat across from Tannin's desk. Gaul stood beside one, shock written across his expression. He lowered his hand, which had been raised in a fist. A freshly crumbling scar cut through the floor of the well-appointed office.

Beside him was the only unfamiliar person—Eris. She looked up at Dahlia with frank curiosity, legs swinging as they dangled from her chair. Long, dark curls cascaded over her shoulders, framing a youthful, heart-shaped face with a smattering of freckles. She wore jeans, a red t-shirt, and scuffed-up sneakers.

A child.

In her hand, she twirled an icicle with a wicked tip. "What offer?"

Tannin's cufflinks caught the light as he folded his arms. "In exchange for her friends' lives, I offered to accept Dahlia back into my service."

Dahlia forced herself to stand tall. She couldn't let him see her fear. Their abilities pressed in on her, each of them possessing centuries of power beyond her own. She focused on Gaul's pestilence, preparing to grab it as soon as she managed to get close to Tannin.

Eris' voice pitched upward incredulously. "Why would you want an infant Grigori at your side?"

Cyrie spoke up. "She's not just any young Grigori. She's a mimic."

Eris' attention shot back to Dahlia, far more interested now. "A mimic! You've been holding out on me, Tannin."

"He does that," Danel said, stepping up behind Dahlia.

Eris' lip curled. "Danel. How charming."

The tension in the room shifted as he leaned against the doorframe, wearing a crooked smile. The tension in his back belied his fear. Still, his voice was light as he spoke. "Am I missing a party?"

Gaul closed his eyes, hands clenching.

Tannin eyed Danel with disdain. "I hope you're not expecting to work together again."

"Not with you," Danel said. "I'm only here to make sure you honor your agreement with Dahlia."

Eris barked a laugh. "Honoring agreements. That's rich, coming from you."

It was disconcerting, watching her. She was every bit

as ancient as Tannin, but she looked no older than ten.

Tannin gestured to a chair across from his desk. "Please take a seat. I will explain the contract."

Danel gave a low laugh. "You haven't even knocked her out first. I'm impressed by your hospitality."

"Dahlia." Gaul turned to her, eyes intense. "Reconsider. I can handle this."

She didn't answer. Instead, she walked forward, legs wooden. Unshouldering her backpack, she let it rest against the chair. "I'd prefer to stand."

"Suit yourself. I have a standard contract for my employees." He opened a drawer and brought out a plain white folder. He set it on the desk and opened it with a manicured hand. Inside were two pieces of paper: a simple contract written in plain English and a symbol that, theoretically, stated the same stipulations.

"Feel free to review it." Tannin glanced at Cyrie, who was peering at the paper. "I will, of course, ask my Artist to make additional adjustments to ensure your loyalty."

"My loyalty." The words were bitter, and she stiffened to hide a shudder. Eris, on the other hand, heaved a bored sigh.

Tannin carried on. "There's a fairly short term, one hundred years with the option to renew. You'll be provided with living quarters, food, and a generous salary. And, of course, in return, your sister's crimes will be forgotten."

The rapid flutter of her heart seemed capable of drowning out the whole world. All eyes were on her. It was crowded—too crowded—but she wouldn't find a better opportunity. She'd sent herself into the heart of danger, and she needed to make her move.

Now.

"What's this part mean?" Dahlia asked, pointing at a swooping line.

He leaned in. "I'm afraid Cyrie will need to explain the—"

She grasped for Danel's speed, pushing through the membrane of resistance around his trapped abilities. Tannin's voice pitched lower, like a video in slow motion. She snatched his hand, then shifted her focus to seizing Gaul's power.

She shoved illness and decay into Tannin, as forcibly as she could. At the same time, her hold on Danel's speed faltered.

Time stuttered back to normal. Tannin hissed and yanked his hand back. She tried to keep her grip, but a blast of icy air slammed into her, knocking her into the chair.

Eris was on her feet, eyes bright. "That was a cute trick."

An acrid, rotten taste filled her mouth as Tannin drew himself up. His hand was covered in a red rash, the skin blistering and flaking. "That was extraordinarily unwise."

Gaul's horrified eyes were on Tannin's hand. "For once, I agree. I came here to negotiate."

Dahlia's voice was shrill. "How'd that work out for Ret?"

Inky darkness billowed behind Tannin. "Negotiations are over. Eris? Help me escort these traitors out."

An eager grin spread across the girl's face. "With pleasure." The temperature plummeted and ice crystals crackled along the walls.

Cyrie shrunk into the corner. "Wait!"

Tannin ignored her. Black smoke shot toward Dahlia, but Gaul leapt in front of her. The blast knocked him into the wall, and he fell to the floor with a grunt of pain.

Dahlia scrambled back, searching for an ability to grasp. But they were a jumbled knot, and her adrenaline was screaming.

Climbing to his feet, Gaul stretched out a hand. A boom filled the space, the floor ripping upward.

"Sir?" Cyrie cut in. Dahlia glanced over. Still in her corner, electricity crackled over her skin, but she didn't attack. She seemed nervous in these close quarters.

Gaul pulled the stone toward him, gathering it close, and then—

It froze. Ice crystallized around the rock, and it fell to the ground. Eris flicked her hand toward Gaul, and he shivered violently, frost crusting in his hair. Ice crawled up his legs, wound around his arms. Like an exoskeleton, it forced him to walk backward through the door.

Dahlia scrambled for the threads of Danel's ability. Speed could help her again. She grabbed at it, but with so many others flaring their powers she couldn't—

A wall of thick ash and brimstone slammed into her, knocking her back to the ground. It crawled up her body like burning vines.

The smoke hoisted her and Danel off the ground, binding tightly. She writhed, trying to break free, but she didn't have any leverage.

A low growl emanated from Gaul. The ground beneath him shuddered. A fissure snapped up through the ice, and he broke free with a snarl. Stalking back into the room, he lifted a hand to attack.

"Don't take another step," Tannin said, eyes on Gaul.

Gaul halted, but he didn't lower his arms. "Release them."

With a twitch of Tannin's finger, the smoke wrapped around Danel's forearm. It tugged sharply, and a snap rung out. He let out an anguished cry.

"Back into the room directly across the hall." The length of thick soot leisurely made its way to Danel's other arm. "Or I'll break both of your protégés, piece by piece."

Cyrie spoke up. "Sir, please reconsider. They may still be useful. The mimic especially."

He ignored her. "Don't wear my patience further, Gaul. You know we're more powerful than you."

Eris came to stand beside Tannin. She had formed another icicle and tossed it casually from hand to hand.

Dahlia grimaced, tears flowing down her cheeks as embers burned her skin. Her vision was tunneling.

"Don't listen to him," she tried to say. But the word caught in her throat, coming out as a strangled sound of pain. She wanted to tell Gaul to fight, to destroy, to hurt Tannin as much as possible. But instead, he lowered his hands.

His eyes on Tannin, Gaul walked backward, into the hallway and through the open door.

A moment later Dahlia flew, tossed through the hall like a ragdoll.

She hit the floor hard, rolling a few feet into the next room. She heard a grunt as Danel was thrown in behind her. Groaning, she propped herself up. Beside her, Danel made a quiet whining sound, holding his broken arm against his chest.

Tannin stood in the doorway, the black of his suit almost indistinguishable from the dark, tumultuous mass of darkness behind him. The smell of sulfur was so strong Dahlia gagged. He shook his head, eyes on her. "A shame. You could have done great things for our people."

A growl ripped through her. The hot fury that had simmered for months burst into flames. His lies pressed on her—lies he himself probably believed. In his world, Grigori restoration would *always* mean the subjugation of those who didn't obey.

She grabbed Danel's power and rushed him.

An explosion of bright light knocked her off balance. A shock jolted through her. She stumbled back, Danel's speed wisping away as she blinked against the retina burn. When her vision cleared, a crackling web of electricity stretched across the open doorframe. Standing on the other side, Tannin watched with disappointment. His smoke crawled back toward him, dissipating around his feet. The smell of rotten eggs lingered.

Dahlia blinked, trying to banish the spots. "What—"

"I've upgraded my security measures. I do hate that you've been locked away again, but Cyrie is right. You may prove useful in other ways."

Tannin turned and strode back into his office, leaving her behind a fresh set of bars.

THIRTY-FOUR

As they turned onto the freeway and pointed the car north, the beacon's light flickered, then sped up.

Bridget looked up. "It's working. We're going the right way."

From there, it was a game of hot and cold, following its mute directions like a map-less GPS. She hoped James would stay safe, and Viri could find a solution buried in Ret's histories.

The possibilities about the symbol were a punch to the gut. All that work, all that hope, and they may have chosen the wrong sketch entirely. If the powers it imbued *did* unlock the path between worlds, what would it mean for James? Could he still learn how to harness the ability? Could he ever wake up?

She had more questions than ever, but right now, she had to put her trust in Viri to protect him. She simply couldn't be two places at once.

Eventually, the beacon led them off the highway and to the cracked parking lot of an abandoned service station. Two cars sat there, including Gaul's unmistakable cherry red Mustang and Nuriel's more practical sedan, adorned with its French flag bumper sticker. Nuriel pulled up beside his car and they all piled out.

Some small piece of Bridget had hoped to see Dahlia waiting for them. But of course, the cars were empty, and no one was hanging around the outside of the building.

Eisheth placed a hand on the hood of the Mustang. "Cold. It's been parked for a while."

As they strode up to the building, Bridget added, "Okay, we need a plan."

Eisheth's eyebrows shot up. "Miss Keene, are you ill?"

"We don't have time for it to be a *good* plan."

Nuriel gave a small smile but was then back to business. "What did you have in mind?"

Neither Eisheth nor Nuriel had been to Tannin's collection before, but the memory of the place was seared into her mind. "We'll come out in a small room where the tattoo supplies are. Behind that is his collection. That's all in the basement, though. Based on everything Dahlia has told me, Tannin spends most of his time upstairs."

"So, we'll have the benefit of surprise," Eisheth said. Their shoes crunched over broken glass and pavement.

"Sort of. There's at least one security camera."

Nuriel said, "We'll need you to direct us, but Bridget, stay behind Eisheth and me. We can protect you."

Bridget bristled. "I'm not coming along to be a liability. Tannin has useful items in his collection. I bet I can find the sword James used." During the battle that had ultimately killed him, the sword had left wounds rapidly decaying. If he could wield such a weapon, so could she.

Eisheth cut in as they approached the gas station, "Try not to get far from us. Our first goal is to get a sense of the situation." She paused in front, turning to face them. "Wait here."

Eisheth disappeared into the building, leaving Bridget and Nuriel to hover near the entrance.

"You're sure about this?" Nuriel's eyes were on her.

Bridget nodded firmly, fingers tight on the beacon. "Positive."

A tense minute later, the door squealed open and Eisheth reemerged.

"All clear. The portal is in there."

They filed inside, past discarded trash and empty shelves to a windowless bathroom. In the dim, dusty light, Bridget spotted the unmistakable graffiti. Seeing it there, painted on the grimy wall, made her feel lightheaded. It took her back to the abandoned building where she'd first seen an identical symbol with James. He'd been thrilled by the discovery.

She touched the paint. A golden glow spread from beneath her hand, too beautiful for the ramshackle space. It gave a humming, buzzing sound, as if alive. She pulled away and it darkened once more.

"I'll go first," Nuriel said.

She gestured for both of them to go ahead and took up the rear, letting the portal's light surround her.

The white, thick air clung to her skin like mist with substance and form. In front of her, two figures created a rippling wake. One was composed of brilliant flame, the other a shimmery liquid. Eisheth and Nuriel.

Bridget held the air in her lungs, closing her eyes against the crawling sensation of otherworldly beings watching them. She focused on the cool, solid feeling of the beacon in her hands. It was a small thing—but it contained hope that they could get everyone out of this situation in one piece. This time, when Dahlia needed her, she'd be there right away.

Gravity returned and Bridget pitched forward. She hit the ground feet first and windmilled her arms to keep from falling.

Eisheth took her arm to steady her. "Thanks." A thread of nausea crept through her as she looked around. "That's where he keeps the bodies." She gestured to the closed door, then turned her gaze down to the polished floor. "And this is where James died."

They were quiet a moment, but Eisheth spoke first, voice surprisingly gentle. "Come on."

Bridget steeled herself. The beacon was flashing faster than ever. She led them toward the collection door and eased it open.

The temperature plummeted. Goosebumps raced up Bridget's arms and her stomach dropped. She caught a glimpse of the brightly lit cabinets, but her attention was pulled to the person standing in front of them.

A dozen feet away, a young girl leaned against one of the clear cabinets. Her lips quirked into a sharp smile when she caught Bridget's eye, breaking any illusion of innocence.

Bridget took an involuntary step back, gaping as the girl held up the beacon's match. It pulsed frantically.

"Hello, there. Looking for this?"

THIRTY-FIVE

A deep chill sent Bridget's skin prickling. White puffs of air accompanied her exhales, obscuring the cabinetry of Tannin's collection.

Eisheth grabbed Bridget's arm, pulling her back. She obliged, too stunned to protest as the detective and Nuriel stepped in front of her.

The girl was short, compact, and straight-backed. She regarded them with interest. "Tannin sure is getting a lot of visitors today."

The beacon's match strobed in the stranger's grasp. At her feet, Dahlia's backpack rested. Bridget's breath caught.

"Eris." Eisheth moved more firmly in front of Bridget. "What are you doing here?"

The girl looked amused. "Why, helping my old friend

balance the scales of justice." Her eyes raked over the detective. "You must be Eisheth. Danel has told me so much about you."

Bridget's stomach roiled. "Where's my sister?"

Instead of responding, Eris gave Bridget an appraising once-over and continued to address Eisheth. "You brought the human. That saves us some time."

A shiver crept through Bridget. "Where did you get that backpack?" Her voice was miraculously steady.

"Dahlia left it for me. Don't worry, she's safely tucked away."

This was the person Ret had thought to trust? To help advocate for them?

Nuriel must have been having the same thought. "Eris, we're here to talk, not fight. We want our friends back. You've already taken Ret from us."

A flicker of flames caught Bridget's eye. They licked Eisheth's fingers greedily. The detective didn't seem to have much interest in talking, but she held herself back.

Eris blew out a loud sigh. "All I hear about is Ret. You would think that overly sympathetic fool was actually a god."

Bridget winced at the casual dismissal. "He was a friend, wasn't he? He went to you for help. Why would you hurt him?"

She fixed Bridget with a disparaging look. "I *did* help him. He wanted your names cleared. His death provided a step in that direction."

"That's not—"

Eris interrupted with a petulant stomp of her foot. "Shut up! Sometimes the fastest way through an obstacle is to destroy it entirely. Ret's kindness blinded him to reality. He's spent centuries buried in books instead of helping our people. He would rather pontificate about a potential *alliance* with you humans than protect what little we have left."

She spat the word alliance like a curse. This girl—this Grigori—hated humanity. Hated Bridget. So strongly it was almost a physical force.

Nuriel drew in a steady breath. Even his immeasurable calm seemed on the verge of cracking. "Trying to imagine a better future for everyone isn't a crime."

Eris' lip curled. "It is when it leads to our further subjugation. Enough of this. I'm sure Tannin wants to say hello to his new guests. You're going to come with me."

For a second, everyone stood still, sizing one another up. Then, they burst into motion.

Eisheth shot fire at Eris as she flung up an ice barrier—its edges immediately beginning to drip away.

Nuriel glanced at Bridget. "Find cover."

Then he turned away, gathering the melting water into a shimmering shield.

Bridget burst into a sprint, but her escape was short-lived. A stinging cold slammed into her ankles and she stumbled. Ice rushed up her shoes and legs, pinning her in place.

"Eisheth!" Bridget twisted, but the detective was preoccupied. Fire pushed against the encroaching floe, which shimmered, glowing red. The shifting ice prevailed, pressing forward and crashed over the detective's hands. It melted and reformed around her, snuffing out the flames.

When the floe finally groaned to a stop, all three of them were ensconced up to their waists, hands trapped. No matter how hard Bridget twisted, she couldn't break free. It was as solid as stone. Beside her, Nuriel grimaced and struggled. Eisheth, on the other hand, held completely still, glaring at Eris from her prison.

"There. Much better."

A chill seeped through Bridget's body. She exhaled in a vain attempt to expel her fear. "You can't kill us."

"No?" Eris moved closer to Bridget, sliding the beacon into her pocket. The hatred in her eyes was as chilling as their icy shackles. "Why not? You humans flirt with death easily enough. Or have you forgotten?"

Bridget tried to shrink back, but Eris' hand shot out and grabbed her by the arm. Her fingers were surprisingly warm as they gripped her, digging into the skin and—

Smoke and dust curled in the air, bringing Kai in and out of focus. He was smiling at her, lips bloodied and hair wild. Embers fell around them as towering pines crackled like torches.

Bridget's chest spasmed. Kai had stolen the air from her lungs. The world was darkening into a single black tunnel, and at the center of the tunnel was Kai, Dahlia's murderer. She'd died just like this.

Her heart thudded like a sledgehammer. The only thing keeping her on her feet was the solid weight of the gun in one hand.

She brought it up and squeezed the trigger.

Crimson sprayed onto the ground.

"Bridget!" Nuriel's voice. Coming from... where?

—she gasped for air as the world snapped back into focus around her. She wasn't in a ravaged, fiery parking lot; she was in Tannin's basement. The cold enveloping her now was jarring compared to the heat of the remembered battle.

Eris backed up with a self-satisfied expression. "You think he deserved it, don't you? I could feel your rage."

The memory faded, but the nausea remained. Eris had thrown her into her own past, pinpointing a moment she desperately wanted to forget. Could she access anything Bridget knew with a touch? If so, the implications chilled her.

"Stop hurting someone who can't fight back." The detective's voice cut through Bridget's spiral. Eisheth's fingers pulsed with flame from within her block of ice. Bubbles formed around her hands—heat slowly melting away the prison.

Eris leered at Eisheth, eyes glinting dangerously. "You'd rather me hurt you?"

Whatever Eisheth was about respond with was lost in a rumble coming from the ground itself. Artifacts began trembling in their cabinets. Another earthquake, even more powerful than the previous ones.

A cabinet toppled toward Bridget, and she flinched back, unable to defend herself. It missed her by inches, its sharp edge landing on her icy prison with an ear-splitting *crack* and leaving a deep fissure behind. Eris danced out of the way of another falling cabinet.

While Eris' back was turned, Bridget shoved her knee toward the crack. The weakened ice splintered and crumbled. With a gasp of relief, she stumbled free.

Bridget braced herself against the fallen cabinet as she regained her balance. From it, a braided leather belt had fallen to the floor. Near it, a plaque read, *Dream hopping. Circa 990 CE, Siberia.*

"Hey!" Eris' voice shot through Bridget. The grating sound of the earthquake had ebbed, and in its wake, Eris was glaring right at her. She pushed herself into as much of a run as she could manage on numb feet. Keeping low, she weaved through the cracked display cases and over shards of glass. She peered into the cabinets, searching for anything that could help. Each object had a label, some more helpful than others. Many only listed a year and a part of the world. Others indicated their function. A flat stone reportedly alerted the owner if intruders appeared. Beside it, a pair of shoes granted the wearer great speed.

Her eyes fell on a beaded necklace made out of lapis lazuli. Its door was shattered open. She read the label.

Perfect.

She took it, fingers closing around the cool stones.

Something glanced off of Bridget's arm. It knocked the necklace from her hand. She stumbled forward as a dagger of ice hit a case in front of her, shattering the glass.

Another *thunk* knocked her into the case. For a moment, she only felt off-kilter. Then pain blossomed in her shoulder. She drew in a hissing breath and reached behind her. Her fingers touched something cold and sharp. Closing her eyes, she gripped it and pulled.

Pain arced through her as the ice-knife came free. It was already melting fast, warmed by the bright crimson blood covering the blade.

"Humans," Eris said the word like a curse. She strode calmly down the aisle toward Bridget. "You never know when to stop, do you?"

Frozen shards spiked out from Eris' feet, twisting into a fresh arsenal of throwing knives, waiting for her to pluck them free. Bridget staggered, putting distance between them. She'd seen Nuriel turn water to ice, but Eris' control of it was something else entirely. She didn't *use* ice. It was part of her.

Bridget turned to run, and her foot slid out from under her. Her stomach flipped as she flew backward and hit the ground hard. A burst of pain turned her vision black. She rolled onto her side, coughing.

Leisurely steps approached, and Eris came to a stop overhead. Her fresh dagger extended outward, growing into a long spear, the ice so tightly compacted it shone a cerulean blue. She pressed a foot against Bridget's chest, pinning her in place.

Bridget scrambled to escape, but the icy restraints locked down her wrists and ankles.

The tip of Eris' spear touched Bridget's throat. "Humans are a plague," Eris whispered, eyes manic. "And they need to be snuffed out, one by one."

Bridget had come so far, gotten so close.

And it was for nothing. Dahlia was a prisoner again, James was lost in his own body, and Nuriel and Eisheth...

She squeezed her eyes shut and waited for the spear to cut her throat.

THIRTY-SIX

Dahlia paced the length of her new cage. Across from her, Tannin's office door remained shut no matter how many times she screamed his name. She'd given up trying to get his attention, instead prowling back and forth, red spots popping in her vision. She'd been so close. If she hadn't lost her grip on Danel's powers, Tannin would be dead now.

"Dahlia."

She ignored Gaul's voice, pressing the heels of her hands against her eyes. She couldn't be trapped again. Not here, not now. She'd sooner die.

"Dahlia!"

She whirled on him. "What?"

Gaul crouched beside Danel, who was clutching his broken arm. Beside him was a filing cabinet, a heavy desk, and a rolling chair.

"Why did you come here?" His voice was tight with anger as he stood.

"Isn't it obvious?"

A red flush crept up his neck, into his cheeks. "You've put all our lives at risk with your foolishness."

He walked toward her, and she thought he might lash out. But he brushed past and went to the doorway instead. She joined him.

The hairs on her arm stood upright as she got close to the electrical field. "I'm not sorry. I had a chance to hurt him. So, I took it."

He shot her a glare. "This is why I've been warning you about relying on strength."

"I'll be more *creative* next time." She rolled her eyes.

"No." Gaul's expression was tense. "There will be no next time. We need to leave this place as quickly as we can."

Frustration coursed through her. "And let him get away with everything he's done?"

"If you hadn't barged in on us, I *may* have been able to reach some sort of agreement. Instead, we've essentially declared war against someone far stronger than us. We cannot win. So yes, we run."

"Good luck with that." She turned on her heel and strode to where Danel leaned against the desk. "You okay?"

"What's it look like?" He steadied himself with a grimace. "Sorry. Been better." In addition to his broken arm, they were both covered with stinging burns. Gaul had tried to assure them it was a good sign; if they could still feel pain, their nerves were intact. It wasn't a comforting thought.

Danel leaned his head against the wall. "At least Tannin didn't snap my neck. I'd hate to die the same way twice."

She winced. She'd believed she could get the upper hand against Tannin. But seizing two powers at once had been too hard in the pressure of the moment, and he and Eris had reacted too quickly.

"Hang in there. We'll get out of here. Then we can get you to Viri."

Gaul grumbled. "It's not going to be so simple, I'm afraid."

Dahlia turned back toward him. "What's wrong?"

Instead of answering her, he gestured at the symbol etched into the open doorway. She returned to his side and crouched down to examine it. After so long staring at different Grigori contracts, she still didn't understand how to interpret them. It was a frustrating reminder of how much she still had to learn. "What's it mean?"

"It's not what it means, it's what it's made of. That's not stone."

She shifted her attention away from the design itself, to the material it was cut into. The entire doorway was as hard as rock, but the colors and patterns were subtly different from the marble dominating much of the bank. "Is it resin?"

"Could be. Whatever it is, there isn't enough rock in it for me to manipulate. And look." He pointed to the walls.

They each had a symbol carved into them—even the ceiling had one. "Well. So much for your escape plan."

"What do they do?" Danel asked.

Gaul straightened and pulled his fingers into a fist. "Stifle my earth ability. I can't access it at all in here."

"Oh." Danel managed a weak smile. "Welcome to the club."

She shoved her irritation at Gaul aside and closed her eyes, focusing. She could sense his power, just like Danel's. But when she tried to grasp it, it eluded her. No matter how hard she tried, she couldn't hold onto it long enough to use.

"What about your other one?" Dahlia asked, shifting her attention.

"Don't." Gaul's tone broke her concentration, and she opened her eyes. "That one is fine, but it's of no use to us right now."

The bright smell of ozone reached her, pulling her attention away.

Cyrie came into view in the hallway, her silver hair pulled back. Frown lines creased her forehead, but she brightened when she saw them behind the crackling doorway. "Isn't the new security system lovely?"

Gaul glowered. "What did you do?"

"Implemented a few of those clever symbols in Dahlia's notebook. Plus a few of my own."

Dahlia started. So, they had been working on the sketches—just not the same ones.

Gaul's eyes narrowed. "Danel and Dahlia need medical attention."

Cyrie eyed Danel. "I'm sorry. Tannin isn't particularly happy with them right now."

"Feeling's mutual," Danel grunted as he pulled himself into a sitting position.

"Please help us." Dahlia needed this woman to listen. She gestured to Tannin's door with a burned hand. "He's shut himself in his office. He won't notice if you let us out."

Cyrie's voice turned regretful. "I wish I could. But Tannin's orders are clear. The three of you are to remain here."

"Don't you see Tannin is using you?"

She tutted. "He respects my knowledge."

Dahlia laughed. "Does he respect *you*? Or are you just a useful tool? Another item for his collection?"

Her voice took on a defensive edge. "Tannin wants to improve our lives."

Gaul shook his head. "Then why'd he lock up Dahlia for nine months? Why'd he let Ret get killed?"

Cyrie's expression darkened. "Not my department. I focus on symbology."

Fury flickered through Dahlia. "You can't ignore when he hurts people because it *isn't your department*. You're not innocent because you stick your head in the sand."

Her words hit their mark. Cyrie looked away, grimacing. "I'm sorry about what happened to Ret, and to you. I... didn't agree with the decision."

"Then why didn't you *do* anything?" Dahlia demanded, fingers clenching at her side.

A quiet laugh bubbled up from Cyrie. "I tried to say something. But you've seen Tannin. Once he's focused on something, nothing will stop him. Eris is even worse. Besides, their strength—I'm five hundred years old, they're millennia."

Dahlia shook her head. "But you're an Artist. You have something they need, and that gives you leverage."

"I'm sorry." Cyrie sounded sincere. Almost pleading. "If you would listen to Tannin, come to a compromise, we could end all of this death."

Dahlia scoffed and abandoned the discussion. Cyrie wasn't going to change her mind. Instead, she focused on the woman's abilities. She yanked on a humming thread of her electricity, sending a pulse through the security field in an effort to overload it.

The light splintered menacingly. Sparks shot out, and Dahlia stumbled backward, into Gaul. He caught her before she could fall.

"Don't do that unless you want to get hurt," Cyrie scolded.

Dahlia bit back a retort and turned away. The hairs on her arms stood upright from the electric shock, and her heart felt like it was running a marathon. She forced herself to breathe as she went back to Danel's side. "We'll get you help soon."

"Sure. Until then, I've still got one working arm. We can play a mean game of table tennis."

Dahlia forced a smile as she sank onto the floor beside Danel. She closed her eyes, blocking Cyrie out. The weight of her captivity was oppressive, threatening to take over.

Gaul was right. She *had* been foolish. Instead of freeing one person, her plan had given Tannin additional hostages. Now they were all trapped, barred in with no way to access help. Her windpipe felt tight and sweat sprang up on her palms.

She pushed back the panic, counting her inhales and exhales.

Breathe through it. This is different than before. It felt like it took several minutes, but finally, her muscles relaxed a little. Eyes still closed, she began thinking through her options. If the doorway was her only possible exit, she needed to disrupt the electricity. Using Cyrie's abilities wouldn't help; they'd only exacerbate the problem. Maybe if she—

A low rumble interrupted her thoughts. She opened her eyes. The floor trembled and an empty coffee mug skittered off the table, shattering on the marble floor. Gaul jumped back, then dove under a desk.

Near them, a file cabinet's drawers slid open. It tilted, and Dahlia grabbed Danel, yanking him back as it slammed to the ground, files scattering everywhere. He cried out in pain as she tugged his injured arm, but she ignored him, pulling them both half-under the desk with Gaul.

"Cover your head!" she cried, her voice lost in the sound of the earth screaming. She huddled with arms slung over the back of her neck.

She counted to five before the shaking subsided, leaving behind only the sound of her ragged breath. Danel's eyes were white around the edges. "This isn't going to get better on its own."

Dahlia peered out from under the desk. Cyrie had backed away from the doorframe and was looking around uneasily. The electric blockade was still very much in place. It was too much to hope the quake would have disrupted it.

Her heart stuttered as the door across from her opened. Tannin peered out, expression neutral. He ignored Dahlia entirely. "Cyrie, go to the basement. We have guests."

Dahlia's heart jolted. More reinforcements for Tannin? Or had help arrived? She crawled out from under the desk and stood.

"Understood, sir." Any sympathy faded away, replaced by obedience.

Tannin gave Dahlia a flat look, then shut the door again.

Cyrie grimaced. "I'll bring back a splint for your friend's arm."

"Think about what I said. You're better than Tannin."

Cyrie's smile was troubled as she turned away. "Maybe I am, dear. But I'm not the one in a cage."

THIRTY-SEVEN

The tip of the spear bit into Bridget's neck. She tried to squirm free, but her shoulder screamed with the motion. Frost rose up to pin her to the floor.

"Stop!" a new voice called.

Bridget cracked open her eyes, straining to look toward the sound of running footfalls. A silver-haired woman came around the corner, slowing to a trot as she eyed the slick floor.

"Cyrie." Eris' voice was laced with irritation. "So good of you to join us."

Cyrie closed the distance between them. "Tannin wants the human. Unharmed." She squatted beside Bridget, tutting as her eyes turned to the blood seeping onto the floor. "Looks like I arrived just in time."

Eris glared down at them, jaw tight. "She tried to run."

"Probably because you were tormenting her."

"She's useless." Petulance crept into Eris' tone.

"Tannin has plans for her."

"I don't answer to him." Still, Eris pulled the spear back and removed her foot from Bridget's chest. The ice dissolved into slush and Bridget rolled onto her side with a gasp. She wiped her neck, palm coming away with a streak of blood.

Cyrie slid her hands under Bridget's uninjured arm. "Can you stand?"

With a quiet grunt of assent, Bridget used Cyrie's help to get to her feet. The cold and adrenaline left her shaking so badly she could barely stay upright.

A loud *crack* made all three of them jump. Eris looked back toward where Nuriel and Eisheth were trapped.

"Fine, take the human. I have more interesting prey to hunt." She spared one more disparaging look at Bridget, then jogged toward the back of the room.

Bridget tried to twist free of Cyrie, but her feet slid on the icy ground, and she fell to one knee. Fresh pain radiated up her leg.

Cyrie made a sound of irritation. "Come with me. Your sister is upstairs."

"Nuriel and Eisheth—" Bridget's teeth chattered, making it hard for her to form words. She tried to push herself upright, but her sneaker slid, bringing her down again.

Her gaze landed on the necklace she'd dropped before Eris' attack. It was shadowed beneath a broken cabinet.

Two dozen feet away, a flash of fire shot upward,

licking the ceiling. Cyrie watched the glow. "Your friends will have to take care of themselves."

Taking advantage of Cyrie's distraction, Bridget lurched forward. Her fingers closed around the necklace, and she yanked it free. She'd just shoved it in her pocket as a zap of electricity stabbed through her. She gasped in pain.

"Besides, you'll only be in their way. Best you come with me." Cyrie's voice was apologetic as she pulled Bridget back to her feet. "Come along, dear, or else I'll have to force you."

Bridget's pulse skittered as Cyrie tugged her toward the main aisle. Each step sent a jolt of pain through her, but she gritted her teeth and did her best to ignore it. Her entire body tingled as Cyrie forced her upstairs, out of the cold, and away from the fight. The thick metal door to the basement clanged shut, cutting off the shouts from below.

Bridget emerged into a high-ceilinged atrium with several hallways extending outward. Like Tannin's basement, it felt sterile—in an older, more immutable way. The stodgy leather furniture looked stiff and unused, more decorative than functional. A vase lay shattered on the floor, possibly a victim of the most recent earthquake. Otherwise, the area was pristine.

With her free hand, Cyrie lifted a walkie-talkie. "I have Bridget."

There was a brief pause before Tannin's voice crackled over the speaker. "Good. And the others?"

"Eris is keeping them occupied."

A crackling sigh. "I'm sure she is. That's fine. They're disposable; just bring me the girl."

Cyrie hooked the walkie back onto her waistband.

"Where's my sister?"

"This way." Cyrie gave Bridget's arm a tug. She led her down one of the hallways, past several doors. Most were closed, and the few she could peer into only housed offices or storage.

Cyrie stopped in front of a closed wooden door. A series of symbols were etched into it—one around the handle, one in the center, and two more near the hinges. When Cyrie touched the handle it glowed softly, followed by a click.

Every rapid pulse of Bridget's heart sent a stab of pain through her. She steadied herself, preparing for whatever state Dahlia might be in.

The door opened into an empty room.

It was barely larger than a coat closet, with a single ceiling light fixture. No windows interrupted the walls. Instead, they were engraved with Grigori symbols, surrounding the space with magic she couldn't guess at.

Her own inhospitable cage.

"Inside," Cyrie said.

If she was going to make a break for it, this was her only chance.

Cyrie's grip loosened slightly as she reached the threshold of the prison.

Now.

With a sharp jerk, Bridget yanked her arm free. She sidestepped the open door and shoved Cyrie as hard as she could.

Cyrie's eyes flew wide with surprise, and she stumbled forward. Her foot caught on the edge of the doorframe, bringing her to her knees.

Before the other woman could respond, Bridget grabbed the door, slamming it shut. The handle flashed gold, then went inert.

A loud thud shook the door. Bridget threw her weight against it to keep it in place. The symbol on the handle pulsed and the door shook again, but did not give. She took a slow step back. Magic was keeping Cyrie locked inside.

Bridget gasped from the exertion. Her shoulder throbbed, but she'd have to tend to it later.

From inside, there came another series of echoing thumps on the door, followed by a muffled, "Hey! Hey! Let me out of here!"

Then Cyrie's walkie blipped, followed by her agitated voice, too low to hear. Bridget cursed. Tannin could arrive to free Cyrie at any moment.

In the meantime, Bridget was the sole person in a position to help her friends. She needed to stay hidden.

She reached into her pocket and pulled the necklace out, slipping it over her head.

As soon as it nestled against her skin, the stones warmed. A gentle hum pulsed through her.

She looked down and, despite expecting it, started when she couldn't see herself. Even her shadow was gone.

Invisibility granted.

THIRTY-EIGHT

Panic gnawed at Dahlia. Everything they'd attempted to break themselves free had failed.

Danel watched as she paced back and forth. "They'll deactivate the electric fence eventually. We might be immortal, but they know we can still starve." He'd propped himself up against a bookshelf. Sweat slicked his blond hair to his forehead.

Gaul stood near the doorway, watching the empty hall with the ferocity of a caged animal. "I'm not counting on Tannin to do anything." He turned to Dahlia. "You'll need to leverage your abilities."

She started. "Now you *want* me to use my powers?"

"I'm not asking you to attack indiscriminately." Gaul folded his arms. "Start by helping us figure out where everyone is."

She fought back the urge to snap at him—to tell him to stop ordering her around. Instead, she closed her eyes, focusing on the distant webs of power. Maybe, if she could separate them out, she could figure out where they were and what they were doing.

Even stifled, Gaul and Danel's were like a physical presence, but she forced her attention beyond them. Tannin was just across the hall, where his aura bubbled and hissed. Dahlia's muscles went rigid, hot anger washing over her. She had to find a way to eliminate his cruelty from their lives.

With effort, she tore her focus back to the building as a whole. Where were the others? She searched for Cyrie's snaps of electricity and found them below her. She was overshadowed by an icy blast of strength. Alongside them, two familiar, weaker pulses.

She opened her eyes. "Eisheth is here. And Nuriel. I think they're downstairs with Eris and Cyrie."

Danel set his jaw. "We have to help them."

"What do *you* intend to do?" Gaul's voice was sour. "Even if we get out of here, you're useless."

Danel scowled. "I'll manage."

"No. You'll hide and stay out of the way."

Dahlia returned her attention back to the basement. Flashes of fire, water, and ice flared to life. She closed her eyes and pressed her hands against her forehead. The pulsing vibrancy of their abilities provided her with a loose mental map of the building. "Cyrie's coming back upstairs. Nuriel and Eisheth are trying to fight against Eris, but—"

She cut off, wincing as Eisheth's fire sputtered and weakened.

"But what?" Danel grunted, holding his broken arm against his chest as he climbed to his feet.

Gaul ignored Danel, coming to stand in front of Dahlia. "Focus on Eris. She's the strongest. See if you can steal her powers from her."

"I can't, she's too far away to grab them." Dahlia chewed her lip. "Hang on, I'm trying something else." Instead of pulling, she *pushed* on Eris' aura—not trying to use them but instead, pressing down on them.

Eris' powers dimmed ever so slightly.

Dahlia tried again, this time shoving hard.

In that moment, the watery thread of Nuriel and Eisheth's abilities sparked brighter.

"Yes!" Dahlia opened her eyes.

"Quiet, don't attract Tannin's attention." Gaul leaned closer. "What did you do?"

"I'm pretty sure I managed to keep Eris from an attack."

Danel's cut in. "Do it again!"

Dahlia closed her eyes once more. She was beginning to see why everyone was so interested in her mimicry. What she'd originally thought of as inferior—simply producing a weak echo—was so much more. She could tell when enemies were approaching and when friends were in danger. From an entire floor away, she could impact an ongoing battle.

"Dahlia!" The shock of hearing her sister's familiar voice made her jump, ruining her focus.

She darted to the open doorway, but the hall was empty. "Bridget?"

"Oh good, now we're hearing voices. That bodes well," muttered Danel. Gaul shushed him, moving to stand by Dahlia.

Bridget simply materialized on the far side of the electrified door. A brilliant blue necklace dangled loosely from her fingers.

Dahlia gasped. "Bridget!"

"I know. It's from downstairs, it—"

"You're hurt!"

Bridget's t-shirt, once a sky blue, had a crimson stain covering the sleeve and spreading down her side. Her skin, by contrast, was pale—except the streak of blood seeping from a shallow wound on her neck. Her ponytail was askew, and the blonde flyaways gave her a wild look.

"I'm alright," Bridget insisted, though she grimaced as she shifted her arm. "It looks worse than it is. How do I get you out of here?"

Gaul approached. "We don't know yet."

Dahlia dropped her gaze down at the floor, where Cyrie's pulsing symbol created the electric field. It made sense for Tannin to stifle earth abilities. Within this facility, it could easily cause the most damage. But that didn't mean they were completely helpless.

Think creatively. She looked back up at her sister. "I need help from one of the others."

"Nuriel and Eisheth are downstairs. I can try to draw them up."

"No." Gaul's firm denial surprised Dahlia. "It's too

dangerous for you to rush into battle. You should've stayed hidden at Viri's."

"I can stay hidden *here*." Bridget held up the necklace.

Danel grunted. "Let Bridget help us. Dahlia can try to weaken Eris from up here."

Gaul heaved a sigh, pinching the bridge of his nose.

Dahlia hesitated. Getting Nuriel or Eisheth had been her idea, but fear seized her as she took in Bridget's injuries. "I don't know how well my abilities will work. And Bridget—Eris is every bit as powerful as Tannin."

"She won't even know I'm there." Bridget replaced the necklace, disappearing from view. "Wait a few minutes before you do anything, so I have time to get down there."

As much as she wanted to refuse the help, she needed it. Bridget may have joined the battle for the wrong reasons, but she was still useful. And with the necklace, she'd be safer. She let go of a shaky breath. "Please be careful."

"You too." Then the sound of footsteps moved away.

"She'll be okay." Danel, of all people, gave her a reassuring smile.

"You think?" In the periphery, she could sense how outpowered her friends were downstairs. And she'd sent her all-too-human sister right back into the fray.

He laughed, despite his grimace of pain. "Yeah. If anyone could brute-force themselves into staying alive, it's Bridget."

A flicker of hope warmed her. They were only words, and they didn't lessen the danger. But she felt better. "Thanks, Danel."

THIRTY-NINE

Bridget's invisibility didn't hide the white puffs of air accompanying her exhales. She hid behind a cabinet, keeping one hand close to her mouth to stifle her breath as she peered around the corner.

She tried to shake off the dread gathering in her body. *Why* had Dahlia returned to this place? When given a choice between seeking out vengeance and helping James, her sister had chosen to stoke her anger.

It was reasonable, given what she'd been through. And also, it was the action of a new Dahlia.

A shout cut through her thoughts. Now that she was close, it was evident how much trouble Nuriel and Eisheth were in. Eris' icy presence far outshone her friends, and she was clearly enjoying herself.

Eisheth and Nuriel tried, though.

Nuriel siphoned water from the melting ice on the

floor, building it into a growing reservoir.

Bridget had seen Nuriel scald a man, encase him in a watery prison, and cause a tsunami. Eisheth had single-handedly started a roaring fire in a lakeside park. They were forces to be reckoned with.

But Eris was even more so. She flicked her hand, and Nuriel's reservoir of water broke free, knocking him off his feet. It covered him entirely before the top layer hardened. Nuriel thrashed beneath the surface, trying to break through.

Bridget rose from her crouch, desperately wishing she could help. But if Dahlia was right, Eris' abilities would be stifled at any moment. She needed to be ready to run in and pull her friends away.

Eisheth sent a blast of fire into the icy crust. Nuriel rammed his elbow against it from the inside. He burst through, soaked and gasping.

The rescue was short lived. The water leapt forward, knocking Eisheth to the ground and the air from her lungs.

"You two are adorable," Eris said as she approached Eisheth. Nuriel was still gasping, shivering violently. "Shall I make you relive your worst memories?"

The child Grigori darted forward, grabbing Eisheth's wrist. The detective tried to pull back—then froze. Her eyes went glassy as Eris' fingers tightened. From Bridget's vantage point she could see Eris also losing focus on her surroundings, the nearby ice beginning to melt.

With Eris distracted, Nuriel lurched forward and snagged her by the ankle. She paused, looking suddenly confused.

The detective gasped, her eyes refocusing as she tore out of Eris' grasp. Searing heat filled the space as she launched a wave of fire directly at Eris. It slammed into her arm and the girl Grigori went down with a shriek of pain. The smell of blistering flesh made Bridget cover her mouth.

This was Bridget's moment. She darted around the cabinets toward Nuriel. She grabbed his wrist and pulled. He recoiled, spinning toward the new threat.

"It's me," Bridget whispered urgently. "Dahlia needs you upstairs."

He stared, searching empty space for her. "What?"

Bridget urged Nuriel toward the nearest cabinets, away from the battle. His eyes tracked, searching for her. "How?"

"An artifact." Bridget glanced through a break in the cabinets as Eisheth and Eris battled. Eris was backing Eisheth into a corner, not about to let her guard down again.

Nuriel looked around wildly. "This is a trick."

"It's not, I promise. Please, she's trapped up there."

"But Eisheth—" Nuriel looked toward her.

"We've got this."

Nuriel hesitated, clearly torn, but Bridget whispered urgently. "Eisheth needs reinforcements. The two of you alone can't beat her. Gaul's with Dahlia, so bring him back with you."

"Eris is going to kill her. *And* you," Nuriel whispered back.

"We won't let her." Bridget knew how ridiculous the words sounded. What could they possibly do against such powerful Grigori? But Nuriel fumbled for her arm, then squeezed it gently.

"Be careful. Don't let her see you. Or touch you."

"I won't. Hurry."

Nuriel cast one last glance at the fight, then turned and ran up the stairs.

Bridget waited until Nuriel was out of view, then hurried down the nearest row, searching for a weapon. She kept low as she hurried from cabinet to cabinet, treading over splintered glass, shattered vases, and waterlogged books. She'd seen no sign of James' sword.

She caught a glimpse of Eisheth through a gap in the cabinetry. The detective was propping herself up against the back wall, glaring at Eris. Her hair had swung free of its bun, hanging in tangles around her face. Blood darkened her shirt.

"I'm bored of playing with you." Eris punctuated her words with a blast of cold that reached Bridget, several aisles away. The detective cried out, thrown into the wall. Bridget returned to her search. James would have to wait. Right now, she needed to survive long enough to help him.

There: a dagger lying inside a broken cabinet with no label.

"You should be embarrassed to live in the shadow of humans." Eris spat the word like it tasted bitter.

Bridget snatched the dagger from its setting. She shoved aside caution and rushed toward the fight.

Coming around the corner, she saw Eisheth with her back against the wall, feet dangling. Serrated rows of ice wrapped themselves around Eisheth, pinning her to the wall and freezing her there. They extended over her hands, which flickered with failed attempts to ignite.

Bridget rushed forward, gripping the dagger tightly. She had almost reached Eris when her foot fell on a pile of broken glass. It crunched loudly underfoot.

Eris whipped around at the noise, swinging a disc of ice blindly in Bridget's direction. It glanced off her injured shoulder, sparking a new flash of pain. "Who's there!"

Bridget stumbled back, tripping over a fallen cabinet with a cry of surprise.

Eris' eyes snapped toward the sound and fumbled for her arm, seizing her wrist.

Bridget tried to twist away—

Sitting in a chair on a hotel balcony, shielded by the rain, she begged Dahlia. "James died helping me find you. If you can find him a Grigori name, we can help him."

Dahlia searched Bridget's eyes, expression haunted. "He won't be the same. He won't be James."

"I don't care," Bridget said. "You might not be the same, but it's better than you being gone."

Then the scene changed.

Danel's boat swayed, making her stomach churn. She resisted the urge to run to the rail and instead watched as Dahlia pressed her hand against the newly tattooed symbol on James' back. Golden veins of light wrapped around the black lines, bringing it to life. A jolt almost sent her flying, as the contract activated and sent power rolling outward.

Bridget gasped, back in Tannin's basement. She could feel Eris digging through her mind, searching for the memories she wanted. "Wait, no—"

Another earthquake had rattled the walls of Viri's

house. Bridget hovered over Ret's histories, dread mounting.

"Nuriel?" she shouted.

He and Viri raced down the hallway. "Coming! What is it? Are you alright?"

Her breath felt thin. "James' symbol is the key."

Confusion puckered his brow. "I suppose they all are, in a way."

Viri looked between them. "But that's not what she means, is it?"

"Not a key. The Key."

The memory ended, thrusting Bridget back into the present. She gasped as the basement came into focus.

Eris stood in front of her, shock in her eyes. The necklace dangled from her fingertips. Bridget hadn't even noticed her pull it off. She'd dropped the dagger.

"You found the Key." Eris' voice was breathy. Then, it sharpened. "You *created* a Key." Glee chased her surprise, and she laughed in delight. "Oh, that poor creature. This changes *everything*."

Bridget shook her head, trying to clear away the memory. "That wasn't anything. It's not—"

But Eris gave a flippant wave of her hand, sending a wave of icy projectiles toward Bridget. Yelping, she ducked back to avoid the onslaught, but they were impossible to dodge. A block of ice glanced off her skull, and she fell to the floor with a moan. Sticky blood seeped through her hair.

"Thank you so much for the information. Truly." Eris giggled, her childlike glee returning.

By the time Bridget climbed to her feet, Eris had disappeared into the portal room.

FORTY

Dahlia felt Nuriel's aura shift away from Eris and Eisheth. The telltale movement of his woven abilities moved up to the ground level of the building. She opened her eyes and the mental map of the battle fell away. "Nuriel's coming."

She used the wall to help her climb to her feet. Burns screamed in protest as she straightened. Once upright, she drew in a few deep breaths, steadying herself.

"Are you okay?" Danel's eyebrows furrowed in concern.

She waved his comment off. "Fine."

"Be careful," Gaul said. "You need to conserve strength. We need to be ready to run."

The sound of Nuriel's footsteps preceded him. He stumbled into view, water dripping from his fingers, curls drenched. His dark eyes raked over their prison.

Dahlia hurried forward, Gaul's warnings forgotten. "Nuriel! You can get us out of here. You just need to—"

An electric pulse slammed into him. He dropped to the ground, twitching violently.

"Nuriel?!" Eyes wide, Dahlia pushed as close as she could to the open doorway. The electricity made the hair on her arms stand on end.

"I truly don't want to hurt any of you." Cyrie's voice came from further down the hall. She sounded pained. If Dahlia twisted her head, she could barely make out the woman's silver hair as she continued approaching.

Gaul came to stand beside Dahlia. "Then don't. It's pretty damn simple."

"Don't make me," Cyrie responded.

Dahlia turned her attention back to Nuriel. He wasn't unconscious, but he didn't move other than to blink slowly.

She told him in a hushed voice, "I'm going to use your powers, alright?" She grasped his primary ability, pulling the water from his clothes, his hair, his skin. She gathered the droplets into a floating ball of liquid, turning slowly in midair. It was small, but it would have to be enough.

Cyrie raised a hand, electricity pulsing between the fingers. But she didn't attack. If anything, she seemed fascinated by Dahlia.

With a sharp push, Dahlia slammed the water down on top of the active symbol. It crackled and hissed as sparks shot up. Cyrie jumped back in surprise.

With a desperate push, Dahlia willed the water to harden into ice, cracking the resin and breaking the shape design.

It splintered apart into milky-colored shards, and the security field fizzled away.

Immediately, Dahlia dropped Nuriel's powers and grabbed Danel's. His speed carried her through the door and into the hall. She came to a stop in front of Nuriel, putting herself protectively between him and Cyrie. "You okay, Nuriel?"

He groaned. "Yeah. That hurt."

Cyrie's eyes were wide with fascination. "Incredible. I've never seen anything like it."

Dahlia risked a glance behind her. Nuriel had rolled onto his side and was slowly climbing to his feet.

Gaul helped Danel out of the room, hand on his back. His eyes focused on something beyond her. "Dahlia!"

She spun around. A tendril of black smoke snagged her wrist, sending shards of agony across her skin. Tannin's office door was open, and he stood in the threshold. His eyes were black slits. "I am trying to work."

Hatred zipped through her, outpacing the burning sensation. Her lip curled.

Tannin advanced as his smoke tightened around her wrist, spiraling up her arm. Like acid-covered vines, they grabbed her arms, her legs, her torso. She tried to twist free, but the sulfuric restraints only crawled higher.

So much for running.

Gaul snarled. "Let go of her." Cracks started forming along the walls, puffs of marble dust filling the air. Free of their prison, his powers worked again. The hanging lamp above Tannin started to swing erratically.

In a fit of desperation, Dahlia reached for Tannin's ability, trying to shove the smoke off herself.

Tannin flared his powers in response, and Dahlia let out a shrill scream. He laughed quietly. "What have I told you about trying to use my abilities?"

Nuriel staggered to his feet. "You're stronger than all

of us combined. But you begrudge her trying to get free? You're a bully."

Cyrie was still watching Dahlia in fascination. "Sir, maybe it's best if we spare the mimic."

"She had her chance." The dark puddle of ash roiled around Tannin's ankles, uncoiling into arms that stretched upward.

A wordless yell burst from behind her. Danel launched himself at Tannin. He looked like a linebacker attempting to make a tackle—but without his speed, he made for an easy target.

A coil of darkness separated from the boiling mass around Tannin's feet. It slammed into Danel, knocking him backward into the wall.

The light fixture fell, crashing to the ground. Gaul raised his hands, summoning huge chunks of the marble-clad walls to hurl at him. A few found their mark, and Tannin grunted in pain as blood bloomed along his side. The smoky bindings weakened and dropped Dahlia to the floor. Whimpering, she rolled away.

Nearby, Danel scooped up a jagged shard of stone and climbed to his feet. His eyes met Dahlia's, and he set his jaw.

"Enough!" He rounded on Tannin, expression twisted with pain and fury. Gripping the length of stone like a wicked dagger, he rushed him.

This time, Tannin whipped his full attention toward Danel. A thick arm of smoke lashed around him seconds before the stone weapon made contact. It constricted, and Danel let out a strangled wheeze. He kicked and squirmed, but Tannin just tugged Danel so close the two were almost nose-to-nose.

"I hope you know how much I enjoy this." Tannin's

voice was like sandpaper.

He plucked the dagger free from Danel's hand. Then, with precision, he drove it deep into his abdomen.

Danel made a choking sound, his eyes going wide. "No!"

Dahlia had no sense of who had screamed. Danel's powers flickered erratically across her awareness. She tried to run to him, but a river of sulfuric ash washed over her. Tears streamed down Dahlia's cheeks as she squirmed to escape. She was gagging, burning.

It couldn't end like this.

Tannin victorious. Her friends and family in danger. Herself—a memory.

A blast of blue-white electricity lit up the inside of Dahlia's eyelids. She opened her eyes, squinting against the maelstrom. Directly in front of her, crackling lightning raced around Tannin's chest, mixing with his smoke. Abruptly, it exploded outward.

Dahlia flew into the wall. Her ears rang, a tinny, high-pitched sound. She coughed, and looked up, trying to get her bearings. Nuriel and Gaul were nearby, coughing violently on their hands and knees.

Tannin... where was Tannin?

She found him on the ground a dozen feet away, clutching his chest with one hand while he stared up in rigid shock. Danel lay on the floor, a pool of blood spreading outward with shocking speed.

Cyrie was the only one who remained standing, her jaw set. "I know you want to help us, Tannin." Her voice sounded thin and far away. "But this isn't the way forward."

Using the wall for support, Tannin slowly pulled himself to his feet. He laughed—a low, incredulous sound. "You would breach your contract for *them*?"

Cyrie responded with a level stare. "You're murdering our kind. Stop, I beg you. We're all we have." At her feet, the marble fuzzed and blurred. She dropped her gaze. Smoke pooled around her shoes. She gasped and backed up. The smoke followed.

Tannin shook his head. "Everyone is replaceable. Even Grigori. There's another Artist here with us right now, and a third in training."

A length of smoke snagged Cyrie's ankle. She shook it free and hurried back. "You've lost your mind. Or you're more of a zealot than I realized."

Tannin watched her with coal-black eyes. "You're at fault here. Once a contract is broken, even I can't prevent the consequences. You know this."

Nuriel grasped Dahlia's hand. "We have to go."

But Dahlia was transfixed by Tannin's cruelty and Cyrie's mounting fear. And Danel—he was a few feet away, unmoving. She tried to find his powers, to reassure herself they were still there.

Nothing.

They were gone. He was gone.

Her raw hands came up to cover her mouth in shock, eyes flooding with tears.

"Get back," Gaul grasped Dahlia and Nuriel's arms.

Tannin stepped closer to Cyrie. "Was it worth it?"

She didn't have the opportunity to respond. Coils of black smoke seeped from the marble floor, the walls, the doors. She turned to run, but the ropes shot after her, lashing her arms and legs as she screamed.

Dahlia watched in horror as one of the long coils arced high. It paused, considering its prey. Then it dove downward into Cyrie's throat. She gagged, her voice cut off into a choked keen of pain.

In seconds, Cyrie's thrashing vanished beneath folds of blackness. Sulfur drenched the air.

The smoke dissipated into a haze. In its wake it left a barely recognizable body. The smoke had cut deep, blackening her flesh and burning away her clothing and hair.

Silence rang through the hall, the absence of Cyrie's screams visceral. Dahlia was frozen with shock and horror. Her stomach lurched, threatening to spill its contents. All of the rage she'd felt toward Tannin had been upended, replaced with a deep, aching fear.

What kind of monster was he? Uncaring, unfeeling, unhinged.

He was too strong, and she was too tired. Her heartbeat throbbed in her skull and her arms trembled. Every bit of her felt wrung out. All she could do was watch as Tannin strode to Cyrie's corpse. He looked down at her, lips pursed in disappointment. Then he turned to Dahlia, Gaul, and Nuriel.

"I'm sorry you had to see that." He straightened his cuffs and ran his palms down the front of his suit, smoothing the scorched fabric. "Now. Where were we?"

Dahlia met her friends' eyes. Gaul looked utterly stricken, his eyes on Danel.

Nuriel had his own unshed tears, and he squeezed her hand. She imagined the gesture was meant to be reassuring, but they both knew the truth.

The fight was over, and they had lost.

FORTY-ONE

"Bridget!" The detective's voice cut through the ringing in Bridget's head. She winced and touched her scalp. It came away red.

"Eris..." She gestured toward the portal room, trying to string together a full sentence.

Eisheth sank down beside her. How had she gotten free? Bridget's vision blurred as the detective touched her head gently. "Hold still. You might have a concussion. Look at me."

Obeying, Bridget lifted her gaze to the detective. Eisheth was soaked, goosebumps running up her arms. Her hair was a dark, bedraggled mess, but her expression was firm and strong. Bridget held onto that small assurance.

"James," she managed to get out. Her teeth were chattering. Without Eris present, the ice around them was beginning to melt, but the basement was still frigid. "We have to follow her. She knows what we think he is."

Eisheth took this in. "We're not going anywhere until I bandage you up."

She stood and walked into the portal room. The sound of rummaging floated back to her. The detective returned with a roll of gauze and a cloth bandage. Bridget remained still as she pressed the cloth against her head injury and secured it in place. The throb in her skull matched the one radiating from her upper back.

"Come on." Eisheth hoisted Bridget upright.

Bridget blinked back black spots in her vision and steadied herself. Her thoughts felt muddled and disjointed. "Okay, um. Dahlia's upstairs. I sent Nuriel to help, but I don't know what happened." She turned toward the stairs. Maybe she should go check.

"Oh no you don't." Eisheth didn't release her. "You need medical attention. Viri's your best choice with Ret gone."

"But Dahlia..."

"You're no help to her like this."

Bridget knew Eisheth was right. Pain pulsed through her head, making it hard to focus.

The detective pursed her lips. "Let's go back through the portal. Viri and I will handle James. Stay hidden until he can treat you."

Hidden. Something about that word— "Wait."

Bridget pulled away from Eisheth and stooped down,

searching the ground until she found the necklace. The dagger lay beside it, unused. She snatched them both, head throbbing as she straightened again.

"Here. This necklace will make me invisible."

Eisheth blinked. "Interesting. Keep it close."

Tucking the necklace into her pocket, Bridget kept the dagger gripped in one hand as she allowed herself to be guided toward the portal. Her chance to use it had passed, but she still felt reassured by its grip. It helped distract her from the guilt. She'd come here to save Dahlia, and instead, she was walking away. But she *had* sent Nuriel to help, and she was in no shape to help.

And James was in more trouble than ever.

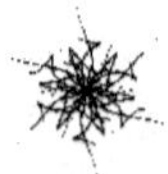

The two of them spilled out of the gas station and into the bright parking lot. Bridget took in their surroundings. A moment later, she realized what had changed.

"Where's Gaul's car?" The cherry red Mustang was gone. Beside it, Viri and Nuriel's cars sat waiting.

Eisheth sighed. "Eris probably took it."

"How does she know where to go?" Bridget felt like her chest was constricting. Every second that passed, the danger to James increased.

"The car's GPS will show her where he was last. Come on." The detective guided her to Viri's car. She held the passenger door open for Bridget, who sank onto the sun-warmed seat. Her thoughts felt less fuzzy and scattered, but sharp pain still pierced through her head. Two competing thoughts waged war in her mind.

Dahlia needs me.

I have to protect James.

Eisheth closed the door and limped around to the driver's side. "Call Viri. Let him know what's happening."

"I don't—" She patted her pockets with her free hand, but all she carried was the necklace and the dagger. The symbol etched into its pommel reflected the sunlight.

"Here." Eisheth reached for her pocket, then cursed. "Lost my phone. Never mind. Let's hurry." She turned the key in the ignition as she buckled up and then pressed down on the accelerator. They exited the parking lot onto the country highway. Bridget watched the speedometer tick up past seventy, far above the speed limit. It still didn't feel fast enough.

"What's the plan?" Bridget asked, pressing a hand against her head. Her vision was still blurry, and the sun hurt her eyes. She hunched to shield her face.

"You stay in the car. I'll go in and help Viri."

"I can't just—"

Eisheth cut off Bridget's protest. "You're injured."

"I can get to James without being seen." Bridget touched the necklace for reassurance.

The detective hesitated, poised to argue. Then she relented with a sigh. "Not a terrible idea. If you can get him to the car, drive to safety."

"And leave you and Viri to deal with Eris? You're hurt, too." Bridget eyed a bloodstain on the detective's shirt.

"We'll be okay. He'll probably stuff her in a giant Venus fly trap." She nodded to the dagger. "Hang onto that, but don't use it unless you absolutely have to. God knows what it can do."

The rest of the drive was silent. Bridget would have argued further, but talking only exacerbated her pain. Instead, she closed her eyes and the throb began to subside. None of them could beat Eris, and they both knew it. There was no ignoring the growing pit of dread she felt.

As they drove up the long stretch of driveway, Bridget put the necklace over her head, disappearing from view.

They passed the grove of trees, and the house came into view. Gaul's Mustang was parked haphazardly in front of the damaged porch.

Eisheth parked beside Gaul's empty Mustang. "I'll keep my car door open so you can follow me out. And I'll leave the keys on the seat."

"Got it." Trust a detective to think of the little details. On the off-chance Eris was watching, Bridget shouldn't spoil the element of surprise by opening and closing her own car door.

"Don't put yourself in unnecessary danger, Bridget. If it's too hard to get James out, hide. And if anything happens to Viri and me, take the car and warn the others when they come back through the portal."

If they came back through the portal. Bridget knew their return was far from guaranteed, but she appreciated Eisheth's vote of confidence.

"Okay. Let's do it." Her heart pattered as the detective exited the car. She waited until Eisheth reached the front landing before levering herself over the center console.

She followed Eisheth up the front porch. The front door was cracked open. Viri was speaking in the foyer. "I don't know what you're talking about."

"Liar." Eris drew out the word. "Come now, Viri. I can call Tannin right now and tell him to release your boyfriend, unharmed. I just need you to cooperate with me."

The detective nudged the door open. "That's not going to happen."

Inside, Viri and Eris stood facing one another. At a glance, it looked as if Viri was Eris' father, preparing to scold her—especially with Eris' arms folded across her chest. Her expression was petulant, but it brightened when the door opened.

"Eisheth! Welcome!" Eris beamed venomously. "Viri was about to tell me where he's tucked away the Key."

Eisheth held the door open as she took in the scene, standing still long enough that Bridget had time to sneak under her arm and into the house. "I thought you'd be at each other's throats by now." The detective regarded them cautiously.

Viri's posture was stiff, whites showing around his eyes as he looked at the detective. "Is Gaul okay?"

"I never saw him." Eisheth closed the door behind her.

"I did," Eris said in a sing-song. "We put him in a cozy little room."

Viri's gaze darted toward her. "Alive?"

Eris heaved a melodramatic sigh. "This is a simple exchange. You tell me where it is, and I'll help you retrieve Gaul."

Bridget wished she could tell Viri she *had* seen Gaul, and he'd been very much alive. But she couldn't reveal herself. Instead, she inched along the wall of the foyer, silently sidling around them.

"You're mistaken. There's no key here," Viri said firmly.

Eris let out a scornful laugh. "I saw the human's memories. I know what she created, and I know it can't hide without help. So where is it?"

"It?" Eisheth echoed, disdain thick.

Bridget bit the inside of her cheek, indignation coursing through her. She kept moving through the foyer, keeping one ear on the conversation.

"Why would you even care? What use is a key without a door?"

"Oh, Viri." Eris tutted and held up one hand. The sound of cracking ice drew Bridget's attention, and she peeked behind her. A latticework of ice grew from Eris' fingers, forming a pristine sculpture of a door with an oversized lock. With her other hand, she created a silvery key that entered the lock. As it turned, the door opened. Glacier blue emanated from the other side. "A key is half of a whole. With one, we are that much closer to the other. And with both, we have no need for this endless hunt for symbols."

The detective shook her head. "You're speaking in riddles."

"No, I'm speaking in inevitabilities." Eris closed her fist. The model gateway crumbled, ice crackling to the ground. "You may have a *broken* Key, but you *also* have the symbol that created it. Come now. This is your chance to change everything for our people. To reject the human world."

Bridget had made it to the hallway entrance. She was only a dozen feet or so from the door to the guest room where Viri had placed James. So far, no one had taken notice of her. She continued into the hall.

"It's *not* a human world," Eisheth said with a snort. "We share it with each other."

"No!" This time Eris shouted, and Bridget jumped. "Humans own it, we only lurk in the shadows, collecting scraps. You have no idea how much we lost. How much we stand to gain."

Viri's response was terse. "I understand it must—"

A low rumble interrupted their conversation. The ground leapt beneath them. A picture frame hanging in the hallway fell to the floor with the sound of cracking glass.

Bridget huddled in the hall, throwing her hands over her head and squeezing her eyes shut. Some part of her subconscious began to count the seconds, like she'd counted thunder as a child. *One Mississippi, two Mississippi.* A crash sounded upstairs.

The quake lasted seven seconds—the longest yet—before the shaking subsided. Slowly, Bridget uncurled herself.

Dust hung in the air. She looked behind her at the foyer. From her vantage point, she could only see Viri, whose hands were stretched upward, forcing vines to run up the walls to reinforce the house.

The room rang with silence. Then Eris said, "Look what your reluctance is causing. Have you fallen in love with humanity so much that you'd protect a corpse while the world falls down around us? Enough. I'll find the Key myself."

Bridget hurried down the hall, trying to avoid making the floorboards creak.

Behind her, Viri shouted, "Hey, stop!" It sounded as if they were moving away, giving her a precious few seconds.

Bridget slipped into the guest room, silently closing the door behind herself.

The knot in Bridget's stomach loosened ever so slightly when she saw James on the bed. Uninjured and oblivious to the commotion, the covers were wadded up from his thrashing. She went to his side and grasped his hand. "It's alright. I'm here."

From the hall, Viri was shouting at Eris to leave, and his voice was coming closer.

She needed to get James out. Now.

With fumbling fingers, she tucked the dagger awkwardly into her back pocket. Then she set about disconnecting the IV. Once he was free of the line, she slid her arms beneath his and tried to lift him.

Screaming pain lanced through her shoulder, and her head throbbed from the effort. She laid him back on the blankets with a gasp. There was no way she'd be able to carry him to the car. She eyed the window, but it was too high for her to lift James through. And the door could burst open at any moment.

Time for Plan B. If she couldn't run, she'd have to hide.

She shifted her grip. This time, she slid James off the bed then dragged him across the floor, toward the closet. Each step sounded impossibly noisy to her and sent a throb of agony through her pounding head, but she kept moving.

Awkwardly, she opened the closet door. Thankfully, the inside was nearly empty. A few of Ret's button-down shirts hung from the rod, but the floor was bare. Bridget pulled James inside, then shut the door, closing them in together.

She leaned against the wall in the darkness, gasping. The effort of bringing James this short distance had left her lightheaded, fresh pain blossoming across her forehead.

Nearby footsteps in the hall made her heart rate burst into high gear. The bedroom door unlatched.

Hurriedly, Bridget pulled the necklace on, then looped it over James' head, too. She hugged him close, listening. The footsteps circled the room and paused.

"I told you there's nothing here." Viri's voice, from the doorway.

Eris responded with a scoff. "The bed is clearly slept in."

"I've had half a dozen guests."

"Do they all use IV poles?"

Bridget shrunk back, holding her breath, as the closet door wrenched open, lighting up their hiding spot.

FORTY-TWO

Dahlia clung to Nuriel's hand. Gaul stood behind them, frozen in shock.

She reached out feebly for Tannin's powers, to stifle them, or to use them, but he swatted away her attempts with ease. Her attention kept gravitating to Danel's body, motionless on the floor. Anger and pain and fear coursed through her, making her feel lightheaded.

"Hartu."

Dahlia's breath caught at the name. "What?"

"I never liked him much. He let his emotions guide his actions, and it got him killed. It's unfortunate history has to repeat itself."

A dark rope shot out from the bubbling mass. White hot pain flooded her senses, too all-consuming to breathe.

She was vaguely aware of Nuriel shouting beside her, but then he flew back with a *whump* against the wall. He crumpled near Cyrie's corpse.

"Not to be pedantic, that's not how he died." Gaul stalked forward, wearing an expression Dahlia had never seen on him. "Hartu died sick as a dog." He made the floor buckle, then lunged. His fingers closed around Tannin's neck.

Dahlia's noose slackened, then released. She fell to the ground, gasping for air.

When she looked back up, Tannin had sunk to his knees. Gaul still gripped him, lips twisted in disgust. The skin under his fingers had darkened with dark red pustules. They spread up his throat and over his cheeks. They swelled and burst with pus, leaving dying flesh behind. The thick scent of decay hit Dahlia, and she gagged.

Placing his hands flat on the floor, Tannin let out a wordless yell. The ground beneath him cracked, and the building shook. Gaul released Tannin to windmill his arms as he stumbled forward, and Dahlia braced herself on hands and knees to ride out the Grigori-made earthquake.

Tannin crawled to his feet. He moved slowly, but Dahlia could still feel the strength of his abilities. They weren't dimmed in the least by his new illness.

A hand fell on Dahlia's back, and she looked up to see Nuriel. His gaze was fixed on Tannin, even as he helped her stand. Together, they backed up toward one of the nearby doorways.

"We can't win this fight. Where's Eisheth?" His arms were covered in deep burns. Her own were also crisscrossed with angry marks.

Dahlia searched for her, trying to find the flicker of fire. Fear stuttered her heart. "She's gone. Eris, too." What did that mean for Bridget?

"What do you mean gone?" Nuriel asked.

"I can't sense them. Either they left or they... they died." The image of Danel's body crashed into the forefront of her mind's eye.

"The portal is down there. It would take them closer to—" His eyes widened. "Eris is going after James. She must have realized what he is."

"What?"

"We think James' symbol is a key to—"

Gaul cried out, and both of them flinched. Tannin bore down on him, a roiling darkness clawing its way up his body.

If what Nuriel said was true, Bridget would be following Eris. Her sister and Eisheth were in danger. But escape would only draw Tannin through the portal, after them. She couldn't risk the fight spilling out into Cleveland.

Unless.

An idea crystallized in an instant. Dangerous, shaky. But it might work.

She looked at Nuriel. "We need to get downstairs."

"I'll need an opening." Nuriel didn't take his eyes off of Gaul. The redhead knocked Tannin's smoke back in a spray of rock, but it was only a matter of time before he was overwhelmed.

"Working on it." She closed her eyes, trying to reclaim the focus she'd felt when dampening Eris' powers. Despite her pain and mounting weariness, anger fueled her. And that sharpened her attention.

She shifted her focus outward. Her mind found purchase and clung tight. Extending her arms, she thrust Tannin's abilities back on him.

She was rewarded with a new cry of pain. She opened her eyes to see Tannin's own smoke wrapped around his torso. His anguish brought Dahlia a deep sense of satisfaction. She moved closer, hands outstretched. Beyond him, Gaul fell to the ground, free but nursing blistering skin.

Sparing a fraction of attention, she glanced over, finding Nuriel. "Downstairs. Now!"

Nuriel burst into a run, hurrying to Gaul's side and pulling him to his feet. They began stumbling down the hallway, toward the stairs.

Adrenaline pushed Dahlia forward, even as she trembled to hold the ability. *This* was what Bridget couldn't understand. Her sister would have her abandon her new talents in the pursuit of normal. But *normal* couldn't do *this*.

A burst of ragged laughter cut through Tannin's pain. "Sweet, isn't it? The power?"

Dahlia didn't respond. He wasn't worth her words, or the focus they would cost her. Instead, she tried to squeeze more tightly.

It didn't respond. Her grip almost slipped. Her entire body shook, a wall of fatigue waiting for her. She'd given Nuriel as much of a head start as possible. Now it was her turn to run.

Dahlia dropped Tannin's abilities. The smoke dissolved, and he hit the floor hard. He rolled onto his side, coughing, hands grasping his blistered neck.

Weariness enveloped her, and she half-fell into the wall. *Go.* She pushed off, breaking into a sprint.

Without Danel's speed, she felt terribly slow. But she ran past where Tannin was climbing to his knees and turned the corner to the top of the stairwell.

She clambered down the stairs, meeting Nuriel and Gaul at the bottom. The world spun until Nuriel gripped her arm to steady her.

"He's close behind," she gasped. Black spots crowded her vision. She took a step forward, then found herself falling. Her knees had simply given out in weariness. Nuriel hoisted her upright.

"On it." Gaul lifted his hands. "Nuriel, help me. Dahlia, go to the portal."

Water drenched the floor, making it smell like a cave. Tannin's cracked cabinets dripped, shards of glass littering the floor. Artifacts lay among the debris, books slowly soaking in water.

Gathering herself, she made her way over the wreckage, glancing back to see Gaul breaking apart the floor until he reached the clay underneath. Nuriel drew in the water that coated the basement. Together, they created a concrete-like mixture to bar their path. Nuriel then drew the water from the newly constructed wall, hardening it instantly.

She turned away, continuing to stagger to the portal room. Once inside, she paused, leaning heavily against the metal table. Nuriel and Gaul came through seconds later. In the shaky silence, she took them all in. Burned tatters of Gaul's shirt hung from him, revealing scorch marks on his pale skin. Nuriel's sleeves were gone, and Dahlia's neck felt like it was on fire.

"We only have a minute." Her voice was hoarse, head throbbing. "Nuriel, can you get home on your own?"

"What?" Gaul asked, eyes hazy, brow furrowed as he listened. "No one needs to stay here. Tannin—"

Dahlia cut him off. "Trust me. This is our order: Gaul, me, Tannin. Nuriel, you'll have to hide until he goes through, okay?"

"What do you need me to do?"

She told them her plan. They listened with various levels of skepticism, but when she was done, Gaul spoke. "It could work. Nuriel, use our funds to catch the first flight out."

Nuriel looked concerned, but he nodded in agreement. "Alright. Be careful."

Dahlia tried to sound as firm as possible. "You be careful. Stay hidden."

A distant thud made them all jump. Tannin was breaking through their defense.

"Get started," Dahlia urged Gaul, heart thumping nervously.

He limped to the symbol and touched it. Familiar golden light illuminated the stark burns covering him. He looked back at Dahlia, one hand flat against the wall. "Don't do anything stupid. Again." The golden light enveloped him, and then he was gone.

She turned back to Nuriel.

"Be careful." He touched Dahlia's shoulder gently. A tingle ran up Dahlia's arm that had nothing to do with Grigori powers. "What Tannin said upstairs, about Hartu? It's wrong. You get to choose who you are."

Dahlia nodded, throat tightening. "Thank you."

She knew it wasn't so simple, and she suspected he

did, too. Hartu was a part of her. If she didn't want to lose his fury... would that be so bad? With it, she'd held Tannin back.

Outside, a loud crash rang through the basement. Dahlia pulled back. "Hide. Now."

Nuriel hurried to the freezer. He ducked inside, emitting a brief wave of frosty air.

Dahlia went to the door again, letting herself out into the destruction of the collection room. Her stomach twisted itself into knots as she waited.

A web of smoke tore through the remnants of the mud wall, shattering it apart. Tannin ignored the rubble, eyes landing on her. His jacket was unbuttoned, dark red stains on the shirt beneath. Diseased black splotches marred his neck. Brimstone flared behind him like wings.

He stalked toward her, lifting his voice so it carried across the space. "Kai was right. Mimics are incapable of loyalty unless forced."

Rage flared up. She fanned the flames, no longer attempting to hold them back. Let him see her fury.

"I'm loyal to people who actually care about me." She held his gaze as she backed up, heart banging in her ears.

He walked straight through the rubble, kicking aside broken glass. The cloud of darkness at his back was so thick, she couldn't see behind him. "You're as much a tool to your so-called friends as you are to me."

Dahlia pressed her hand firmly on the portal as Tannin's smoke lashed out, wrapping around her ankle and searing her flesh. He tried to yank her back to him, but the portal pulled harder, and she tumbled through.

Inside, she barely registered the black lightning, the

thickness of the air. But she couldn't avoid the myriad eyes and the overlapping voices whispering to her. *Little sister, what are you doing?* They sounded anxious, rising and falling like ocean waves.

She twisted to look behind herself as she was drawn forward. Golden light split the space open, and another presence joined her. In this alien place, Tannin appeared as a dark, smoky smudge.

But no matter how powerful he was, in this space between worlds, they were both helpless. The energy of the portal pulsed through her, pushing her forward. Anticipation made her hands shake.

The golden glow behind Tannin flickered. It went dark—leaving behind a black, gaping hole.

Nuriel had done it.

Exhaling sharply, fingers steadying, Dahlia turned forward again. She let the golden light embrace her.

She stumbled through the other side, and an arm stabilized her. The air around her thinned to normal. The gas station bathroom came into focus—and Gaul, bracing her upright.

"Now," she rasped.

She grabbed his earth ability. Gaul pulled away, and they both lifted their hands.

Together, they turned their powers toward the wall. It shuddered, then buckled. Slabs of painted cinder block broke free, tumbling to the ground.

The portal collapsed, trapping Tannin inside.

FORTY-THREE

Bridget held her breath as the temperature in the closet plunged. She covered James' mouth with the edge of her bloodied t-shirt, blocking his misty exhales.

Eris' scuffed sneakers came to a stop only inches from her. The young-looking Grigori peered into the closet, eyebrows drawn together. Bridget didn't move. Didn't breathe. Willed James to stay still.

"Viri," Eris said, "do you know what my name means?"

"I hardly see how this is relevant."

Bridget slowly exhaled to ease her burning lungs. Beside her, James shifted silently. She counted her heartbeats, urging them to slow. It was like hiding during childhood games of hide-and-seek with Dahlia. This moment would pass. They would make it through this. She had to believe that.

"Strife. And discord."

Dahlia. After everything, Bridget had left her sister behind. The lure of hope crumbled. How could she live with abandoning her? What was Tannin doing to her while she hunched in the shadows of the closet?

Viri came into view, following Eris into the room. For the first time since Bridget met him, he looked angry. He jabbed a finger toward the door. "I don't care. What you're looking for isn't here. Please go."

Footsteps sounded in the hall, announcing Eisheth's arrival. She paused in the doorway, leaning heavily against the frame. The bloodstain on her shirt had grown. "This is ridiculous."

"Eisheth, you're injured. Please go sit down." Viri looked at her in concern.

Eris turned from the closet door to regard them. "But you *should* care, Viri. Because it's who I am. And I'll gladly rip every nail from this house if it brings me the Key."

Eisheth growled, balling her hands into fists at her side. Flames sputtered, then leaped upward, licking her arms and eating away what was left of her sleeves. "You'll get the hell out."

James shivered. He tried to twist away from Bridget. She held him tightly to keep him still.

A wordless sound of protest escaped him.

Eris spun around, staring directly at their hiding spot. "Interesting."

Bridget's own breath came in short gasps, escaping in puffs of fog. Her heart was in her ears.

Before Eris could act, Eisheth launched a spray of fire at her. At the same time, a vibrant green vine burst from the floor, throwing up splinters of wood. It wrapped itself around Eris' leg and tugged. Eris hit the ground hard and held her arms up, shielding herself from the raining flames.

Bridget pressed herself deeper into the closet, watching for an opening that might allow her to escape with James in tow. The grip of the dagger pressed into her, but she couldn't grab it and maneuver James. She could leave James and join the fight, or trust her friends and try to drag him to freedom.

Eris flung a hand toward Viri and Eisheth. They both threw their arms up defensively. Then, they froze in place, a thick sheet of glossy white ice settling over them. Frost latticed over their open eyes and their expressions stiffened in place.

Both Eisheth and Viri toppled to the ground, blanketed beneath icy plasters. The vine holding Eris withered and fell away. Bridget shrunk back in horror. Effortless. Like her friends were bugs.

Eris crawled to her feet, kicking away dead plants and scowled down at her unmoving foes, shaking her head. Then she turned back to the closet. Bridget's heart thudded as Eris approached. "You all seem to think this is personal. It's really not."

Bridget turned wide eyes from her friends up to Eris. She pulled James close to her, covering his mouth and holding still.

Eris squatted down in front of the open closet door. She was so close, Bridget could see each individual freckle covering the bridge of her nose.

"That invisibility trick will only work once, human."

Bridget drew her legs up to her chest and kicked hard.

She caught Eris in the hip. The Grigori fell back with a surprised cry. Bridget tugged the necklace from her head, leaving it on James, and launched herself forward. Head throbbing, she tackled Eris around the waist. They fell onto the blackened carpet with twin grunts.

Sudden cold blossomed through her veins, spreading to her extremities. It sunk deep into her muscles, freezing them in place. She tried to grip Eris' shirt more tightly, but the child Grigori shoved her aside. Bridget hit the ground, numb. She fell face-to-face with Eisheth, who remained trapped beneath a sheet of ice—but her eyes tracked Bridget's movements.

Bridget tried to sit up, but she only managed to roll over. Her body was frigid and sluggish.

"Let's see what we have here." Eris recovered her balance and turned her full attention to the closet. She grasped the doorframe and kicked sharply. James let out a grunt and she bent down, fumbling until her fingers found what she was searching for. She drew the necklace from James, who popped into view. He was slumped, shivering, in the corner.

Bridget trembled. "Let him go." The words slurred, barely audible. Her tongue felt like a block of ice in her mouth. "P-please."

She sneered. "*Him?* This creature is useless. Unimaginable power trapped inside a worthless vessel." A blue-white knife formed in her hand, serrated and gleaming. Her smile was bright. "Relieving him of this symbol will be a mercy."

James was still shivering, oblivious to the world around him. With a surprisingly gentle motion, Eris laid a hand on his chest. Frost crept outward from her fingers, crawling up his throat and over him.

Bridget tried to scream, managing only a strangled, guttural sound. She thrashed the best she could against the ice, but her body didn't listen. It *couldn't* end like this. She couldn't watch him die, again, at the hand of her enemy.

But there was nothing she could do as frost slithered from Eris' fingers, pouring into James' body and freezing him from the inside out.

FORTY-FOUR

Dahlia and Gaul staggered from the gas station building, burned and bruised. Nuriel's car sat alone in the parking lot, drawing a curse from Gaul. He patted his pockets, coming up with a useless Mustang key. "One of them must've hot-wired it."

It was disorienting, emerging from Tannin's lair and into the early evening sunlight. On the road, cars whisked by—people going about their business, earthquakes or no. Dahlia shook herself. "I have Nuriel's key fob."

The two of them piled into his Prius. The same strange disorientation settled over Dahlia as she backed out of the parking spot. After everything they'd been through, it felt *too* normal.

"Why is Eris is going to Viri's?" Gaul gripped the handle above the door as Dahlia turned onto the main road and punched the accelerator.

"I'm not sure, exactly. Nuriel said something about James and his symbol being a key to something. I think he might've been talking about—"

"The Gateway." Gaul finished her thought. "Drive faster."

She sped down the straight stretches of road. When they reached a slowdown, she tried to channel Danel's devil-may-care driving habits.

God. Danel.

Her throat tightened. Every physical ache and burn screamed, but the pain of losing him was shocking by comparison.

She still hated him. His actions were irredeemable. But he'd only come along to help her. He didn't deserve to die, and certainly not at Tannin's hand.

"Will Nuriel bring him home?" Her voice shook.

Gaul met her gaze, then nodded. He didn't have to ask who she meant. "If he can, I'm sure he will."

She turned her eyes back to the road. "He—he had a niece. Great-niece. Whatever. Her name is Morgan. Someone should tell her... and Eisheth. God, she's going to be..." She trailed off, her thoughts scattering.

All she could picture was Tannin's cold, flat eyes as he ended Danel's life.

He's trapped. He can't escape. She steadied herself with those words of reassurance. Her plan had finally eliminated Tannin as a threat. She should feel relieved.

Instead, she just felt angry.

Gaul's response was measured. "Let's focus on what's in front of us right now."

She steadied herself. "Okay, yeah. Um. What happens

if Eris gets to James?"

"I don't know, but I have guesses. None of them good. Most likely, she'll kill James and take the symbol for herself. Once she has it, she can search for a more suitable owner."

Dahlia changed lanes. "Can it be reused so quickly? Naming symbols can't."

"I don't know."

She nodded. She was too focused on the road to delve into the nuance of Grigori magic. "And then?"

"It depends. If she can also find the Gateway, everyone on this planet will face the most dramatic shift in our reality we've seen in millennia. We won't need tattoos anymore. All of us will be at full power, as if we were thousands of years old. The door between our worlds would be thrown open.

"I don't know as much about this as Ret did. There was a time when the Gateway was open and it *didn't* destroy both of our worlds. But it doesn't take many megalomaniacal Grigori to cause a hell of a lot of trouble."

Dahlia turned onto the country road that led to Viri's house. She could easily imagine how bad the fallout would be if enough Grigori were like Tannin and Eris— apathetic to the pain they caused. "Okay. So, we won't let her get to James."

"Right." Their earlier conversation wasn't lost on her. From the beginning, Gaul had known eliminating James was an option. Now, though, he seemed prepared to fight for him. For that, she was grateful.

As they pulled into Viri's driveway, it was clear Eris was here. The closer they got to the house, the colder it got. As she parked, frost formed on the windshield and dusted the flowerbeds.

"Let's go." She threw the door open, but was stopped by a hand on her arm.

"Are you sure you're up to this?" Gaul's eyes raked over her, taking in the burns. "This is going to be every bit as dangerous as fighting Tannin."

She *was* exhausted. She was hurt and still reeling from the death of Danel.

But she also wasn't done.

Dahlia pulled her arm free. "Let's go." She let herself out of the car, trusting Gaul to follow.

The foyer was empty, although it showed signs of the most recent quake. Water dripped from the ceiling, where melting ice soaked a complex tangle of climbing plants.

There was a swell of powers to her left, centered around the guest bedrooms. With relief, she recognized Eisheth and Viri's abilities. They were alive, at least.

Eris was there, too. And James, his strength outshining them all.

Hopefully Bridget was out of harm's way.

She beckoned for Gaul to follow her into the hallway. One of the doors was open wide, ice fractals spreading from it.

"Let's see what we have here." Eris' high-pitched voice was impossible to mistake.

A whisper of a response. Dahlia couldn't make out the words.

Gaul leaned in, "Do what you can here without revealing yourself."

Eris spoke again. "*Him?* This creature is useless.

Unimaginable power trapped inside a worthless vessel. Relieving him of this symbol will be a mercy."

Her words were followed by a horrible, stifled scream she'd recognize anywhere. Her eyes went wide. Bridget.

Gaul rushed toward the doorway. He raised his hands, and the room shuddered.

A flare of ice. Dahlia felt the edges of the blast of cold air that hit Gaul. He hit the back hallway wall, encased in ice.

She rushed to him, dropping to her knees. "Gaul!" His eyes met hers, but he didn't move otherwise.

Tremors of rage rolled through Dahlia as she stood. Approaching the open door, she saw two more icy lumps lying on the floor—the frozen-over forms of Eisheth and Viri. Bridget was nearby, moving sluggishly toward James in an army crawl. Only Eris was standing.

They locked eyes, and Dahlia didn't see a young girl at all. This Grigori had murdered Ret, stifled the abilities that might have saved Danel. And now she was standing over James as if she had any right to his fate. Confident. Smug.

Angry spots sparked across her vision, but Dahlia knew she couldn't beat Eris. No more than she could face down Tannin. In a one-on-one match, she was dust beneath Eris' feet.

Except... she *had* beaten Tannin, hadn't she?

And Eris' powers weren't the strongest in the room.

This time strength would have to prevail.

She closed her eyes and focused on James, funneling the Key's power into herself.

Her entire world exploded into gold.

FORTY-FIVE

Bridget's heart jolted as James trembled. His eyes opened wide. He was awake.

But no. His eyes appeared to register nothing—unmoving, unflinching. Then he fell forward, folding on himself. His back came into view, tattoo glowing a lurid yellow.

The glow peeled back from James entirely. It puddled in the air over him, a pulsing orb. And then it streaked away, over Bridget's head.

She turned her eyes to see Dahlia standing in the doorway. A shock of adrenaline. In the fog of her pain, she hadn't realized her sister had arrived. Relief crashed down on her—she'd made it out of Tannin's alive.

The ball of light slammed into Dahlia. She staggered back, back arching. Piercing gold light poured into her eyes. And then she swayed and slumped to the ground.

Bridget willed herself to her knees. A prickling sensation raced up her extremities as she shuffled to her sister. She grasped Dahlia's arm, then drew back in shock. She was hot to the touch. Her skin flickered, luminescent. It was as if the golden light was boiling her from the inside.

Terror pulsed through Bridget. Whirling back on Eris, she demanded, "What did you do?!"

Eris watched, eyes bright with interest. "Nothing at all."

Bridget tried to stand, but her achingly cold legs buckled. She crawled forward and shook Dahlia. "Dahlia, can you hear me?"

The golden light in her eyes sputtered, dark brown coming back through sporadically. "It hurts." Her voice came out as a rasp.

"It's okay. I've got you. We'll fix this." Tears stung Bridget's eyes. The promise felt hollow. She didn't know how to help Dahlia. She couldn't heal James. All their friends were trapped. She even caught sight of a frozen Gaul in the hallway.

"You can't possibly hold that power," Eris said.

Dahlia reached out for Bridget. "Run."

Then she stood. Golden arcs of light continued to crackle around her, making her glow. She fixed her gaze on Eris. Her eyes sparked and glittered. "Danel is dead."

Shock froze Bridget in place. Dead?

No, that wasn't possible.

Was Nuriel gone, too? He hadn't come back with Dahlia and Gaul.

The girl's eyebrows lifted. She was watching Dahlia

intently. A fresh icicle dagger had formed in one hand, but she didn't attack. "Is he? Well, I suppose he had it coming."

"So is Cyrie." Dahlia advanced. "Both thanks to Tannin. And now *Tannin* is gone. He won't hurt anyone ever again."

Eris paused. "You're lying."

"Now it's your turn." Dahlia clenched her fists and a wave of frigid air rolled toward Eris, knocking her back. It hit Bridget too, and she staggered into the doorframe.

"Go, Bridget. I've got this." Dahlia's voice was ragged.

Bridget felt locked in place, rooted by confusion.

The blast of light had knocked Eris into the bed. She steadied herself. "You think you can kill me with a power you don't even understand?"

She flicked her hand, sending a shock of arctic air toward Dahlia. But where the same move had rendered Eisheth, Viri, and Gaul motionless, Dahlia waved it away, conjuring a wall of flames. The two elements met and fizzled.

Eris hesitated. For the first time since Bridget had met her, uncertainty flickered across her features. Dahlia took advantage of the pause, raising her hands and summoning a fireball in each palm.

"Wait." Eris dropped her own hands. "The Key isn't meant for a Grigori. You can't possibly hold it. But you *can* use it. Think about it. If we find the right vessel for the Key—a *living* human, not a corpse—you could help free all of our people." She gestured toward Bridget. "We have one right here."

Bridget flinched back instinctively as Eris' attention turned to her. The soggy rug beneath her feet hardened into slick ice, and her feet slid out from under her. She landed on the floor with a painful thump.

"Leave her alone." Dahlia moved to throw the fire, but it sparked and fizzled out. Gold light rushed across her and she doubled over.

"Let it go before it consumes you, child. Work *with* me. If Tannin is truly gone, we will need someone to replace him. A mimic could—"

"Stop!" Dahlia thrust her hands out, clenched her fists, and *pulled*. Eris gasped, falling to one knee. The air between them shimmered with frost as Dahlia siphoned the power toward her.

"I will *never* side with you." Her sister staggered closer to Eris. She thrust a hand out, grabbing the Grigori's arm. Eris' eyes went wide, then blank.

Bridget watched in horror. She knew exactly what was happening. Dahlia had thrust Eris into the depths of her own memories, forcing her to relive them.

Giving Bridget an opening.

She edged toward the closet, where James lay. Unconscious. Alone. Ignored. His eyes were still open, staring blankly up at the ceiling.

She grabbed him under his armpits. Her shoulder screamed in pain, her heartbeat thundered like a jackhammer in her head, as she began dragging him across the floor on half-numb legs. It took all of her willpower not to watch as Dahlia struggled to cling to Eris, to keep her trapped in the past. Her sister had fallen onto one knee, her body shaking.

Passing Viri, Eisheth, and Gaul, Bridget dragged James' dead weight down the hall. Step by anguished step, she brought him into the foyer, then out onto the front porch.

There, she paused to catch her breath. She released her grip on James, and he slumped to the ground. Somehow, with his eyes open, he seemed more like a corpse than he ever had.

Bridget's entire body trembled. Her stomach churned, her head felt like it had an icepick lodged in it. She swallowed hard to keep herself from throwing up.

Just a little farther. The car was right there. If she could get him inside, she could take him... somewhere. Keep him safe until—

Until what? Until Dahlia destroyed Eris, like she had Tannin? Whatever had happened in Athens had left Dahlia almost unrecognizable, overflowing with vindictiveness.

And what would happen once Eris *was* gone? The earthquakes would continue. It wouldn't be long before other Grigori found them. Tannin and Eris were only the beginning.

James wasn't safe. Would never be safe.

Bridget brushed back blood-encrusted hair and looked back at the house. The weight of reality was crushing. James was beyond her help. And Dahlia...

Golden light flickered in the windows, coiling and snapping angrily.

She couldn't leave, not yet. Not with Dahlia allowing raw power to consume her.

Bridget squeezed James' hand, then let go. She was the only person who could save Dahlia from herself. Taking the necklace, she put it over her head and hurried back into the house.

FORTY-SIX

Dahlia was burning alive. The power she'd taken from James seethed within her, desperate for an outlet. Static overtook her, blinding her, distracting her. A jarring pain coursed through her—not to her physical body, but to her whole being. She tried to focus on Eris, but jumbled voices filled her mind, speaking in ideas more than words. One voice spoke above the rest.

This is yours.

The Key had unlocked a bottomless well of strength. Every other ability was magnified. Abilities that weren't just hers to manipulate, but to take for herself. It required barely more than a thought.

So. This was what it felt like to have full access to her Grigori self.

This is what it would be like to open the Gateway.

No wonder Gaul had been nervous. She'd swatted Eris down like she was nothing.

There was no end to what she could do.

Don't question this. Seize it.

And yet, she was locked in a battle with her own body. Willing herself to move, to think, to focus. James' condition now made sense. He hadn't been unconscious—he'd been overwhelmed, at war with himself. How could a dead man possibly harness this kind of power?

Eris was watching with fascination. She'd regained her abilities when a wave of crackling pain overwhelmed Dahlia, and now she was saying something.

Focus, the voice urged. It felt familiar, somehow.

"This fight is counterproductive, mimic." Eris' eyes flashed. "We can restore the Gateway together, so you can always have this kind of strength."

Eris was a snake, and her words only stoked Dahlia's anger. With barely a thought, she siphoned off a sliver of Eisheth's fire and sent a blast of flame toward Eris. A shield of ice erected itself in defense. The hot and cold consumed one another.

Stabbing, noncorporeal pain overtook her. She doubled over, losing Eisheth's fire.

When she blinked away the sparks, panting in the wake of the jolt, Eris had surrounded herself with a protective ring of ice daggers. Eagerness lit up her eyes. "Listen to me. I was alive when the Gateway fell. We can open it again, together."

You don't need her.

"I don't need you." It felt true.

Eris lifted her chin, standing with the confidence of a

queen. "You with the Key, me with the Gateway. Together, we'll change the world."

"No." Anger clawed at Dahlia's throat. "You're a snake. No better than Tannin. Everything that comes out of your mouth is a lie."

"Little child." How strange to have someone so young-looking call *her* a child. Eris' eyes were ablaze with intensity. "I don't lie. This is my reality, after millennia of diminishing freedom—thanks to short-lived, small-minded humans."

She's right. But she wants the power for herself.

Dahlia bristled. "You can't blame all humans for something that happened millennia ago."

"Please. As if your own sister wouldn't wish our world away if she could?"

Dahlia flinched as if slapped. "Leave Bridget out of this."

Of course, Eris was right. That's exactly what her sister wanted—for both of them. Normal life. Normal school. Normal relationship.

A smile slithered across Eris' face at Dahlia's hesitation. "She has no power over you. You're a mimic. She's nothing. A breath in time that will die and turn to ash before you even fully understand yourself."

The words slipped into Dahlia like bitter medicine. There was truth to them, and that truth bubbled up into a pain she hadn't allowed herself to feel yet. Grief. She *would* outlive her sister. By centuries, millennia.

Bridget *didn't* have any power over her.

But that didn't mean her sister wasn't important.

Her flawed, overprotective, controlling sister had gone through hell and back for her. Twice. And Dahlia knew she'd do it again in a heartbeat.

Eris crooned, "You'd be better off without her."

Anger zinged through Dahlia. She called thick vines up through the window and floorboards to ensnare Eris. She squeezed her hands, and they constricted across her waist, her throat, her legs.

Eris gasped, clawing at the coils of greenery. They froze and withered under her fingers.

Dahlia dropped Viri's ability for a new one. Pestilence tingled at the tips of her fingers. She stalked forward, grabbing Eris by the shoulder, pouring disease into her. Eris fell to her knees. Sweat broke out along her forehead, and she began coughing—a deep, hacking sound of liquid settling in the lungs.

A cacophony of possibilities crackled through Dahlia's veins, sparking with potential. She bore down on sickness and grim satisfaction filled her. Why Gaul hated this power was a mystery to her. It was shockingly effective. Eris' breathing came in wet, heaving gasps, her whole body trembling.

The presence in her mind stirred again. It didn't say anything, but it was watching intently.

Dahlia bore down on Eris. She would no longer be a threat. Just as Dahlia had locked Tannin away, she'd end Eris' pitiful campaign for supremacy.

Dahlia's vision sparked gold, and she doubled over again. Her head was in a vice, a war of voices and power and electricity coursing through her.

When her vision cleared again, Eris had broken free and staggered toward the hallway. She tripped over Viri's fallen form, catching herself in the doorframe. Her shoe cracked the melting ice, and it spiderwebbed open. He sucked in weak breaths.

This strength is yours. Use it.

Dahlia gathered powers toward her. It didn't matter whose, or what they did. They swirled together, a tempest of strength and fire and sickness. Gold light set her whole body ablaze.

She lifted her hand, preparing to release the maelstrom. To destroy Eris once and for all. And then? And then *she* could decide what would happen with the Key.

Eris stiffened and staggered forward, as if hit from behind. Dahlia paused.

The girl's eyes widened, sparking with sudden fear. She wavered, then toppled forward, falling face-first onto the ruined floorboards.

Down her back, a ragged line sliced through her shirt. Blood seeped through the tear, a deep slash bisecting the tattoo on her back. It flickered with a golden pulse, then went dark.

Dahlia stared, uncomprehending. All of the power she'd been about to unleash pulsed, desperate for escape.

The shadowy voice echoed her bewilderment. *That's it?*

In the silence that followed, Bridget snapped into view as she pulled the necklace off. In her other hand, she held a bloody dagger. Her cheeks were pale as she stepped around Eris' body. Her wide eyes fixed on Dahlia. "Release it. Please. It's over."

Heat flushed through her. Eris was supposed to be *her* kill. And Bridget took it with one simple slice through the tattoo?

Were they all that vulnerable?

All this power... all this fragility.

Bridget took Dahlia's hand, squeezed it. "You're safe. We're safe. Let it go."

Don't, the voice warned. *Keep it. You need it.*

Dahlia wavered. She wasn't safe, not really. Not when any one of them could be destroyed so easily.

She clung to her grip on the Key. If she let go, she'd be weak again. A tool for others to kidnap and manipulate.

But there was no one left to battle, only her sister staring at her, her friends thawing from their prisons of ice.

She remembered Nuriel's sense of betrayal when she'd taken his power without asking.

Bridget's desperation to anchor Dahlia in her humanity.

Gaul's reluctance to train her, and her own promises that she wouldn't use her ability to destroy—the way Hartu had.

This is a mistake.

With a shudder, she pushed the power outward, away from her. It evaporated, golden light dissipating around her.

In its place, darkness crowded in.

She could feel herself falling, but she was unconscious before she hit the floor.

FORTY-SEVEN

Bridget rushed to her sister's side, falling to her knees. Dahlia's eyes were closed, her skin hot. But she was breathing and no longer glowing. Sweat beaded along her brow, and Bridget brushed it away.

"You're okay," she whispered.

"Are *you* okay?" Gaul's ragged voice caught her attention. With Eris' death, her friends had been freed from the icy bindings. Now Gaul sat in the hallway, his tattered clothes soaked through. His lips were tinged blue, and he was shivering.

She cradled Dahlia's head in her lap and glanced at Eris. "I didn't know if it would work, but I couldn't think of anything else."

"It was smart. And it had to be done." Gaul turned his attention to Dahlia. "I've been remiss in my mentorship.

I promise I'll be more present to help your sister going forward."

She tucked a dark, wavy strand of hair behind Dahlia's ear. Yes, Gaul *should* have given her more guidance. But Bridget couldn't fault him for his reticence.

She'd felt the same way. Grigori magic was dangerous. The more Dahlia leaned into it, the more alien she would become.

She'd proven it. She *had* become dangerous. She *had* changed. Given the chance, she'd seized the Key and become a weapon.

A weapon to save them all.

Bridget squeezed her hand. Would Dahlia have released the power if it hadn't been eating her alive? She couldn't know, not for certain.

But it was undeniable now that her sister had dramatically changed. The rage in her, the way she'd attacked Eris—this wasn't the old Dahlia.

Neither was Bridget the old Bridget.

"Up you get." Gaul knelt by Eisheth, breaking away the remaining ice and helping her sit upright. Then he turned to Viri, doing the same for him. They both looked bewildered and half frozen.

Viri surveyed the damage around him and the dead girl at his feet. He turned away, hand to his mouth, as Gaul slipped a blanket over his shoulders.

Eisheth grabbed a pillow from the bed and handed it to Bridget. "What happened? I could barely see, couldn't hear anything at all."

She slid the pillow under her sister's head. "Dahlia saved us." With a deep exhale, she stood and walked to where Eris lay prone. She was so small. Devoid of life, she simply looked like a child, broken on the torn hardwood floor. That marked two Grigori she had killed. Two people. She felt sick.

An escalating roar interrupted her morose thoughts. The ground shook, a discontented rumble sending plaster falling around them. One of the walls cracked like a gunshot. A ceramic pot holding a frost-bitten plant fell to the ground with a crash. Immediately, Bridget hurried to cover Dahlia, but Gaul was already there, protecting her unconscious form with his exhausted body. Eisheth cursed as the lintel above the door fell, scraping her arm on the way down.

The world wasn't free from danger yet. Now that Dahlia had relinquished the Key's power, the earthquakes had resumed. Bridget swallowed hard.

"Where is James?" Eisheth held her scraped arm against her.

"On the front porch."

Viri shook himself. "I can help bring him back to the bed. Once we... once we're able to regather, we can talk about how to help him."

An ache settled in Bridget's chest as Viri spoke. His words were kind and hopeful, but Bridget was hollow.

"I know how to help him." She gave her sister one last glance to reassure herself she was still safe. "Someone watch over her?"

"I will," Gaul said. She met his green eyes, and he reached out to squeeze her hand. No words passed between them, but there was a gravitas to his expression. He understood.

He turned his attention to the detective, the corners of his eyes tightening. "Eisheth, stay with me. I have difficult news for you."

Standing shakily, Bridget picked up the dagger she'd

dropped. She climbed past the wreckage in the doorway and into the hall. Out of the crowded room—away from Eris' body—she could breathe a little easier. But that only stirred up dread.

She started down the corridor but stopped again as she heard footsteps behind her.

Viri was following, his expression somber. "I don't have to come with you. But I thought, maybe..."

Bridget's heart panged in sorrow. In gratitude. "I appreciate it." She continued her progress through the house. A few more walls had enormous cracks running through them, and there was an inches-wide crevice between the slats of the formerly tight hardwood floor.

James was exactly where she'd left him, curled up on the porch. Shattered glass sparkled around him, but he seemed unharmed. Healthy, even.

He moaned softly, rolling over. Golden light flickered over him, like iridescent flames. Bridget didn't know if it was the power re-entering his body, or if the Key was becoming harder to contain. But it didn't really matter. The situation was untenable, and it wouldn't get better on its own.

"James?" she ventured quietly.

He didn't respond. Kneeling beside him, Bridget pressed a hand to his back. His tattoo was hot under her fingers.

She choked a sob. Guilt swirled within her. Hadn't she just been reflecting on how much death she'd caused? But James wasn't truly alive. He'd been gone for weeks now. There had been no hint of his affable personality since his revival. Only a shell of his former self, animated by a power that made him a target.

Viri's voice was gentle from the doorway. "I can help

ease this process for both of you. If you want."

She looked back at him, studying the compassion in his eyes.

More than anything, she wanted to run away from this moment. To put it past her. To anesthetize herself to it. Viri's abilities gave her that option.

She'd tried so hard to save James, throwing herself into it with the same desperation as when Dahlia had gone missing. She *could* keep trying. She could pour over Ret's books, dig deeper into Grigori lore. Find another symbol.

But what would he want?

What would excitable, loyal James ask for, if he could?

Not this. Not eternity caught between worlds. She slid her free hand into his.

Bridget's obsession with saving him had only hurt more people. She saw that clearly now, surrounded by the damage to Viri's house. Seeing her friends—yes, her *friends*—nursing injuries caused by the pursuit of power. Knowing Ret was dead, Danel was dead.

She owed it to herself and to James to feel this with all its sharp, unfair poignancy.

"Thank you, Viri. Help James. But not me."

She hadn't meant to do *anything* but give James another chance. One he deserved. One he'd never have.

But now, the greatest honor she could give him—the most dignity she could afford him—was to let him go peacefully.

Viri knelt down opposite her, taking James' other hand. Light trickled from his fingers into James' skin.

Tears spilled down Bridget's cheeks as she tightened her grip on the dagger.

There would be time later to grieve, to accept he was

gone. First, she had to let him go.

"I'm so sorry, James." Her voice was a reedy whisper. "I hope the next life is an adventure. You deserve a good one." She leaned down to kiss the top of his head.

Then, vision blurry, she shakily brought the blade to the skin above his shirt collar. It was the same motion she had used with Eris. But now, she was filled with tenderness rather than desperation. Sorrow rather than hate. Love rather than fear.

She readied herself, hoping for James' forgiveness. And for an ounce of his courage. With a stone weighing down her heart, she pressed hard and pulled downward.

The metal met resistance at first, then pierced the skin. It sliced through the fabric of his shirt and the tattooed symbol beneath. A gash opened, an arc of blood seeping out. Cut in half, the design flashed gold and sputtered. The dagger's pommel drank in the failing light.

James fell limp.

She dropped the dagger, pressing her fingers against his neck, feeling for a pulse, for breath, anything. But he was still and silent. It was as if he'd been dead all along.

Sobs welled up, wracking her as she huddled over James' body. A wail tore from her throat, becoming a discordant whine. Viri put his arms around her, and she sobbed.

She doubted she would ever be able to scrub this memory from her mind. And she wasn't sure she wanted to. He was her friend, and she'd honored him the only way she knew how.

Letting go was an important step toward healing.

Right?

FORTY-EIGHT

Dahlia had no sense of time. She floated in a brilliantly white world. The air around her was thick and welcoming, like a heavy quilt in winter. Inverted lightning pulsed on the horizon, unaccompanied by thunder.

"You released it." The voice startled her. She spun around, searching for its owner.

He materialized in front of her, a creature that pulsed and changed with every heartbeat. Flames, smoke, darkness. Electricity rushed down the semblance of arms then fizzled into a cloud of vapor. Through it all, the vague sense of a body appeared.

"Who are you?"

"I think you know."

She did. It was the voice that had followed her through

battle, urging her to take the Key, to use it to destroy. The shadow pressing on her since her transformation, filling her with a splintered sense of reality.

"Hartu."

The ghost of an inclined head. "I've been wanting to speak with you more directly."

She spun away from him, searching for anyone else. But they were alone.

Hartu continued, "We seem to have been matched. Improperly, perhaps, but any human body is preferable from life in this realm." Smoke swirled around where his face should be, giving the impression of a grimace.

"I don't understand. How are you here? How am *I* here?"

His gaze weighed heavily on her. "When you used the Key, you created a tear between these worlds."

Did that mean she was trapped here? "How do I get back?"

"Your mind will return, soon enough. But let's not waste this opportunity."

His voice felt so foreign, yet so familiar. She'd nursed it in her nightmares, followed it to Tannin's. It had led her to steal powers and stoke fury. "I want you to leave me alone."

He laughed. It was a sound like grinding rock. "Impossible. We're suspended together. Your human consciousness never let go, and mine could never fully embrace that body of yours. So here we are."

"Will it always be like this, between us?"

"As long as you're alive." A flat tone.

She shivered, wrapping her arms around herself. Suddenly, the blanketing air felt smothering. "Is Ret here? Danel?"

"You should have held onto it, Dahlia." Hartu didn't have eyes, but she had the sense he was staring at her intently. "The Key—"

"Was destroying me."

An ambient buzz crept into her awareness. It made the air tremble faintly.

Hartu sighed in disappointment. "Yes. Well, it isn't lost to you. You know the symbol, which means you can find a proper human host. Release our people from this place." He spread his arms wide.

"Your world, you mean. Why not just stay here?"

Another laugh cut through Dahlia. "This isn't our world. It's a prison. Devised to keep us quiet and complacent."

The buzzing sound was getting louder. She felt something pulling at her waist, and knew it was consciousness, trying to drag her away.

"I won't be far, Dahlia. Together, we can change the world."

He vanished in a waft of smoke, and the world funneled down to a bright point of light, surrounded by darkness.

She woke up gasping and trembling, covered in sweat.

FORTY-NINE

Summer had finally arrived in earnest. Embracing the warmth, Bridget sat on one of the wrought-iron benches of Viri's garden, a piece of paper between her fingers. On it was the symbol Dahlia and Nuriel had worked so hard to complete.

The earthquakes had been gone for a week—ever since she took James' half-life. Around the world, geologists were scratching their heads. But most people had moved on, repaving roads, rebuilding structures, fighting insurance adjusters. Viri's own home was a hodge-podge of construction, supported by magically sourced wood and dirt.

"Bridget."

She turned at the sound of Nuriel's voice, her heart lightening a little at the sight of him. "When did you get back?”

“Just now. Viri picked me up from the airport.” His hands were in his pockets, dark curls smooshed on one side like he’d been sleeping on the plane.

“Sorry you had to go the long way around.” She scooted over on the bench to make space for him.

“We all had a role to play, and I’m glad it worked out. Your sister thought faster than all of us, the way she trapped Tannin. I’m proud of her.”

So was Bridget, although she still felt some reluctance articulating it. She shifted the subject. “What happened to Tannin’s collection?”

He sat beside her. “I emptied it. Some I brought back with me, some I found a safe place for in Europe. Then I left an anonymous tip with the police. They’ll identify the bodies and reunite them with their families.”

“What about Danel?” Her voice was small.

“He’s at Charlie’s. Viri’s offered to inter the body here.”

Bridget nodded, pressing her hands against the pit in her stomach. She had complex feelings about him, but she wasn’t glad he was gone. Eisheth was a wreck. And his niece... would she ever even know?

Nuriel’s other updates offered some relief. Not only were Tannin and his collection no longer a threat, but his victims’ loved ones might receive some peace.

Of course, they weren’t free of danger. With Tannin gone and Eris dead, it would only be a matter of time before word spread to the rest of the Grigori population—including their own mentor, Notos.

They had a decision to make: remain in hiding indefinitely or accept responsibility for the growing body count.

And she had a choice of her own. The siren's call of normal life had lost its luster. Without James, with Dahlia changed, what was normal anymore? It had been a dream from the moment Dahlia had first gone missing.

She smoothed out the drawing on her lap. "Viri wants to hold a memorial here. He's already grown a garden in remembrance of everyone we lost."

She gestured toward a newly sprouted addition to the backyard. Not far from the grove of trees, an expanse of yellow wildflowers fluttered in the breeze, bright and bold and full of life.

Nuriel's eyes followed the movement of her hand. "It's beautiful."

"Yeah." She'd missed James' funeral, of course. Eisheth and Viri used back channels to anonymously return him to his family, and they'd held the service shortly after. Bridget didn't ask for details. She'd been too wrapped up in her own sorrow.

She'd cried for several days after losing James once and for all. But she'd been surprised by her capacity for happiness too. She'd spent a fair amount of time on this bench, watching plants sway in the wind. Thinking about everything she'd been through, everyone she'd lost, and what came next.

Nuriel looked down at the drawing in her hands. "What do you want to do with James' symbol?"

"I've been asking myself the same question." She folded the paper, hiding the lines of the artwork from view.

"I'm not sure this world is ready to have the Gateway thrown open."

"Yeah." She'd placed so much hope into the symbol, and the others like it. Dahlia's sketchbook had dozens of unfinished sketches. Dozens of possible paths to power. Dozens of possible paths to grief.

He placed a hand on hers. "We don't have to decide now. I can keep it safe."

Relieved, she passed it over to him. Too many life-or-death decisions had fallen to her lately. Right now, all she wanted was to rest.

"How is Dahlia?" Nuriel asked, turning the paper idly in his hands.

"For the first few days, she was barely conscious. She's been a little distant, but she's recovering. We all are." Her own shoulder still ached, and without Ret around, they all needed to wait out their injuries, allowing them to heal the old-fashioned way.

It was clear Dahlia's injuries went beyond the physical. The nightmares had gotten worse, and she kept staring off into space, lost to the world.

"She's going to need your help," Bridget said.

"Mine?" Nuriel looked startled. "Gaul told me he was taking over training her."

"Not for training."

He shook his head, bewildered. "I'm not sure I follow."

"She needs people who care about her as a person. More than just me."

Nuriel fell quiet, looking out over the wildflowers. Then he drew in a slow breath. "I've been thinking about what you said. About how I feel about her." His tone was confessional. "You're right. I *do* care. Quite a lot."

"I know."

In the past, Bridget would have felt wary of someone

interested in Dahlia. But this time, all Bridget felt was comfort. Dahlia would never be a kid again. Would never be human again. Bridget couldn't protect her forever, and Dahlia could do much worse than grow closer with Nuriel. "And I'm really glad."

He responded with a surprised, grateful smile. "Thank you. That means a lot."

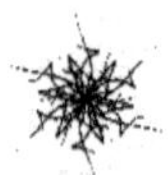

They held a private memorial service in Viri's garden. They released Eris' ashes, everyone watching them dissipate with stony expressions. Danel's ashes went to Eisheth, who promised to take them to the *Mercy* and release his remains into the lake. The detective clutched the urn to her chest, hollow-eyed.

Bridget wondered after his niece, living across the water in Canada. She wished she'd asked Danel more about her—the connection to humanity he'd kept close to his heart.

Once the service was over, Gaul erected three markers, one each to honor Ret, Danel, and James.

After, everyone stayed up sharing stories. There were a great number of tales about Ret, as long as his life had been. He'd been a fatherly presence in Gaul's life that, over the centuries, had become a friendship of equals.

Bridget told stories about James—about his love of ghost stories, his goofy likeability, and dogged loyalty.

Finally, Nuriel began the stories about Danel. His less-than-legal antics. His stubborn selfishness. His surprising kindness when he thought no one was looking.

Eventually, they drifted away from the topic of their

departed friends. At first, Dahlia was distant, but Bridget drew her into the conversation by asking her to share her college antics.

Eisheth, who'd refused to talk about Danel, instead regaled them with stories from her years as a detective. As Bridget shared memories of her and Dahlia's childhood, she caught glimpses of Gaul and Viri holding hands. The two men slipped out of the gathering together.

Loss still weighed on her like a physical burden. But for the first time since she'd entered their world, being here with these familiar faces was comforting. Viri's house felt like a home.

It was late by the time Bridget excused herself to bed. Her heart felt full, despite the grief dwelling in her bones.

Opening the door to the bedroom she shared with Dahlia, Bridget let the weight of the last few weeks fall away. It was cool and quiet in the room. An open window let in the sound of crickets, and in the distance, lightning bugs winked on and off. Overhead, a ceiling fan hummed quietly, and a spider plant wafted in the gentle breeze.

The house was far sturdier now, thanks to their daily efforts to reinforce everything that was broken. They'd added a bit of color to the walls, and Dahlia had contributed a mural of flowers in the hallway.

Bridget finished the herbal tea she'd been nursing, brushed her teeth and changed into her pajamas, listening to the occasional murmur of laughter from downstairs. The sound made her heart swell. After so much fear and grief, they all deserved a peaceful evening.

Drawing a brush through her hair, Bridget walked over to the bed, sitting among the bunched-up comforter and pillows.

Footsteps came up the stairs, and then Dahlia opened the door. "Hey. Had enough for the night?"

"Yeah. You too?"

Dahlia gently closed the door behind her. "It was nice."

Bridget's heart panged for her sister. "You've been through so much, Dahlia. And life's going to keep changing for you."

Dahlia perched on the edge of the bed, kicking off her slippers. "I don't know how most Grigori do this without their family. Honestly, I'm so lucky."

The words sent a familiar pang through her, but she breathed through it. Yes. Her sister was a Grigori. And yes, she was becoming a new version of herself. There was no point denying it anymore. "I'll be here for you as long as I can."

"I *want* that. But I also can't ask you to give up your life to help me." Dahlia's wavy hair shimmered in the moonlight as she shook her head.

"There's no point in making plans for the rest of my life right now. We never know what's coming next. So, I'm letting you know I'm here *now*. And I love you."

Dahlia held her gaze steadily. "I love you too."

Despite the peaceful darkness, sleep didn't come for Bridget. Dahlia had been breathing heavily for an hour before she finally gave up. She sat upright in bed, eyes scanning the darkness. There were plenty of books in the house. Surely, she could find one to quiet her mind.

Maybe she'd return to one of Ret's journals.

She pushed back the comforter, letting her legs dangle off the bed, and she adjusted the pillow. Then she paused as her fingers brushed something smooth under the fabric. Grasping it, paper crinkled.

She turned it over in her hands, running her fingers along the four sides. Then, careful not to disturb Dahlia's sleep, she slipped out of the bed and into the bathroom, closing the door behind her.

Flicking the light on, she read *Bridget* scrawled across the envelope in an unfamiliar cursive script.

With a frown, Bridget turned it over in her hands. An uneasy sensation settled over her. With Tannin gone, she'd been assured no one else knew of their location, outside of those sharing the house with her. She was safe here.

Right?

She ripped the envelope open and pulled out a single piece of paper.

It was almost entirely blank. An address was in the center, written in the same loopy writing. Beneath it:

Bring no one, tell no one.

- Morgan

ABOUT THE AUTHORS

Jes Honard (they/she) is a queer sci-fi/fantasy writer and professional coffee inhaler. Their co-authored debut, Unrelenting, won several awards, including the 2022 New Mexico-Arizona Book Awards LGBTQ title. It was also a finalist for the 2020 Book Pipeline Unpublished Manuscript Competition. Jes has also published short stories and poetry in several anthologies, including the Lesbians in Space anthology and Antifa Lit Journal, Vol. 1.

Jes finds their best words when writing about found family, queer identity, and what happens when we build bridges instead of walls. They currently live in Kalamazoo, MI with their wife and two cats.

Marie Parks (she/her) is a queer fantasy author living in New Mexico, where she hikes, camps, and eats copious amounts of green chile. In addition to winning multiple awards for Unrelenting, Marie was a finalist for the Futurescapes Award for Most Promising New Author for her social justice fantasy heist, Flightless (Shadow Dragon Press, 2026). Marie also received a 2025 New Mexico Writers Grant to support her next writing project.

She is the founder of Sandia Starforgers Writers Retreats and Workshops and is a speaker for conferences such as Dragonsteel and WriteHive. She's delighted by the birds at her feeders, the veggies in her garden, and asexual representation anywhere in the world.

ACKNOWLEDGEMENTS

The nuts and bolts of writing may be solitary (or as solitary as it gets with two authors), but we have been fortunate to be surrounded by a supportive, loving community.

Thank you to Benjamin Gorman and Chrys Gorman at Not a Pipe Publishing for believing in this story. We are also grateful to Heather Tracy for her copyediting expertise.

Lauren Raye Snow, your cover art is simply gorgeous, and it captures Dahlia and her magic so elegantly. And thank you, Gigi Little, for your beautiful and intricate Grigori symbol designs.

Mary Robinette Kowal, thank you for your artistic direction, for connecting us with Lauren in the first place, and for being such an encouraging and supportive friend and mentor. We are forever grateful. Readers, if you haven't yet listened to Mary Robinette's absurdly talented audiobook narration of *Unrelenting*, get thee to an audiobookery this instant.

We remain indebted to our writing friends we've met through Writing Excuses, The Potted Plant, and our various writing communities and critique groups. To our subscribers on Patreon, your continued support makes a difference every month and encourages us to continue telling stories.

Taormina Lepore and Drew Overmier, thanks for enduring our early morning writing sessions and for your unwavering encouragement.

To Jes' mom, Robin, thank you for always asking, "So, what's going on with your book?" to keep them on their toes. To their dad, Mark, who sat Jes down in front of *Star Trek Voyager* as a kid and fostered their love of imagining new worlds. And to Jes' siblings and in-laws, Valerie, Sean, Caitlin, and Katrina, for their constant cheerleading.

To Nancy and Barry Parks, you've always believed in Marie, and she is so grateful. Barry has become a beloved part of Marie's writing community, including by supporting the retreats she coordinates; Sandia Starforgers isn't Sandia Starforgers without him.

Dear reader, these next few paragraphs talk about the death of parents, so please exercise caution for your emotional well-being, or skip ahead to the final paragraph, if needed.

Nancy, Marie's mom, was a brilliant woman and a voracious reader. When Unrelenting came out, she wrangled her book club into discussing it, got it placed in all her local libraries, and continually encouraged us to make a splash with public events. In the summer of 2023, as we were writing Undeniable, she had a life-threatening and devastating brain bleed.

Incredibly, against all odds, she recovered. She got back to work and was able to retire with much fanfare. Six months after her initial bleed, she fell, hit her head, and was gone in two short days.

It was only after finishing *Undeniable* that we realized how closely James' story and Nancy's last few months paralleled one another. Tragedy, followed by hope, snuffed out by a final goodbye.

Jes and their wife also suffered a deep loss as we wrote this book. No one was more effusive about the release of *Unrelenting* than Jes' mother-in-law, Marlene. She shared it with their entire (extremely large) extended family and was a constant voice of support, even as her health was diminishing. The "F*CK CANCER" cross stitch in Charlie's basement? That's for you, Marlene.

We wanted to keep James alive, we truly did. We love his affable personality and relate to his nerdy obsessiveness. And also, we've experienced the reality that sometimes death is abrupt and cruel and senseless. However, death never negates the love we've shared with those who have passed. Grief makes us softer, gentler, more empathetic. Grief teaches us how to give comfort to those newly grieving. Grief reminds us of how very real and important our loved ones were and are.

Finally, thank you to our many friends, family, and readers of *Unrelenting* who are back for more of Bridget and Dahlia's story in *Undeniable*. We look forward to completing the series soon.